THE HEALERS

THE HEALERS

Jack Kriege

ROPER PRESS
Dallas, Texas

THE HEALERS by Jack Kriege

Cover Design: Schechner & Associates
Cover Illustration: Stephen Marchesi

First printing, 1993
Printed in the United States of America

Library of Congress Catalog Number 93-84280

ISBN 0-86606-325-0

PUBLISHER'S NOTE: This is a work of fiction. Names, characters, places and incidents either are the product of the author's imagination or are used ficticiously, and any resemblance to actual persons, living or dead, events or locales is entirely coincidental.

To Jean,
my wonderful wife,
for her patience, encouragement and love.

1

I rarely recall the events surrounding the initial session of any of my patients. Psychiatry is not the exhilarating career that many suppose, nor which I had anticipated when I embarked on it, and the preliminary session is seldom more than a plodding inquiry into a series of mundane facts. But this case was different. I subsequently tried to explain my vivid recollection by the fact that I had been unusually testy in training my newly hired secretary all week or by the tension generated by the gathering later that night. But neither of these could possibly have caused the events to remain so indelibly etched on my mind. No, the case was spectacular from the beginning, and in less than two months my life had been changed because of it.

I had always tried to get out of the office early on Fridays. I was sure that I had made that point clear to Cheryl. And I was even more certain that I had insisted that I never meet with "walk-in" patients prior to a complete review of the written history -- a history that she was expected to obtain. Nevertheless, at 4:00 p.m. on that Friday afternoon, just after I had dismissed my last scheduled patient, Cheryl stepped gingerly into my office, smiled, and tapped lightly on the open door.

"Dr. Summers . . . "

"Yes, Cheryl, what is it?"

"I know I'm not supposed to do this, but . . . " She glanced furtively back toward the waiting room, hunched her shoulders, and spoke in a harsh whisper. "She won't leave."

"What?"

"This woman," said Cheryl. "She came in an hour ago, and said she just had to see you today, and she won't leave until you do."

I was irritated that Cheryl had let the woman sit there and allow her anticipation to build. "Did you have her fill out a fact sheet?" I asked.

Cheryl shook her head. "She refused to do it."

"Well, then, how am I supposed to . . . " I stopped myself abruptly. I detest rhetorical questions, and when I find myself resorting to them, I realize all the more how meaningless they are.

"I'm sorry, Dr. Summers. Maybe . . . maybe I should just turn off the lights, or . . . " Cheryl was stammering, and I found myself suddenly chuckling at her inability to handle the situation.

"No, never mind, Cheryl," I said quietly. "Send her in."

Cheryl closed her eyes, sighed, and started to leave. Then she turned back. "Dr. Summers."

"Yes?"

Cheryl stepped inside the office and closed the door behind her. "She's really strange, and I guess I was just a little frightened."

"Strange people come to see psychiatrists, Cheryl," I responded somewhat sarcastically. "You're going to have to get used to that."

"Yes, sir." Cheryl opened the door, and made a gross beckoning motion toward the waiting room. That was an annoying mannerism that I had already spoken with her about on several occasions, but I ignored it this time.

The woman stepped past Cheryl and assisted in closing the door behind her. She was very tall, and wore a brightly designed floor-length dress. A thick mat of black hair, clearly a wig, hung eight inches below her shoulders, and her face was partially concealed by a pair of large, darkly tinted sun glasses, which she did not remove. As she stepped closer to my desk, however, the shadow of a beard was visible. It was obvious that "she" was a man.

"Dr. Summers?" he asked with a forced falsetto.

"Yes?"

"I hope you don't mind my barging in like this." The statement was punctuated by a nervous laugh. "That's just the way I am. Your nice young lady out there wanted me to fill out some papers, but I have a thing about signing anything until . . . "

"I'll need your name, at least," I interrupted.

"Mrs. Smith," he said quickly.

I raised my eyebrow slightly, but he seemed committed to that pseudonym. "Very well," I said finally, pointing to a chair opposite me. "Why don't you sit down, Mrs. Smith, and tell me what you need to see me about."

He pulled the chair up behind him and sat with a very masculine carriage. In the process, a heavy gold necklace smacked against my desk. At the end of a long chain was a large mandala. The series of concentric squares in the center joined to a surrounding circle by four small circles was a very familiar symbol to me. I had been trained in the Jungian school of psychiatric analysis, and this was particularly intriguing to me, since Carl Jung had devoted considerable attention to the significance of the mandala. But I knew also that this could be merely a coincidental piece of costume jewelry.

"Thank you," continued Mrs. Smith in the forged voice. "I won't take much of your time."

"What seems to be the problem?" I asked.

"I just need to pick up something to help me sleep."

"I see." I studied his expression as well as I could beneath the concealing glasses. His mouth twitched slightly as I paused before responding. "If you just need a sedative, why didn't you just go to your general practitioner?"

He shifted grossly in the chair. "Well . . . but there's a reason, isn't there? I mean, when I say I need something to help me sleep, I naturally assume that you will ask me why I'm having trouble sleeping."

"Why are you having trouble sleeping?" I asked condescendingly.

"Well, it could be many things, couldn't it? I mean . . . I have been so very busy." He laid his head back for a moment, and the wig separated slightly from his head. "But the dream doesn't help." He laughed nervously.

"The dream?"

"Yes."

"So that's why you thought I could help you."

"Yes. I mean . . . " He sat forward and placed a pair of masculine hands on my desk. " . . . that's what you do, isn't it?"

"Sometimes."

He glanced at his hands. Then he quickly pulled them away and sat back in the chair.

"How did you happen to choose me?" I asked.

"You were referred," he said.

"By whom?" I asked.

Instead of responding to my question, he crossed one leg over the other heavily and leaned his face on one hand while he gestured with the other. "We have two options, as I see it. You can either prescribe something for a really deep sleep, or you can prescribe a dream suppressant. They make those, don't they?"

"Well . . . "

"Isn't it amazing what they can do with drugs lately? Sometimes I wish that I had followed a pharmaceutical career."

"What *is* your career?" I slipped in quickly.

"I'm an entrepreneur." The response was immediate and rehearsed.

"I see."

"So money is no object, you see, and if you can just dash off a prescription, I'll be out of your way."

"I'll have to know more about your dream first," I probed. "Tell me about it."

"Varied."

"The dream is varied?" I asked.

"Oh, did I say *dream*?" He laughed nervously again. "I meant *dreams*, of course. I have many dreams. I've been so busy, you know."

"Do you have any idea what's causing them?"

"That's *your* job, isn't it?"

"I mean . . . have you been troubled by anything lately?" I asked.

"Oh, no. Absolutely not." He shifted in the chair again and dropped the crossed leg heavily to the floor. "I have a marvelous life. I'm an entrepreneur, you know, and I'm just so busy. There are so many thoughts rushing around in my mind. That's probably the reason. All those thoughts . . . incubating all day long, struggling to be free. Then at night . . . " He smiled and raised his hands. "They hatch!"

I nodded and waited for him to continue the thought, but it was clear that he was through. "That's an attractive mandala," I said finally.

"Thank you." He picked up the necklace and dangled it between two fingers.

I thought that it might be significant that he knew the term.

"I like to wear it when I get this way," he continued.

"What way?"

"So busy . . . like running around to the four corners of the world. And the four winds blowing . . . just like my tumbling thoughts. To and fro . . to and fro . . . "

"And the circle?" I asked.

"I feel like I'm going around in circles," he said, suddenly letting the chain drop. "Are we getting anywhere here?"

"I'm at a disadvantage, Mrs. Smith."

"Why?"

"Communication is significantly aided by eye contact," I said.

"Oh, these?" He tapped his finger lightly on the frame of the sun glasses. "Do they bother you?"

"I would prefer that you removed them," I said.

"No, that shouldn't make any difference."

"I would really prefer that you removed them," I repeated, trying to spark a reaction.

"Haven't you treated entrepreneurs before?" he asked with a sudden rush of hostility. "Haven't you ever heard the term *incognito*? I'm very busy, you know. And there are many people wondering how I do everything. People are watching me. Don't you understand?"

"Do you think that people are in here watching you?" I asked, gesturing vaguely about the office.

"The walls have eyes," he responded curtly.

"Very well." I decided not to push the removal of the sun glasses this time. But it is very difficult to detect feelings and motivations without being able to see the eyes. "Perhaps you can give me some information which will help me know what to prescribe." I removed my pen and began scribbling on a pad. "Do you have any allergies?"

"Is that the best you can do?" he asked disdainfully.

I had to chuckle despite myself. He had made a very astute observation. I had asked an absurd question in this context.

"Very well . . . " he continued aimlessly. "I'm allergic to life. That's a common entrepreneurial disease I've been told."

While he was responsive, I tried to press further. "Perhaps if you could give me the name of your general practitioner . . . "

"Varied," he responded mechanically.

"Your GP is varied?"

"I've had several."

"The latest, then," I pressed.

Mrs. Smith suddenly sat forward and spoke harshly. The falsetto voice crackled beneath his anger. "All these questions for a little dream suppressant! It's absurd! Perhaps I should go elsewhere."

"Just a moment, please . . . " I put my hand forward, and he sat back again. I could tell that I wasn't going to get any further today. Mrs. Smith clearly had a problem, and I was intrigued to discover more about it. I opened my bottom drawer and removed two sample packages containing sedatives.

As I placed them on the desk before me, he smiled and sighed deeply. "Good. I thought you'd listen to reason."

"I'll give you enough for two nights . . . " I began.

He reached out impulsively to take the packages, but I placed my hand over them. "There's a condition," I said. "You have to promise to see me again on Monday."

"Well, if they don't work, I certainly will see you."

"Regardless," I insisted. "See me again on Monday."

"I'm so busy, you know," he said.

"Monday," I repeated emphatically.

"Oh . . . very well."

I picked up my phone and pressed the intercom button.

"Good afternoon. This is Dr. Summers' office. May I help you?" Cheryl's crisp, inaccurate message greeted my ears. She realized quickly what she had done. "Oh, I'm sorry, Dr. Summers. This is the intercom, isn't it?"

"Mrs. Smith will be coming out momentarily," I said, ignoring her embarrassed response. "Schedule another appointment for Monday afternoon."

"Yes, sir."

"And get a telephone number where she can be reached in case a change is necessary." I thought perhaps this informal arrangement would elicit some information about Mrs. Smith.

"Very well, Dr. Summers."

I hung up the phone and turned back to Mrs. Smith. "Stop by Cheryl's desk on the way out and she will set up a time for you."

"Of course." He reached out and impulsively grabbed the sample packages from the table. Then he stood and walked heavily toward the door.

"Oh, Mrs. Smith . . . " I called after him.

He placed his hand on the knob, opened the door a crack, and then turned slowly back toward me without answering.

"When you come in on Monday . . . " My words were suddenly interrupted by the buzz of the intercom. I had told Cheryl several times not to interrupt me while I was in session. I raised my hand toward Mrs. Smith. "Wait a moment please." I picked up the receiver, and spoke harshly. "Cheryl, don't you remember that . . . "

"I'm sorry, Dr. Summers," she said softly. "Your wife is on the phone."

"I doesn't matter if the president is on the phone," I mumbled inaudibly. And then I spoke gruffly. "Put her on hold. I'll get back with her in a moment."

"Yes, sir."

I hung up the phone and tried to collect my thoughts. Mrs. Smith shifted impatiently at the slightly opened door. "Mrs. Smith . . . " I said, trying to reestablish the tone."

"Yes?"

"When you come in on Monday, I think we can make much more progress if you drop the female impersonation."

He stood without moving for a moment. Then he shrugged. "Perhaps." The voice had suddenly changed to its accurate male range, and he spoke in a slow, threatening tone. "I'll know by then. I'm going to have you checked out thoroughly over the weekend." The door opened, and the figure swept out, slamming the door behind.

I sat back in my chair and sighed heavily. My mind was somewhat muddled with the recollections of the encounter with Mrs. Smith and my irritation with Cheryl's incompetence. Out of the corner of my eye I could see a blinking light on the telephone. I reached over and picked up the receiver. "Hello, Meg."

"It sounds like I interrupted a patient," said Meg. "Sorry. I thought you'd be through by now."

"Well, I should have been, but . . . "

"Do you want me to call back?" she asked.

"No . . . no."

"I just wanted to be sure you remembered to get home on time," continued Meg.

"On time . . . "

"Your parents' fiftieth anniversary party," she reminded.

"Yes, of course," I said. "What time are we supposed to be there?"

"Eight o'clock," she said. "We should leave by seven-thirty."

"I'll be there by then."

"John, I'm having a little trouble with Diane." Meg's voice was somewhat strained. The sound was so familiar. "She says she doesn't want to go tonight."

"Well . . . "

"I'd appreciate it if you could come home as soon as possible and speak with her," she said.

I was exhausted from my session with Mrs. Smith. I wasn't in any mood to run home and counsel a fifteen-year-old."

"John . . . When do you think you'll be home?" asked Meg.

"As soon as I can, Meg," I responded noncommittally. "As soon as I can." I laid the receiver gently back in its cradle.

I heard a light tapping at my door, and looked up in time to see Cheryl push the door open slightly and step partially inside.

"I saw that you were off the phone," she said softly. "So I thought it would be all right if I . . . "

"Yes. Come in, Cheryl. Come in."

She smiled, pushed the door fully open, and stepped briskly up to my desk.

"Did you schedule Mrs. Smith for Monday?" I asked.

"At 4:00 o'clock Monday afternoon," she said.

"Good. Did you get a phone number?" I asked.

Cheryl shook her head. "She said she couldn't give it to me."

"How about the check?" I asked. "Did that have an address on it?"

"She paid by cash," said Cheryl.

I must have responded with an angry look, because Cheryl's smile suddenly vanished. "That's all right, Cheryl," I reassured her. "I didn't really expect to get anything . . . not yet."

"I hope you're not angry."

I shook my head. "Oh, by the way . . . Mrs. Smith should be coming in on Monday minus the impersonation."

"Impersonation?" A quizzical look crossed her face.

"Oh, I thought you had noticed . . . " I began. But then I realized. Of course she wouldn't have. "Mrs. Smith is a man, Cheryl."

"Really?" Her eyes grew wide.

I had made a list of things that I wanted to discuss with Cheryl about procedures in the office, but there wasn't time to go over them tonight. Besides, I wasn't at all sure that she was going to work out. She seemed to lack certain intuitive skills. As an example, even though I had made a clear implication that our conversation was over, she still stood expectantly in front of me, waiting for me to speak. I decided to oblige her. "How long have you been working for me now, Cheryl?" I asked.

"Four days, Dr. Summers."

"Hmm . . . "

"I hope I'm doing all right," she said eagerly. "I really enjoy the work, and I'm trying really hard to learn how to do things the way you want."

She was disarming. I had to admit that. I decided that I'd give her until the end of next week. "Thank you, Cheryl," I said. "You may go now."

She smiled and slipped quietly out the door, closing it behind her.

I glanced at my watch. It was nearly five. If I left right away, I could get home in time to listen to Meg complain about Diane, and then try unsuccessfully to talk to Diane about her attitude problem. But if I had that much energy, I would talk to Cheryl about her inadequacies. It would be nice, I thought, to begin next week with a smoothly efficient office operation. I owed that to my patients. Home was more flexible. And I knew there was nothing that I could say tonight that would make Diane any less belligerent than when Meg called. It was a good thing she called, though. I had almost forgotten my parents' fiftieth anniversary. Fifty years . . . It seemed like so long a time. And yet I'd been in practice for over ten. Diane was only five when I opened my office. Things were easier then. I couldn't imagine what Meg would want me to say to her.

I rather dreaded going to the party myself. All the people from my father's law firm would undoubtedly be there, and I was barely acquainted with any of them. Lloyd and Kate would be there, of course, but that was likely to cause contention. Lloyd . . . He was my brother, but we were so different. I had a sudden desire to skip the weekend and proceed directly to Monday. I was beginning to be excited about treating "Mrs. Smith." There were so many things to think about -- strategies to plan, questions to formulate. I couldn't let Meg and Diane's problem detract my train of thought. I decided to stop for a drink on the way home. That would make for an easier transition, anyway. It always did.

2

It was eight-fifteen when we pulled into the broad drive leading to my parents' home. I told Meg that we could easily have been here on time if she had not insisted on describing the details surrounding Diane's latest rebellion when I arrived home at seven-thirty. The only really important issue tonight was Diane's attendance at the party, and I had resolved that by telling her to get into the car. At any rate, we were here, and as we pulled to a stop at the entrance, a young man stepped up and opened the passenger-side doors. Then he opened my door and waited for me to step out so that he could park the car. Many years ago my father had crossed over the economic line that led him to the belief that his social functions should be presented with the trappings and procedures of an elegant club, complete with parking attendants and hired greeters. I recalled with amusement the time that he had invited Meg and me alone to dinner, and our car was parked by a formally attired youth. I had promised myself that night that, no matter how financially successful I became, I would never be that ostentatious.

I walked around to the other side of the car. Meg had already gotten out, and was waiting on the steps. Diane still sat sullenly in the back seat, her arms crossed tightly across her chest. I beckoned with my hand, and she emerged without uncrossing her arms and stalked past me. We joined Meg at the front door, where we were ushered in by a stern white-haired man. As we passed through the spacious entry into the living room, I was surprised to see only about ten people there.

"There, you see." I took Meg's arm and pointed to them. "We can't be all that late."

Meg looked at me and frowned. Then she shrugged, and whispered , "Maybe not."

My mother was standing with a group of women across the room, and as she saw us, she waved and walked quickly over to us. Her hair was completely white now, but her face seemed no more wrinkled than it did when I was a boy. She set a drink she was carrying on a small table and embraced me.

"Hi, mother. Good to see you," I said, giving her a tight hug.

"Hello, John." She turned to Meg and patted her on the arm. "Meg . . . It's good to see you."

"Hello, mother," responded Meg.

"And Diane!" My mother put her arms around Diane's rigid form and squeezed. "I'm so glad you could come."

"Hi, Grandma," Diane responded quietly, her arms now hanging at her side.

"Not many here yet, are there?" I asked my mother.

"What?" She looked about the room. "Oh, almost everyone. Charles decided not to invite the entire office this time. Just the partners. Make it more of a family affair, you know."

"John!"

I looked up to see my father leading two men across the room. His tall, muscular frame seemed to tower over them as they approached. When I was a boy I always thought that he was indestructible, and my opinion hadn't changed much over the years. At seventy-three he was still the undisputed senior partner of his law firm. His lips parted in the familiar forced smile as he introduced us.

"I know you've met my son before, but it's been a long time, I'm sure," said my father.

"At least five years," agreed one of the men.

"These two have been with the firm nearly as long as I have, John," said my father. "James Haley . . . and Donald Klein. This is John's wife Meg, and their daughter Diane."

We all greeted one another.

"How's the practice going, John?" asked Klein.

"Very well, thank you," I replied.

"Good . . . good." He and Haley drifted back into the center of the room.

My father turned his attention to my mother. "Louise, why didn't you take John and Meg to the bar?"

"They just arrived, Charles," said my mother.

"Oh, trying to become socially correct, eh?" asked my father. He laughed mechanically and pounded my back. "No matter. Go on over now, and help yourselves. We won't eat for a few minutes." He pointed to a formal bar in the corner of the room and walked off to join his friends. My mother picked up her drink from the table, waved, and walked back toward the group of women.

I started to lead Meg toward the bar, but I realized she was resisting me. "What is it?" I asked.

"I thought maybe you'd already had your quota," she said.

"Oh, Meg . . . that was two hours ago."

"What am I supposed to do?" asked Diane. Her arms were crossed again.

"Just go . . . mingle, Diane," I said.

"There's nobody to mingle with!" she said bitterly.

I laughed lightly, grasped Meg's arm, and led her reluctantly across the room. I understood her concern. She had no way of knowing that I'd had only one or two drinks on the way home. But I wished that she wouldn't act that way . . . especially here. I had the red-jacketed bartender make me double scotch and soda, and Meg insisted on having just a wine cooler.

It had actually been ten years since I had met my father's partners. It was just after I had begun my practice. He'd had a reception for me at his office. Meg wasn't invited. It was just for his partners and me. He introduced me as a brilliant new psychiatrist who lacked only patients, and he urged them to recommend that their neurotic and otherwise troubled clients come to me for therapy. I thought at the time that he was joking, but I soon realized that easily three-quarters of my quickly growing practice was the result of referrals, directly or indirectly, from the members of his firm. I remember the feeling I had at that reception of being put on display. And tonight that uncomfortable perception crept up my spine. Meg and I stood alone at the bar, and it seemed at that moment that the eyes of those in the room were directed solely toward me.

I closed my eyes, took a large swallow from my drink, and relaxed momentarily as the smoothly bitter essence permeated my consciousness. When I opened my eyes, I saw my father motioning for us to join him.

"He wants to introduce us to the others," I told Meg.

"Us . . . or *you*?" she asked. "Maybe I should go over with your mother."

"C'mon . . . " I took her by the arm, and led her over to the group of men.

"John, you remember Richard Walker and Marvin Phillips, don't you?" asked my father as we joined them.

"Of course," I lied, and shook their hands cordially.

"And this must be Peg," said Walker.

"Meg," I corrected.

"Meg! We've heard so much about you." Walker leaned over and gave Meg a sloppy hug. She pulled away, and he nearly lost his balance.

"Easy, Rich," cautioned a less inebriated Phillips. "You're not as young as you used to be." The two of them laughed.

"How's the practice going, John?" asked Phillips.

"Fine," I responded. This was surely one of the things my father wanted from me tonight -- a progress report for his friends. "And I certainly do appreciate the referrals that you've sent me," I added.

"Well, Marvin knows a lot of crazy people!" said Walker, and he doubled over with laughter.

"By the way," continued Phillips, ignoring Walker, "one of my clients owns the yacht club. He tells me you're quite a speed boat enthusiast."

"Yes," I responded.

"And motorcycle racing, and underwater exploration, and sky diving . . . " rattled off my father. "John is, unfortunately, involved with a number of high-risk activities. I've told him that if I were an insurance broker rather than a lawyer, I'd have to drop him as a liability."

The others laughed and began pressing me to describe my experiences. I wished that my father had not brought this up. I was here tonight as a successful psychiatrist, thanks largely to the recommendations of his friends. I was ready for that role. I was not prepared to share with them my private pleasures. Besides, Meg was getting nervous.

"Charles!"

It was my mother's voice. I looked back and saw her standing at the entrance beside Lloyd and Kate and their children. I was happy for the opportunity to break away from this conversation. I excused myself and led Meg across the room.

"I'll be back in a moment," I heard my father tell the men, and he joined us.

Meg seemed suddenly very relieved. She walked quickly over to Kate and embraced her. "You don't know how happy I am to see you," she said.

"Good!" responded Kate cheerfully.

"Hi, Lloyd," I said, grasping his hand firmly.

"Hi, John." He pulled me toward him, tossed his other arm around me, and patted me warmly on the back. "How've you been?"

Lloyd's children greeted us warmly. His son Patrick was twenty-one, and his daughter Amy was fifteen -- the same age as Diane.

"Hello, Lloyd," said my father, extending his hand. "I'm glad you could make it."

"Hi, Pop," responded Lloyd. He stepped closer, but my father backed away. Lloyd just smiled, and held firmly to his hand for a moment before releasing it.

"Where's Diane?" asked Amy.

I glanced around the room. Diane wasn't anywhere in sight. "I don't know, Amy," I said.

"I'll find her," she responded quickly, and bounded off.

"The bar's over there," said my father to Lloyd. "But I don't suppose . . . "

"Do you have any lemonade?" asked Lloyd with a smile.

"You should take a little wine . . . for your stomach's sake," said my father sardonically.

"No, thanks. My stomach's fine," responded Lloyd.

My father frowned, shook his head, and left to join his friends.

"Dad, did you bring in the gift?" Patrick asked Lloyd.

"No, I don't think I did," said Lloyd.

"I'll go get it." Patrick turned and walked slowly out of the room.

Meg and Kate had joined mother and the women. I saw that my glass was empty, so I motioned for Lloyd to come with me as I went for a refill. There wasn't any lemonade, so the man gave Lloyd a lime twist in a glass of sparkling water.

I hadn't seen Lloyd for over a year. When Meg and I were first married, we used to visit them periodically, but after I began my practice, and Lloyd was appointed as head pastor at his church, we began to drift apart. He and my father didn't get along well, anyway, and I always sensed that he held some hostility toward me because I had maintained a good relationship with our parents.

"You still at that church over on Eleventh Avenue?" I asked.

He nodded. Then he smiled and raised an eyebrow. "You still at that practice over on Elm Street?"

"Touché!" I chuckled. "Has Dad been to one of your services yet?"

"No. But then you've been only once, as I recall," he said.

"Yeah, that's right." That was at his first service as senior pastor ten years ago. Things were still pretty bad between my father and Lloyd then, and father simply refused to go. I thought it would be better if I declined also, but Meg insisted that we go, so we did. "But you shouldn't feel bad. I haven't gone any place else, either," I laughed.

Lloyd smiled and nodded. "You're still following the Jungian approach in your analysis, aren't you?" he asked, changing the subject.

"Sure," I responded.

"I'd really like to sit down with you sometime, and discuss his theories," he said.

"You mean his ideas on spirituality?"

"Yes."

"Sure, Lloyd. We'll have to do that some time." I tried not to sound condescending. He had asked me this several times -- first, when I was attending the Jung Psychiatric Institute, and then when I first started my practice. I had always put him off, because I knew that he only wanted to use this as a lead in to try to convert me. I was sure that our relationship would be a lot more amicable if I avoided confrontations like this.

A high-pitched ringing filled the room. I looked up to see my father banging a wine glass against a metal lamp stand. When everyone had stopped talking and looked toward him, he stopped.

"It's time to eat, everyone. The buffet is set up in the recreation room. Fill up there, and take your plates to the dining room."

"I'd better get Kate and the kids," said Lloyd.

"Yeah."

Everyone began to move toward the doorway. I asked the bartender to top off my drink, and I turned to look for Meg. I saw her walking toward me, dragging Diane by the arm with one hand, and holding a drink in the other.

"Look at this, John," said Meg angrily. "Amy never did find Diane. Do you know where she's been all this time? She's been off in the bathroom with *this*!" She thrust the glass up to my nose, and the strong smell of liquor invaded my nostrils.

"Oh, Diane . . . " I took the glass and set it on the bar. "Why did you do that?"

"You told me to mingle . . . " Her speech was slurred. The alcohol had definitely affected her.

"You shouldn't have done this, Diane," I said, with as much sternness as I could muster.

"Why not?" she asked. *"You* do."

"You know that's different, Diane," I insisted.

"Why?"

"You're going to have to do better than that, John," said Meg angrily. "I think this should make it clear to you that we have a problem."

"Meg, this isn't the time or place . . . "

"Why not?" asked Meg. "There's never a time or place!"

"Stop it!" Diane turned around suddenly, brushed her hands awkwardly across her skirt, and staggered toward the recreation room.

"Later, Meg . . . later," I said. We walked quickly up beside Diane and accompanied her to the buffet.

My father had the long dining table set up for the occasion. He and my mother sat at the head. Below them, my family and Lloyd's family sat opposite each other; my father's partners and their wives filled in the remainder of the table. This arrangement would have been beneficial if my father had spent the majority of the evening talking with Lloyd and me, but the biggest part of the conversation was carried on loudly between him and his partners, discussing the boring details of some recent corporate lawsuit. After a while, it apparently became clear to my mother that her children weren't participating in the discussion. She turned to my father, and tugged at his sleeve.

"What is it, Louise?" he asked.

"Can't we talk about something that everyone is interested in?" she asked.

The expression on my father's face became suddenly very dark. He glanced quickly toward the end of the table. Then he pulled my mother roughly toward him and whispered coarsely, "Don't embarrass me in front of my friends!"

The sound of the harsh message didn't carry far, but I heard it clearly. So, apparently did Patrick, who sat directly across from me, next to my father. He reached out impulsively and tapped my father on the arm. "Grandpa . . . "

My father suddenly released my mother and looked at Patrick. "What is it?"

"I've been wondering . . . " Patrick was clearly trying to come up with something . . . anything that would defuse the situation. "I've been wondering," he repeated. "Does your firm ever deal with criminal cases?"

"Well . . . " My father brushed his hands together aimlessly. "Some of our clients have been accused of being criminals . . . " He smiled broadly toward his partners, and they laughed in response. "But no. We deal only with civil law. Mainly corporate."

James Haley leaned forward and directed his voice toward Patrick. "There are too many headaches and too little money in criminal law young man. If you lose, your clients hate you, and even if you win, they frequently can't pay you."

"It just seems as though it would be more rewarding, though," said Patrick. "I think it would be nice to be able to help some innocent people."

"There are no innocent people anymore," said Marvin Phillips. "There's no black and white . . . good and bad. Everyone is guilty of something."

"You want a good example of that?" Richard Walker had been quiet throughout the meal, but now he spoke loudly. "Case in point . . . How many have there been now?"

"What do you mean?" asked Donald Klein.

"The prostitute murders," he said. "How many have there been now? Six . . . seven?"

"I believe the police have linked seven in the last year and a half," said my father.

"Case in point," repeated Walker. "Everyone's guilty of something. If we were in criminal law, we'd have to defend someone. Who would we defend?

My father suddenly got a gleam in his eye, and he slapped his hand on the table. I remembered that mannerism of his; it always meant that he was about to make a joke . . . or make fun of someone. Everyone else must have recognized it too, for they looked at him expectantly.

"I just got a brilliant notion! If we were placed in that position, we'd just issue a subcontract to my two sons. Lloyd would lead the prostitutes to Christ, and John would dampen the libidos of the murderers!"

My father smiled broadly and scanned the table slowly for approval. His partners and their wives responded with loud laughter, and I joined them.

"How is it that your sons *didn't* follow you in the legal profession, Charles?" asked Felicia Klein.

"Too long a name," responded my father casually, and he passed his hand across an imaginary sign: "Summers, Summers, Haley, Walker, Phillips and Klein."

"I'd have to retire," said Klein, and everyone laughed.

"No, I tried to convince John to go into law," said my father, more seriously. "But he decided he'd rather *heal* crazy people than *represent* them in court."

Even my mother laughed this time. Patrick's detraction had done its job.

"I don't know about you, Louise, but I'd like to open our gifts," said my father. He pushed the plates away from them, stood, and placed three gifts on the table. He and my mother stood. "Let's see . . . " He passed his finger slowly across the gifts, and then picked one. It was an envelope. "This one's from my faithful co-workers," he said. "Good things come in small packages . . . except retainers." He tore open the envelope and pulled out an impressive looking coupon. "Well! A trip to Hawaii!" He held the coupon up, and he and my mother smiled. "That's great! We haven't been to Hawaii for two years!"

"We keep trying, Charles," said Phillips. "One of these years you're going to stay there, and our firm can start making money!"

"No chance," said my father. "I'll outlast you all!" He picked up the next gift. It was the one from Meg and me. "All right . . . this one's from John." He pulled off the paper, opened the box, and removed the two gold watches that we'd bought -- a pocket watch for him, and a necklace watch for my mother.

"Oh, those are lovely, John . . . Meg," said my mother.

"That's very good, John," said my father. "You finally replaced the watch of mine that you lost when you were twelve!"

"He's just trying to help us," joked Walker. "Your time is measured!"

My father pointed ominously at him, and picked up the final gift. "Well . . . this must be from Lloyd and Kate." He picked up the gift, removed the paper, and raised his eyebrow as he looked at it. It was a Bible.

"Oh, how beautiful!" My mother took it quickly from his hands. "And look at the gold inscription." She held the Bible up and pointed. "See . . . *Charles and Louise Summers.* Thank you, Lloyd and Kate. It's beautiful!"

"Sure, Mom," said Lloyd.

"We can put that on the shelf next to the one that you gave us for our *twenty-fifth* anniversary, Lloyd," said my father. "You remember that, don't you, Lloyd?"

Lloyd shook his head self-consciously. "Don't, Pop . . . "

"Tell us about it, Charles," said Walker loudly.

"Well, you all know that I've given my boys a good Catholic upbringing," explained my father, with a deliberate smile on his face. "Well, twenty-five years ago, when Lloyd was twenty-two years old, he went to some tent revival meeting and became . . . *saved.*" He formed imaginary quotation marks around the word with his fingers.

"It wasn't a tent," mumbled Lloyd.

"And then he invited me and Louise to come to his baptism," continued my father, without listening to Lloyd. "Can you feature that? I told him that his getting baptized was completely unnecessary, because I'd had him baptized when he was three weeks old." The look on my father's face became suddenly stern, and it was clear that he wasn't joking anymore. "That was an affront, Lloyd, and so is this!" He pointed toward the Bible, but continued speaking ominously toward Lloyd. "It suggests to my friends that I haven't done my job . . . when the *opposite* is the case. I took care of every one of you boys' needs . . . including your salvation!"

The room was deathly silent for what must have been a full ten seconds. Meg grasped my leg and pleaded silently with me to do something . . . say something. But I didn't know what to say.

Finally, Donald Klein leaned forward and spoke to my father. "Come on, Charles . . . lighten up! I'll have to accuse you of violating your son's first amendment rights."

The other partners laughed lightly in an attempt to lighten the hostility.

"There are many forms of religious expression," said Mary Ellen Haley haltingly. "I think your son is just trying to say that . . . that everyone needs to express themselves religiously in . . . in love."

"That's right, Charles," agreed her husband. "You see them on TV all the time. There are gospels of social responsibility, gospels of self-awareness . . . even gospels of success. You ought to subscribe to that one!"

"And what your son is trying to say is that one gospel is just as good as another, Charles," continued Mary Ellen. "Isn't that what you're trying to say, Lloyd?"

"No . . . No, that's not what I was trying to say," mumbled Lloyd.

"So, come on Charles . . . lighten up!" repeated Klein, ignoring Lloyd's response.

My father frowned toward Lloyd for a moment longer, and then he looked up with his broad forced smile. "Well . . . I was just joking, anyway. That's something Lloyd never could understand. I don't care what kind of religion he follows . . . as long as he doesn't drag me into any lengthy discussions about guilt and sin. I have enough trouble dealing with this life. I'll let the priests worry about the next life!"

My father's partners laughed lightly, relieved that the tense atmosphere had been broken.

"Well, I think it's time for an after-dinner drink," said my father conclusively. "Who's going to join me?" He left the table, and his partners and their wives quickly followed him toward the living room.

My mother sat down, placed the Bible on the table before her, and leaned toward Lloyd and Kate. "Lloyd . . . don't pay any attention to your father. He's just . . . "

"It's all right, Mom," said Lloyd.

"I love the Bible, Lloyd," she said. "I really do! I never told you, I don't think. I have a very special secret place . . . where I put things that are really important. That's where your other Bible is. I'm going to put this one there, too."

"I'd rather you read it, Mom," said Lloyd.

"It's very special, Lloyd," said my mother, without listening to Lloyd. "I'm going to put it in my very special place." She took the Bible lovingly, rose, and left the room.

"Mom!"

I turned at the sound of Diane's voice. Meg leaned over toward her.

"Mom!" Her face was contorted. Suddenly she reached forward and grabbed a salad bowl. She placed it on her lap, leaned over, and began to vomit.

"Oh, honey!" Meg held her head and rubbed her shoulder gently.

"Let me help you, Meg," said Kate. She jumped up from her place and ran around to our side of the table. She and Meg helped Diane up and guided her toward the bathroom.

"Well . . . " I raised my hands in a futile expression. I couldn't think of anything to say.

"How about you, Amy?" asked Lloyd. "You don't look so good right now, either."

Patrick took the hint. "Let's go get a breath of fresh air, Amy," he said. He took her by the hand, and they quickly left the room.

I thought Lloyd needed an explanation. "She's been in the booze," I said.

"I know," said Lloyd.

"Oh?"

Lloyd nodded. "Amy told me she saw her make one up from leftovers."

I laughed lightly at the thought of the concoction, and I was surprised to see that Lloyd was joining in my laughter. "Amy tells you these things, huh?"

"Yeah. We have a good relationship," said Lloyd.

"Yeah . . . I know . . . I know . . . " I wanted to say, I know what you mean . . . So do Diane and I. But, of course I couldn't. So I had to talk about the more obvious topic of the evening. "I don't know what got into Dad," I said. "That was really uncalled for."

Lloyd shrugged. "I know, but I'm pretty much accustomed to it by now. I just hate it that the kids have to see him like that."

"It's just that some things seem to set him off more than others," I said.

"What do you mean?"

"Well . . . This probably could have been avoided if . . . " I stopped myself. I really didn't want to get into this discussion with Lloyd.

"If what, John?" asked Lloyd.

"Never mind. It isn't important," I said.

"It *is* important!" Lloyd sat back in an exasperated stance. Then he leaned forward again and spoke intensely. "This is just like when we were growing up. I used to have to drag things out of you."

"Well . . . because then, too, you used to do things that set Dad off."

"How did I set him off tonight?" asked Lloyd.

"Well . . . did you have to get them a Bible for a gift?" I asked.

"Oh . . . " said Lloyd, dragging out the syllable. "Don't you think he'd have found some provocation, no matter what the gift was?"

"Maybe. But that's his sorest spot," I said.

"I have to follow God's lead in what I do," said Lloyd, "not some vague fear that what I do may upset Pop."

"It wasn't God's lead when you were eighteen, though, was it?" I asked.

Lloyd smiled, shook his head, and sat back in the chair. "No, it sure wasn't, John. It sure wasn't."

My recollections of Lloyd's rebelliousness against our father started from my earliest recollections. I was just ten when Lloyd graduated from high school. But I remember vividly his violent departure. That was the last time we saw Lloyd until the baptism incident four years later. But we knew that during that time he was following a rough, carousing life.

"Yeah, I had stormy four years after I left home," said Lloyd, as if in response to my thoughts. "And if I could change all that I sure would. But once I became reborn . . . all that was washed away, anyway." He smiled. "I like to think of it as my own personal B.C. and A.D. -- Before Christ . . . and After Deliverance!"

"But do you have to talk about it?" I asked him.

He nodded. "I have to talk about it," he said quietly.

I noticed that the drink that I brought with me to the dinner table was still sitting before me. I picked it up and began to drink. Then I stopped and looked accusingly at Lloyd. "I suppose you feel you have to talk about *this*, too," I said, lifting my glass.

"Do you want me to?" he asked.

"Not now," I said.

"Then I won't."

"Good." I lifted the glass, and let the warm, pungent liquid pass through my mouth. I felt a sudden hostility toward Lloyd, and I couldn't identify the reason. I didn't like that. It reminded me of the time he left home. I thought it was terrible for him to treat our father that way . . . but I envied him for his strength. I think that's why I decided not to follow the legal profession. It was my own rebellion -- my own way of proving that I was just as strong as Lloyd. But I didn't break the relationship with my father. What was there about Lloyd and he that became so . . . terminal? If Lloyd had been sanctimonious in his faith, I could have understood it, but he never was.

"I'd rather talk to you about Jung's theories," said Lloyd.

"What?" My mind had lost the flow.

"You asked me if I was going to talk to you about . . . "

"Oh . . . all right . . . all right." I was back on track.

"And I get the distinct impression that you're avoiding the topic," continued Lloyd.

I was, of course, but that didn't relate to the point that I was trying to make. "You know, I treat born-again believers from time to time," I said finally, in an attempt to find some disparaging link that might explain the confrontation.

Lloyd shrugged. "No one said Christians don't have problems."

"Yeah . . . I know." But *he* didn't seem to have any. Not with his family, anyway. He said it tonight. Amy confided in him, because they have a good relationship. And he and Kate . . . They always seemed so . . . content. I took another drink, and let the dulling potion divert my hostile feelings toward . . . toward what? I began to think that if Meg were more understanding things would be better, and I hated myself for falling into that rationalization. It was better at the office, though. I was in control. There was order, and purpose . . . That's why it was so important for the procedures to be followed.

I suddenly remembered Cheryl and her struggle to do the right thing, and I wondered if I would have to get rid of her. Then my mind played an amazing trick on me: it superimposed the incompetence of Cheryl onto my own unsuccessful dealings with my family. This was absurd. I had placed myself on my own couch, and was stepping myself through analytic hoops.

No . . . I had to concentrate on Lloyd's problem. I was sure that he could have prevented this confrontation . . . If he'd just had a little more psychological training . . . I drained the remainder of the drink, and settled back as the buzz of unresponsiveness soothed my unnecessary self-punishing thoughts. Things would be better Monday. That was a life that I could control.

3

Our car's tires thudded rhythmically across the regularly spaced dividers, and I found myself slapping my fingers against my knee in cadence with the dull sound. Meg had insisted on driving home, since I'd had so much to drink. I'd told her that in another hour or two the effects of the alcohol would have worn off, but she was eager to leave. Lloyd and his family had departed before eleven, and Meg wasn't inclined to spend any more time with the wives of my father's partners. We hadn't spoken a word since leaving. I glanced into the back seat. Diane was huddled in the corner -- either asleep or pretending to be.

Meg pulled into our driveway while retrieving the garage-door remote control from beneath the visor. As she pressed the button the door began to rise, and the timer-governed light inside the garage came on simultaneously. She drove slowly in, pressed the button for the door to close behind us, and turned off the ignition. I started to get out of the car, but I felt Meg's hand on my arm.

"John . . . " She glanced back at Diane, and then continued talking in a low voice. "We have to talk to her about what she did tonight."

"Yes . . . well, I'll try to find some time tomorrow, or . . . "

"No. Tonight, John!" she said emphatically in a forced whisper. "Otherwise, it will just . . . drift off into another forgotten episode."

The familiar feeling of discomfort rose from the base of my spine. I glanced at my watch. It was after eleven-thirty. I could make a plea on the basis of the late hour, but tomorrow was Saturday, and Diane didn't have to get up early. That would have been an irrelevant argument, anyway. Meg was right, of course. The issue should be dealt with while it was fresh in everyone's mind.

"I'll get the door and wait for you inside," continued Meg, assuming that I had capitulated. "You wake Diane and bring her in." She left the car and climbed the narrow steps leading to our back door.

I got out of the car, walked around to the other side, and opened the back door. Diane was still huddled in the seat, her eyes closed tightly. Perhaps she *was* really asleep. I put my hand on her shoulder and shook gently. "Diane . . . Diane, wake up."

"Hmm . . . " She stirred restlessly, and her eyes opened a crack.

"We're home," I said. "Let's go in."

Diane's eyes opened fully, now, and she moved her head from side to side with a disoriented gaze. I helped her out of the car and closed the door. As we walked toward the door to the house, the light suddenly went out. The timer had reached its programmed limit. The garage was in total darkness. Diane emitted a hushed moan, and clutched my arm.

"It's all right, honey," I reassured her, and guided her up the narrow steps.

As I opened the door, the light from the house flooded our entrance. Diane squinted and turned her head aside. Meg was waiting in the kitchen. An opened container of cocoa sat on the sink, and Meg was holding a large cup under the hot-water tap in our refrigerator door. She pointed toward the round kitchen table. I led Diane to a waiting chair, and sat beside her. Meg stirred the cocoa and placed the spoon on the sink. Then she sat across from us and pushed the cup in front of Diane.

"What's this all about?" asked Diane.

"It's for you," said Meg. "I thought it might taste good."

"Yuk!" Diane shoved the cup aside and turned away."

"We need to talk, Diane," I said.

"About what?" she asked.

"About your behavior at the party tonight," said Meg.

"Oh . . . Mom!"

"Why did you do that, Diane?" I asked her. "You surely knew that it would embarrass your mother . . . and me."

"I wouldn't have embarrassed anyone, if you'd just left me alone," she said.

"I still need to know why you did it, Diane," I persisted. "You were in a really sullen state before we left . . . and then sneaking drinks . . . "

"Just forget it!" murmured Diane angrily.

"We're not going to forget it, Diane," said Meg. "We have to know what's bothering you."

"Let's start with tonight," I suggested. "Why were you so upset about tonight?"

Diane frowned at both of us, sighed deeply, and sunk down gloomily in her chair. "I hate going over there," she said.

"Why? They're your grandparents." I said.

"They don't act like grandparents," said Diane.

"How are grandparents supposed to act?" I asked.

Diane shook her head. "Every time we go, he starts some kind of argument. He's mean! He's just a mean old man!"

"You shouldn't talk about your grandfather that way, Diane," I said.

"She's right, John," said Meg suddenly.

"What?"

"She's right," Meg repeated. "Your father is a mean old man."

"Meg . . . " I leaned across the table and spoke threateningly to her. "It's not going to help me discipline Diane, if you agree with her."

"This isn't about discipline, John," said Meg. "It's about understanding."

"Nevertheless, you don't establish an understanding atmosphere by casting insults at my father," I said.

"But we have to recognize facts," persisted Meg. "Look at the way your father behaved tonight. Look at the way he treated Lloyd."

"Ahh . . . " I waved my hand toward her contemptuously, and sat back in my chair.

"How can you toss it off like that?" asked Meg. "He was brutal!"

"Lloyd was partially responsible for that," I told her.

"How can you say that?" she asked with an astonished look on her face.

"Well . . . giving him that Bible . . . He should have known."

"I don't believe what I'm hearing!" Meg responded, her voice rising in anger.

"You just don't understand how that . . . "

"You're always doing this!" She interrupted. "Your father cuts Lloyd down, and you go along with it. You never defend your brother. What's the matter with you two?"

"There's nothing the matter with *me*," I said petulantly.

"So it's all Lloyd's fault?"

"Stop it!" Diane suddenly rose and backed away from the table. "Stop it!" she yelled again. "It always turns out like this! You two are as bad as Grandpa!" She turned and ran from the room.

Meg started to go after her, but I grasped her wrist, and pulled her back down into her chair.

"We can't just let her walk out like that," said Meg.

I held tight to her wrist and shook my head. "We blew it tonight, Meg."

"But . . . "

"The minute we started at each other, we lost our chance," I said.

Meg sighed. Then she shook her wrist free and stood up. She took the cup of cocoa over the sink and poured it out. "I don't think you realize how worried I've been lately, John," she said. "I thought it would be better when school let out for the summer break. But she still associates with the same people."

"Well, what's wrong with that?" I asked.

Meg cast a hateful look toward me, and shook her head. "The same thing that was wrong in April!"

"Oh . . . you mean the beach thing . . . "

"Of course!"

During spring break, Meg had asked to go to the beach with some of her friends for a week. Meg had refused, but I had persuaded her to let Diane go for three days, since one of the girl's parents would be staying with them. Unfortunately, the parents had not done an adequate job of supervision, and the girls had become involved in a wild party with some boys in an adjacent house.

"You surely haven't forgotten that already have you?" continued Meg.

"Of course not," I said. "That was an unfortunate incident. But the police stopped it before anything really serious happened."

"You mean I picked Diane up and brought her home before anything serious happened," she corrected.

"Well, that's over with now," I said.

"But she's running around with the same kids, and . . . " Meg sighed, and sat down across from me again. "But it's more than that, John. "Ever since then, Diane has withdrawn into her own little world. I can't even talk to her anymore."

"Yes . . . I've noticed that."

"Well, that's why I'm asking for your help. I mean . . . you're a psychiatrist, for heaven's sake!" she said irritably. "Surely you should be able to understand her."

"I do . . . I think I do understand," I said. "But I'll admit to you that understanding problems is a lot easier than solving them."

Meg cast a vacant expression toward me, raised her hands in frustration, and sat back in her chair.

There was more to it than that, of course. Meg had touched her finger on a sore spot, and I wasn't willing to let her massage the wound. I knew that Meg thought my being a psychiatrist should make it possible for me to "fix" things in Diane's behavior. I used to think that it should, too. I'd certainly had success with my patients. Why not Diane? Meg even suggested once handling our family disagreements in my office -- treating Diane like a patient. But I knew that wouldn't work. I couldn't let my home life interfere with my career life. They were two separate and distinct entities. Allowing them to merge would result in the failure of both. At least, now, I was succeeding with one.

"Why don't other people have these problems?" Meg asked aimlessly.

"What?"

"Why don't other . . . "

"I *heard* you," I said. "I just can't believe you'd make such a statement. Everyone has problems with their children."

"No. *These* problems," she corrected, pointing first toward Diane's room, then toward herself, and then toward me. "It's not just Diane," she continued. "Why do you suppose . . . " She bit her lip lightly and shook her head.

"What?"

"I know how you're going to react to this," she said.

"Go on . . . go on," I prodded her, somewhat tauntingly.

"Why do you suppose Lloyd's children are as well adjusted as they are?" she asked quickly.

"Oh, so that's it!" I slammed my hand against the table and turned away.

"Well, haven't you ever thought about it?" she asked.

I shouldn't have reacted so defensively. Of course I'd thought about it. Just tonight . . . Amy confided in Lloyd, didn't she. Of course I'd thought about it. I just wasn't ready to deal with it. "Of course I've thought about it," I mumbled. Then, almost without thinking, I stood, walked to the cupboard, and pulled out a glass and a bottle of bourbon.

"What are you doing?" asked Meg.

"Getting a nightcap," I said, pouring a double shot into the glass.

"You've been drinking all night long," she said.

"That's an exaggeration," I responded.

"We need to talk about this, John," said Meg. "Why do you insist on escaping?"

"Escaping? Oh . . . Now *you're* the psychiatrist," I said sarcastically. I shook my head in irritation at myself. What was making me act this way? I bit my tongue, and turned toward the sink.

"John . . . "

"Hmm?" I turned to see Meg standing beside me.

"Maybe we just need to get away somewhere . . . you and I . . . and Diane. Why don't we just jump in the car tomorrow and drive somewhere."

"Can't," I responded abruptly. And then I suddenly realized that I'd forgotten to tell her about tomorrow.

"Why not?" she asked.

"I . . . ah . . . I'm taking hang-gliding lessons," I said.

Meg backed away and squinted her eyes. "Hang gliding?"

"Yes . . . " I knew how ludicrous it must have sounded, and I suddenly laughed at the thought of it. "I know what you're thinking. But it's true. I met this guy at the club last week who's an instructor, and I arranged to meet him tomorrow for lessons." I laughed again.

"You . . . you know I hate it when you do these dangerous things," she said.

"Well . . . yeah . . . "

"Take us along," Meg said suddenly.

"Huh?"

"If that's the only way we can spend time with you, then . . . "

"No." I hadn't intended to sound so dogmatic. It just slipped out. "Not while I'm learning. That would make me too nervous. Maybe later. Maybe after . . . " I let my voice drift off. That was a put-off, and we both knew it. I'd refused her too many other times -- the boat racing, the sky-diving, and the water-skiing . . . She couldn't understand. Even I couldn't fully understand, for that matter. I just knew that this was another aspect of my life that I couldn't allow to mingle with my family life. Not yet, anyway. Not until I found some meaning . . . for all of them.

"What about Sunday, then?" continued Meg.

"This just isn't a good weekend, Meg," I said. "I got this new case Friday . . . and I'm going to need to spend some time at the office on Sunday preparing . . . "

"There's always a reason, John!" she said angrily.

"Next weekend, Meg," I said. "I promise."

"Unless something else comes up." She crossed her arms and leaned against the sink.

"Meg . . . " I set my drink down and approached her. Her eyes were closed, and her short dark hair brushed lightly against the cupboard. She appeared suddenly very alluring to me. I placed me hand on her shoulder. "Meg . . . Let's put this evening behind us." I pulled her around toward me. "C'mon . . . Let's set these ridiculous problems aside . . . and be . . . close . . . "

Meg opened her eyes, and tears gathered in the corners. "The only ridiculous problem is a nonexistent problem," she said softly. "And our problems definitely exist. You can't just push them aside like they aren't there. You can't just push us aside, either . . . not for long . . . " She turned and started walking out of the room.

"Meg . . . Wait a minute."

She put her hand up without turning around. "See you . . . whenever." She left the room.

I considered following her, but then thought better of it. When Meg got this way, my attempting to reestablish communication always resulted in further frustration. I picked up my drink and walked into the living room. The light from the kitchen spilled dimly into the spacious room, casting faintly discernible shadows across the dark furnishings. I found my way to the plush couch and sat heavily. I tried to recall the point in our marriage that Meg and I had begun to have trouble communicating. During the first five years of our marriage, Meg had worked, either full-time or part time, to help support us while I was finishing my education. Then, during the first few years of my practice, while Diane was in elementary school, Meg and I seemed content to look forward to the comforts that we would enjoy as the result of my successful practice. Three years ago we bought this house. I thought that may have been the turning point. The house had been the pinnacle of our motivation and, once that was attained, we no longer spent much time together planning for future acquisitions. I was sure that was the point at which I began to spend more time with my career. Success is a merciless taskmaster; it requires greater and greater commitment toward a never-attainable state of perfection. Of course, Diane had become a teenager by then -- that magic period of life at which children suddenly know more than their parents. Lloyd had certainly exhibited that with our father. I tried to recall my own teenage years. I had adjusted . . . coped with the relationships. What was the difference? After Lloyd left home, my father had become more affluent, of course . . . and there was the horseback training . . .

I sank more deeply into the couch and swallowed half of my drink. I closed my eyes as the dulling sensation swept slowly through the recesses of my perception. People should be able to cope. I certainly did. And it wasn't easy. Not everything a person does is going to fall into the realm of wished-for experiences. That's why it was so important to separate myself into aspects of performance. I had performed better as a child than Lloyd had . . . that was surely the case. And Lloyd should certainly not be sanctimonious with our father, and definitely not with me, because Lloyd had experienced more immoral acts during those four years after he left home than I had in my lifetime. That was one thing that I had definitely acquired from our father -- scrupulous personal morality. That had always been a point of pride . . . as well it should have been.

I swallowed the remaining portion of the drink, and set the glass clumsily on the low table beside the couch. No, that part was unreproachable. I had always been a good ethical role model for Diane. What, then . . . I began to be faintly dizzy from the effects of the alcohol. I had the sudden feeling that my head was spinning off my body and rising slowly toward the high ceiling. But my visual system was still firmly attached, and as I rose, I looked back at my disembodied self, sitting on the couch. The dizziness increased, and the image split, and there were now two . . . three of me, sitting on three semi-disjointed couches. I chuckled at the entertaining illusion, and pursued it. The figure in the center appeared to be taking a beating from the others. The figure on the left was counseling it on successful coping skills . . . and the figure on the right was enticing it toward daring escapades. The figure in the center wanted to cope . . . wanted to be excitedly involved . . . but it was rooted to the couch . . .

The figures merged again, and my spinning head plummeted back and attached itself to my body. I breathed deeply and clasped my hands on my stomach. If it were only as easy as that . . . screw my head on and merge the lives. Surely it was possible . . . and if it was possible, surely I, above all people, could accomplish it. I would work on it . . . another day.

4

Mondays are usually difficult for me. I generally plan some stimulating activity on the weekend, and the following tightly scheduled office routine seems dull by comparison. But today was different. Even as I was being instructed on the exciting sport of hang-gliding on Saturday, I was looking forward with anticipation to my next session with "Mrs. Smith." Of course, I had no way of knowing whether this strange person would even show up again, and I had already qualified my expectations with that fact in mind. Nevertheless, I experienced a tingle of excitement as Cheryl knocked lightly on my door and stepped into my office at 4:00 p.m.

"Dr. Summers . . . "

I merely looked up from my desk and nodded.

"He's here . . . or she . . . or . . . " She laughed nervously.

"That's good, Cheryl," I said.

"You were right, Dr. Summers," she whispered. "He is a man."

"Yes."

"He introduced himself today as '*Mr.* Smith.'"

"Have him come in."

She nodded, opened the door fully, and began to make her objectionable beckoning motion.

"Cheryl . . . " I cautioned.

"Oops!" She giggled lightly. Then she gracefully pointed her arm into my office, and spoke softly. "Mr. Smith . . . The doctor will see you now."

I nodded in approval. "Mr. Smith" walked briskly through the doorway, and Cheryl closed it behind him. He wore a long trench coat today. The same darkly tinted sunglasses covered the upper part of his face, but what was apparently his own flowing sandy-colored hair was revealed. He walked directly to the chair opposite me, and sat.

"Good afternoon, Mr. Smith," I said. "I'm glad that you came in again."

"I always keep my appointments," he said. His voice was firmly masculine today.

"That's good," I said. Then I pointed toward my eyes. "But I still would prefer the opportunity to experience eye contact."

"We'll see," he said without moving. "Perhaps later."

"I thought you were going to have me checked out over the weekend," I reminded him.

"I did," he responded abruptly. "But now I have to complete my personal verification of the data."

"I see. Well, tell me, how did the medication work?" I asked.

"As expected, I assume," he said. "You gave me only two doses."

"Yes. When did you take them?" I asked.

He held up a hand slowly with a single finger extended. "Friday . . . " he said, touching that finger. Then he extended a second and touched it. "And Saturday."

"And those nights?"

"Restful," he said tentatively. Then he extended a third finger, and hit the three rhythmically. "But Sunday . . . "

"Last night," I said.

He nodded. "Why did you plan it that way?"

"Sometimes the effects of two restful nights carry over," I explained. "That's something we had to discover."

"Discovery can be exciting . . . if you're not a participant."

"So . . . last night was not restful?" I asked.

"Of course not," he said, beginning to become agitated.

"Tell me what happened," I said.

He sat rigidly without responding. His fingers clutched at the arm of the chair, and perspiration beaded on his forehead.

"You dreamed again," I coaxed.

"Worse . . . " he mumbled. "You made it worse!" The perspiration now trickled under his sunglasses, and down his cheek.

"It's rather warm in here, Mr. Smith," I said. "Why don't you take your overcoat off. I'm sure you'll be more comfortable."

He stood mechanically, removed his trench coat. He wiped his forehead with the tail of the coat, and then he tossed it on the floor beside him. Underneath, he wore a tight-fitting light blue turtle-neck shirt that revealed a muscular body. Around his neck hung the same golden mandala that he had worn on Friday, and it thumped against his chest as he sat down again.

After he had sat for a moment, I pursued the conversation. "You said, 'worse.' Were there more dreams?"

"Just one," he muttered. "There's always just one."

"You told me Friday you had many dreams," I reminded him.

"Yes . . . many dreams," he agreed. "But always just one."

"I see."

"It's really quite simple." He sat forward, and spoke with a self-assured tone. "You displayed a degree of competence in the medication you gave me. I suggest that you give me a prescription for some more of it, and we'll give it a try. Say . . . a three-week supply."

"I can only prescribe medication during the course of treatment, Mr. Smith," I said. "And if I'm going to treat you, I'll need some additional information."

"Of course, I'll tell you whatever you really need to know."

"Very well . . . " I could see that he was going to be very resistive, so I decided to begin with something that should be non-threatening. "Why don't you begin by telling me who referred you to me."

He sat silently, drumming his fingers on the arm of the chair.

"Or, if you'd prefer, we could begin with what you do for a living."

"Dr. Butler," he said impulsively.

This got my attention. "Dr. Leonard Butler?" I asked.

"Our relationship wasn't on a first-name basis," he responded.

That was a *yes.* That would help. Leonard was a friend of mine. We had done our undergraduate work together at the State University. But he had followed the Freudian school, whereas I had elected to attend the Jung Psychiatric Institute. "Yes, I know Dr. Butler," I said. "How long did he treat you?"

"I didn't say that he was treating me," he responded angrily.

I merely looked at him, expressing facially a repetition of the question.

He shifted uncomfortably in the chair and turned his head away. "Three months," he said finally. He brushed his hand three times across the arm of the chair as if to emphasize the number.

"What ailment was he treating you for?" I asked.

He shifted again, and turned his head in the other direction.

"I can ask Dr. Butler, of course," I told him, "but it would be better if you would tell me yourself."

He sat facing me again, and a faint smile crossed his lips. "I've been so busy, you know . . . especially for the last three months. And, of course, there are so many thoughts rushing through my head . . . I don't know if you've ever experienced that. So, naturally, Dr. Butler thought I'd gotten a little 'schizi.' He assured me, of course, that it was a result of the demands of my work."

He paused for a moment, so I pursued his last statement. "Your entrepreneur career, you mean?"

"He's a competent doctor, I'm sure," he continued without responding to my question. "But he didn't seem to be getting anywhere, and he thought that you might have a little more success."

"I see. Did he tell you why he thought that?" I asked.

"Oh . . . something about your being a follower of Jung, I believe," he said casually. Then he leaned forward. "Is that correct?"

"Yes."

He sat back again and gestured aimlessly. "Jung . . . Freud . . . It makes little difference to me, as long as the doctor finds some way to tame these pesky thoughts . . . and dreams. I do need my rest, you know. I'm so busy."

If Leonard had, in fact, diagnosed Mr. Smith as being schizophrenic, I could understand his referring him to me for treatment. Leonard held a dismal view of the prognosis for treating schizophrenia. I was a little surprised that he had given up after only three months, however. "What did Dr. Butler tell you about schizophrenia?" I asked.

"Well . . . " He laughed nervously. "He told me it *didn't* mean a dual personality."

"No, that's a common misunderstanding," I agreed.

"But he talked about a splitting . . . the false self . . . the true self . . . " He laughed again. "Too many *me's.* No wonder I have so many thoughts."

"All of us have different selves," I assured him. "We just have to find a way to make them work in harmony."

"Harmony . . . yes." His mouth remained open in silent continuation of a thought. Then he spoke testily. "Dr. Butler did tell me . . . He said there was very little chance for complete cure . . . "

"I disagree with that view," I interrupted.

He sighed, and smiled faintly. "Of course . . . as do many of your esteemed colleagues, I'm sure."

"Yes."

"I was quite certain that Dr. Butler was incompetent," he said. "Why . . . he couldn't even hypnotize me."

"How often did he attempt hypnosis?" I asked.

"Oh . . . several times," he said. "I'm sure you'll have more success, though."

I shook my head. "I rarely use hypnosis."

"Why not?"

"Well, first of all, many people simply can't be hypnotized. It sounds as though you may be one of those."

"That's what Dr. Butler said."

I nodded. "Also, the historic facts derived through hypnosis may be distorted beyond their level of importance. Most will have no relevance to your current problem."

"But how will you learn my secrets?" he asked. "There are so many secrets."

"We start with what you know. Every fact . . . every feeling . . . "

"I can deal with what I know," he said. "It's what's beneath . . . the shadows . . . they're everywhere . . . "

"We'll find them," I reassured him.

He glanced about the room, and his eyes fell on my therapy couch. "Will I have to lie on that?"

"Well, it's usually helpful during the initial phase," I said.

"Dr. Butler said it could take years," he mumbled without looking back.

"Well . . . " He had apparently gotten a lot of negative information from Leonard. Accurate, but counterproductive. He shouldn't have to focus on the required length of therapy at this time. "That depends on how quickly we obtain the information we need," I told him. "Some therapists spend an inordinate amount of time in the discovery process. I'm counting on you to provide me with a lot of good information very rapidly."

He smiled, and quickly sat forward and placed his hands on my desk. "I like the way you talk!" He said, with a slight crack in his voice. Then he stopped, pushed himself back slowly to a casual sitting position, and folded his hands on his lap. "I think I'll give you a short try, Dr. Summers. I'm very busy, of course, but I'll try to work you in for a few sessions."

"Very well." I sat back in my chair, and looked at him without speaking for a moment. "The very first task, Mr. Smith, is to establish a feeling of trust between us."

"Trust is essential," he agreed.

"Then you'll need to demonstrate that," I said, pointing to my eyes again.

He sighed. Then he slowly removed his sunglasses and laid them on his lap. He sat forward and looked at me as if he were anticipating a response. "Don't you know who I am?" he asked.

I shook my head.

"Hmm . . . " He got a perplexed look on his face, and sat back. "I'm Peter Lumen," he said finally.

I shrugged and raised my hands questioningly.

"You still don't know?" Then his head nodded vigorously. "Of course . . . You're a psychiatrist!" He reached to the floor and pulled his trench coat over his lap. Then he placed his hand in the coat's inside pocket, and retrieved a tightly rolled document. He removed a rubber band from the document, and tossed it on my desk. "There . . . that should help." He turned partially sideways in the chair and looked out the window.

I unrolled the document, and found it to be a small promotional poster. Peter's figure was featured as the center of attention. He wore a flowing white robe, and his arms were outstretched. He stood in front of a colorful backdrop, which included a waterfall, and a large tree. In bold letters across the top of the poster was the enticing message:

THE LIGHT ON THE ROCK

THE HEALING MINISTRY OF PETER LUMEN

An emoting singer was displayed in the midst of a crowd in the foreground, and several names were listed in the corner. My interest in this case suddenly doubled. Peter's presentation and actions had already intrigued me; the knowledge that he was an evangelist left me initially in a state of shock.

Peter glanced in my direction. "You seem surprised."

"I am," I admitted. "What did you mean before, when you said, 'Of course . . . You're a psychiatrist?'" I asked.

Peter shrugged and turned his head away again. "I shouldn't have expected you to recognize me, since you're not a Christian."

There was too much meaning implicit in that statement. I decided not to pursue it at this time. I anchored the corners of the poster with ash trays and pen holders to prevent it from rolling back up again. Then I sat back and studied first the poster, and then Peter. "Tell me what you do," I said finally. "In your ministry, I mean."

He turned toward me again. He glanced at the poster momentarily, and then he laid his head back on the chair and closed his eyes. "I was appointed by God. I heal people. Like Christ did, you know." He opened his eyes, but left his head on the back of the chair, and rolled it back and forth slowly. "It's so exhausting . . . being a Christ figure for so many thousands of people . . . " He continued moving his head from side to side for a few moments. Then he suddenly sat upright, and spoke in a businesslike manner. "How would Jung deal with that?"

"With what?" I asked.

"With the Christ figure," he said.

"Jung treats Christ as an archetype," I explained slowly, not knowing where he was leading. "He finds that people through the ages have assimilated the Christ figure in their dreams or fantasy projections of heroic existence."

"I've read some Jung, you know," Peter said smugly. "I studied Freud, too, while I was being treated by Dr. Butler. That's how I found out about the negative prognosis and the dreadfully long therapeutic time. I studied some Jung before I came to you. I'll be watching you."

"I believe you've already made an accurate value judgment," I said. "It shouldn't really be necessary for you to distrust me any longer."

His mouth slowly lifted into a smile. "Flattery will get you everywhere!"

"Please continue describing your work," I urged.

He sighed, closed his eyes, and placed his head back against the top of the chair again. "People come to me . . . They know that I was appointed . . . and anointed . . . " He laughed giddily, and repeated it without opening his eyes. "Appointed and anointed!" Then his lips turned into a frown. "The sinners come to me . . . and I heal them. Just like Christ. But it's harder for me. I understand their sin. Christ didn't have an evil side, you know . . . that was a definite character weakness. It's harder for me. I feel the . . . I feel their sin . . . "

He was silent for several seconds. When he did not continue, I decided to be more directive. I glanced at the poster before me. "Tell me about the people who work with you."

"Hmm?"

"There are several listed here on the poster," I said. I read one of the names: "*Greg Hatcher -- Stewardship Minister.*"

"Mr. Money-bags," he said without raising his head.

"Does your ministry bring in a great deal of money?" I asked.

"So I'm told," he mumbled.

"But you don't get involved in that aspect of the ministry?" I asked.

"Greg realizes I have too many important things to do," said Peter. "He handles all that."

"Do you trust him?" I asked.

Peter's eyes popped open. "I've studied some economics," he said deliberately. "I'm watching him. People have to be watched."

"How about this name," I said, reading again: "*Kyle Wingate -- Worship Leader.*"

Peter closed his eyes again and smiled. "Kyle would like to be a Christ figure," he said softly. "I know that he lusts after it."

"Does he ever substitute for you?" I asked.

"The people would stone him," he said ominously.

"I see . . . " I looked back at the poster. "Who is the girl . . . the one singing?" I asked.

Peter sat up abruptly, and brushed his hand across his trench coat, which still lay across his lap. "Oh, that's Julie . . . Julie Peters. She's our featured singer."

"She's very pretty," I said.

"Yes, she's . . . " He paused, looked intently at her picture for a moment, and then looked away. "Naturally, I'm not involved with her . . . with any of my workers . . . in anything but a professional manner."

"Why?"

"Oh . . . " Peter smiled coyly and nodded. Then he sat forward and shook his head. "No. I know what you're getting at. I'm not a homosexual, you know. Dr. Butler wondered about that, too. He told me that is frequently the case with schizophrenics. I've studied Freud, you know. I know what he thinks."

"Jung does not insist on that interpretation," I said.

"And you?"

"No."

Peter studied me coldly for a moment, and then he sighed and sat back. "Remember that. I'm not a homosexual. There are simply other more taxing responsibilities."

"That's understandable," I said. I glanced at my watch. The time was flying, and there were several other items I needed at least to touch upon. "Last night, Peter . . . " I began.

"Sunday nights are the worst," he interrupted me. "I knew that I should have saved the medication until then."

"Tell me about last night," I said. "The dream."

"Many dreams," he mumbled. "Each time . . . they conspire . . . gather together . . . become one . . . "

"Tell me about last night's dream, Peter," I said. "Can you do that?"

Perspiration rose on his forehead again. He clutched at the necklace, and then brought the mandala up before his eyes. "You'll probably think it comes from this . . . " He dropped the mandala. "But it's more . . . so much more."

"Describe it, Peter . . . as well as you can."

Peter sighed and began speaking slowly, almost dispassionately. "I was at the top of a long flight of stairs, standing in my white robe. At the bottom . . . there was a glow. As I descended, I could see it. It was a mandala . . . like this one, but . . . different. Snakes jumped out from the wall and wagged their tongues at me as I walked by. Someone called out -- 'Protect yourself . . . protect yourself . . . ' It was because of my robe. The serpents hate purity, you know. But it was only a robe. I could put it on and take it off, whenever I wished. I walked away from my robe, but I could still see myself wearing it. I was in both places. The me in the robe smiled and walked back up the stairs. The other me couldn't leave. The serpents were all around. And the mandala was there, drawing me . . . and Satan was there, smiling. The mandala was beautiful, and I wanted to put it on. I continued down, and the stairs became narrower and narrower . . . and they began to crumble. But Satan called out and told me that he would save me. And he stuck his tongue out at me . . . but it had been torn out, and all that was left was a bloody stub. The mandala was burning, and its warm flames licked my body like serpents, and I was drawn to it . . . deeper, and deeper . . . "

Peter picked up the tail of his trench coat and wiped it across his perspiring face again. Then he sat silently for several seconds.

"Is that it?" I asked.

He suddenly focused his eyes on me, sat erect, and began speaking formally again. "Much ado about nothing, perhaps, but . . . yes, that's it."

"And each time it's the same dream?"

"Or with an element added, or modified," said Peter. "Last night, the flames enticed me. The time before, they burned my flesh."

"I see. And what was the very first element to surface?" I asked.

A vacant expression crossed Peter's face, and he responded slowly. "The white robe." His face then became abruptly more alert, and he spoke quickly. "So, if you can just interpret my dream, I'll know who my enemies are, and I can go to battle with sword in hand."

"I couldn't possibly interpret a single dream, Peter," I said.

He gave me a hateful look. "Why not?" he asked. "Didn't I describe it in sufficient detail?"

"You did an excellent job of relating it," I said.

"Then you should be able to interpret it," he said. "Let me remind you that in the second year of Nebuchadnezzar's reign, he had dreams, and the Chaldeans could not interpret them . . . and he set out to destroy them for their incompetence!"

"Nevertheless, I cannot interpret a dream in isolation," I continued, electing not to push him into an explication of his Biblical reference at this time. "I must relate it to other information I learn about you, and to other dreams that you have, before . . . "

"I don't want to have any other dreams!" he shouted. "Don't you understand? I expect you to stop them!"

"I know, Peter," I said. "And I will. It's just going to take some time."

"Time . . . time . . . " He began flopping his head from side to side against his knuckles. "Tick, tock . . . tick, tock . . . tick, tock . . . "

"I will prescribe some medication for you, though, Peter, to relieve the symptoms while we are in therapy."

Peter put his hands on the arms of the chair and spoke coldly and rationally again. "I've tried them all. Nothing works."

"Oh? What medication did Dr. Butler have you take?" I asked.

He snorted contemptuously, and quickly rattled off the names of several drugs: "Chlorpromazine, Haloperidol, Fluphenazine, Mezoridazine . . . " He shook his head. "Nothing worked," he muttered.

"There are others," I told him.

"Guaranteed to work?" he asked.

I shook my head slowly. "Some people don't respond to any of them, but that's rare. We have to try several until we find the right one." I pulled a pad from my desk drawer, and wrote a prescription for Acetophenazine. I was impressed that Peter remembered the medications that he'd already tried, and that didn't work. I looked up from writing the prescription, and I saw that Peter was sitting slumped in the chair, with tears rolling down his face.

"We'll find the answer, Peter," I said. "Take the medication, and trust me. There is a road out of your jungle. We'll find it."

"It isn't really all that bad, you know," he mumbled. "It's just my fear of it. When I think about it . . . the flames are warm, and the serpents nestle harmlessly about my body. It isn't all that bad . . . who else can experience that?"

"Your fear is good, Peter," I said. "Your fear is healthy. It's warning you of something that needs to be corrected."

"At what cost?" he asked.

"We'll find the answer," I repeated. I handed him the prescription, and then I picked up the telephone receiver and pressed the intercom button.

"Yes?"

"Cheryl, would you step in for a moment?" I said.

"Yes, Dr. Summers."

I hung up the receiver, and looked past Peter to see the door open, and Cheryl step briskly into the office. She walked around to the side of my desk.

"Cheryl . . . this is Peter," I said.

Peter suddenly looked at me, and then at Cheryl. He fumbled for his sunglasses, put them quickly on, and then stood, holding his trench coat bundled in front of him. He extended his hand toward her. "Peter Smith," he said.

"I'm glad to meet you, Mr. Smith," said Cheryl.

"Why don't we just make it *Peter*," I said. "All right?"

Peter glanced at me and nodded.

"I want you to schedule Peter for three sessions each week, Cheryl," I said.

"Sure, Dr. Summers," she said brightly. "Come on with me, Peter."

Cheryl and Peter left the office and closed the door behind them. Cheryl had done all right today. Just a little . . . I couldn't put my finger on it. There was just something lacking. But it was just Monday, and I had concluded that I would give her until Friday.

Leonard Butler . . . We hadn't remained as close as we had been in undergraduate school, but we met socially from time to time. I couldn't understand why he didn't call me . . . tell me that he had referred one of his patients. Perhaps he felt bad about having to admit failure. But Leonard always said you could never cure a schizophrenic. He wasn't the only one, either. Many psychiatrists believed that. It was only my heavy indoctrination at the Institute, and Bernadette's constant help that made me a believer. But still . . . it was so theoretical. I had treated only five or six schizophrenics since I began my practice, and my success with them had been only moderate. I regretted the fact that I hadn't spent some time working in the State hospital. Working with schizophrenics in the hospital setting would have given me valuable experience. But my father would have none of that. He insisted that State hospital assignments were meant solely for economically deprived interns who used them as a means of repaying government loans. Since he had financed my college education, there was no need for government loans. And since he had set me up in private practice, and provided the majority of my patients, there was no need for an experience-filled resume.

I struggled to recall the details of my previous cases of schizophrenia. If I were to be honest with myself, I would have to term them borderline. Peter's case, on the other hand, was clearly a full-blown psychosis. So many of the symptoms were clearly illustrated -- the bizarre behavior, the impersonations, the hallucinatory dreams, the paranoia . . . I had never dealt with anything approaching his condition. A feeling of utter inadequacy swept suddenly over my body. My mind drifted aimlessly back to Friday night, and I recalled sitting in the kitchen, grasping hopelessly for some magic solution to my problem with Diane, and Meg . . .

That was a self-destructive notion, and I pushed it aside. I had already decided not to merge my family life with my career, and that decision had to apply to these spurious comparative relationships as well. I was a successful psychiatrist. Even my father admitted that. If I couldn't solve Peter's problem, no one could.

5

Peter arrived promptly at the Wednesday and Friday sessions, and was quite communicative. The Acetophenazine that I had prescribed on Monday seemed to be diminishing his state of dread, so I had him continue with it. The dream had persisted nearly every night, but Peter's attitude toward it had become more analytical, and he described the details with a somewhat detached attitude. This was helpful in the recording of needed facts, but it did not allow me to differentiate those aspects which were the most threatening to him. Dreams are often a blend of trivial and significant incidents from recent and past events, and the mind forces the distorted montage into a single whole. It would be necessary for me to derive considerably more collateral and historic data before I could even begin to venture a reasonable interpretation. My reluctance irritated Peter, and that hindered our communication to a degree. By Friday, however, he had begun to trust the moderate success of the medication, and I had persuaded him to allow me to begin couch therapy. This seemed to allow Peter to open up more in his narrative. He spoke glowingly of his calling, and his work with the Light on the Rock Ministry. His account seemed somewhat superficial, however, and I was unsuccessful in probing beneath the surface.

The fact that Peter had just concluded three months of therapy with Leonard, of course, had a positive influence on his progress with me. I had called Leonard Tuesday to discuss Peter's case, but he was away at a conference all week. I knew that Leonard enjoyed playing golf, so I had his secretary schedule a round with me at my father's club Sunday morning. I had completely forgotten my promise to Meg that I would spend time with her and Diane this weekend. And I had another hang-gliding lesson on Saturday, so that day was out. I hit on what appeared to be a solution to this dilemma: I asked Meg to bring Diane and meet me at the club; I told her that, after my game and consultation with Leonard, I would take them to lunch. This arrangement seemed particularly positive when I called Leonard on Friday night to confirm our game. He said that he would also bring his wife, Grace, and that she and Meg could visit while we golfed.

I am not particularly good at golf. Leonard, on the other hand, while not perhaps possessing the skill of a professional, does exhibit a professional's attitude and concentration. He refused to talk business during the course of the game. I was glad that we had elected to play only a nine-hole round, because I was becoming very impatient. As we reached the last hole, Leonard sank a long putt for a final score of 39. I tapped the uncooperative ball several times, and finally finished with a score of 53.

"You're too impulsive, John," said Leonard. "You need to exhibit more patience, and the ball will follow your lead."

"I much prefer the more action-filled sports," I replied.

"You were always that way," said Leonard. "When we were in college, I attributed it to youthful abandon. But I see you're still following that bent."

"I can't find meaning in activities that don't challenge all of my instincts," I said.

"I don't play golf for meaning," responded Leonard. "I play golf for relaxation."

"I *sleep* for relaxation," I said.

Leonard laughed and motioned for the caddy to drive the golf cart up to where we were standing. Leonard took our putters, and slid them methodically into the bags on the cart. "You drive on back," he told the caddy. "We're going to walk."

The caddy nodded, and drove rapidly over the green mounds toward the clubhouse, which was three hundred yards away. We began walking slowly toward the attached terrace, where we were to meet Meg and Grace.

"Now do I have your undivided attention?" I asked.

"Of course," said Leonard. "Peter Lumen . . . " He shook his head. "He *requires* our undivided attention."

"I'm certainly glad that you finally recognized your inability to deal with so complex a case," I joked.

"Actually, it was a charity referral," he retorted. "I knew you were struggling to make a go of it, so I thought I'd give you one of my easy ones."

We laughed. I always enjoyed talking with Leonard, even though we had followed different schools of analysis. Meg and I had met with Leonard and Grace socially on several occasions, but our discussions invariably reverted to our careers, and Meg never seemed to appreciate that.

"Peter told me that you treated him for three months," I said.

"That's correct," said Leonard. Then he laughed. "I should say, he came to my office for three months. Usually very little treatment took place. It took me five sessions just to discover his true identity."

"I know what you mean," I said. "On his first visit to me, he came disguised as a woman -- *Mrs. Smith.*"

"Really? With me he was a bearded, homeless street person -- *Mr. Brown.*"

"And wearing sunglasses?" I asked.

"Of course," he said, smiling. "When I finally found out who he was, though, I was really intrigued, as I'm sure you were."

"Yes."

"But I'm afraid I let my fascination get the better of my common sense," said Leonard. "By the end of the first month, I had no doubt that he was an advanced paranoid schizophrenic. I probably should have concluded therapy at that point."

"Why?" I asked.

"Therapy is futile with schizophrenia," he said.

"That's an unfounded Freudian bias," I argued.

He smiled and shrugged. "Nevertheless, I *was* fascinated, and I let my ego convince me that I could provide him with some relief -- work toward, if nothing else, encapsulating the psychosis. So I tried a number of medications."

"All of which were unsuccessful, apparently," I said.

"Each one worked for a while," he said. "But then the effectiveness diminished . . . actually aggravated the hysteria in some instances."

"All the more reason to continue pursuing an analytic solution," I said.

"That's what I told myself," said Leonard. "But after two and a half months of couch therapy, I couldn't make a dent in his resistance. Toward the end, he began to be disturbed by dreams, but he would never reveal their content."

"He wouldn't?" I was surprised at this. "He's given me a complete description," I said.

"Really?" Leonard gave me a pensive look. "Really . . . " he repeated. "Well . . . no . . . he never revealed any of his dreams to me. That's when I decided to try hypnosis."

"You don't use hypnosis in therapy very often, do you?" I asked.

He shook his head. "Almost never. But I have used it successfully a few times for extremely resistive patients . . . like Peter."

"Peter told me you were unable to hypnotize him, though," I said.

"That's right," said Leonard. "I tried three . . . no, four times. On the fourth attempt he actually *pretended* to be hypnotized. That's when I realized I was butting my head against a brick wall."

"And you decided to let me give my head a beating, instead," I said.

"Precisely!" He laughed lightly, and then became more serious. "Actually, I thought perhaps my own negative prognosis was getting in the way of progress. Don't get me wrong . . .

I really *don't* believe schizophrenia can be cured. But far be it from me to prevent an attempt by someone who believes that it *can*."

"I was a little surprised that you didn't call me . . . alert me that he would be coming," I said.

"I frankly didn't believe that he would contact you, John," said Leonard. "I've seen so many like him . . . They drift until the psychosis becomes so overpowering that they need to be hospitalized. The fact that he actually went to you is a good sign, though, isn't it?"

"I suppose."

"I'd give you my notes, but I can summarize them in a nutshell," said Leonard. "Clearly the career that he's chosen illustrates a narcissistic tendency, and that fits in well with the diagnosis. I'm sure there is some sexual anomaly in his background at the root of his problem, but I was never able to get further into his past than the previous day's activities."

"Of course you realize that I don't believe that a sexual tie is not necessarily implied in cases of schizophrenia," I told him.

"Jung's argument with Freud on that point becomes primarily semantic," said Leonard. "Let's just say that there has to be some libidinal relationship."

I laughed. "Peter tells me you accused him of being homosexual."

"Absolutely not!" he said. Then he joined my laughter. "He got that from his reading."

"I gathered that from something he said later," I said.

"He's really very intelligent, you know," he added.

"Yes."

"I frequently got the impression that he was giving me information that he thought would fit in with my analytic approach," said Leonard. "It was almost as though he were taking charge of the session."

"Hmm . . . "

We walked for a few moments without speaking. Then Leonard pointed his finger toward an indiscriminate point on the ground. "Nevertheless . . . I definitely believe his psychosis relates to some sexual problem in his childhood."

"Well . . . " I was about to argue with him, but I realized that we were approaching the terrace. Meg and Grace sat at a round metal table, which was shaded by a large, brightly colored umbrella. They waved at us. "I'm afraid we'll have to put that discussion on hold," I said to Leonard, as we joined the two women.

"What discussion will you have to put on hold?" asked Grace.

"John and I were just discussing the finer points of the libido," said Leonard lightly.

"Ooh!" cried Grace, her voice swooping, and trailing out the syllable. "Continue your discussion . . . please!"

That was another reason they seldom met socially with Leonard and Grace. She was loud, and somewhat crude. Meg didn't care for her much, and her expression today showed a somewhat disdainful tolerance. Leonard and I sat down.

"Where's Diane?" I asked.

"She's in the game room . . . playing the video machines," said Meg.

"You should see some of the great games they have there, Leonard," said Grace. "We have to bring Melissa here some day."

"You should have brought her along today," I said. "She's the same age as Diane, isn't she?"

"She likes to sleep in on Sundays," said Grace.

The waiter approached, and took drink orders from Leonard and me. Meg and Grace ordered refills. I noticed for the first time that she'd had a margarita. I was surprised, since she usually orders just wine.

"So, how did the game go?" asked Meg.

"He killed me!" I said.

"John has a problem," said Leonard. "He has more *patients* than I do . . . but not nearly as much *patience*!"

Grace slapped the table and threw her head back and she laughed loudly. "I think you need a little more of what *he* has."

"Quality is what counts, my dear . . . not quantity," said Leonard with feigned haughtiness.

"And it's a little less quantity, now," said Grace. "I understand that Leonard gave you one of his schizophrenic patients."

"That's . . . ah . . . that's right," I said, somewhat surprised that Leonard had told Grace about it.

"Do you know how Leonard found out that this guy had a split personality?" asked Grace, with a sly smile on her face.

"No. How?" I asked.

"He walked in one day, and said, "Doctor, I'm simply beside myself!" She laughed raucously again.

Leonard and I joined in her laughter. Grace was somewhat uncouth, but she did have a knack for bringing the conversation to an informal level. Meg merely smiled.

The waiter brought the drinks and set them before us. Leonard insisted on paying for them. Meg quickly placed hers against her lips and drank.

"Seriously, Leonard," said Grace, still chuckling. "Why should John be any better suited to handle this patient than you?" she asked.

"It's the difference between the Freudian and the Jungian approaches to analysis," explained Leonard. "Some cases are better suited to one, and some to the other."

"Hmm . . . " Grace sipped her drink, and then smiled. "Maybe you should have followed the other school." She cupped her mouth toward Meg. "Leonard spends most of his time with neurotic women!"

"Well . . . I'm sure that John doesn't turn away any neurotic women who come to him for help," said Leonard.

"Only one," said Meg impulsively. Then she slumped down and continued drinking.

There was a moment of tense silence. I tried to question Meg with a silent look, but she avoided my eyes. Then Grace broke the silence.

"Ooh!" she whooped again. Then she licked her finger and made an imaginary mark in the air. "Score one for Meg!"

"Tell me, Leonard . . . How are you and Grace getting along with Melissa?" I asked, trying to change the subject.

"She's a teenager, John," said Leonard. "What can I say?"

"So you think . . . " I looked purposefully toward Meg. "You think it's normal for parents to have problems with their teenage daughters?"

"Of course," said Leonard.

"The schools help a lot more than they used to," said Grace. "Melissa was in the tenth grade last year, and she had this course that taught her values clarification. Frankly, she does a better job dealing with tough decisions now than I do."

"But what if she makes decisions you don't approve of?" asked Meg.

"Listen . . . It's her life," said Grace. "I can't live it for her. She's learning the consequences of her behavior. That's the important thing."

"That's not enough for me," said Meg. "There are some values that I *want* her to hold."

"Boy . . . you're in for a confrontation, aren't you?" laughed Grace.

Confrontation was the word, all right. But I had to agree with Meg. "No, Meg is right," I said. "There are some decisions that Diane makes that are simply . . . well . . . not appropriate."

"Based upon what standard?" asked Leonard.

"Well . . . based on . . . " I paused for a moment. The word *standard* had given me a fleeting recollection of my father, towering over me . . . "There are acceptable standards of behavior," he had said. "And you *will* adhere to them!"

"Based upon what standard?" repeated Leonard.

"My standard . . . " I glanced at Meg. "Our standard."

"That works fine for a five-year-old," said Leonard. "But we're talking here of a young lady. And young ladies must develop strategies for dealing with life based on their own sense of morality." He leaned over and hit my arm with the back of his hand. "Surely you've dealt with enough neurotic women in your career to realize that is true, haven't you?"

Of course I realized that. A person can't continue to govern his behavior by standards superimposed by his parents. But, somehow, with Diane, I couldn't make my psychological awareness of this fact jibe with my own reality.

"How about you, Meg?" asked Grace. "Do you think that Diane should believe a certain way just because you believe that way?"

"No, of course not. But there have to be rules," said Meg.

"And as society changes, the rules are modified to adapt to its new moral principles," said Leonard.

"But what if society is wrong?" asked Meg.

"Society can't be wrong," said Grace. "Not totally, anyway. Society is people . . . and whatever is good for the people will eventually end up being the rules for society."

"Golly, Grace, I didn't know you were such a philosopher," I said.

"I got that in Ethics 1-A, in my second year in college," she laughed.

"I don't think everyone would agree with that, though," said Meg, pursuing the issue. "I'm sure that Lloyd wouldn't."

"Lloyd?" asked Leonard.

"My brother," I responded. I bristled inwardly at the mention of his name in this conversation, and hoped that Meg wasn't going to push the comparison of Diane with Amy again. "He's a pastor," I explained.

"Oh, well, then he's operating from a different frame of reference," said Leonard. "But his kids aren't . . . " He paused and looked at me. "Does he have children?"

"Yes," I answered.

Leonard nodded. "Well, his kids aren't likely to follow his line of thinking, and he's going to have real problems trying to match his outmoded standards with their realistic view of life."

"But I don't think they have a problem with . . . " began Meg.

I caught her attention and shook my head. I really didn't want this subject continued, and I was sure that she knew it.

Meg glanced toward Grace and Leonard, then she frowned, and took another drink.

Leonard waited for a moment for Meg to continue. When she did not, he turned to me and changed the subject. "The last time we were together, John, I recall that you were looking for a new secretary. Have you had any luck?"

"Yes, I hired one about two weeks ago," I said.

"Good," said Leonard.

"Well, I'm not so sure," I said. Cheryl had done a little better last week, and I had decided to give her a little more time. But I still wasn't completely satisfied.

"What seems to be the problem?" asked Leonard.

"I just have an idea of how the office should be run," I explained. "And she doesn't follow that idea very closely."

"Having some problem with your standards again, eh?" laughed Leonard.

I hadn't thought of it that way, but he had a point. I just nodded.

"How many secretaries have you had in the last year, John?" asked Leonard.

"Four," I said.

"Well . . . " Leonard smiled and nodded. "Have you ever considered the possibility that you're part of the problem?"

I smiled, but shook my head. I knew that Leonard was being only partly facetious. And I'd thought about this myself, too. "No, I don't think so. I've told all of them very specifically what I expected . . . how I wanted them to act. People just aren't competent in what they do any more."

"Well . . . perhaps this one will work out," said Leonard.

"I hope so," I concluded.

I looked up to see Diane approaching the table. She pulled up a chair from an adjacent table, set it next to Meg, and plopped down heavily on it, with her arms crossed in front of her.

"Hi, honey," said Meg. "Did you have fun?"

Diane just shrugged.

"Hello, Diane," said Leonard. "Were your ears burning?"

Diane gave him a quizzical look.

"We were talking about the perils of being a teenager," he explained.

"Oh . . . " She smiled faintly and shook her head.

"They have some really neat games in there, don't they, Diane?" asked Grace. "I was telling Leonard that we should bring . . . " She glanced at her watch and placed her hands on the table. "That reminds me . . . I promised Melissa that I'd take her to the mall this afternoon and let her go shopping for a new fall wardrobe."

"Yes, I guess it is getting to be that time," said Leonard. He downed the rest of his drink. "Thanks for the game, John." He patted me on the back and stood up.

"Sure," I said. "Anytime you want to have a water-skiing contest, let me know."

"Hah!" He rounded the table and helped Grace to her feet.

"Nice talking to you, Meg . . . and John," said Grace.

"You, too," said Meg quietly.

"I really did give you about everything I had on that case, John," said Leonard. "But if you have any questions, be sure to call me."

"I will," I said. "Thanks for the information."

Leonard and Grace waved and hurried off. I was relieved that they had gone, but the sudden absence of conversation fell upon the table like a cloak.

"Did you get your fill of the arcade, Diane?" I asked finally.

"An hour ago," she said.

"How about you, Meg," I continued after a lull. "Did you and Grace have a good talk?"

"What do you think?" she asked, and finished her margarita.

"How many of those have you had?" I asked. I tried to make it sound like a joke, but I was serious.

Meg held up two fingers. "Do you have a problem with that?" she asked.

"No, Meg. I don't have a problem with that," I lied.

She chuckled. "I guess you think you kept your promise, don't you?"

"What . . . "

"Inviting us to come and wait here while you and Leonard played golf."

"And then we're going to lunch," I reminded her.

"We can eat together at home," she said bitterly.

Diane slouched lower in her chair, and looked back and forth between Meg and me. I shook my head at Meg again, and she sighed and stood up.

I struggled to find something to say that would change this mood. Then I remembered what Grace had said. I stood and walked over behind Meg. "Hey . . . I know what! Why don't we take Diane shopping -- buy her some clothes."

Diane looked up and frowned. "I don't need any clothes."

I gave her a mock look of reproach. "Do we have to do everything just because we *need* to?" I held on to Meg's arm with one hand, and bent over and grasped Diane's with the other. "Come on! It'll be fun!"

Diane shook her head, and stood slowly. "Whatever . . . "

I released Meg's arm, and then placed my hand on her shoulder and squeezed. "Come on . . . It'll be fun," I whispered.

"John . . . " Meg looked at me intently for a moment, her lips trembling. "Can't you see that I'd rather just . . . be together . . . talk . . . together."

I pulled her gently toward me and smiled pleadingly. "Come on . . . "

Meg nodded slowly. I put my arms around both of them, and we started toward the exit. We were going to buy Diane some new clothes. We were going to have a good time. I would see to it.

6

I decided that Leonard was probably right about one thing: I was very possibly part of the problem that I had experienced keeping a secretary. Four in a single year is certainly not normal. Two of them had resigned after having worked for me for four or five months, and a third one I had let go because she simply couldn't adjust her way of operating to my bookkeeping system. And then there was Cheryl. The billing procedure didn't appear to be a problem for her, and she was outwardly very willing to learn. But she had certain mannerisms that grated on my nerves. A psychiatrist's office shouldn't be rigidly formal, but a general atmosphere of respectability is required, to provide patients with a feeling of quiet assurance. Cheryl was a little too relaxed, a little too . . . effervescent. But perhaps I hadn't given her sufficient training.

I always scheduled my first session at 9:00 a.m., and usually arrived at the office by 8:30 to prepare for it. When I arrived Monday morning, Cheryl was already there, and she sat behind her desk, studying a booklet on office procedures that I had put together. A large bouquet of fresh flowers sat on the corner of the desk, and their fragrance filled the room. As I entered, she looked up from her studying and smiled broadly.

"Good morning, Dr. Summers," she said.

"Good morning, Cheryl."

"Did you have a good weekend?"

"Yes. Very nice. Thank you." No better time than Monday morning. I knew that it would be a while before my first patient arrived, so I thought this would be the best opportunity. "Cheryl, I'd like to speak with you for a few minutes this morning," I said.

"Sure, Dr. Summers," she said brightly. "I'll be right in."

I smiled at her, unlocked my office door, and went in. By the time I had placed my briefcase on the low file and sat behind my desk, Cheryl had already entered the room, closed the door behind her, and taken her place in the chair across from me, pencil and pad in hand.

"I thought we'd just spend a few minutes this morning . . . talk about how things are going," I began.

"Okay."

"Do you find the work interesting, Cheryl?" I asked.

"Oh, yes. It's fascinating, Dr. Summers," she said enthusiastically. "I worked in a dentist's office before, you know. And I really enjoy this a lot more."

Perhaps that was it. When people go to the dentist they need to be greeted with cheerful encouragement, rather than restful assurance. "Do you think that people coming into my office should be treated in any different manner than people coming into a dentist's office?" I asked her.

Cheryl put on a thoughtful look. "I don't know," she said after a moment. "Whether they have a problem in their teeth or in their head, they just need to know they're at a place where they'll get help." She laughed good-naturedly.

"Hmm . . " I thought perhaps another approach might be better. "Do you think there are any different confidentiality requirements?" I asked.

"Maybe," she said. "But that's needed in both places. I mean, I would never go around talking about people's tooth problems."

"But if you happened to meet one of the dentist's patients on the street, you might ask him if his root canal was still bothering him, wouldn't you?" I asked.

"Probably," she said. "That would just be the friendly thing to do."

"And if you happened to see one of my patients on the street, would you walk up and say, 'Hi! How's your neurosis?'"

"Oh, no!" She laughed, and put her hand over her mouth self-consciously. "I see what you mean. I guess there is a difference."

I thought that I had struck on the ideal example. "I was sure that you would see that, Cheryl," I said. "And do you think, perhaps, that there might be a different way of acting in a psychiatrist's office . . . different from how you'd act in a dentist's office, that is."

"Hmm . . . I never thought about it," she said. "Maybe there would be . . . "

Before she could finish, the door to my office suddenly flew open, and Peter ran in. When he saw Cheryl, he stopped abruptly, adjusted his sunglasses, and pulled the lapels of his trench coat together.

"Peter . . . what are you doing here?" I asked.

"I . . . I have to . . . have to see you," he stammered.

"Your appointment isn't until four this afternoon, Peter," said Cheryl.

"I can't . . . can't wait. Something came up." His eyes weren't visible beneath the sunglasses, but his hand clutched tightly about the lapels of his coat.

"Dr. Summers has another patient at 9:00, Peter," said Cheryl. "I don't believe there's an opening."

"Just a moment, Cheryl," I said. "Peter . . . what is it?"

He didn't speak, but he slowly removed his sunglasses. His eyes were pleading . . . fearful.

"Who's scheduled at nine, Cheryl?" I asked.

"Mrs. Mandell," she said.

I glanced at my watch. It was just eight-forty. Mrs. Mandell lived just a few blocks away, and she was frequently late. "Why don't you call Mrs. Mandell, Cheryl, and change her time to nine-thirty. And then make any other adjustments throughout the morning that are needed."

"Sure, Dr. Summers," said Cheryl. "I can handle that."

I winced slightly at her objectionable expression, and waved my hand to dismiss her. She rose and left the room, closing the door quietly behind her.

Peter watched her leave. Then he tossed his coat and sunglasses carelessly on a chair near the door and began pacing back and forth.

"What is it, Peter?" I asked. "Why couldn't you wait until this afternoon?"

"It stopped working," he said. "The medication stopped working."

"When?"

"Last night . . . it didn't work . . . the dream came . . . "

"You were able to handle the dream last week, Peter," I reminded him.

"It's different . . . it changed," he said. "It's worse."

"Can you tell me?" I asked.

He paced more quickly, speaking loudly and haltingly. "I didn't walk down the stairs this time. I was already there . . . in the fire. But the other me was on top still, and the robe was torn and dirty. And I laughed, and I called for me to come down . . but I wouldn't . . . the other me. So I took my snakes, and I threw them . . . up the stairs. I laughed because the flames were warm and the other me was so frightened. I tried to speak, but I couldn't, because my tongue was torn out! And I remembered what you said, even in my dream . . . deny the delusion . . . I can fix it. And I woke up, and I looked in my mirror . . . " He began to cry. "And it was just a stub! It had been torn out, and the blood filled my mouth, and spilled out on the sink!" He was now screaming.

"That was just a residual hallucination, Peter," I assured him. "That's not unusual just after awakening from such a traumatic dream. You're all right now, aren't you?"

He sat without responding, breathing heavily, his eyes filled with fear, and his mouth rigidly shut.

"You're all right now, aren't you?" I repeated.

Slowly, he opened his mouth. He tentatively set his tongue on his lower lip. Then he grossly thrust it out, and moved it from side to side. Without taking his eyes off me, he reached up and touched his tongue. He pushed it gently back into his mouth, and closed his lips on his fingers. Tears gushed from his eyes, and he walked slowly over and sat in the chair opposite me.

"You have the power, Peter," I said. "When you're asleep, your dreams will be the master for a while yet. But when you're awake, you have the power over your delusions."

"It's so hard!" he mumbled.

"I know."

"And it's going to take so long," he said. "I don't think it's worth it."

"There's another thing you should remember, Peter," I said. "Last night was Sunday, and Sunday is always your worst night."

"Yes."

"Later this week I'll give you a heavy sedative to take next Sunday," I said. "That may be necessary temporarily."

"Why not every night?" he pleaded. "I just want to sleep . . . sleep."

"That's natural, Peter," I said. But you must remember that your psychosis is a journey . . . from life . . . to hell . . . and back to life again."

"I'll never come back," he mumbled.

"Yes, you will, Peter," I said. "But we have to continue the analysis . . . aggressively, to find the key to your problem."

"No one ever comes back," he said. "Dr. Butler said so."

"Dr. Butler didn't say that, Peter," I told him. "And if he did, he was wrong. Many people have come back to completely normal lives from deep schizophrenic states." This may have been an exaggeration, but certainly there were examples. The most marked was probably the man who brought himself back from catatonic schizophrenia while in the confines of an early twentieth-century madhouse. I didn't think this would be a productive example to bring forth at this time, however.

Peter sighed deeply. Then he closed his eyes and began to chant. "I renounce you . . . I renounce you . . . I renounce you . . . " He opened eyes again and spoke with inexplicable composure. "Very well, Dr. Summers. Let's begin."

I pointed to the couch.

"Must we?" he asked.

I nodded.

Peter frowned. Then he stood slowly, walked to the couch, and reclined awkwardly, one foot still resting on the floor. I sat in the chair beside his head.

"You revealed quite a bit of information last week about your current ministry, Peter," I said. "I think it's time we searched for a little history."

"History is a collection of forgotten moments," he mumbled.

I recalled Leonard's statement that he could never push Peter beyond the previous day. And I realized that everything that he had revealed to me thus far had been either present . . . or timeless. "It's also a heritage," I said. "And a teacher for today . . . if we will only learn."

"But when we know everything, yesterday's facts become irrelevant," he said.

"Do you know everything, Peter?" I asked.

"Everything I need to know," he answered softly. "And what I don't . . . he tells me."

"Who tells you?" I asked.

He raised his forearm and twirled it slowly in a circle, and then dropped it to the couch again.

"There was a notation on the poster you gave me . . . it said the Light on the Rock ministry was in its tenth year," I said. "How did you begin?"

"I was born to be anointed," he said.

"But how did this particular ministry begin?" I asked.

"One night . . . I was in bed," he began. "A messenger came to me . . . a messenger of God . . . told me that I was going to be a rich and famous evangelist . . . heal people of their sins . . . renounce their hurts. I knew it was a messenger of God, because my whole body began to tingle. From the center outward . . . just like the mandala." He grasped the mandala which again hung from the chain around his neck. "From the center outward, in waves of rapture . . . until my toes and the tips of my fingers ached and trembled. And my mouth became an instrument of the Holy Spirit. But clear, and precise . . . not like some who mumble and stammer after their righteousness." He lifted his foot from the floor and laid it across his other leg. "The messenger came to me. That's how I began."

"Was this immediately before you began the ministry, or was it earlier than that?" I asked.

"Time is irrelevant when miracles occur," He said. "It may have been *then* . . . Or it may have been . . . *then*."

"Or might it have been when you were a child?" I asked.

"Perhaps. I was born to be anointed," he said.

"Your mother must have been very proud," I ventured cautiously.

"Pride is a sin," he said.

"Pleased, then," I corrected myself. "What did they think about your calling . . . your parents, I mean?" I asked.

"It doesn't matter," he said.

"Surely they must have had an opinion," I said.

"Everyone has opinions about everything," he said. "That doesn't mean they matter, does it?"

"Perhaps." I paused for a moment, and watched as he moved his hand nervously across his leg. "Tell me about your parents, Peter."

Peter suddenly stood up and began pacing again. As he spoke, his words came rapidly, almost automatically. "My father is a mechanic. He's very skilled. He fixes things . . . things that are broken. My mother is dead. There's nothing important there. They're just people. It's the messenger that's important."

"How did your mother die?" I asked.

He stopped pacing and glared at me. "I knew you'd get around to that. Just like Dr. Butler. All you doctors think there has to be some kind of Oedipus complex. Well there's not! My mother is dead."

"All right, Peter." I decided not to pursue the mother relationship any further now. "Your father is a mechanic, you say?"

"He fixes things," he said.

"When you were a boy . . . did your father punish you?" I asked.

"No. He doesn't punish me. He's a mechanic. He fixes things." He walked over and sat on the couch. "It's the messenger who punishes me. That's why I have the dreams . . . the visions. They are miracles . . . evil miracles. It's the messenger . . . but my body doesn't tingle any more. I'm exalted in pain because there are so many . . . so many to heal."

I wouldn't be able to force any more information about his parents today. I pointed to the mandala. "Do you wear that all the time?" I asked.

Peter took the mandala between his fingers and focused his eyes on it. "It's like the one in the window at my temple," he said. "It helps me remember all there is to do. It's like the universe . . . waves from the center out . . . It's how I reach out and make my words known to all about me. The circle is the world. The circle makes me whole."

"Do you think it brings you luck . . . or gives you power?" I asked.

"If I wish it to, it will," he responded. "But I have the power without it. That's what being a Christ figure means." He closed his eyes for a moment, and sighed. "It's a terrible responsibility. I sometimes think that's my problem -- the fear of failure."

"Do you fear your power?" I asked.

"I don't have any fears. I can do anything," he said quickly. "Maybe the dreams are sent to me to fix things. But then it would be done. I don't know why I can't heal myself. But then even Christ couldn't do that, could he? He died on the cross. But his journey was only three days. Mine is so long . . . so long . . . I wish I could just sleep . . . fall into a restful state of nonexistence."

He seemed to be utilizing the journey symbol that I introduced in the description of the psychotic episode. And his continued reference to the Christ archetype must have signified some deep-seated religious relationship, but I wasn't quite sure how to approach it.

"Do you fear nonexistence?" I asked.

"How can you fear something that doesn't exist," he responded.

"But you *wish for* nonexistence," I said.

"Yes, because you *can wish* for something that doesn't exist," he said.

"And your journey to health can be . . . " I began.

"A journey is a circle," he interrupted. "And life is a journey."

"Is that the circle you're thinking of?" I asked. "The end of life . . . Is that the nonexistence you seek?"

Peter reached out suddenly and placed his hands on my knees. This was the first time that I fully realized that he wasn't lying on the couch any more, but sitting directly across from me. His willingness to extend the communication into areas which I thought would be helpful caught me off guard, and there was nothing I could do to alter it now.

"What do *you* think?" he asked. "Do *you* seek the restful nonexistence of the end of life?"

"I must . . . I must ask the questions, Peter," I stammered. "That's the only way we can make any progress."

"We make progress when we find the truth," he said firmly. "What is your truth? Do you seek the nonexistence?"

The session had turned. He was taking control. I had to ease him back . . . turn him toward his own feelings . . . his own fears. "There is nothing to fear, Peter," I said. "All life . . . You said it yourself. How can you fear something that doesn't exist?" I found myself struggling for words. I shouldn't have pursued the issue of nonexistence. The fears of my own childhood suddenly rushed into my mind . . . sitting on the edge of my bed one night, crying . . . so terribly afraid of death . . . and my father coming in, shaking me . . . cursing me for fearing the silence of nothingness . . . think about life, he told me . . . forget about death. But I never could . . . not until I became older, and wiser, and cast my thoughts into the realm of forgotten memories.

Peter still grasped my knees, but his head was turned upward, and he was smiling. "Yes . . . I'll tell him," he said. "I'll heal him." He lowered his head, and his eyes were deep, and intense. "There is no nonexistence," he said loudly. "There is no *nothing* . . . only eternal bliss . . . or eternal damnation! You need to be healed!"

I backed away slightly, but I couldn't escape the grasp of his gaze. He was reverting to the power of his ministerial personality. I knew that rationally, but I couldn't avoid the image . . . He was so close that the chain holding his mandala looked like a rosary, and vague recollections of Catholic rituals swept through my mind, and I saw the priest, chastising the sinners lest they die unblessed . . . but it didn't matter, because my grandfather didn't repent, and when he died the priest came and blessed him, and everything was fixed . . . I remember thinking that salvation must be easy, as long as a priest is around . . . or my father. He said he took care of that for us. Why couldn't Lloyd understand that. But it didn't matter anyway . . . it was all meaningless . . .

Peter's rambling voice crept vaguely into my recognition again. I forced my own delusion clearly before me . . . and I banished it. I took Peter firmly by the shoulders and shook him. "Peter! Peter!"

Peter stopped talking, and sat silently before me with a distant expression.

"This is another delusion, Peter," I said. "Think about what you were doing . . . saying. It's another delusion. Pull it out, and look at it. Be aware of it . . . and then get rid of it."

Peter ran his fingers slowly down his chain and rested them on the mandala. Then he looked blankly past me, and chanted methodically: "I renounce you . . . I renounce you . . . I renounce you . . . "

"Remember that technique, Peter," I urged him. "You have the power. You can fix things."

Peter smiled, leaned back in the couch, and spoke calmly again. "That's really quite effective. I believe I'll continue with you for a while, Dr. Summers. You definitely show promise. You may be competent enough to deal with my pesky nervous problem, after all."

I was relieved by the added distance between us. I knew that I must never let him take control of the session like that again. It was counterproductive. I stood, walked over to my desk and removed a prescription pad. "I'm going to change your medication," I said formally, as I wrote the prescription. "I think we should try some Molindone. And then when you come on Friday, I'll give you a sedative for Sunday night."

"Yes, I would really appreciate that," Peter responded coldly. "Although I doubt that I'll need it. However . . . just in the event . . . "

I tore the prescription from the pad and held it out. Peter rose slowly, walked over to me, and took the sheet between his fingers.

"And you must try to maintain consistency in your sessions, Peter," I told him. "Regularity and consistency in your patterns will show that you are in control."

Peter waved the prescription toward me, smiled, and walked toward the door. "I do apologize for departing from schedule today. It's just that I've been so busy, you know." He picked up his sunglasses and placed them on deliberately, pressing the bridge into his nose. Then he picked up his trench coat and tossed it over his arm. "See you Wednesday," he said, and he opened the door and walked slowly out.

I sank heavily into my chair. I was completely drained from today's experience. I couldn't believe that I had let the session slip away like I did. That had never happened before. But I recalled Leonard's statement that Peter often appeared to take charge of the session by giving him information that he thought would fit in with his analytic approach. Peter was very bright, but also very troubled. I was more intent than ever on finding a way to lead him back to health.

In retrospect, the delusional experience that I'd had in the midst of our session today filled me with a strange sense of excitement. I had actually slipped into a brief hysterical state myself, and pulled myself back by the power of my own conscious will. My skin tingled at the recollection. It was like the rush of adrenalin that shot through my body as I stepped off the cliff with the hang-glider. No . . . it was better.

The door to my office opened, and Cheryl stepped inside. "Dr. Summers . . . " she said quietly.

"Yes?"

"Your brother is on the phone," she said. "He told me he'd like to meet with you for lunch some day. I can just go ahead and schedule an appointment, but I thought, since you were between sessions, you might want to speak with him."

I wondered what Lloyd wanted to talk to me about. "Yes, Cheryl," I said absently. "I'll talk to him." But then sudden reluctance came over me. "No, wait . . . "

"What?" She stood expectantly in the door way.

I experienced a strangely impelling need to distance myself from any outside associations at this time. If I spoke to Lloyd now, the conversation would lead inevitably to irrelevant ramblings that would detract me from my work. I had a busy schedule ahead of me today. "No . . . Just go ahead and arrange it yourself," I told Cheryl.

"As it turns out, you'll have time today," she said. "And tomorrow looks good, too, if you'd rather . . . "

"Wednesday," I said abruptly. "Tell him I'll meet with him on Wednesday at noon -- at the Chart House Restaurant."

Cheryl tilted her head with a quizzical expression. Then she smiled, nodded, and stepped back, closing the door before her.

The image of Cheryl's young face hovered before my recollection for a moment after she had left. We hadn't finished our discussion about office demeanor, but I hoped that she had gotten the point. And yet she seemed somehow so . . . fragile. She did well, and seemed to honor my wishes as long as I was supervising her, but as soon as I entered my office and shut the door, there was a barrier, preventing my control. I smiled, as I mused that what went on in my outside office was like what occurred in Peter's dream -- bits and pieces of his experience, merged with some indefinable extension of his motives and desires . . . but all operating somehow autonomously, and beyond his grasp. And if what occurs during his sleep becomes destructive, he can waken, open the door, and scatter the pieces -- I renounce you . . . I renounce you . . . renounce you . . .

I chuckled at the comparison. And yet it was relevant. The important thing was that we were in control -- Peter and I. Control was the word. Whenever it was possessed, delusions would lose their power. But then I recalled the harrowing experience in this session. Peter was supposed to gain strength from my sense of composure and my control. That was the whole idea of the psychological transference, which would take place at some point in the therapy. But I wondered whether Peter and I could ever exercise control jointly, or whether control by one would necessarily strengthen the power of the other's delusions. I had made good progress today, though. The armor covering his past had been breached. His parents had definitely had some influence on the development of his psychotic conditions. But that was nothing new . . . the universal archetype . . .

I thought the rest of the day would go well. Perhaps it was good that Peter had arrived the first thing in the morning. That challenge had passed. And I felt good about how things turned out yesterday; we had bought Diane a raft of new clothes, as I had suggested. And even my unilateral determination of the day of my luncheon appointment with Lloyd added to my sense of well-being. There was just Cheryl. I decided that I'd step outside between each session today and see how she was doing. If she didn't work out, I would just renounce her. Yes, it was going to be a good day.

7

I usually ate lunch at the Chart House Restaurant at least once a week, so my meeting Lloyd there on Wednesday made sense. And the more I'd thought about it since Monday, the more I realized that I might be able to gain some insights that could help me with Peter's case. Both Peter and Lloyd seemed to be involved with . . . I thought the term was *evangelical ministries.* And at this point, I would welcome any clues that I could gather about Peter's character.

I arrived at the restaurant a little before twelve. The tall, attractive hostess stood, smiling, at the entry to the dimly lighted areas into which the restaurant was divided. She waved at me as I approached.

"Hello, Dr. Summers," she said. "It's nice to see you again."

"Hello, Delia," I responded. "I'm expecting my brother, and . . . "

"He's already arrived," she said.

"Oh?"

"Yes. Won't you come with me?" She smiled, and pointed gracefully toward the dining area. Delia had been with the restaurant for several years, and always handled her job with class. I always thought she would make an excellent secretary.

Delia led me to a secluded booth near the back of the restaurant. Lloyd sat there, perusing the menu. He looked up and waved as we approached.

"There you are, Dr. Summers," Delia said as she ushered me to my seat. "You gentlemen enjoy your lunch."

"Thank you, Delia," I said as she walked off. Then I reached my hand across the table. "Hi, Lloyd!"

"Good to see you, John," he said, grasping my hand firmly. "I've never been here before. I'm glad you suggested it."

"I thought you'd like it," I said.

A short, blond waitress stepped up to our table. She must have been new, because I didn't recognize her.

"Good afternoon, gentlemen," she said. "Can I get you something to drink?"

"I'll have some coffee," said Lloyd.

"Coffee for me, also," I said.

"Don't give up your lunch drink on my account," said Lloyd.

"No . . . No, I never drink during working hours," I said.

"Oh?" Lloyd gave me a quizzical look.

"So . . . it's two coffees, then?" asked the waitress.

"Please," I said.

"And are you ready to order, or would you like a few minutes?" she asked.

Lloyd picked up the menu and opened it. "Well, I think I'd like . . . "

"Their seafood special is outstanding," I interrupted. "That's what I'm having."

"Is that right?" Lloyd glanced quickly at the menu. Then he closed it and set it on top of mine. "All right. Make it two."

"Thank you," said the waitress. She picked up the menus and walked briskly off.

"That's interesting," said Lloyd.

"Hmm?"

"Pop used to have that rule," he said.

"What rule?" I asked.

"He never took a drink during working hours." He laughed lightly. "But, boy, did he make up for it afterward!"

"Yeah . . . " I said absently. "I'm sure he still follows that rule. I've never known him to break any restrictions he's placed on himself."

"You're probably right," said Lloyd.

"He was drinking a lot at the anniversary party, though, wasn't he?" I asked.

"Well . . . special occasion."

I could have told Lloyd that our father always drank that much, but I didn't see any purpose in that. "He doesn't hold his tongue very well when he's been drinking, though," I said. "I don't think he'd have laid into you like that otherwise."

"Well . . . I thought about what you said after Kate and I got home," said Lloyd. "You were probably right. I could have prevented the scene if I'd bought them a crystal vase . . . or something." He let out a low chuckle.

The waitress set our coffee on the table.

"Oh, thank you," I said.

"Your lunch will be right up," she said as she left.

Lloyd took a sip of his coffee. "So, I'll remember that the next time," he said.

"What . . . at their seventy-fifth?" I asked. We both laughed.

"It may be that long," said Lloyd. "He just won't come to our house, and he seldom invites us to his."

"I never could understand why Dad was so hostile toward your religious choice." I said.

"Well, a lot of it has to do with my rebelling against him . . . leaving home," he said. But it's more than that." He sipped his coffee again. "Yeah . . . a lot more. Pop is really a paradox," he said slowly. "He isn't religious at all, and yet he insists on being considered a good Catholic."

"Well, I think he probably has been," I said.

Lloyd frowned and shook his head. "Does he ever go to church?" he asked.

"Well . . . Christmas and Easter," I admitted. "But he always speaks well of the faith, and . . . "

"And gives financial support," interrupted Lloyd. "And, of course, he had his children baptized when they were babies."

I shrugged. "I think he'd say that he's following the spirit of the law."

"The law being the church," said Lloyd.

"I suppose."

"I think that's why Pop likes the Catholic Church," said Lloyd. "There are so many rules, and dogmatic practices, that it has the appearance of *controlling* him."

"Controlling Dad?" I said incredulously.

Lloyd raised his hand to silence my question. "The *appearance*," he emphasized. "He likes that, because he's a controlling person, and he relates to that. But he likes it even more, because he can ignore all the rituals and rules that he espouses to support, and feel even more powerful in his own right."

"When may I schedule a therapy session with you, Doctor?" I questioned jokingly. But I realized that he was probably right. And I recalled the mixed message I'd always received from this behavior of his when I was a child. Lloyd had felt much more strongly about it. I remember vividly when he left home his calling our father a filthy hypocrite.

"So when I broke away from both him and the church, it was a double insult to him," said Lloyd.

"He needs to be more broad-minded," I said. "He should realize that religion is a matter of personal choice."

"But there's a lot more to it than that, John," he said. "You should know that better than anyone."

"Why is that?" I asked.

"Because you're the expert on Jung," he said. "And you must be very familiar with Jung's views of religious experience."

I smiled. "You're going to coax me into a discussion of Jung's religious views, after all, aren't you?" I asked.

"I've only been asking for about thirteen years," he said.

"I've been letting my opinions ripen," I joked.

"Why?" he asked smiling. "Your opinions have been rotten all along!"

We laughed. I hadn't felt this relaxed around Lloyd for years. He was right. I had been avoiding the discussion, mainly because

I didn't want to muddy my intellectual, analytic views with his specious religious arguments. But he and Peter seemed to have followed the same direction in life. I thought that the more I found out about Lloyd's views, the better I could understand Peter.

"First of all, you've got to promise never to tell Dad that Jung wasn't a Catholic," I said, smiling. "I think that's the only reason he sent me to the Institute."

"He may as well have been," said Lloyd. "He favored the Catholic religion in his writing."

"But of course he was a Protestant," I said.

"Actually, Jung's religion of choice was neither Catholicism nor Protestantism, but mysticism," said Lloyd.

"Well, I don't think I'd go so far as to say that," I began. But then I decided not to initiate a quarrel on this point. "Of course some might argue that *all* religion is mysticism," I said. "At any rate, Jung looked upon religion as an important aspect of man's unconscious. And he liked the Catholic religion because it possessed a large array of dogmatic ideas which could be used as helpful symbols by the unconscious."

"And he saw the priest as the symbol of the intercessor," added Lloyd.

"That's right," I said. "And the church and all its trappings provided an archetype -- the spiritual safeguard."

"Pop bought into that one, didn't he?" asked Lloyd. "Remember, at the party, he said that he only wanted to deal with this life, and that he'd let the priests worry about the next one?"

"I don't think he looked at it as a spiritual safeguard, though," I said.

"Well, think about it," said Lloyd. "What did Jung mean by *safeguard*?"

"The unconscious mind is a naive maiden," I said. "And unguided thoughts and feelings can ravish it like a whirlwind. And an unbridled religious experience will pounce on an unguarded unconscious and become absorbed in a state of chaos."

"And so the intercessor is needed," said Lloyd.

"Yes. To protect the person against the forces waiting for liberation in the unconscious mind," I said.

"A shield against the immediate religious experience," added Lloyd.

"Jung's exact words," I agreed. "But of course you can relate to that from a Biblical perspective," I added. "I mean, doesn't the myth of Moses relate to his face becoming a radiant glow as a result of his immediate encounter with God?"

"Moses was not a myth," said Lloyd.

"Well, for the purpose of discussion . . . " I began.

"The issue remains the same," concluded Lloyd. "And the people couldn't even look directly upon Moses' face when it glowed, or upon the Holy of Holies in the midst of the temple."

"Right," I agreed.

"But that was the Old Testament," said Lloyd. "When Christ died on the cross, the veil of the temple was torn in two from top to bottom. That's why Paul told the Corinthians that when one turns to the Lord, the veil is taken away."

"That was precisely Jung's point," I explained. "When Protestantism took away the intercession of the church, in the figure of the priest, man lost all his protection against the unaccountable forces of the unconscious; he had to deal with God alone."

"That's what Jung said," agreed Lloyd. "But Jung was wrong. We are not left to deal with God alone. Christ is our high priest. And he is our *only* intercessor."

This was a slightly different view of Jung's point, and I thought it might prove helpful. "So, what you're saying, then, is that the archetype of the protective safeguard remains," I said.

Lloyd shook his head slowly. "Christ is not an archetype."

"Well, not from the standpoint of religious ritual, perhaps," I conceded. "But I'm a psychiatrist, and in Jungian psychiatric therapy the Christ archetype is a powerful and useful model."

"John . . . " Lloyd placed his elbows on the table, and bounced his folded hands lightly against his lips. Then he separated his hands slightly and placed them on the table before me. "This is a critical point that has major implications for every aspect of your therapy." He punctuated the words that followed by tapping the edges of his hands on the table. "Christ is not an archetype. Christ is God!"

I realized that we had reached that point in our discussion that I had dreaded -- the point where religious belief interferes with reason. And yet it was important for me to pursue the point, for I thought surely that Peter would hold the same opinion. "Do all Protestant ministers follow the same line of reasoning as that?" I asked.

Lloyd sat back and smiled. *"All* is too broad a term." He chuckled. "For that matter, so is *Protestant.* "Can you be more specific?"

I didn't want to reveal that I was particularly interested in Peter's theology, so I tried to find a way to generalize my definition. I believed that I knew the category that his ministry would fit under. "Oh, let's say . . . these new charismatic religions," I suggested. "Would they be in agreement with your theology?" I asked.

"I'm not a charismatic," said Lloyd. "But I'd agree with some of them." He smiled. "On the other hand . . . others I wouldn't. So . . . "

"So can I be more specific . . . " I concluded for him.

Lloyd smiled and nodded.

I really didn't want to reveal Peter's identity, but it was clear that I wasn't going to get any substantive information until I did. "Well, let's say . . . someone like Peter Lumen," I said finally.

"The Light on the Rock," Lloyd responded.

"You're familiar with his ministry, then?" I asked.

He nodded. "That's a good illustration of the point I just made. Light on the Rock has a dynamic ministry, and many people have been won to Christ through their work. I know one of the ministers quite well . . . Kyle Wingate."

"Yes . . . "

"And I have no particular problem with him."

"But that isn't the case with Peter Lumen?" I asked.

He shook his head. "No. I am definitely *not* in theological agreement with Peter Lumen."

"Why is that?" I asked.

"Well, you remember what we said about Jung's idea of the immediate religious experience, and how he avoided the intercession of Christ?" he asked.

"Yes."

"I view Peter Lumen's approach that way," he explained. "His primary message is that people should rely on their own power, their own . . . divinity."

"He has made the statement, I believe, that he was appointed . . . even anointed by God," I said cautiously.

"I know. And he's treading on dangerous doctrinal ground with that belief," said Lloyd. "You see, he places his personal revelations on the same level as the Bible . . . even above the Bible in many cases."

"And that's *verboten*, of course," I interjected.

"Are you kidding?" Lloyd reached into his inside coat pocket and pulled out a small Bible. He placed it in the palm of one hand and touched it with the other as he spoke. "It says in Revelation that if anyone adds to the prophecy of this book, God will place on him the plagues that are written in the book."

An uncomfortable tingle rose from the base of my spine. I wished that Lloyd hadn't started on this tack. I definitely didn't want this to turn into an evangelistic session. "I think I'd rather not broach the spiritual . . . but concentrate on reality, if you don't mind," I said.

Lloyd smiled. "One day, I hope, you'll discover, as I did . . . " He held the Bible up before me. "This is the *only* reality."

"But for now . . . "

"But for now . . . " he conceded. He placed the Bible back in his pocket. "All right . . . from Jung's perspective, then," he continued, "he is placing himself, and his congregation, in the path of the immediate religious experience, without the protection of Christ's intercession."

"But he talks about Christ," I said. "In fact, he refers to himself as a *Christ figure*," I added.

"Ah . . . exactly!" said Lloyd, raising his finger in the air. "And to the extent that he assumes that role, he becomes the intercessor."

"Like the priest in the Catholic Church," I suggested.

"Yes," he agreed. "But probably with a different motive."

"A different style, certainly," I agreed. "But isn't that what it comes down to ultimately?" I asked. "Individual doctrinal preference?"

Lloyd shook his head. Then he reached into his inside coat pocket again.

"No!" I raised my hand toward him. "No more Bible lessons."

Lloyd smiled and removed his empty hand.

I know that Lloyd didn't agree with me on the issue of relative doctrinal validity. One of the most important things that I learned from my study of Jung was that the psychologist is a scientist, and as such, he must assume a scientific attitude, and disregard the claim of any creed to be the unique and eternal truth. If I let myself be swayed from that fact, my whole rational approach to therapy would crumble.

I was relieved as the waitress returned, and placed our plates in front of us. "Oh, good! Here we are," I said.

"That looks delicious!" exclaimed Lloyd.

"Enjoy . . . " she said insincerely, and ambled off into the semi-darkness.

We were both silent for a few moments as we began eating. I had obtained a good deal of helpful theological information from our discussion so far, but I was eager to pursue the point of the religious person's psychological frame of mind. I wasn't sure that Lloyd could relate to that issue without reverting to religiosity, but I decided to give it a try.

"There's something else I've been meaning to ask you, Lloyd," I said.

"Hmm?" Lloyd asked through a mouthful of fish.

"I've treated thousands of patients in the last ten years," I said. "And I think I told you that a lot of professing believers come to me for help."

"Mmm-hmm. And I told you that I never said that Christians don't have problems," he said.

"But what about ministers?" I asked. "Do they ever have psychological problems?"

"Ministers are people," he said. "Sure!"

"How about charismatic ministers?" I asked.

He took on a pensive look. "Charismatics generally resist seeking psychiatric help, but that doesn't mean they don't have problems." He shrugged. "People with different views may have different kinds of problems."

"So a charismatic minister who holds a different view from yours might not be as neurotic as you," I joked.

"Or more!" he said. He joined me in laughter. Then he stopped abruptly. He placed his elbows on the table, rested his chin on his clasped hands, and smiled wryly. He glanced to the side, and then he looked back with an intense gaze and spoke softly. "You're treating Peter Lumen, aren't you?"

His statement struck me with a jolt, and I sat back impulsively. I was irritated with myself for having introduced so much information that this fact was detected by Lloyd. I had breached professional confidentiality, and I suddenly viewed that as dent in the armor of my competence.

Lloyd must have read my discomfort, because he leaned closer and spoke reassuringly. "I guess you didn't want me to know that, did you?" he asked.

"Well . . . "

"Don't worry," he said. "I'll naturally keep my knowledge in strict confidence. Besides, you can just look on this as a consultation," he added. "You wouldn't feel bad about talking to another psychiatrist about the case, would you?"

"No, but that's a professional relationship," I said.

Lloyd smirked. "How about his clergyman, then?" he asked.

"His cler . . . " I thought about that for a moment. Of course I had often spoken to my patients' clergymen when I thought they might be able to provide some relevant information. "Yes, I suppose," I said.

"Very well." Lloyd winked and gestured with his fist. "I'll be his clergyman." He returned to his eating.

I was filled with a strange sense of relief. As Lloyd sat across from me now, I viewed him as a fellow professional, rather than as my brother. I knew that I would even feel comfortable calling on him again with questions, and I felt good about that. Furthermore, I hadn't revealed the fact that Peter was schizophrenic. For all Lloyd knew, he might be just suffering from stress because of overwork. And I was pleased that he hadn't asked. I sat forward and began eating.

"Have you attended one of his services?" Lloyd asked.

I looked up. "What?"

"The Light on the Rock," he said. "Have you gone to any services there?"

"No."

"You really should," said Lloyd. "I think that would give you a lot of insight on Peter's personality."

"Yes," I agreed. "Yes, I think you're right."

"And while you're there, try to detect the difference between his approach and Kyle's," he suggested.

"Peter distrusts Wingate," I offered tentatively. "In fact, he says that he also wants to be a Christ figure."

Lloyd shook his head. "No. Kyle knows the difference between speaking *for* Christ . . . and speaking *as* Christ."

We ate in silence for a while. Then it suddenly occurred to me that Lloyd was the one who asked me to lunch, and we had spent the entire time on my agenda. "You know what . . . I don't think we ever got around to what you wanted to talk about," I said.

Lloyd finished the last of his lunch, pushed his plate aside and wiped his mouth with the napkin. "You're right."

"So . . . what . . . " I ventured.

"I told you that my daughter Amy and I have a pretty good relationship," he said. "She told me something last week that I thought you should know about."

"What's that?"

"She spoke with Diane just briefly at the party two weeks ago," he said. "And, of course, Diane was pretty . . . well . . . verbal at that point."

"After she'd been drinking," I said.

"Yes. Anyway, they were talking about their friends and activities," Lloyd continued. "Amy knows about the people that Diane said she was associating with, John. And she really became concerned."

"Why?" I asked.

"Well, of course school's out for the summer, and all of the same people aren't as frequently clustered together," he explained. "But the core group of kids still gets together on a regular basis, and Diane told Amy that she often goes places with them."

"Yes, Diane has a group of friends that she meets with periodically," I said. "But what does that . . . "

"Amy says that group of kids is definitely into drugs, John," Lloyd said somberly. "And she suspects . . . immoral behavior."

I was shocked by that statement. First by the possibility that it might be true. But more, by the fact that the information came from the unsolicited statement of my fifteen-year-old niece. I was filled with a strange mixture of contradictory feelings. I was definitely concerned that Diane might be involved in some dangerous activity. But I was also offended by the fact that my brother had to bring it to my attention. My view of him as a fellow professional abruptly departed, and I began to look at him again as a conservative fundamentalist. And, of course, the information was hearsay. I wondered if Amy had something against Diane. I was sure that she felt as if she were better than Diane was from a moral point of view. I'd certainly detected that feeling between Lloyd and myself on occasion. And Diane was very popular, also. I wasn't sure about Amy's social status. Perhaps she was just reacting with typical teenage jealousy.

Lloyd waited for a moment for me to respond. When I remained silent, he continued. "Of course this may be blown all out of proportion, too," he said. "But it sounded serious enough to me, that I thought you out to know about it . . . in case you don't already, that is."

"Sure. Sure, Lloyd. Thanks." I said finally.

"I know bringing kids through this time in their lives can be very trying," he said. "And we need all the help we can get."

"Really? The way Meg tells it, you don't have any problems with your kids." I tried to make my statement sound like a joke, but I realized that it had come across with an acrid tone.

Lloyd apparently picked up my hostility. He chuckled self-consciously, and brushed some crumbs off the table with the back of his hand. "No. We have plenty of problems with our kids," he said. "Just like everybody else. Patrick's pretty much on the straight and narrow, now. But, I'll tell, for a while . . . whew!"

"Well, that's reassuring," I said.

"Anyway, if there's ever anything I can do to help, I'll sure be happy to," he said brightly.

I was really offended by Lloyd's notion that he could help me raise my child, but I tried to hide my irritation. "A second opinion, you mean?" I asked lightly.

"Well . . . " He laughed lightly. "I didn't mean from a psychological point of view. But there are some good Biblical principals that Kate and I have had a lot of success with, and we'd be happy to share those."

"Well, that's all right for a church-and-Sunday-school family," I said. "But I have to treat my situation in the context of our life style." I was becoming more and more uncomfortable with the way the conversation was going, and I wanted to end it. "But, listen, Lloyd . . . I really do appreciate what you told me. And I'll look into it right away."

"Yeah . . . good." Lloyd nodded and sat back.

The waitress stepped up to our table again, excused herself, and picked up our plates. "Is there anything else you'd like, gentlemen? Dessert, or . . . "

"Oh, not for me, thank you," said Lloyd.

"No, I don't think . . . " But I felt very tense, and I hated the idea of going back to the office harboring this hostility. "Wait, Miss . . . "

The waitress turned back with an expectant look.

"I think perhaps I'll have a glass of white wine," I said.

"Very well, sir," she said, and stepped quickly off.

I know that Lloyd would disapprove of my decision to have a glass of wine. And as I recalled that I told him I never had a drink during working hours, I became suddenly irritated with myself for having ordered it. But this was only a glass of wine, after all. It wasn't as though I had violated my principle. And Lloyd had brought out such a feeling of resentment in me that it really was necessary for me to relax before resuming my professional duties. Lloyd could certainly understand that. And if he couldn't, I really didn't care.

8

Lloyd had made a good suggestion at lunch Wednesday. I generally don't like to see my patients outside the confines of my office, but Peter's psychosis was so clearly linked to aspects of his career, that I decided to observe him in his work environment. I thought that I could probably view the service without his knowing that I'd been there, but I didn't know until I actually went there on Sunday morning how correct this assumption had been. Peter had referred to his church building as a temple, and it was easy to see why he had; it was a huge, semicircular structure, nestled into the side of a rocky mountainside. I arrived early, but because of the jammed parking lot, I had to park on the street. As a result, I entered the building just before the service started.

The huge auditorium was packed -- even the circling double balconies. I stayed downstairs, and remained near the back so that it would be virtually impossible for Peter to recognize me. The actual setting of the temple put the poster to shame. The raised stage appeared to be a hundred feet wide and fifty feet deep. A richly colored sky backdrop swept across most of the stage. In front of this was a huge rock-mountain, with a running waterfall, its waters plunging into a clear pool at stage level. To the right of this was an immense live tree -- that is, it appeared to be live. After noticing that, however, I wondered how that could be, since there didn't seem to be any access to sunlight. To the right of the tree was a many-tiered choir loft that was filled with at least a hundred robed singers. On the left side of the stage was a tall, triple-segmented structure that contained graphic displays. Across the top in large letters was the phrase:

THIS WEEK'S SUCCESSES

And each segment was headed by a bold printed word:

SALVATIONS -- HEALINGS -- COMMITMENTS

Above this board, in what appeared to be a window formed from rich cut glass, was a gigantic mandala, similar to the one that Peter wore. Several television cameras were placed in strategic positions throughout the auditorium.

Music began to play loudly. I didn't see an orchestra, so I assumed that it was being electronically transmitted. The choir began to sway back and fro, and the congregation clapped in rhythm to the music. Then two people appeared on the stage and sat in plush chairs near the display board. They waved at the congregation and began clapping in rhythm. I recognized the men from the poster. One was Greg Hatcher, the Stewardship Minister; the other was Kyle Wingate, the Worship Leader. A third man entered from the other side of the stage and stood facing the choir, his arms outstretched.

The music built to an emotional introduction, and the choir began to sing. Hatcher and Wingate stood and invoked the congregation as the music rose in excitement, and they led the people into clapping and swaying to the beat of the music. From the sides of the auditorium twelve or fifteen young people ran out and stood in front of the stage. They were dressed in sparkling costumes, and they clapped and sang along with the choir. The words were clear, and very upbeat:

Oh, there's a light (see it glowing)
Shining in the dark.
Yes, there's a light, (feel it growing)
Showing us the way
Oh, let it shine, (shine, shine, shine)
Bring it in your heart.
And let it lead us from the night
Into the brilliant day!

Oh, there's a rock (strong foundation)
Standing on the ground.
Yes, there's a rock, (our liberation)
Precious cornerstone
Oh, let it stand, (stand, stand, stand)
Lean upon it now.
And let it give us such a strength
We'll never be alone!

Light on the rock, (I see it.)
Light on the rock, (I know it.)
Light on the rock, (Let's feel it.)
Light on the rock, (Let's show it.)
Standing on the ground
And shining in the night --
Rock, rock . . .
Give us light!

Oh, there's a light and a rock,
Shining in the dark and standing on the ground.
There's a rock and a light,
Precious cornerstone, showing us the way.
Oh, let it shine and let it stand!
Lean upon it now and bring it in your heart!

Lead us from the night, give us all your might!
Never take your love away!

Light on the rock, (I see it.)
Light on the rock, (I know it.)
Light on the rock, (Let's feel it.)
Light on the rock, (Let's show it.)
Standing on the ground
And shining in the night --
Rock, rock . . .
Give us light!
Rock, rock . . .
Give us light!

The young people led the congregation in rousing applause as the song concluded, and motioned for everyone to be seated, as they themselves sat in chairs which lined the floor in front of the stage. Kyle Wingate rose from his chair and stepped briskly to the front center portion of the stage. There was no lectern or microphone, but Kyle appeared to be wearing a lapel mike. He raised his arms and smiled as he nodded to the crowd. He had a broad smile and pronounced features.

"Welcome to The Light on the Rock this glorious Sunday morning," he said enthusiastically. His voice was high and resonant. "We have an outstanding message from Peter this morning, and a wonderful healing service tonight. So it's going to be another miraculous day . . . Praise God?"

"Praise God!" shouted the congregation in response.

"All right!" shouted Wingate. "And I'll tell you, we have some outstanding successes since last week." He looked over toward Hatcher and motioned for him to stand. "Brother Greg . . . Bring us up to date."

Hatcher stood and raised his thick lips into a tight-lipped smiled. He straightened his coat tail and stepped to the side of the display board. "You're absolutely right, Brother Kyle," said Hatcher in a deep, rich southern accent. He pointed to the first segment. "Since last week . . . Salvations -- sixty-three!"

Kyle and the congregation responded with applause.

"Healings -- twenty-one!" continued Hatcher, pointing to the second segment.

The audience responded again.

"And commitments -- two hundred thirty-three thousand!"

The congregation cheered, and the choir responded with a resounding, unaccompanied reprise of the chorus of *Light on the Rock*.

Wingate stepped forward again. This time he carried a Bible in one hand. "Well, we have a blessed congregation, and a magnificent viewing audience!" he exclaimed. "And this is a brand new week, and a brand new opportunity for all of you out there to participate, and help us honor Christ's word!" He smiled and raised the Bible. "Our telephone workers are waiting for you to call in. Do it! I just know that many of you have established a personal relationship with Christ because of this ministry. Tell us about it! And if you can you can bless us with a financial commitment, God will honor you greatly."

Hatcher stepped forward again. "And your responses will be registered on our display as they are received!" he said.

As he spoke, the three graphs began inching upward.

"Praise God," shouted Hatcher, pointing to the display.

"Praise God!" responded the congregation.

Wingate nodded slowly and stepped back.

"I can't think of a better time to go into our sharing time," said Hatcher. "The choir will sing, and the Light-on-the-Rock Singers will pass among you for the offering. Join in as you feel led. This is a time for praise!"

The electronic music blared, and the choir began to sing another exuberant song: *Give and So Receive.* The young people at the front took offering bags from beneath their chairs and began circulating through the auditorium, singing and clapping their hands. They passed the bags cheerfully down the aisles, and paused occasionally to embrace members of the congregation. As the choir sang, the figures on the display board rose more, and the congregation responded with increased excitement and weeping. By the time the offering bag reached the row I was sitting in, the music and emotional level had reached a tremendous pitch. It was difficult not to respond in some manner. I turned to observe an elderly, poorly dressed woman next to me. She removed a crumpled fifty-dollar bill from her jacket pocket and placed it in the bag. Then she held the bag toward me with tear-filled eyes. I tried to take it and pass it on, but she still held it, waiting for me to contribute. Impulsively, I took a hundred-dollar bill from my wallet, stuffed it in the bag, and sent it on down the row.

I had to admit to myself that I actually felt good about having made such a large donation. This was an extremely effective emotional hype. And the timing was superb. Just as the energetic youths ran back down the aisle and out the wings, the choir concluded the song.

Suddenly, the lights went out, and the auditorium was thrust into pitch darkness. Immediately following this, a hush fell over the congregation, and the choir began chanting the words: "Light on the Rock." One by one, colored, circling lights beamed down on the mountain scene until the entire center section of the stage was flooded with blinding illumination. Hatcher and Wingate were gone. The choir members were barely visible in now shadowed portion of the stage, as they repeated the phrase. Then from the congregation rose a growing chant: "Peter . . . Peter . . . Peter . . . Peter . . . "

A white-robed figure stepped out from a crack in the rock behind the falls and walked down the winding path between the falls and the tree. His flowing sandy-colored hair was brushed neatly into place, and his skin looked tanned and unblemished. He was expressionless. He walked to the front center portion of the stage to the growing chant of the congregation and then stopped.

Peter raised one arm to the side and shouted, "Cry!"

"Salvation!" responded the crowd with a deafening roar.

Peter raised the other arm to the side, and shouted again, "Cry!"

"Salvation!" answered the crowd, even more loudly.

Then Peter raised his head toward the ceiling, and placed both arms high above his head and called emotionally, "Cry!"

"Salvation!" returned the congregation, with a tumultuous, lingering sound.

Peter lowered his arms, and the congregation became silent.

"Bless you all!" said Peter more softly. "This is life. This is about life, isn't it? All of you out there, you're here because you're alive. Alive! And God wants us to live fruitfully and abundantly."

"Praise God!" responded a few scattered members of the congregation.

I felt as though I were out of sync with reality. The man I was watching was not the same frightened, bizarre individual who was coming to me for therapy. Peter was doing an extremely good job at concealing his psychotic behavior. He displayed presence, charisma . . . even dynamism.

"I want you to begin today by looking inwardly," continued Peter. "To the very core of your being. God is there. Can you see Him? He's waiting to serve you, as He's told us so many times. Do you have a hope? God hopes it, too. Do you have a wish? God wishes for you. Do you have a dream? Do you have a dream?"

Soft music began issuing from the speakers. Peter motioned toward the side of the stage, and a trim blond girl in a flowing white dress emerged, carrying a cordless microphone. I recognized her as Julie Peters, the girl on the poster. She smiled as she walked slowly toward him.

"I want you to concentrate on your dream," Peter said as the music grew louder. "Concentrate on your dream. God wants you to have it. Concentrate on it. Julie will help you."

Julie stepped toward the front of the stage, on a parallel with Peter, as the music concluded its introductory notes. Then she began to sing in a low, inviting voice.

Only in my dreams
Did I imagine the Lord.
Only in my dreams was He real.
Silly as it seems,
I had no need for the Lord --
Never knew what His love could reveal.
Then one day I stumbled,
I couldn't find my way.
I saw a dark and hollow me.
But somehow, He touched me,
And I could hear him say,
"Arise . . . Arise, and follow me."

Now only in my dreams
Could I imagine myself
Drifting in the darkness alone.
He is by my side,
I'll never walk by myself --
Never try to live on my own.
And if ever the shadows
Should slip into my mind,
Some dark and fearful night . . .
I'll remember, even in my dreams
I will kneel,
Knowing all the peace that I'll find.
For even in my dreams, He will bring His light.
Even in my dreams, He is real.
God is real!

As Julie concluded, the music continued, and Peter spoke over it with an impassioned voice. "How about you?" he asked the congregation. "Are you stumbling in the darkness, because you're afraid to follow your dream? Are you filled with doubt?"

Peter nodded toward Julie, and she began to sing the second verse of the song again. He waited for cue words, and interspersed his message with these. Julie watched him intently, following his lead. I remembered his bizarre denial of involvement with her in our second session, and I wondered if perhaps there were some relationship, or at least fantasy, that he was repressing. Julie was very attractive. And in their brief shared presentation, she certainly appeared to be quite taken with him. Of course it was difficult to be sure from this distance.

"And if ever the shadow should slip into my mind . . . " sang Julie.

"Don't let the shadows slip into your mind," urged Peter. "Take hold of your dream. God wants you to grasp it. He is within you!"

"Even in my dreams, He is real. God is real!" concluded Julie.

"He is real, and he awaits you," said Peter.

Julie lowered the microphone, and bounced off the stage as the music picked up in tempo. The lights played on the stage in circles of color, producing a kaleidoscopic effect.

"Are you ready for your dream?" asked Peter. "Don't make it a small one. Make it worthy of the God within you. Close your eyes! Though blinded, you may see. You have the power! Visualize your needs and your desires. Toss out all those petty, insignificant hopes. They aren't worthy of you."

I looked around the auditorium and discovered that I was the only person not gazing intently on Peter. People of all ages were there, and all of them enthralled by his message. And as I listened, I could understand why. The content was certainly appealing, but, more than that, his presentation was captivating . . . almost hypnotic. People wept occasionally, and a periodic supportive "Amen" or "Praise God" arose from the still auditorium. But other than that, people sat transfixed.

The music began, slowly at first, and then rising in pitch and intensity. I glanced at my watch, and realized that Peter had been speaking for over thirty minutes. Lines of people began go emerge from rows throughout the auditorium and file toward the stage. Peter was still speaking emotionally as the music rose, and the choir backed him now with a rousing rendition of song entitled *Think Big -- God is on Your Side.* The congregation became more and more emotionally involved, and greater numbers of people started filing toward the stage. Wingate and three or four other men appeared from the side of the auditorium and stood below the stage as people came forward by the scores, weeping, swaying to and fro, and mumbling unintelligible syllables. Wingate and the others met with them . . . soothing them, embracing them . . . as Peter spoke.

The choir finished the song, and Peter continued unaccompanied. "If we do nothing more this hour than to allow you to recognize the power you have, we will have accomplished our miracle for this morning," said Peter. "Be the divine person that

God wants you to be. Live your dream today. Be your dream today. Be alive!"

Now shouts of "Praise God!" and "Amen!" filled the auditorium. The elderly woman next to me embraced me, and her tears streamed down my coat sleeve. Impulsively I returned her embrace, and I realized that my own eyes were welling with tears.

The music exploded, and all the lights came up on the stage as Peter turned abruptly and disappeared into the crack in the rock. The choir swayed and clapped, and sang a loud reprise of *Light on the Rock*. Wingate ran quickly up the stairs and hurried to the center of the stage, clapping in rhythm with the music. Then he checked his lapel mike, nodded toward the back of the auditorium, and addressed the congregation in a loud voice.

"This has been a miraculous morning!" he shouted. "Praise God?"

"Praise God!" responded the congregation.

"Bless you all for coming," he continued. "And you people in our television viewing audience . . . we wish you could be here with us. But keep those calls coming. I really felt the Holy Spirit surging in me today. I know there are some salvations and healings going on right now. Make those calls. Bless you again. Don't forget to come back tonight at seven for our regular Sunday Evening Healing Service. Remember what Peter told us . . . Live your dream. Say it with me . . . "

And at Wingate's signal, he and the congregation shouted in unison, "Live your Dream!"

"Praise God!" shouted Wingate. Then he nodded again toward the back, and the auditorium lights came on. "You're dismissed." He walked quickly off the stage as the choir sang the concluding refrain: "Rock, rock . . . Give us . . . Light!"

The congregation began moving in a huge mass toward the exits. Since I was near the rear, I was caught up in a surge which moved toward that opening. As we reached the spacious lobby, I stepped aside to escape the crowd, and I found myself standing before a long counter. Brightly colored signs advertised the sale of audio tapes from this morning's message and video tapes from last week's entire service. Several of the Light-on-the-Rock Singers were there working. I happened to be standing directly across from the blond in the flowing white dress. It was Julie.

"Yes, sir . . . May I help you?" Julie asked me.

"Well . . . ah . . . yes," I said. "I'll buy a video of last week's service." Since they were available, I thought it may be helpful to have one for further research into Peter's personality. "How much are they?"

"Twenty dollars," she said as she handed me the video. "No tax."

I removed a twenty-dollar bill from my wallet and gave it to her. "I really enjoyed your singing," I told her.

"Oh, thank you," she said. Then she smiled and pointed toward an attractive display of tapes. "Perhaps you'd be interested in purchasing one of the Light-on-the-Rock Singers' tapes."

"No. Not this time, thanks." As I was replacing my wallet, I looked behind her at a long row of small, glass-enclosed cubicles, each of which held a person speaking on a telephone. "What's that?" I asked pointing.

Julie glanced toward the cubicles. "Oh . . . those are our telephone workers," she explained. "They're still taking calls from people who have watched the service on TV."

"Impressive!" I said.

"It's all for the Lord," she said.

I gestured toward the workers, and the singers behind the counter. "It must cost a great deal to run an operation like this," I said.

"Well, it does, of course," she said. "But all of us singers and the telephone workers are volunteers."

"Really?"

"Mmm-hmm."

The crowd was beginning to thin as it departed through the doors, but another surge of people was beginning to enter.

"Are they coming for the next service?" I asked Julie.

"Yes. It doesn't start for another thirty minutes, but they come early to get their choice of seats," she said.

"I believe it," I said. "How many people does the auditorium hold?"

"Five thousand," she said.

"And the auditorium is filled for both services?" I asked.

"Oh, yes," she said. "And at our evening healing service, there's always an overflow, and people have to watch on the monitor in the recreation hall."

People behind me began to bump me, in an attempt to get to the counter. I stepped aside. "Thank you," I said to Julie.

She waved and turned to the next customer.

I found the least cluttered exit and stepped outside. The fresh air felt good, and I walked over to a low railing and leaned on it as I watched the people stream by. The reality of my experience was just beginning to set in. Peter's performance was unbelievable, considering the depth of his psychosis. And it wasn't only his competence that impressed me, but my reaction to it. I had been caught up by the service . . . moved by it. I had never witnessed a church service like this. I recalled that, as a boy, I'd had an emotional reaction once to a high mass. The image was still vivid: the priest marching slowly down the aisle, chanting in Latin, and the mechanically swaying men's choir, singing in slow, dirge-like tones, and the smell of incense filling my nostrils. Even now a tingle crossed my spine as I recalled that experience. But this was different. This was personal and . . . exciting. And the thousands of people who attended. All of them clearly felt the same way. And how many were watching on television? More thousands . . . or, perhaps . . . millions?

I smiled at the recollection of Peter's name for Hatcher -- Mr. Money-bags. But that was probably a very accurate label. I chuckled as I recalled that I had casually tossed a hundred dollars into the bag, myself. How much money must they be bringing in? And what could be so troubling to Peter that in the midst of all this success and wealth he could feel so lost and frightened?

I suddenly became very impatient to see Peter at tomorrow afternoon's session. This was without a doubt the most intriguing and baffling case that I'd ever treated. And the anticipation of the challenge of therapy was even more exciting than the service that I had just witnessed.

9

I was glad that I had given Peter another sedative to take on Sunday night, because when he arrived at our session on Monday afternoon he was calm and lucid. He had dreamed again, in his typical cumulative, additive format, but he was able to maintain a relatively objective stance toward his experience. Since I had witnessed Peter in his ministerial role, I was more convinced than ever that this was related somehow to his psychosis in general, and more specifically to the content of his dream. But I was as far away from discovering the link as I had been before. This wasn't surprising to me. I remembered Jung's statement that the deity or the demon speaks in symbolic speech to the sleeper, and the dream interpreter has the riddle to solve. The discovery process wasn't taking any longer than normal, but Peter was continuing to grow impatient with my lack of answers. And I was as impatient as he. I was tempted to tell Peter that I had seen his service . . . use that as a springboard toward the exploration into other hidden facts in his psyche. But I knew that his initial reaction to this revelation would be one of aversion, and would likely lead to a breakdown in our relationship. I was unwilling to take this chance, especially now that I sensed that a positive transference was beginning to take place.

I realized that I needed to speak with a colleague about the case in an attempt to broaden my view and, perhaps, identify some inadvertent blockage that my own biases were bringing about. Leonard wasn't sufficiently grounded in Jungian analysis to be of much help. I concluded that I should settle for none but the very best -- my former teacher and mentor, Bernadette Keating. I hadn't seen her since I had completed my postgraduate work at the Institute nearly twelve years ago, but I thought she would be willing to see me. I had Cheryl call her and arrange for me to visit with her at her home on Tuesday evening.

Bernadette lived several miles out of town on a secluded, wooded plot about a quarter mile off the road. Her house was a rambling shingle-covered structure, nestled in the midst of a heavily landscaped section of her property. I parked my car beneath a drooping pepper tree, and stepped through a vine-covered entryway. I didn't see a doorbell, so I knocked loudly on the dark wooden door. I heard an electronic buzzing above my head, and I looked up to see a tiny speaker concealed in the eaves.

"John . . . Is that you?" Bernadette's voice crackled through the device.

When the buzzing subsided, I responded. "Yes. It's me, Bernadette."

The buzzing recommenced. "I'm in the greenhouse," said Bernadette. "Look to your left. . . . The iron gate."

I looked. The gate faced the edge of the long porch, about forty feet away, and it appeared to lead to a structure adjacent to the house. "All right," I said.

"I'll be waiting," Bernadette's voice responded.

I walked across the dusty floor to the end of the porch, placed my hand on the gate and pulled. It was locked. Then a buzz sounded. I pulled again, and the gate swung open. As I stepped inside a small secondary foyer, another large wooden door swung open before me, and Bernadette stood in the entrance. She immediately thrust her hand forward.

"John!" she said enthusiastically. "It's so good to see you again. Come in! Come in!"

I took her hand and followed her inside. Bernadette's white hair sparkled in the glimmering light of the greenhouse. The last time I saw her, it had been just streaked with gray. Her skin seemed as smooth as it was then, however, and she as attractive and stately as I had always remembered her being.

"I thought that, since you had become rich and famous, you were no longer interested in your old teacher," she said.

"None of the above statements is accurate!" I said emphatically.

"I'm so glad you came," she said. "Since I stopped teaching I have precious little contact with the outside world."

"You're still practicing, aren't you?" I asked.

"Oh, yes. I still have a few patients," she said. "I conduct the sessions in my home. Just enough to keep the juices flowing!"

"I'm glad."

"But this is my main career now," she said, gesturing broadly across the large greenhouse. "Come. Let me show you around."

The greenhouse was filled with exotic plants and vines, and Bernadette took great pride in describing the history and significance of each. She seemed particularly fond of a sort of willow tree that had long shoots of green mistletoe hanging from its branches.

"This is somewhat of a hybrid," she said in definition of the willow. "I've been nurturing it for eight years. It's very symbolic, don't you think? The maternal image of the tree, superimposed by the clinging, dependent parasite. The mistletoe isn't aware of its role, of course. It just flourishes in dreadful subservience, robbing both itself and the mother image of their right to freedom. I often bring my oedipal patients here during our sessions. I never make an overt point of the similarity, but invariably the symbol thrusts itself upon their unconscious minds, and they begin the road back to health."

"That's fascinating, Bernadette," I said. The heat and humidity of the greenhouse was beginning to become oppressive. I took a handkerchief from my pocket and wiped the perspiration from my forehead.

"Oh, how thoughtless of me," she said. "It is rather unpleasant in here for the uninitiated, isn't it? I was prepared, however." She pointed toward a white wrought-iron table and chairs in a small clearing, under a slowly revolving overhead fan. A pitcher and two glasses rested on the table. "Let's sit."

We sat at the table. The hard chairs were somewhat uncomfortable, but the cooling flow of air from the fan soothed my discomfort from the heat. Bernadette picked up the pitcher and poured the drink and a few tinkling ice cubes into the large glasses.

"Lemonade," she said. "I made it myself from my own fresh lemons."

"Thanks." I drank, and the sweet tangy liquid cleared my head. I chuckled in the recollection that Lloyd had asked for lemonade at our parents party. I thought perhaps he should visit Bernadette.

"Now . . . enough of *my* passions," said Bernadette. "Tell me about you. How is your family."

"Doing well," I said evasively. "Meg isn't working any more, and . . . "

"Meg is your wife," confirmed Bernadette.

"Yes," I said. "And our daughter Diane is fifteen."

"My!" She shook her head slowly. "And how about your father?" she asked. "Do you see him often?"

"Occasionally," I said. "In fact, just a couple of weeks ago, I went to my parents' fiftieth wedding anniversary."

"Yes . . . " She nodded her head slowly. "The years do slip by." She took a long drink, and then set her glass down. "I haven't seen Charles for ten years," she said. "Is he still working?"

"As hard as ever," I said. "He's the senior member of the firm, and I sometimes doubt that he'll ever retire."

"He's a strong man," she said. "Retirement would be difficult for him."

It sounded strange to hear Bernadette talk about my father this way. I knew that he had met with her several times to help me schedule my course of study at the Institute, but the way she spoke, she must have known him outside that relationship. "You've apparently seen my father under other circumstances, too," I said.

"Yes. I thought he told you," she said. "Charles handled my legal affairs for many years."

"No, I didn't know that," I said. I smiled remembering her statement of the time they last met. "And you haven't had any legal affairs for ten years?" I asked.

Bernadette threw her head back and laughed lightly. "Well, actually, very few," she said. "I've become somewhat less . . . venturesome in my therapy."

"You're not becoming too conventional, I hope," I said. "I need your advice with a tough case."

"Ah, splendid, John!" she gushed. "You've come to me for consultation. I'm honored."

"No, the honor will be mine, Bernadette," I said. "I still regard you as my infallible mentor." I leaned forward ominously. "So don't disappoint me."

Bernadette laughed again. "Well, I'll try not to. Very well." She pushed the pitcher and glasses aside and leaned on the table. "Tell me about your tough case."

"It's a schizophrenic," I began.

"All right . . . "

"I actually inherited him from a friend of mine," I added.

"Who?" she asked.

"Leonard Butler."

She grimaced. "Isn't he Freudian?" she asked.

"Yes."

"No wonder he gave up," she said.

"He admitted his inability to continue successfully," I said. "But I believe he actually made more initial progress than he was willing to acknowledge."

"Well, of course," she said. "We haven't *relinquished* Freud. We've simply added the necessary archetypal layer to his psychoanalytical foundation."

"I've told that to Leonard," I said. "But, of course, he doesn't see it that way."

She nodded. "I always relate it to Christ's words: 'Do not think that I came to destroy the Law or the Prophets. I did not come to destroy but to fulfill.'"

"It's interesting that you should make that Biblical reference," I said.

"Why is that?"

"My patient is an evangelist," I said.

Bernadette's eyebrows rose, and her mouth parted in a wide smile. "This sounds intriguing, indeed! You used the term . . . *evangelist*. Is he successful?"

"Very," I said.

"So he has a large following," she added.

"Thousands at least," I said. "His services are also transmitted on television."

"And he presents himself in this role with complete control and charm," she said confidently. "Is that not correct?"

"Completely," I agreed. "But I was very surprised when I discovered that. In therapy he slips randomly from anxiety to megalomania to paranoia to composure."

"Not unusual at all," she said. "His false self needs an audience. And he's apparently used that need to create a very successful facade."

"Yes."

"But, of course, the false-self system is extremely fragile," she said. "And any breach in the illusion will send him headlong into a psychotic response." She pursed her lips and sat back. "He's not one of these 'touchy-feely' evangelists, is he?"

"What?" I laughed.

"He doesn't go out among his congregation . . . mingle, embrace . . . "

"I've only been to one service," I said. "But he certainly didn't then. He came out on stage, delivered his message, and left." Then I recalled that Kyle Wingate had gone out and personally joined those coming forward. I wondered if this was one of the differences Lloyd had asked me to detect in their approaches. There was another, of course. Wingate had used a hand prop -- the Bible.

Bernadette nodded. "You'll probably find that's his pattern. He dare not become personally involved with his followers; they've become *things* to him -- objects of his illusion."

My mind raced to reach out for Bernadette's wisdom. I had forgotten how brilliant she was. She hadn't even met Peter, and yet, from my brief description, she had described him precisely.

"You're very fortunate, John," she continued. "There are precious few full-blown schizophrenics around . . . at least outside the institutional setting. And it sounds as though you've really gotten a plum."

"I have to admit that he's captured an inordinate amount of my attention."

"Of course!" she said. "It's extremely difficult not to become intellectual gluttons with cases like this."

"I agree."

"He's exhibited hysteria, I'm sure," she said.

I nodded. "Most blatantly manifested in a troublesome recurring dream. And that's what's bothering me," I said. "I can't seem to make sense of it."

"Tell me the dream," she said.

That was easy. Not only had Peter described it with vivid details on several occasions, I had mulled over in my own mind countless times, searching for significant links. I told her the setting -- Peter in a white robe, walking down the long flight of narrow, crumbling stairs toward a mandala. And I described the serpents jumping out and wagging their tongues at him as he splits from his white-robed self. And I told her of his trying to cry out, only to find that his tongue has been ripped out. She seemed particularly intrigued by the fire around the mandala and the figure of Satan emerging from the flames and beckoning to him, and his irresistibly being drawn, away from his disconnected self to the fire. But then when I told her that Satan had stuck out the stub of a torn-out tongue, and that Peter had become this figure in later dreams, she looked perplexed.

"In a way, I'm happy to see that you're confused over that last aspect," I said. "That's the part I've become stumped on." I smiled. "But I'd rather hoped you could help me with it."

"Well, if he were not so successful . . . " She paused and shook her head. "Naturally, there's a link with his calling. But the details are somewhat baffling, aren't they?"

"Yes."

"Much of it fits in nicely," she continued. Then she closed her eyes and began mumbling: "The myth is a fragment of the infantile soul life of the race, and the dream is the myth of the individual. The dream is the myth of the individual . . . "

I recognized that quote; it was directly out of Jung's book, *Psychology of the Unconscious.*

Bernadette opened her eyes and sat forward. "Naturally the elements of evil, as well as good are there," she said. "The aspect missing in the Christ Archetype."

"He referred to himself as a Christ figure," I said. "And he claimed a harder challenge because of possessing this aspect himself."

"Of course . . . of course . . . " She chuckled. "And your friend Leonard would like the flame symbol," she said. "There are definite Freudian sexual overtones in that."

"He exhibits a radical denial syndrome at any suggestion of sexual involvement," I said. "Particularly at the notion of homosexuality."

"Methinks you deny too strongly . . . "

"That's what I thought initially," I said. "But now I'm not so sure."

"No. That would be too easy . . . too obvious," she agreed. "No, we're dealing with a rich, complex personality here. We mustn't jump to the obvious interpretation, because that will invariably be wrong." She rubbed her chin lightly. "Have you explored the symbol of the moth and the flame?"

"No. But that sounds promising in this case," I said.

"Yes . . . The self immolation for the promise of rebirth."

"I'll remember that," I said.

"Do you have a good historical work-up?" she asked.

"Almost nothing," I admitted reluctantly. "He displays marked resistance to any attempt to discuss his parents."

"There again, that may be an indication of a significant link . . . or nothing at all," she said. "It may even be a ruse used by the patient to divert you from the actual core of the problem."

"He's very bright," I said.

"Most schizophrenics are," she said. "And, of course most are spiritually motivated." She looked at me with an instructive glance. "In the clinical sense, I mean, of course."

"I understand."

"So a schizoid individual who has ostensibly found his spiritual outlet would be expected to avoid the psychosis attached to the frustration from the lack of discovering it."

"I've bounced that troubling observations around more than a few times," I said.

"Well, you will need eventually to find out about his parents," she said. "You can't afford any missing links. Until then, you'll just have to deal exclusively with his communication regarding his ministry."

"I haven't decided whether to reveal that I've seen him in this setting," I said. "I'm afraid it will disturb the patient-physician relationship."

"Possibly," she agreed. "But therapy could advance more rapidly if you could step boldly into mutually understood experiences."

"I know."

"Do you believe that a transference has taken place yet?" she asked.

"I sense that it has," I said. "But, of course, I have no idea at this point what person or experience in his life I am becoming the substitute for."

"Not necessary initially," she said.

"But there are times . . . " I paused as I recalled our session last week . . . Peter grasping my knees, gazing at me intently . . . and his words . . . Do you seek the restful nonexistence of the end of life? I breathed deeply, and I felt a trickle of perspiration on my cheek.

Bernadette tilted her head coyly and raised an eyebrow. "Has your patient taken occasion to grasp control of the session, John?"

"Yes," I responded abruptly. She had read me too easily. A nauseated feeling swept across me, and I sat back. "That is . . . he's attempted to."

Bernadette did not speak, but a low laughter rippled across her body. "They will do that, John," she said finally. "Especially the really bright ones. You must exercise caution."

"I know."

"On the other hand, that's probably a sign that a positive transference is at least in the making," she added. "I think you're on the right track."

"I . . . I hope so . . . " The heat and humidity of the green house suddenly fell upon me like a blanket. I had trouble getting my breath. Bernadette's face faded in and out of focus, and it periodically merged with my recollection of Peter, sitting across from me. I heard Bernadette repeat . . . You must exercise caution . . . or was that my recollection of it? I removed my handkerchief again, and wiped it heavily across my face.

"Restful nonexistence . . . " Bernadette seemed to be saying.

"Wh . . . what?" I mumbled.

" . . . restful in here, but the humidity can be a threat to your existence."

"Yes . . . yes . . . "

"Would you like to get some fresh air?" she asked.

"I think I really should be going," I said.

"Oh, so soon?" she asked.

"Yes. I need to get home." I stood awkwardly, and the chair tipped backward.

"Watch it!" she cautioned.

"Sorry . . . " I walked back through the greenhouse, past the willow with its parasitic mistletoe, and pulled open the door.

"Thank you so much for coming, John." Bernadette was right behind me, and her hand fell lightly on my shoulder. "And remember . . . you will probably end up learning a great deal more from your patient than he learns from you."

"Yes." I swung the door open, and a blast of warm summer evening air cooled my face. I saw my car under the pepper tree, but it seemed to be moving, and the feeling of nausea rose again. "Bernadette . . . "

"Yes?"

"Do you remember William James' example for the feeling of dread?" I asked without turning toward her.

"Of course," she answered. "Walking along a curb stone elicits no sensation of dread; therefore, no sense of ominous reality is sensed, and we are sure we will not fall. But if the curb were placed at the edge of a cliff, the sickening emotion would make us quite unable to function, even though the particulars of the muscular involvement are identical."

"In dealing with schizophrenic patients . . . have you ever experienced the feeling of walking that curb stone at the edge of a cliff?"

"Once or twice," she said. "And it's both terrifying . . . and exhilarating!"

"Yes . . . "

"Stay in control, John," she said.

"Yes." I waved at her without looking back, and headed toward my car.

It was nearly nine when I arrived home. When I walked into the living room, I saw Meg sitting in a straight chair, reading a book. I wondered why she wasn't relaxing on the couch, as usual. And then I realized with a rush of guilt that I had forgotten to tell her that I would be late. She looked up as I entered and cast a cold glance in my direction.

"Meg . . . I'm so sorry!" I said. "I just . . . I just forgot."

"I know."

"It's just . . . when it's on my calendar . . . I assume you know."

"You're not blaming Cheryl for *that*, are you?" she asked crisply.

"No . . . " And then I chuckled at the thought of what she had asked. I smiled and threw my hands up. "No. I assume complete responsibility."

"So, where were you?" she asked.

"I went to see Bernadette Keating," I said.

"Bernadette?" she asked incredulously. "What for?"

"I needed her advice on this case," I said.

"Hmm . . . " She looked back down at her book. "Does she do family counseling?"

"Come, on, Meg . . . " I tried to change the subject. "How'd your day go?"

"Fine," she said noncommittally. "I visited with Sally this afternoon."

"Oh?"

"She told me that you and Lloyd had lunch last week."

"Oh . . . yes," I said. "Yes, we did.

"You didn't tell me," she said with growing bitterness in her voice.

"I know. We just . . . we just talked about a case."

"Same case?" she asked.

"Yes . . . well . . . " I recalled of course the full details of my meeting with Lloyd. I walked over to where Meg sat. "No. There's more than that. We talked about Diane, too. I don't know why I didn't mention it to you. I've just been so busy. And this case has me . . . "

"This case has you turning into a zombie!" Meg suddenly shouted. "There's no communication . . . no warmth . . . no . . . " She shook her head in frustration. Then she slammed the book shut and tossed it on the floor, beside a stack of some other books and magazines.

"You're right, Meg . . . you're right . . . " I squatted down on the floor in front of her and tried to take her hand, but she pulled it away. I glanced around the room. "Where is Diane?" I asked.

"That's a new record." She looked at her watch. "You noticed something in less than five minutes!" she said sarcastically.

I never responded to Meg's sarcastic barbs. She knew that. I just sighed and waited for her to make her point rationally.

"She's out with her friends," she said.

"Which friends?" I asked.

"The ones she's always with," said Meg. "The ones I'm so worried about. But I just can't get any support from you."

"Maybe you're right, Meg," I said.

"Maybe I'm right?"

"I mean . . . How long has she been gone?"

"A couple of hours," she said.

I didn't want to tell her everything Lloyd said. I was sure that he was probably overreacting. But I had dropped the ball . . . seriously. I tried to recall the events following my meeting with Lloyd to determine why I hadn't followed up with Meg. There were three more sessions with Peter, of course . . . and the Light on the Rock service . . . No excuse. I needed to make up for it.

"Let's go somewhere next Sunday," I said.

"Where? To your father's club again while you and Leonard play golf?" she asked bitterly.

"No. Just the three of us," I said. "Let's fix a picnic lunch and go somewhere?"

Meg shrugged. "Where?"

"I don't know." Then I had an idea. "Why don't we take the boat out?"

Meg frowned and shook her head. Then she stood and began picking up books and magazines from the floor. Meg didn't particularly like our boat, because she associated it with my racing. But I didn't have that in mind. I stood and walked toward her, and the blood rushed suddenly to my head from having squatted so long. I became dizzy and leaned against the wall to brace myself?

Meg stood up and looked at me suspiciously. "Have you been drinking?"

"Lemonade," I said impulsively. And then I began to laugh.

Meg shook her head and started out of the room.

"Sunday, Meg," I called after her. "Just the three of us. I promise."

The blood was still surging in my head, and Meg's figure blurred as she left the room. I began to walk after her. I glanced down at the floor to avoid stepping on the books, and the image of a curb stone suddenly thrust itself upon me. My feet were balanced precariously on the white concrete . . . and the blurred carpet on either side took on the appearance of a distant valley. My heart jumped, and my feet became frozen in place. I couldn't walk. Slowly, I knelt down and grasped the curb and felt its plush texture push itself violently into my fingertips. I was aware of my lips moving . . . mumbling . . . I renounce you . . . I renounce you . . . And the image of the curb disappeared, and the reassuring flatness of the carpet stretched out before me . . . and left me with a peaceful feeling of nonexistence.

10

The next afternoon I reviewed my notes in preparation for Peter's session. My visit with Bernadette had been helpful, and I was angry with myself for having become nauseous and leaving as early as I did. Bernadette would surely have continued talking for hours, and I could have gained so much more. As it turned out, there was no problem with Diane. She returned home before ten, and I could detect no actions on her part which would indicate that she had been participating in any type of asocial behavior. Of course, Meg had a right to be angry with me; I was not spending enough time with her and Diane. The outing on Sunday would be good for all of us. At any rate, the wave of queasiness that caused my distress was gone now. I had a good night's sleep, and this had been a positive, productive day.

It was not quite four yet, but Cheryl entered the office quietly and closed the door behind her. As I looked up from my work, she met me with her familiar apologetic, self-conscious look.

"I'm sorry, Dr. Summers," she said tentatively. "But Peter is here."

I pointed at the clock on the wall, which indicated that it was only three fifty-five.

"I know, that," she said. "But he's really agitated again today."

It was really extremely important that Peter force himself to follow the rigid schedule. The more he could take control over his personal time, the more he could gain mastery of his delusional departures. But he clearly had the ability to raise Cheryl's level of anxiety, and her sitting across from him in the outside office in this state would not be particularly helpful.

I closed the folder that I was reviewing and placed it in my desk drawer. "In what way is he agitated today, Cheryl?" I asked her.

"He's pacing the floor," she said. "And he's . . . " She pounded the fist of one hand into the palm of another to illustrate his actions.

"How is he dressed today?" I asked.

She looked perplexed for a moment. Then she raised her finger in the air. "Just a minute." She started to open the door.

"No, Cheryl!"

She jumped back startled.

"Don't go out again," I said. "If you can't remember, that's all right."

"I guess I just didn't pay that much attention," she said. Then she smiled. "I do remember that he's not wearing his coat today."

"Oh?"

"I think I avoided looking at him because of the smell," she added.

"What smell?" I asked.

"It's really strange," she explained. "He smells like he's been swimming in perfume."

"Hmm . . . " I glanced at the clock. There were still two minutes to go, but I concluded that it was close enough. "Very well, Cheryl. You may ask him to come in now."

She nodded and opened the door. Then she stepped into the opening, and motioned gracefully toward me. "All right, Peter," she said. "The doctor will see you now."

Peter stormed past her into my office, and watched her impatiently as she closed the door. I realized immediately what Cheryl was referring to. The strong aroma of heavy cologne was overpowering. Even still, I couldn't see how Cheryl could have forgotten his attire. He was dressed in a long-sleeved white shirt and white trousers. The gold mandala still hung about his neck, but today he wasn't wearing sunglasses. I looked on that as progress.

"Good afternoon, Peter," I said.

He didn't answer me, but walked quickly over and sat in the chair across from me. "It stopped working again!" he said loudly.

"The medication?" I asked.

"You're supposed to know about these things," he said. "Why do I have to be the one to discover it all the time?"

"Your body is just building up some type of rapid tolerance response," I told him. I really didn't believe this, though. Each new medication that I had given him had performed perfectly for a few days; and then this cycle reappeared. It was almost as though he were reacting psychosomatically.

"My body is an empty vessel," said Peter. "It has no tolerance to anything."

"There are other medications," I reminded him. "I'll prescribe another. But I told you that the final resolution must be psychological, not chemical."

"Words . . . words . . . words . . . " he mumbled.

"Did you have the dream again last night?" I asked.

"Of course!"

"Were there any changes?" I asked.

"Nothing new, nothing old . . . nothing borrowed, nothing gold."

"What was so upsetting, then?" I asked, ignoring his bizarre verbal departure.

"Time . . . " He placed his hands against his ears and closed his eyes. "My brain took it all and compressed it! So many thoughts . . . I can't stop them. My brain! There must be something wrong with it. Someone should just yank it out! You should just yank it out and fix it! That's what they do with cars. Just yank it out and fix it. It's no good, anyway."

"You know that isn't true, Peter," I told him calmly. "You know that your brain is very good, or you wouldn't be having this trouble."

"Lies . . . "

"You deal with extremely complex issues," I assured him. "Look at all the intricacies in your dream, for example."

"That's not me," he said. "That's someone else. There's someone else in my mind, pretending to be me. That's who the dream is . . . someone else."

"It just seems that way, Peter," I said. "The dream is a marvelous fabricator. It takes aspects of our real life . . . memories of our own existence . . . and merges them in strange and incomprehensible ways. But it is your life, your memories. We just have to unravel the mystery."

"Mystery . . . Miss Tree, Mrs. Tree, and Mr. Tree," he mumbled.

"You're wearing your mandala again, I see," I said.

"Of course," he muttered. "It's part of me."

"Is it exactly like the one in your dream?" I asked.

"It isn't burning," he said.

"What about the one in your temple?" I asked.

"It isn't burning," he repeated.

"The mandala in your temple is much larger," I said.

"Size means success," he said.

I recalled the image if the mandala in the temple, and the large letters below it -- **THIS WEEK'S SUCCESSES**. I thought there might be something significant in that reference, and I decided to venture out with some knowledge I had gained from my attendance at the service on Sunday.

"Do you enjoy your success, Peter?" I asked.

"Success isn't ice cream," he said. "It's intangible." He leaned back in his chair, crossed his legs, and looked vaguely off into the distance.

I thought that perhaps by forcing his recollection of aspects of the service that I could move him past this blockage. I thought the headings on the display board might do it. "What's more important to you, Peter?" I asked. "Salvations, healings, or commitments?"

Peter turned his head slowly back toward me, and his unblinking eyes became riveted to mine. "You've been to my temple," he said slowly.

I couldn't believe that Peter could simultaneously be drifting in a delusional state and holding sufficiently to details of reality that he could immediately be aware of my having attended the service from my mere mention of those three words.

"What were you doing at my temple?" Peter asked, more loudly.

The issue was out in the open now, and so I decided to try to take advantage of it. "If I'm going to be able to help you, Peter, it's imperative that I learn as much about your surroundings as possible," I said.

"But you're here, and that's there," he said.

"*You're* in both places, Peter," I reminded him. "Why can't I be, also?"

"There are more me's than there are you's," he said.

"How do you know?" I asked him.

That question stopped him. He fidgeted nervously in the chair. Then he reached into his pants' pocket and pulled out a small cartridge. He pointed it toward several areas of his body and pressed it, and a strong smell of sweet cologne spewed forth.

"Why are you doing that, Peter?" I asked him.

"What?"

"That," I repeated, pointing the cologne cartridge.

He quickly put the cartridge back into his pocket. "I've been bothered by this terrible body odor lately," he said. "Something glandular, I'm sure."

"That's not an uncommon symptom in schizophrenia, Peter," I told him.

"Glandular problems?" he asked.

"No. Hypersensitivity to your own body parts and functions," I said. "There is no odor, Peter. That's another delusion that you have to deal with."

"I'll deal with my mind," he said. "But my body is my temple."

I had let his actions divert me from the discussion of the service. I had to reinitiate it before the details became lost. "Last Sunday is the service I viewed, Peter," I told him.

He nodded slowly.

"You made a very effective presentation," I said.

"Presentation? Do you think I'm just playing a role?" he asked.

"I didn't say that," I said.

"It doesn't matter." Peter slumped down in the chair. "The role of Christ is so hard to master, anyway."

I decided to pursue the associations that sparked his recognition. "What's more important to you, Peter? Salvations, healings, or commitments?" I repeated.

"I have come not to judge the world, but to save it," he mumbled.

"Salvations, then . . . "

Peter suddenly sat forward and began singing and clapping his hands. "Salvation Army, Salvation Army! Throw a nickel on the drum, throw a nickel on the drum!"

"What's more important, Peter?" I repeated.

Peter slumped back in the chair again, and concluded the song, singing weakly. "Throw a nickel on the drum, and save a soul."

"How many souls have you saved?" I asked.

"It's a function of time," he said. "And it costs dearly to put on an effective presentation. There are the lights, the makeup, the actors, the director . . . "

"Who is the director, Peter?" I asked him.

"The director . . . " He sighed deeply, and looked vaguely about the room, and toward the ceiling. Then he shook his head, and shifted in the chair. "It doesn't matter. It's the actors that count. And they can do splendidly without him."

"Are you one of the actors?" I asked.

He grasped the arms of the chair and sat forward. "I told you . . . I'm not just playing a role! This is reality! I was *called*! Can't you remember that? I was appointed and anointed. And God has hold of my nerves, and He won't let go, and He's stretching them out so far, I'm afraid they're going to snap!" He slumped back down and closed his eyes.

Bernadette had told me that I'd have to deal exclusively with aspects of Peter's ministry until I obtained more historical content. And the current exchange seemed to be the best opportunity I'd ever had to pursue this topic, so I pressed it. "Let's talk about your temple, Peter," I said.

He opened his eyes and looked at me without responding.

"Your stage has a magnificent setting," I said. "An actual waterfall, coming right out of the mountain! What is the significance of that?"

"I use it in the healing ceremony," he said calmly. "It washes away the sins of the world."

"And what about the tree?" I asked.

"The tree of life," he mumbled.

I remembered Bernadette's tree, covered with the clinging, dependent mistletoe. Peter's tree was not like this; it was fresh and vibrant -- a vivid illustration of the maternal symbol -- new life out of the darkness of nonexistence.

"The tree is a good symbol for you, Peter," I suggested. "Strong . . . its branches reaching out in complex interrelationships. And the perennial cycle of life -- death and rebirth."

"No! My tree never dies!" he said abruptly. "Rebirth is not necessary."

"Is it an artificial tree?" I asked.

"What of it?" he asked. "Can't artificial beings have a life of their own?"

"What do you think?" I asked.

"It's possible . . . it's possible . . . " he mumbled. "Christ can do anything."

"The tree is not in your dream, though, is it, Peter?" I asked.

He looked blankly over my shoulder for a moment. Then he shook his head. "There's no tree in my mind. Nothing artificial is in my mind."

"Except the mandala," I reminded him.

He picked up his golden mandala and gazed at it absently. "The mandala is the universe," he said. "The mandala is the world."

"Is the world artificial?" I asked.

"The world is what you make of it," he said slowly.

I had allowed the free flow of our ideas to rush randomly into our conversation. There was something significant here, but it constantly lay beyond my grasp. I thought that Bernadette's suggested moth symbol might open something substantial, though, particularly in light of the elements of his dream.

"Why do you suppose the mandala in your dream is burning, Peter?" I asked.

"There is nothing artificial in my dream," he said. "I had to destroy it."

"But the fire. . . . You are drawn to it," I said.

"It's warm . . . and it reaches out to me."

"Which *you* is it reaching out to, Peter?" I asked.

"The one on the stairs," he said.

"Is that the real *you,* or the artificial *you*?" I asked.

"There is nothing artificial in my mind!" he responded loudly.

"But what will happen when you reach the flame?" I asked.

"It's warm . . . it reaches out to me," he repeated.

"But you remain at the top as well," I said. "Are you safe there?"

"There is nothing safe in my dream," he said.

"Will the mandala be destroyed?" I asked.

He jerked his head from side to side in a spasmodic denial. "Changed! It will be changed!"

"How?"

"Melted down . . . purified . . . restored."

"Is that what you are attempting in your dream? Sacrifice yourself to the flames . . . be destroyed, purified and restored?"

"No! There is no restoration through fire," he said. "The light is the important thing. Can't you see that? The fire is light. And it's heroic, and everlasting. The eternal flame . . . like the Olympics . . . or Kennedy's grave."

There were too many layers of repression blocking further discovery through this route. But I felt that I had made good progress. He still seemed communicative, though, so I decided to switch to other aspects of the service.

"You need a great deal of help in your service, don't you?" I asked.

"It costs dearly to put on an effective presentation," he said.

"And Greg Hatcher takes care of all of the finances?" I asked.

Peter suddenly sat forward with a frown on his face. "You were there Sunday. Was Greg there when the singers brought the bags forward?"

His very literal question took me by surprise. I searched my recollection. "On the stage, you mean? Yes. I believe so."

"Did they give the money to him, or did they leave with it?" he asked.

"They. . . ah . . . they left the auditorium with the bags," I said.

He sighed, sat back and nodded. "They have strict instructions to take the money and put it directly into the safe. But I believe he's been talking to them . . . telling them something different. I've been watching him very carefully. But it's difficult. I've been so busy."

"Why do you distrust Hatcher?" I asked.

"I know things that I'm not supposed to know," he said. "My nerves tell me." He shook his head. "It's a terrible responsibility being a Christ figure."

"But your presentation was very successful," I said. "At the conclusion, many people came forward, and met with Wingate and some other pastors."

"Yes. I saw them out of the corner of my eye," he said. "They used to take the people outside, but I put a stop to that."

"Why?"

"Kyle would like to be a Christ figure," he said softly. "He lusts after it. When he and his helpers are there with my followers, they whisper. He's trying to convince them that it's not really me who has the power," he said.

"Who, then?" I probed.

He squinted and turned away momentarily. Then he raised his arm and moved it about in a circular motion. "Some . . . nebulous . . . " He lowered his arm and turned back. "If they believe him they will be destroyed. I must prevent that."

"But it's you that the people responded to," I reminded him.

"I know." A faint smile crossed his lips. "But when you can't trust people . . "

"Do you trust Julie?" I asked.

He raised his eyebrow and sat forward. "Julie?"

"Julie Peters . . . the singer," I said.

"Julie is a saint," he said. "She brings her spirit into the temple with her song. How can you *not* trust a saint?"

"I noticed during the service . . . she seemed quite taken with you," I said.

He frowned slightly and shrugged. "That's part of the rehearsed repartee. It adds interest to the presentation."

"So it's an artificial relationship?" I prodded.

He frowned at me, and spoke slowly and harshly. "Julie is not artificial."

"Do you ever meet with her outside the services?" I asked him.

Peter folded his arms in front of him and sighed with exasperation. "I believe we put that suspicion of yours to rest at another session," he said. "There is unequivocally no romantic relationship."

"All right."

He nodded with a look of self-satisfaction. "I have no need for that type of thing. Besides . . . all great leaders are hermaphroditic, anyway. There simply isn't time for others. It's such a responsibility . . . there are so many people to watch."

"Have you ever thought of doing something else for a living?" I asked.

"Of course I have." He sat forward again with a desperate expression. "Don't you think I'd rather . . . But God has a permanent hold on my nerves and He won't let go!"

I smiled acceptingly and nodded. Peter sighed heavily and curled back in the chair again. If I had really thought he would continue in this communicative state, I would have moved him to the couch and attempted to probe his history. But I was quite certain that would break the flow. Still, I thought perhaps he might not be too resistive to such a tack if I allowed him to remain seated.

"I don't think you ever told me whether your parents approved of your profession," I said.

"My mother is dead," he said abruptly. "And my father is a mechanic."

"Well . . . your father, then," I said. "Does he approve of your profession?"

Peter suddenly became very agitated. He shifted several times in the chair, and then he stood and began to pace. "I told you . . . he's a mechanic! He fixes things! If he didn't approve of my profession, he'd fix it!"

"How would he do that?" I asked.

Peter looked up momentarily, and then continued his pacing, mumbling feverishly: "I renounce you . . . I renounce you . . . I renounce you . . . "

"What delusion are you trying to renounce, Peter?" I asked, eager to push this into a worthwhile recognition.

"Delusions are artificial, and my father is not artificial. He's a mechanic."

"Then . . . what?"

He suddenly stopped pacing, rushed over and sat again, leaning his arms heavily on my desk. "It's not working! I can't renounce it! You'll have to do something else."

"What do you think I should do, Peter?" I asked.

"I don't care. Anything!" Then a look of fear came into his eyes. Except . . . "

"Except what?"

"Please . . . don't do what the other doctor did!" he pleaded.

"What other doctor, Peter?"

"Your friend," he said.

"Dr. Butler?" I asked

"Don't do what he did!" he pleaded.

"What did he do?" I asked.

"It was so cold . . . the cold water, and the ice . . . " He was mumbling almost incoherently. "And the bathtub was full, and he threw me in, and the water sloshed out. And I told him I was sorry, but he put in more ice!"

"Why did he do that, Peter?"

"I couldn't renounce it," he said. "He had to fix it. But I hated it! It was so cold!"

Obviously Leonard hadn't taken this bizarre action. Peter was pulling it up from something he'd read, or something from his past. But his past was clearly not going to be any more accessible to me today.

"Don't worry, Peter," I said calmly. "You may be assured that I will never place you in a bathtub full of ice water."

"But how will you fix it?" he asked.

"I'll find a way," I said.

He sat poised over my desk, is arms still leaning heavily, and his breathing falling hard and deep.

"You'll just have to trust me," I said.

"Are you a saint?" he asked.

"No. But saints aren't the only ones you can trust," I said.

Tears began welling up in his eyes. "I need . . . "

"You need to trust me, Peter," I said.

He sighed heavily, nodded, and sat back in his chair. I felt suddenly ecstatic. I was positive that a strong positive transference had taken place. We had made more headway in this session than in all the rest combined. I shuddered inwardly as I recalled the session just over a week ago. That one had turned into a shambles. Peter had gained control then, and assumed the leadership role. It was a wonder that I was able to turn things around so quickly and so effectively. I was so glad that I had visited Bernadette yesterday. She had reminded me of my skills . . . and my responsibility to pursue bold, aggressive therapy. I sat back in my chair and looked at the compliant figure across from me. Peter was slumped in the chair, and his arms dangled lifelessly over the arms. His face was expressionless, and he gazed past me with a resigned look. He was an empty vessel . . . waiting to be filled. The battle for his mental salvation could soon begin.

11

We got a late start on Sunday morning, and it was very hot when we arrived at the dock, but as we walked down the ramp and headed toward the boat slip, we were met by a cool ocean breeze. Half way out the ramp to our boat, we encountered the young, heavily tanned dock worker. He was standing in front of an open tool shed, coiling a long hose. He waved as we approached.

"Good morning, Danny," I said.

"Almost noon, Dr. Summers," he reminded me.

"I know," I said. "We got a late start. Is the boat ready?"

"All cleaned and fueled," he said. "That's what you pay me for."

"Thanks, Danny," I said. We walked past him. "He's a good worker," I said to Meg. "I can always depend on him."

Meg cocked her head and smiled coyly. "Maybe you should hire him as your secretary."

I laughed. "Somehow, I don't see him in that role."

"How *is* Cheryl doing?" asked Meg.

"Oh, better . . . better," I said noncommittally.

Diane hastened her step as we arrived at the boat. Then she leaned over and passed her hand slowly over the smooth fiberglass prow. "This is going to be fun, Dad," she said. "You haven't taken us out on the boat for a long time."

"Really? It somehow doesn't seem that long to me," I said.

"It's been over a year, John," said Meg.

"Well . . . " I shrugged. The time had slipped by so quickly, and I realized that, from Diane's perspective, it must have seemed even longer. I helped Meg into the boat and handed her the picnic basket.

"You want me to untie it, Dad?" asked Diane.

I nodded. "After I get it started," I said. I stepped into the boat and started the engine, and the deep powerful throb reverberated through the hull. "All right, Diane," I said.

Diane quickly removed the line from the dock cleat, wound it skillfully, and then jumped into the boat beside Meg. I backed slowly out of the slip, and then engaged the forward gear and headed into the bay. It felt good to have the two of them beside me today. I really hadn't been a very good father for the last few months, and my concern over Peter's case for three weeks had made me even less communicative. But things were looking up with him. Beginning on Wednesday, and then continuing on Friday, he was more responsive . . . even compliant to my suggestions. I felt much more confident today than I had for a long time. I was sure that I could mend our fragile family relationship.

"You're going to stay in the bay today, aren't you, John?" asked Meg.

"I don't know, Meg," I said. "It's always so congested."

She raised her eyebrows slightly, and turned away.

I really hoped that Meg would just sit back and enjoy the ride today . . . take things as they came. That was part of the problem in our relationship. She was frequently so resistive to things that I wanted to do with the three of us. She always told me that the things I did frightened her, and she didn't want to subject Diane to any danger. That really irritated me -- that fact that she couldn't trust me to exercise caution with my own family. I wanted this to be an enjoyable outing, but now her negative comment had already started things out wrong. But this was an important time for us, and I determined not to let my feelings about Meg's statement interfere with our day.

Diane leaned forward with her eyes closed, and let the breeze hit her face as I increased the speed slightly. The engine was still barely above an idle, though, and I could even hear the sound of the gulls as they passed overhead periodically.

"What have you been doing to keep yourself occupied during the summer break, Diane?" I asked.

She shrugged her shoulders, and responded without turning her head. "Summer is really a drag. There's hardly anything to do."

Out of the corner of my eye, I could see Meg yank Diane's arm lightly. Diane opened her eyes and looked at her, and Meg nodded her head inconspicuously in my direction. Diane sat forward on the edge of the seat and turned to face me.

"It's just that there's not a regular schedule like in school," she said. "You know what I mean?"

"Sure."

"So I've been watching a lot more television," she added.

I nodded, and smiled at her.

Something apparently peaked her interest, because she got a bright look on her face and spoke with uncharacteristic enthusiasm. "Did you watch the news last night?" she asked.

"No," I said.

"There's been another one of those prostitute murders," she said.

"Oh, Diane," mumbled Meg with a smile on her face.

"It's really creepy!" Diane continued. "They don't have any idea who the murderer is. Do you suppose that has anything to do with what Grandpa's friend said?" she asked.

"What's that?" I asked.

"Well . . . maybe the police think the prostitutes are as guilty as the murderers, and so they aren't as interested in solving the cases," she said.

"They wouldn't ever admit to that," I said. "But I sometimes wonder."

Diane shook her head. "What makes people do those things?" she asked.

"Which guilty party are you referring to?" I asked with a smile.

"Hmm?" She gave me a perplexed look. Then she laughed self-consciously. "Oh, Dad! The murderer, I mean." Then she looked at me intensely. "Did you ever treat anyone who killed someone?"

"You, mean . . . not like in the war . . . "

"No. I mean, did you ever treat a murderer?" she asked.

"No, I didn't, Diane," I told her. That, too, had been the result of my never having worked in an institution. In that setting I would surely have had that opportunity. My colleagues who had started their careers with this type of assignment had always told me that I was overly glamorizing that experience, and that in reality it was characterized by a high degree of drudgery and a low rate of pay. Nevertheless, I always regretted missing the experience. I thought that the cases would surely be more complex . . . richer.

"I think it would really be spooky to talk to a person who'd killed someone," said Diane.

"The way things are going in the world, if you're not careful who you associate with, you might be talking to someone like that without even knowing it," said Meg.

"No . . . " Diane shook her head. "I'm sure I'd know," she said.

"I don't think you can be sure, Diane," said Meg. "That's why I'm so concerned about the people you're spending so much time with this summer."

"Oh, Mom!" Diane gave Meg and exasperated look. Then she turned toward me. "Dad?"

I could see that one coming. Meg had thrust us suddenly into a confrontational discussion. But she was right. And I did have to support her with Diane. "You really can't tell, Diane," I said. "The human mind is too complex. And people manufacture elaborate schemes and behavior patterns to justify their actions."

"I'm not running around with a bunch of psychos, you know," she said angrily.

"I know," I said vaguely. And yet I really didn't. I realized that I knew nothing about the people that Diane was associating with, except for what Meg told me . . . and what Lloyd had said.

"But sometimes seemingly . . . innocent behavior . . . can lead to other problems," I continued. "For example, a lot of kids today think there's nothing wrong with using drugs," I said cautiously.

Diane knew immediately what I was leading to. She turned away and leaned her face into the wind again.

"Your father's right, Diane," said Meg. "And sometimes . . . when people act a certain way . . . well . . . we have concerns."

"When people act *what* way?" asked Diane, turning toward Meg.

"The people you're associating with this summer, Diane," explained Meg. "Their rough behavior . . . and their language. I just . . . " Meg glanced at me with a pleading look. "*We* just don't like it."

Diane turned her head away again. And when I didn't step right in and support Meg, *she* sat back and crossed her arms in front of her. It was clear that we could either finish the rest of our outing in silence, or I would have to do something.

"Diane . . . " I said coaxingly.

Diane turned her head back slightly, but a frown was on her face.

"Diane, why don't we take a look at what your mother's trying to say," I suggested.

Meg gave me a hostile look, and I raised my hand reassuringly.

"I know what she's trying to say," said Diane. "She doesn't like my friends."

"But why is that?" I asked. "What frame of reference is she coming from that makes her take that stand?"

"What?" Diane grimaced.

"Opinions like that are based on a set of values," I said. "And it's important that you understand what values your mother is using as a point of reference, so that you can understand them in relation to your own value system."

"Oh Dad!" Diane sighed in exasperation. "You sound just like my Social Problems Teacher!"

"Well . . . "

"Can't you talk to Diane like a father?" said Meg. "Instead of like a . . . disinterested counselor?"

"Disinterested doesn't mean *un*interested," I reminded Meg.

"But you're right, Dad," said Diane. "I don't know very much about Mother's values."

"Well, that's why I suggested . . . " I began.

"But I don't know *anything* about *yours*," she interrupted. "And maybe you think *disinterested* doesn't mean *uninterested*, but I don't see the difference."

"Diane, what do you mean by . . . "

"You want to know the truth?" asked Diane. "I don't even *like* my friends!" Tears suddenly appeared in her eyes, and she sat forward, and spoke intensely. "It's just that they're there. And we do things. And they talk to me. I don't know anything about their values, either. But at least they talk to me."

Meg reached out and placed her hand gently on Diane's arm. "You know, Diane . . . I wish I could say that I had made you aware of my values. But I know that wouldn't be true. I'd like to think that I've given you the right kind of guidance in your life. But so many times, I've struggled to know the reason myself, the basis for . . . " She shook her head. "I know that I love you. But that's not enough."

The tears were now running down Diane's cheeks. She placed her hand lightly on Meg's cheek, and then drew it away. "Did you ever feel like you were searching for something . . . but you didn't know what?"

"Yes," Meg nodded.

"I feel like that . . . a lot." Diane turned sideways in the seat and leaned back. "I know you love me, Mom. And I know you have a lot of answers. But my friends have a lot of answers, too. I just don't know . . . I just don't know what the *questions* are."

I glanced at Diane, sitting curled beside Meg. I had never heard her talk like that. I hadn't noticed her enough in the last five years, and it appeared to me today as though these probing words were coming from a ten-year-old.

"We're all too much involved with the world, Diane," said Meg. "Your father has given us a very comfortable life. We certainly have all the material things that we could possibly want."

"But that's not enough, Mom," said Diane.

"But that's not enough," repeated Meg.

"Of course it's not enough," I agreed. "The most important thing is your own . . . your own sense of value. Your own sense of self-worth." I struggled somehow to relate this to some sort of object lesson. "That's why we're concerned about drugs, Diane. They can destroy that sense."

"You know what some of my friends say, Dad?" asked Diane. "They say they never feel so good about themselves as when they're smoking a joint, because they can see inside themselves, and they can feel what wonderful beings they are."

"But that's a . . . " Diane's frank statement about drugs took me completely by surprise, and I struggled for words. I shook my head "No. That's false. That's a false sense of value, Diane."

"Then what is the *true* sense of value, Dad?" she asked. "What is the truth? Maybe that's the question I haven't been smart enough to ask."

"Yes . . . " mumbled Meg.

"What is the truth, Dad?" asked Diane, almost pleading.

I tried initially to pass this off as a rhetorical question, but it clearly was not one. She wanted an answer. "Well, Diane . . . " I chuckled and shook my head slowly. "That's a question that philosophers have been struggling with for thousands of years."

"That must mean there isn't any answer," said Diane.

I squinted slightly, and passed my hand through the air in an obscure attempt to formulate some erudite response.

"Or it may mean that there *is* an answer," suggested Meg thoughtfully, "but they've rejected it."

"Why would anyone reject the truth?" asked Diane. And then she looked at me . . . and her eyes seemed suddenly intense and piercing. "Dad . . . Would anyone ever know the truth . . . and reject it?"

I kept my eyes focused ahead, but I could see her gaze clearly out of the corner of my eye, and suddenly I recalled Peter that day, sitting opposite me . . . the piercing look in his eyes . . . and his pleading words: We make progress when we find the truth. What is your truth? Do you seek the nonexistence? And I remembered . . . that was unproductive, so I handled it. How did I handle it? It had been so simple. Of course . . . I must ask the questions, I said. I must ask the questions.

"I must ask the questions . . . " I heard myself muttering.

Diane looked at me for what seemed a full minute, waiting for a different response. Then she shrugged and shook her head. "I guess that must mean there isn't any answer."

Meg gave me a plaintive look. Then she sighed and turned toward Diane. "Well, some people at least *think* they have some answers," she said. "And they seem to be doing quite well with them."

"Who?" asked Diane.

"Well . . . " Meg glanced toward me again, and then continued tentatively speaking to Diane. "Well, your Uncle Lloyd and Aunt Sally, for instance, and Patrick and Amy. They don't seem to be bothered by this . . . this uncertainty."

The familiar stabbing feeling that I always felt when Meg made comparative statements about Lloyd and me thrust itself upon my spine again. But this time it was followed by a strangely perverse sense of relief. I realized full well that this reference would undoubtedly leave Diane cold, and I thought that would help convince Meg that Lloyd was coming from a completely different, outmoded frame of reference.

"I know," said Diane. "I've always noticed that. I just . . . " She glanced toward me self-consciously. "I just never wanted to say anything."

The cold steel of the knife pushed its way deeper into my spine. I couldn't believe what I was hearing.

"Of course you're reacting on the basis of what you see on the surface," I suggested. "There's no way to know how things are between them in private."

"I don't know," said Diane. "Amy talked to me at Grandma and Grandpa's party. She seemed really . . . I don't know . . . peaceful."

"You know, I've been thinking, Diane," said Meg. "John, what do you think?"

I knew that Meg was speaking, but her words were blurred . . . overshadowed. I thought for a moment the boat's engine had increased its pitch, but then I realized that it was the echo of Diane's words . . . Amy . . . peaceful . . . I turned toward Meg and squinted.

"John, what do you think?" she repeated. "Maybe . . . Maybe we should try going to Lloyd's church."

This suggestion by Meg made me think suddenly of my father's description of his reaction to Lloyd's having become baptized. That was an affront . . . that was an affront . . . no need . . . our father took care of our needs, including our salvation. For a moment a sudden feeling of dread filled my heart as I wondered whether I had taken care of Diane's. But I was not my father. Mine was a different salvation. It was . . . different. And hers would be different, too. She would realize that . . . when she was older. We did not need Lloyd's solution. This was an affront.

"What do you think, Dad?" asked Diane. "Maybe we could."

Then the sudden sick realization struck me. Meg had spoken with Lloyd on Tuesday. For all I knew, she might have taken Diane with her as well. It was clear what had happened. They had spoken with Lloyd about this behind my back, and had conspired to bend my will on this issue. I wanted to say something . . . express my disillusionment with this action. But this wasn't the time. This was our family outing. This was supposed to be enjoyable . . .

I noticed that the water was becoming more choppy, and as I looked from side to side, I realized that we had arrived at the outlet to the ocean. "Let's not talk about that now," I said. I tapped Diane on the arm. "You ready for some speed?"

She nodded enthusiastically.

"No, John," said Meg fearfully.

I thrust the throttle up to half speed, and the boat lurched forward. Out of the corner of my eye, I could see Diane smiling at the sensation. She was enjoying it. Meg should understand that. The boat quickly rose to a speed of forty knots and smacked firmly on the crests of the rolling waves leading into the inlet to the bay. Meg was right when she said that it had been over a year. I remembered now. It was on Diane's fourteenth birthday. I recalled the day vividly . . . her bright, teenage eyes, glistening with excitement. And her words . . . Faster, Daddy . . . faster!

"John! Slow down!" Meg pleaded.

But Diane wasn't asking me to slow down. Her eyes were riveted to the horizon. She wanted to go faster.

I placed my hand on the throttle, and pushed it ahead to three-quarter speed, and the boat shot forward again.

"John! Please!"

We had cleared the breakwater bordering the inlet, and the waves became larger, but our increased speed allowed us to fly from wave peak to wave peak . . . never falling into the valleys. I hadn't been on the boat myself for several weeks, and each time, I remember anew the excitement brought about by the power and the speed. I nudged the throttle forward more, and the bottom of the boat smacked mercilessly against the vanquished waves. The engine screamed with a high-pitched wail . . . crying victoriously against the elements. And then the whine of the engine was joined by a distant cry . . . Daddy . . . Daddy . . .

I glanced to the side, and I saw Diane, screaming almost inaudibly, her face filled with fear. I immediately brought the throttle full back. The boat hung momentarily in the air, between the crests of two waves, and then fell with a painful impact into the liquid valley. I moved the gear to the neutral position, and the boat struggled up to the top of the next wave . . . and then fell smoothly and motionlessly into its hollow.

"You've made her sick, John," said Meg. "You've made her sick with your nonsense!"

I turned off the power, and the low throb of the engine disappeared, and was replaced by the steady lap of water, thrusting itself gently against the gunwales.

"Diane, I'm sorry," I said. "I thought you . . . "

The look of fear was no longer on Diane's face; instead, her mouth and eyes were a stark image of nausea. The boat rolled with another wave, and Diane placed her hand against her mouth, turned away, and hung her head over the side of the boat. Meg placed her arm around Diane's body, and supported her head with her other hand. Diane lurched, and the sound of her vomiting split the air . . . three . . . four . . . five times. Then she nodded, and Meg helped her turn back and sit up. Diane was trembling and wiping her face with her hand. Meg searched frantically, and then took off her coat, tossed it over Diane's chest, and used the tail of it to wipe her face gently.

"I'm really sorry, guys," I said. "I just didn't think that . . . "

"You just didn't think, *period*!" said Meg.

Diane just sat there trembling, her eyes half-closed. I was sure that she'd say it was all right. She was just having trouble getting things together right now.

I sighed and sat back. The gulls were there. I could hear them clearly. And I looked up and saw them flying back and forth . . . back and forth above our silently rocking boat.

"Well . . . " I gestured vaguely, trying to think of something disarming to say. Then I reached into the small opening behind us and pulled out the picnic basket. I placed it on my lap, opened it, and pulled out a sandwich. "Anyone want some lunch?" I asked, waving the sandwich before them.

"Oh . . . Daddy!" Diane frowned, coughed, and turned her head aside.

"Back off, John!" said Meg angrily.

I sighed, closed the basket, and put it back behind me. Then I deliberately unwrapped the sandwich and folded the enclosing paper half-way back upon the cool bread. I took a large bite, and the taste of cold cuts and mayonnaise filled my mouth. "This is very tasty, Meg," I mumbled through a full mouth. "You do good work!"

Meg just looked at me and shook her head. Then she gently brushed her hand across Diane's trembling head.

I decided that I had better just not say anything. I really *was* sorry. I had clearly made a mess of things today. I vaguely recalled what it was that had set me off. In the excitement I had almost forgotten the discussion about values, and truth . . . and Meg's suggestion that we go to Lloyd's church. A hot flash passed across my head as I remembered that I had actually considered that Meg and Lloyd had conspired to trick me into that. I wouldn't go, of course. But my notion of a conspiracy was ludicrous. I was very glad that I hadn't told them what I was thinking at the time.

I took another bite of the sandwich, placed my head back against the firm cushion, and watched the gulls flying aimlessly through the sky.

12

On Wednesday, just before noon, I was making a few notes for my afternoon session with Peter. I was seriously considering increasing his therapy sessions from three times to five times per week. I sensed that we were on the brink of significant progress, and that the added continuity might prevent the possibility of regression. During Monday's session, Peter had been actually more withdrawn and had exhibited stronger delusions of paranoia, but I viewed this as a positive sign at this juncture. In the session he was calm, and compliant, and I was able to direct him much more effectively toward the communication of his feelings and anxieties. It was clear, however, that the root of his fear lay much deeper than even the most wrenching expressions had revealed thus far. I still hadn't a clue as to the full explication of his dream, and until I could link that successfully with related aspects of his current and past existence, I would not be able to lead him to the attainment of the explosive cathartic peak. His calling still presented itself as an enigma, since his true personality was hidden so deeply beneath the blanket of his dynamic fervor.

I was reminded of Jung's description of the sixteenth-century alchemist, Paracelsus, whose deepest passion, Jung believed, was buried in the darkness. I now realized the ironic significance of Jung's term for this -- the *lumen naturae.* He characterized this as the light of the darkness itself, which illuminates its own darkness -- a darkness which only his own internal darkness could comprehend. My task was to force Peter's darkness into the light. I was never more intent upon succeeding at this task. But what potential dangers lurked in the shadows of this course? I might exorcise his demons -- renounce them forever, only to find that I had in reality alienated Peter from his true nature, and had left him standing as but a portrait of his hidden desire . . . an empty shell. But that's the paradoxical covenant of the healer. Even Freud realized that the most we can promise is to transform hysterical misery into everyday unhappiness.

I closed the folder that I was noting in and placed it tidily on the corner of my desk. Then I rose, and left my office. Cheryl was sitting at her desk. I noticed that she was reading a book on Jungian analysis. She looked up and smiled at me.

"Oh, hi, Dr. Summers. This is really interesting!" she exclaimed. "He's a lot more fun to read than Freud."

"Yes." I nodded casually. I marveled at the truth of the adage -- *a little knowledge is a dangerous thing.* But she was sincerely attempting to augment her psychiatric receptionist skills. "Yes," I repeated. "I'm going to lunch, Cheryl. What is the schedule this afternoon?"

"Mrs. Cray is coming for therapy at one-thirty," she answered. "And then there's a new client -- William Morrison -- coming for preliminary consultation at two-forty-five. And, of course, Peter at four."

"Yes. Well, I should return on time." I would have to give Mrs. Cray's case some thought during lunch. All of my other cases paled in comparison to Peter's, and I often had to consciously coerce myself to plan for their therapy. "You can lockup and go to lunch, too, if you wish, Cheryl," I told her.

"Oh, no, Dr. Summers. I'd rather just grab a sandwich here, so I can continue studying," she said.

"As you wish." I waved at her and left the office.

The office building that I was in bordered a spacious off-street parking lot, and I always parked in a distant corner, to allow room for clients near my entry. At this moment, however, two parking places were blocked by a long white limousine, which had heavily shaded windows. As I approached it, the back door swung open, and I could see a bright logo which displayed rays from the sun falling on the outline of a mountain top and a waterfall gushing from a rock. Beneath the logo were the words: *LIGHT ON THE ROCK MINISTRIES*. A stocky man stepped out of the car and raised his hand toward me. It was Greg Hatcher.

"Dr. Summers?" asked Hatcher.

"Yes. I'm Dr. Summers."

Hatcher's heavy jowls raised in a brief smile, and he extended his hand toward me. "I'm Greg Hatcher," he said.

"Yes. I know who you are," I said, shaking his hand.

"Oh?" He tilted his head skeptically. "Well, good. Then you'll know that I'm not from the Mafia, or something." He laughed casually and gestured toward the long car.

"What can I do for you?" I asked.

"I'd like to speak with you for a few minutes, Dr. Summers," he said.

I glanced back toward my office.

"No. I mean, just . . . " He moved his hand quickly between the two of us. "Informally, you know. It's extremely important."

I wondered at the contradiction of an extremely important communication being conducted informally. Nevertheless, this was a very opportune meeting. He should be able to help me learn more about Peter. "Very well," I told him.

Hatcher pointed inside the car. "Will you take a little ride with us?"

"Us . . . "

"It will be more comfortable . . . and private," said Hatcher. He motioned again to the open door and moved aside.

"All right," I said. I leaned down and stepped into the limousine. As I sat down, I saw Kyle Wingate sitting across from me.

Hatcher followed me into the vehicle, sat heavily beside Wingate, and closed the door. "Perhaps you know Kyle Wingate, also, Dr. Summers," he said.

"Yes." I reached out to shake his hand.

Wingate had a somewhat vacant look on his face as he gave my hand a firm grasp. "Have we met?" he asked.

"No," I told him.

"Dr. Summers must have seen us at one of the services, Kyle," said Hatcher. "Is that right, Doctor?"

"Yes. That's right," I said.

Hatcher let out a low laugh. Then he tapped on the window leading to the driver's compartment, and the limousine began to move.

"It's good of you to give us some time, Dr. Summers," said Wingate.

"Let me get right to the point, Doctor," said Hatcher. "We've known for just a little over a week now that Peter has been coming to you for treatment."

"I see."

"And I'm certainly glad that you've witnessed one of our presentations," he continued, "because then you'll have an idea what we're about. And, of course, having worked with Peter for . . . I don't know how long . . . you certainly have an idea what *he's* about."

I nodded slowly. "What is your point, Mr. Hatcher?" I asked.

"I'm sure you detected that we . . . all of us at Light on the Rock . . . we have a very close, cooperative working relationship," he responded. "It's the nature of what we do. And the spirit of our service depends upon it."

Wingate leaned forward and gestured with one hand. "We've been together for years," he said. "We've been a cohesive team."

"And . . . " I said questioningly.

"And we've always told one another when problems have come up in our lives," explained Hatcher. "But this time, Peter has been somewhat reticent to discuss his problem."

"Secretive might be a better word," said Wingate.

I sat forward. "But surely he should be able to seek professional help without telling you what . . . "

"But it shouldn't be necessary!" interrupted Wingate heatedly.

I sat back and raised an eyebrow toward Wingate. "You don't particularly subscribe to psychiatric treatment, do you?" I asked, remembering what Lloyd had told me about charismatics.

Wingate and Hatcher glanced toward one another. Then Wingate leaned forward and spoke, choosing his words carefully. "It's not that we denigrate your profession," he said. "It's just that we are usually able to achieve inner healing through the Word of God and reliance on the Spirit for guidance."

"Healing is our business, too, after all," added Hatcher. "And for Peter not to have come to us, at least at first . . . "

Wingate sat back and turned toward Hatcher. "That's what I mean, Greg," he said. "It's just one more example of . . . "

Hatcher frowned and shook his head, and Wingate sat back.

"One more example of what?" I asked.

"We just want to help," said Hatcher. "That's why we came to you. We hoped that you would tell us what you're treating Peter for."

I shook my head. "I can't do that gentlemen," I said. "Not unless Peter authorizes me to."

"Well . . . " Hatcher laughed nervously and glanced at Wingate. "Normally we'd accept that. But the problem is . . . he might not realize . . . You see, his work is being affected."

"In what way?" I asked.

Wingate glanced at Hatcher and sat forward again. "Peter has always been very . . . well . . . spontaneous in his presentation. And that's fine, because when the Holy Spirit moves you . . . you must respond. But we've always been able to provide a balance, you see."

"Balance . . . " I muttered questioningly.

"Dr. Summers isn't interested in our pattern of worship, Kyle," said Hatcher impatiently.

"But there has to be some connection," continued Wingate. "We haven't wanted to admit it because he's been so successful. But we've seen it growing for over a year. He's taking too much on himself, Greg."

"Well . . . " muttered Hatcher.

"And now this -- going to a psychiatrist. He shouldn't need that. How many times has he said it himself? If a professing believer needs to go outside the realm of the spirit to find healing for the soul, then he isn't really . . . "

Hatcher sat forward abruptly and placed his hand on Wingate's shoulder and interrupted him. "But it's too late to question that decision, Kyle. It's not our place, anyway." Then he turned toward me. "But we do want to help. If you could just tell us

Peter's problem, we could . . . well . . . we could be an extension of your therapy." He laughed lightly.

I recalled vividly Peter's description of these two, and his fears about Hatcher absconding with funds and Wingate trying to usurp his place. These were paranoid fears, to be sure, but I was confident that Peter would not want his case revealed to them. "Even if I wanted to, my professional ethics would not allow me discuss the cases of any of my clients without their permission."

"But you don't understand," said Hatcher. "Peter is a very fragile entity. He has a divine calling. You can't just treat him like some . . . some neurotic person."

"I treat each of my patients in a completely unique way," I said.

Hatcher frowned and shook his head. Then he leaned forward on his knees, and displayed the chubby smile again. "I think we should be completely forthright with you, Dr. Summers." He sighed, and a look of concern covered his face. "Peter has been missing since Monday night."

"Missing?" I asked.

"I believe he had a session with you on Monday afternoon?" he questioned.

"Yes, he did," I responded.

"Well, we haven't seen him since Monday morning."

"Is that unusual?" I asked.

"Very unusual," said Wingate. "We never go without seeing one another for more than a day. Not without saying something."

"Has he ever done this before?" I asked.

"Well . . . not for this long a time," said Wingate. "He has had periods of . . . well . . . temporary detachment from reality."

"So, that's our concern," said Hatcher. "And we believe that he's scheduled to meet with you again this afternoon. Is that correct?"

"Yes."

"Well, we just hope . . . we just pray that his brief journey is concluded, and that he will at least return for his therapy session with you," said Hatcher. "We'd just wait outside ourselves," he added. "But we don't want Peter to think we're spying on him, do we?" He laughed nervously.

"We're just praying that he will be here," said Wingate. "And when he arrives, we'd like you tell him to contact us."

"I will certainly give Peter your message," I promised.

"And tell him that he's all right, and that he just needs to get back into the groove," said Hatcher, laughing lightly. "He doesn't need this -- especially now, what with the national network hookup, and . . . "

"I'll give him the message," I repeated. "That's all I can promise."

"That's all we ask," said Hatcher with a note of finality.

I didn't want to miss a chance to obtain as much information as possible. "But, naturally, the more I know about Peter, the more quickly I can restore him to effective functioning," I said. "Perhaps you can help me with that."

"You mean . . . " began Hatcher.

"Give me some background on his work . . . his relationships."

"Of course," agreed Hatcher. "Whatever we can."

"I understand the ministry is in its tenth year," I said.

"That's right," said Wingate.

"That seems a relatively short time to have grown so large," I said.

"I suppose so," said Hatcher. Then he chuckled. "Especially when you consider that we began in a tent."

"So the three of you have been together since the beginning?" I asked.

"Yes," responded Hatcher.

"How about other relationships?" I asked. "What other people does Peter associate with?"

"Peter is not a mixer," said Wingate. "He really just appears for his part of the service, and then he retires quietly."

"So there's no one that he confides in . . . socializes with?" I asked. "How about that singer -- Julie Peters?"

"No," said Hatcher.

"No," agreed Wingate.

They didn't appear to be withholding any information with regard to Julie. And a reclusive pattern would certainly be a typical style for a schizophrenic. "Then perhaps you can give me some information about his prior background," I suggested.

"What do you mean?" asked Hatcher.

"Well, where he came from," I said. "Something about his parents."

"I . . . I don't know," said Hatcher.

"Or, for that matter . . . his name," I said.

"His name?" asked Wingate.

"Yes. It could be a coincidence, of course," I said. "I mean . . . *Peter* and *Lumen* mean *rock* and *light*. And, of course, the ministry could have been given its name simply because of that. But I rather suspect that isn't his real name."

Wingate glanced toward me, and then leaned toward Hatcher. "Greg . . . Don't you suppose we should . . . "

Hatcher frowned and shook his head. "Peter doesn't want that brought up. He has his reasons. I think we should honor that."

"But if he's really ill . . . I mean . . . not thinking clearly . . . " responded Wingate.

"We're on the brink of going on the national network," muttered Hatcher through his teeth. "If he doesn't get on track right away, that could all be shot down! We can't do anything that would . . . well . . . upset Peter. I'm sure Dr. Summers would agree with that."

"Well . . . "

Hatcher forced a calm expression and leaned toward me. "You'll have to excuse our little diversion, Dr. Summers," he said. "We're just so concerned about the ministry. There are so many millions out there who need salvation. And Peter can save them! This is a very critical period in his ministry . . . in *our* ministry."

"I accept that," I said. "But, of course, I will keep anything you tell me in the strictest confidence."

"Dr. Summers, you told us that there are things you can't reveal because of your professional ethics, and I understand that," said Hatcher. "But you must understand that there are some things that we may know about Peter's past that we can't tell you, because we don't think he'd want us to. Does that seem fair?"

"I suppose," I said. That was a reasonable statement, but I had the strange impression that he was tossing it out more as a bargaining chip to gain information from me about Peter's case. I was not going to barter with these two. "Naturally you shouldn't reveal anything that you believe would be violating Peter's confidence."

Hatcher looked somewhat disappointed. He waited for me to qualify my response, and then raised his hands, smiled, and sat back. "Can we drop you somewhere, Dr. Summers?" he asked.

"Just back at the office," I said.

Hatcher tapped on the window the driver's compartment and pointed. Then he turned back toward me and smiled. "I hope after all this disturbing business is over with, you'll visit our temple again," he said.

"Perhaps," I said.

"You have a lot in common . . . you and Peter," he said. "You heal the mind, and he heals the spirit." He nodded slowly. "You have a lot in common."

Peter did not show up for his session at four. In fact, he did not show up at all. This was the first time that Peter had missed a session, and I was quite concerned. Hatcher had been correct about one thing: Peter was a very fragile entity. And at this point in his therapy, he was particularly vulnerable to attacks from others, from himself, and from that deep hidden part of him that continued to manifest itself in the cloaked recesses of his unconscious.

At five-thirty Cheryl came into my office and placed the calendar for the following day on my desk. She started to leave, and then she turned back and spoke with uncharacteristic sensitivity

"You're really worried about Peter, aren't you, Dr. Summers?" she asked.

"Well . . . it is unusual, isn't it?" I mumbled.

"Do you want me to call . . . anyone?" she asked with a shrug.

"I wouldn't know who to call," I said. I smiled and shook my head. "No, that's all right, Cheryl. Perhaps he just forgot."

She shook her head. "I don't think so, Dr. Summers," she said. "He always acted like these sessions were the most important things in his life. I don't think he forgot."

I nodded. Cheryl was right. Unless some overpowering drive had overcome him, Peter would have been here . . . unless, of course, something had happened to prevent him from coming.

"Would you like me to stay for a while, Dr. Summers?" she asked. "I could watch the phone, or . . . "

"No, Cheryl," I said. "Thank you anyway, but it's already past time for you to go home."

"Are you sure?"

I nodded. "I'll be leaving soon myself. I'm sure there's some logical explanation. We'll just find out at the next session."

"Well . . . all right." She smiled "Good night, Dr. Summers. I'll see you tomorrow." She headed toward the door.

"Good night, Cheryl," I called after her as she left.

I had been studying Peter's folder since four, but after Cheryl left I opened it again, and scanned randomly over my notes from Monday. If he had gone somewhere directly after our session, there might have been something in the therapy that triggered a flight motive. He certainly was plagued by dread, particularly when the dream had been especially vivid, but my office had always been a safe haven for him. I wished that I had increased the frequency of sessions immediately after Monday's visit.

My deliberations were interrupted by the faint sound of the telephone ringing in Cheryl's office. I glanced at my phone, and saw the light blinking. I quickly reached over and picked up the receiver.

"Hello . . . "

"Is this . . . Dr. Summers?" a woman's voice asked.

"Yes. Who is . . . "

"Dr. John Summers?" she interrupted.

"Yes. This is Dr. John Summers," I responded. "Who is this?"

There was no response, but I could hear her breathing.

"Hello . . . " I said again.

"Listen . . . You aren't the police, are you?" she asked finally.

"What? Of course I'm not the . . . Who is this?"

"Well, I don't usually do this for people, but . . . there's this guy here at my place," she said. "And he asked me to call you."

"Who asked you to call me?" I asked.

"He said his name is Mr. Smith," she said.

A shiver crossed my spine. I knew that it must be Peter, but why was someone else calling for him? "Let me speak with him," I said.

"He's asleep," she said. "Can you just come and get him?"

"Where are you located?" I asked.

She was silent for a moment . . . as thought listening for something. "You sure you aren't the police?" she asked finally.

"I said, no!" I responded angrily. "Tell me where he is, and I'll come and get him."

She sighed heavily, and then slowly recited the address: "Twelve-thirty-four South Broadway. Number two-thirty-three."

I hurriedly scribbled the address on a pad. Then I realized where this was: in the sleaziest part of downtown. I wondered what Peter could be doing there. "Who am I speaking with?" I asked.

"Just come and pick him up," she said.

"I have to know who this is first," I insisted.

There was a long pause. Then she mumbled coarsely: "This is Rebah. Just come and get him."

"All right Rebah," I said. "I'll be right there."

"No! Wait. I just remembered," she said. "You gotta wait 'til it's dark."

"Why?"

"He said . . . you gotta wait 'til it's dark," she repeated. "Don't ask me why. Just come and get him . . . after it gets dark."

There was a click . . . and then a buzzing dial tone.

I slowly replaced the receiver, and slumped back in my chair. "Peter . . . Peter . . . " I mumbled. "Where have you gone . . . and what have you done? And what could I have done to prevent it?"

I glanced at the clock. It was nearly six. I could go home, and then go out again afterward. But then Meg would be irritated that I was going off at night for the cause of one of my clients. And there would be questions, and worry. No. I decided to go have a drink while I was waiting . . . maybe get a deli sandwich. I suddenly wished that Cheryl were still here. I'd have her call Meg for me . . . tell her that I'd be late.

13

I didn't want to take my car to that crime-ridden part of the city, so, after I sat impatiently through my light dinner, I returned to my office and called a cab. It had long been my observation that, in many large cities, the central section was characterized by a gradual degradation of property from north to south, as though some latitudinal sifter were scattering the chaff at the lower levels. Such was certainly the case here, and as the cab carried me from the northeastern section of town, where my office was located, toward my destination, the gradation became stark, particularly on Broadway, which was one of the major thoroughfares.

As we arrived at the South one hundred block, the street lights became less abundant and dimmer, and the freshly painted buildings gave way to scarred brick and walls covered with graffiti. Increasing numbers of huddled figures stood, sat, or lay aimlessly on the sidewalks, and the wildly contrasting sounds of rock music merged occasionally with the faint sound of distant sirens. The interior of the cab began to be oppressively hot, and I opened my window partially to get a breath of fresh air. My nostrils were filled, instead, with the smell of smoke, stale food, and sewage that hadn't been adequately dispersed. Still, there was something strangely exciting about *downtown*. When I was in high school, some of my less conservative friends and I made it a point to come here periodically . . . drink in the sights, sounds, and smells of the *wicked city*. My father didn't particularly approve of these excursions, but he never made an issue of it, except to say that if I ever got arrested I'd have to spend the night in jail, because he wasn't about to come to the downtown precinct to bail me out. My mother was a different story; she always seemed petrified at the thought of my having been in this part of the city. I always scoffed at her concern, but in retrospect, I realized that she had a right to be afraid. In my senior year, Harold Palmer, one of my friends, was killed by muggers on one of our treks.

The cab pulled to the curb in front of a grimy, darkly illuminated brick building. The driver turned back and looked at me with a frown on his face.

"Are you sure this is where you wanted to go?" he asked.

I looked above the chipped entryway, and saw the dimly painted numerals: 1234. The building appeared to be an extremely old, dilapidated hotel. "Yes. This is it," I said.

"I ain't waitin', you know," he said.

"No. That's all right," I said. "How much do I owe you?"

He glanced at his meter. "Sixteen eighty-seven."

I pulled a twenty-dollar bill out of my wallet and gave it to him. "There. Keep it," I said.

"Thanks, buddy," he replied. Then he looked at the door as I opened it. "Hey! Close that window!"

"Oh . . . sure." I rolled up the window, stepped out of the cab and shut the door behind me. The engine roared, and the cab lurched from the curb, spun about in the street, and headed back to the north.

Several figures were huddled darkly against the building, but the moment that I headed toward the entrance, three of them approached me. They were scantily clad women, their faces masked with heavy makeup, and their bodies reeking of stale perfume.

"You picked the right corner, Baby!" said one of the women. "I have your ticket to paradise!"

"No, that's not what I . . . "

"She doesn't even know where paradise is," said another, rubbing her plump body against me. "But I know the way."

"No . . . "

But the third one stepped up and pressed a tobacco-stained finger against my lips. "Hey, girls . . . Maybe he likes all three of us."

"I said no!" I pushed them aside and headed for the doorway.

The three of them cursed and jeered, and then returned to the shadows.

I walked up the warped wooden steps, through a narrow door and into a dark lobby. Several shabby looking men sat about on tattered furniture, or on the floor. I smelled the aroma of burning wax. I looked toward the narrow stairwell, and a group of candles was hanging on the adjacent wall in the shape of a pyramid. Inside the burning triangle were the glittering letters: **LOVE**.

I stepped up to a shallow counter. A heavy metal grate rose from the counter to the ceiling, placing a protective cage around a frail, whiskered attendant. He stepped up to meet me, and the stench of heavy cigar smoke drifted through the bars.

"What's your pleasure?" asked the man.

"Where's room two-thirty-three?" I asked.

"You have an appointment, or are you just window shopping?" he exploded in a phlegm-filled laugh.

"No. I'm just here to pick someone up," I said.

"Sure!" he said mockingly. "No matter. You still have to pay the toll."

"Toll?"

"We aren't in this for charity," said the man. "Pay your girl whatever she wants, but the room rent is twenty dollars an hour . . . in advance."

I shook my head in disgust. "Never mind. I'll find it myself."

I left the counter and headed toward the stairwell. Before I could reach it, though, a huge man stepped out from a partially hidden alcove and blocked my way.

"You weren't listening," said the man in a deep, rough voice. "This ain't charity!"

"No . . . *You* weren't listening," I said. "I'm just here to pick someone up. I'm a doctor."

"Doctor?" A high, raspy voice emerged from the shadows. Then a wretched looking man stepped forward. Wisps of gray air hung unevenly from his chin, and his gaping mouth revealed a random interspersion of dirty teeth and empty spaces. "Doctor?" he repeated. "I need a doctor. They didn't warn me. It's in the blood, you know." He reached out and grasped my shoulder with a trembling hand. "They didn't warn me! They said a doctor couldn't help. Is that true?"

"Get out of here, Sammy," said the man behind the counter. "You're giving this place a bad name."

The huge man stepped toward Sammy, and the frail man retreated into the shadows.

"Identify your girl and pay your rent," the huge man told me. "And then you can go up."

"The girl is Rebah," I said. "But I'm not here to see her. If you'll just call her, she'll tell you."

"Is this a raid?" asked the man behind the desk.

"What?" I asked.

"We only call if there's a raid," he said, and he and the huge man laughed raucously.

I could see that I was not going to get upstairs without paying, so I removed a twenty dollar bill from my wallet and passed it through the grating to the man.

"Second floor . . . third room on the right," he said.

"Thanks!" I responded sarcastically.

The huge man made a gross ushering gesture, and I walked past him and up the dark, narrow stairway. I could barely make out the numbers in the nearly unlighted hallway, so I just went to the third door and knocked. There was no response, so I knocked again.

"Hold on!" replied a high course voice from inside the room.

After a moment, the door swung open a crack and stopped abruptly against the link of a security chain. A pudgy painted face surrounded by curly blond hair appeared in the opening.

"What is it?" she asked.

"I'm Dr. Summers," I said.

"Oh . . . " She nodded. Then she closed the door, removed the chain, and opened it completely.

I stepped inside the room and she closed the door again and replaced the chain.

"Thanks for coming," she said. Then she walked over to the bed, sat heavily, and began filing her fingernails.

The interior of the room was dark, too, but it appeared to be decorated considerably more attractively than the rest of the building. A large red heart was pasted on the wall at the head of her bed, and burning candles rested on the small tables to either side of it. Rebah wore a thin pink gown. She appeared to be in her late thirties.

I stepped toward the bed. "Where is he?" I asked.

She looked up from her nails, and pointed the file casually toward the corner of the room opposite her. The room was dark, but I could see his figure huddled on the floor. It was Peter. He appeared to be in a catatonic state.

I walked quickly over to Peter and squatted down beside him. "Peter . . . Peter . . . " I turned his head toward me and spoke again. "Peter, it's Dr. Summers."

Peter merely nodded slowly and turned his head back.

"How long as he been like this?" I asked Rebah.

"All day long," she said.

"All day . . . How long has he been here?" I asked.

"Since last night," she said. "But this morning he started acting real funny. He gave me this card with your name and number on it, and said I should ask you to get him tonight. After dark, though. He was very clear about that. And then he just . . . sat there."

"Why didn't you call me earlier?" I asked.

"Hey . . . look, I don't usually do any favors like this, you know," she said. "But . . . he was a nice guy. Anyway . . . he paid me in advance for twenty-four hours of my time. And all he wanted to do was talk, anyhow, so I figured . . . why not?" She glanced at her watch. "His time is about up, though."

I turned back to Peter, and placed my hand on his shoulder. "Peter, it's time to go. Are you ready to go?"

Peter glanced at me. Then he turned his eyes on Rebah, and a faint smile crossed his lips. "Isn't she beautiful?" he asked.

"Do you know where you are, Peter?" I asked. "Do you know who that is?"

"Of course," he responded softly. "It's Mary."

"Mary?"

"Mary Magdalene," muttered Peter. "And she came to me for redemption."

"What's he talking about?" asked Rebah.

I held my hand up to silence her and turned back to Peter. "All right, Peter," I said. "But it's time to go now."

I stood and helped Peter to his feet.

"But I failed," said Peter. He stepped slowly toward the bed. "I failed, because I'm imperfect. Dark, light . . . good, evil . . . up, down . . . Why do they coexist? It's so much harder for me than it was for Christ."

"He never talked like that before," said Rebah. "What's going on?"

"It's all right," I said. "It's just been a difficult time for him."

"I suppose," she said. "I know he didn't get hardly any sleep."

"There's no time for sleep," mumbled Peter. "The world is so big . . . and all the people . . . they are depending on me. But I'm too weak. The world is destroying itself . . . and it's my fault."

"No, Peter. It's not your fault." I pulled him back to the corner of the room and shielded his view of Rebah with my body. "Take control, Peter," I whispered. Then I placed my hands on his shoulders and shook him lightly. "Take control."

Peter gave me a vague look of acknowledgment and nodded. Then he closed his eyes. "I renounce you . . . I renounce you . . . I renounce you . . . "

"That's good, Peter," I told him.

Peter sighed and opened his eyes. "I suppose you're wondering why I came here," he said.

"It doesn't matter . . . " I began.

"It doesn't matter . . . it doesn't matter . . . " he interrupted. Then he gave me a piercing look and spoke intensely. "Does anything matter to you?"

"Of course, Peter," I assured him.

"Do you think I enjoy . . . " He pushed me aside so that he could get a clear view of Rebah. He looked at her for a sustained moment, and then tears began to well in his eyes. "She was very kind. It's about love, you know. That's what the sign in the candles said. Everything's about love in the final analysis. But look . . . " He pointed toward Rebah, and then let his arm pass vaguely around the room. "I can't stay. And then there'll be another . . . and another . . . and another . . . It's so . . .

artificial. But maybe that's better. There's nothing artificial in my mind. Maybe that's better."

"It's neither better, nor worse, Peter," I said. "It's an experience on your road to recovery."

"Recovery to what?" he asked. "Will I ever feel? Will I ever . . . love?"

"Of course," I told him.

"It's so easy for some," he muttered. "And I long for what others have. But I'm not worthy of it."

"Your actions deny that, Peter," I said. "You are worthy of choice. And at this particular point in your journey, you chose to come here."

"I didn't choose," he said. "It was my destiny. My adventures come from God, who appointed me."

"All right, Peter."

"All right, Peter," he repeated mockingly. Then he looked at Rebah again. "Isn't she beautiful?"

Peter's actions during the last twenty-four hours were not at all uncharacteristic. Schizophrenics usually feel unworthy to establish any kind of meaningful relationship with anyone close to them. This experience provided Peter with an outlet -- a pseudo-closeness that might serve him in later modeling sessions. Because of his actions, however, I thought that Leonard may have been correct in assuming that there was some sexual anomaly in Peter's past. But that would explain only a small part of his psychosis. The important thing now was to remove him from the surroundings of this delusional episode.

"I think we're ready to go now, Rebah," I said.

"Sure," she said. "Oh, he's got a few things." She rose from the bed, pulled a coat from a hook on the wall and tossed it toward me. Then she went to one of the side tables and pulled out a drawer. She removed some articles and walked over to us. "Here . . . " She held out Peter's sunglasses, and the small cologne cartridge.

"Just a minute," I said. I helped Peter put on his coat, and then I took the glasses and the cartridge.

"You're a nice man, Mr. Smith," said Rebah. "You can come back and rent my room for a day anytime you want."

"Thank you," said Peter with forced composure. "Have you met Dr. Summers?" he asked her. "He is a very competent mechanic. He fixes things. He magically fixes things."

"Well, he can come back, too, then," said Rebah with a smile.

"Let's go, Peter," I said.

Peter took the sunglasses and placed them on his face, and grasped the cologne cartridge.

"Oh, listen, Doctor," said Rebah. "If he comes here again, you should really tell him not to travel so heavy."

"Hmm?"

Rebah pointed toward Peter's inside coat pocket. I reached in and pulled out a large roll of bills which appeared to be of large denominations.

"Thank you. I will," I said. We turned toward the door, but then my curiosity got the better of me. I turned back to her. "Rebah . . . the way he is acting . . . why didn't you take the money?" I asked.

"Hey, I'm a prostitute, not a thief!" she said emphatically.

I smiled and nodded. Then I turned back and removed the chain from the door.

"You got your car?" she asked.

"No. I came in a cab," I replied.

"Cabs don't usually go driving by here by choice," she said. "And you don't want to be waiting outside too long. I'll call one for you."

"Thanks," I said. "I'd appreciate that."

Rebah slipped a robe on, stepped in front of us and opened the door. "Phone's down at the end of the hall," she said. She went out into the hall, and then stopped with a frown on her face.

I led Peter out of the room and stopped beside Rebah. Across from us, the huge man was leaning against the wall, cleaning his fingernails with a large knife.

"What are you doing here, Archie?" asked Rebah.

"Keepin' an eye on things," he said hoarsely. "That's what you pay me for. Remember?" He held a hand out and beckoned with his fingers.

"What's the hurry?" asked Rebah.

"I can't wait all night, Rebah," he said. "I got other places to go." He scowled and pointed to Peter. "And this nut's been in there since yesterday."

"You got no cause to worry," said Rebah caustically.

The huge man chuckled and scraped the knife blade across his chin.

Rebah shook her head disgustedly. Then she reached into a large pocket on her robe and pulled out a roll of bills. She pulled several of them off and handed them to the man.

The huge man took the bills, smiled and waved ominously with his knife. Then he turned and lumbered off toward the stairs.

"Are you all right?" I asked Rebah.

"Yeah." Rebah placed her hands on her hips and watched the man head down the stairs. Things have been kinda bad around here for the last year. Protection costs money. Archie's okay. He just gets impatient."

"Why do you . . . " I began to ask her.

"Don't *you* start it!" she mocked good-naturedly. "I've already had twenty-four hours of that!" She looked at Peter. "Good-bye, Mr. Smith." She turned and walked toward the end of the hall.

Peter looked at her and smiled. "Good-bye . . . good-bye, Mary."

I pushed Peter ahead of me down the narrow stairway. As we passed by the pyramid of candles, he halted, and gazed at the flickering flames.

"What is it, Peter?" I asked.

He slowly passed his hand across the outline of the candles. "The eternal flame at the foot of the stairs. Warmth . . . life . . . " He shook his head and continued into the lobby.

The huge man was still here. He was standing at the counter. He frowned at us as we passed. Then the man behind the counter called out.

"You . . . the doctor!" he barked derisively.

"What?" I had Peter by the arm, and I was moving us slowly toward the door.

"We don't like visitors here," he said. "Too many questions. Next time, tell your friend to find his own way out."

I started to open the door. Suddenly, Peter reached his hand out and slammed it shut. Then he turned back toward the desk and shouted. "You . . . seller of harlots!"

The man behind the counter glowered at Peter. "What did you call me?"

The huge man stepped away from the counter, and stood rubbing his hands.

Peter thrust his arm out, and pointed his finger at them. "Beware your city, for Babylon the great is fallen, is fallen, and has become a habitation of demons, a prison for every foul spirit, and a cage for every unclean and hated bird!"

"Get that loony out of here!" said the man behind the counter.

I felt a warm gust of air as I heard the door open and close behind us.

"Get outa the road!" resounded a raspy voice. A short, thin man stepped between us. He had long, greasy black hair, and a pock-marked face. He was barefoot, and wore dirty jeans. A black leather jacket hung open from his shoulders, and a single earring hung from his left ear. It was a cross entwined with a serpent.

The man stepped toward the counter, but Peter suddenly grabbed him by the arm and turned him back.

"What . . . " The man glared at Peter.

"Who are you?" asked Peter.

"What's it to you, jerk?" said the man.

I tried to pull Peter back, but he was intensely attending to the man. He squinted his eyes, and leaned closer to the man's face. It was his earring . . . Peter was staring at the man's earring.

"You got some kinda problem?" asked the man.

Peter slowly raised is arm and held out the cologne cartridge toward the man. Then he pressed three times, and a sickening aroma of perfume mingled with the smell of perspiration and cigar smoke.

"Hey!" The man with the earring raised his fist to strike Peter.

"Peter . . . come on!" I pulled Peter toward the door.

"All right, you creeps!" The huge man stepped between them, and pushed them apart. "None of that in here!"

The man with the earring laughed scornfully. Then he pulled a dirty twenty-dollar bill out of his pocket, tossed it through the grating to the man behind the counter, and bolted up the stairs.

"Come on, Peter," I said. "Let's go." I opened the door and pulled him out."

"Beware the city!" he mumbled over his shoulder as he left. "Mother of harlots!"

I closed the door behind us and breathed a sigh of relief. The stench of the outdoors filled my nostrils, but at this point it was a welcome aroma.

"Why did you do that, Peter?" I asked him.

"I know him," he said softly. "He drifts across the city like a stale breeze."

I couldn't determine whether Peter was reacting to the man, or to the symbol of the cross and the serpent, but I was not inclined to stop and analyze his statement now. I led him off the narrow porch and onto the sidewalk, and the three street walkers approached us like eager beggars.

"You two had enough?" asked one of them.

"Hey wait a minute," said another. "Don't you see who he is?"

The first one cocked her head and glared at me. "Oh, yeah. Mr. High and Mighty. Why didn't you tell us you wanted a boy?"

The three laughed raucously and sauntered down the street.

I led Peter out toward the curb. I thought there was a billow of steam escaping from some nearby vent, but I realized that a low-hanging fog was beginning to fall. I glanced up the street and saw the three women speaking with two large men. The men laughed, and slowly approached us. A vague feeling of anxiety began to creep up my spine. A low hot breeze passed by, and a heavy accumulation of fog settled about us. My vision was distorted, and as I looked at Peter, a frightening recollection passed across my mind. Harold Palmer . . . He had been drinking that night. There were two men then, too. They approached us, and asked for our wallets. But Harold was foolish. He challenged them. They didn't get his wallet . . . but Harold was dead . . .

The two men passed behind us, chuckling softly, and walked slowly down the street, out of sight. A piercing pain rose from my chest, and I realized that I hadn't taken a breath. I drew in the stale air, and marveled at the exhilaration I felt at the sudden, fleeting recognition -- the awareness of the immediacy of life.

Peter raised his arm and pointed down the street. "The eyes of the messenger. Look!"

I strained my eyes into the deepening fog in the direction that Peter was pointing, and a glow of comfort swept over my body. The headlights in the distance grew brighter, and then the glowing illumination of the taxi sign came into view.

14

I immediately placed Peter on daily therapy in an attempt to strengthen the communicative bond that we had established. But a week had passed since I had brought Peter back from Rebah's room, and even after five intensive sessions, I realized that he was actually regressing. I sensed that this might be a problem from the moment that Peter verbally accosted the man at the hotel. He had relied on the artificial courage inherent in his vibrant pseudo-personality . . . and it had worked. He had been encouraged by that experience, and he was letting that feeling of temporary success push him toward greater and greater reliance on his false self as a protective shield against reality. Even his Sunday message at the temple had been delivered with unusual verve. I had witnessed just enough of the service from the lobby to see that Hatcher and Wingate were ecstatic over his apparent recovery. But I realized only too well that this euphoric state would be short-lived. Peter was clearly falling more deeply into the spiral of his unreal, psychotic world.

I had received the most disturbing signal of this regression in today's session. Peter was still having his dream. But this time, he described it in glowing, sensual terms, and insisted that he finally realized that he was not becoming insane at all, but, rather, being transformed into spiritual perfection by the purging of the dream images. I concluded that a break in the daily pattern might force a disturbing element into his consciousness. But he reacted with only mild curiosity and then condescension when I told him that we would have no session tomorrow, but meet again on Friday.

My intercom buzzer sounded, and I picked up the telephone receiver. "Yes?"

"Your wife is on the phone, Dr. Summers," said Cheryl.

"All right." I pressed the button for the active line. "Hello, Meg."

"John . . . Cheryl said you were through," she said tentatively.

"Yes."

"I'd like you to spend some time with Diane tonight, John," she said. "I just . . . I just hope you'll be home on time to eat with us."

"Of course, Meg," I responded.

"I'm just calling," she continued, "because last Wednesday you didn't come home until very late."

"That was . . . an unforeseen incident."

"But ever since then, you've become even more heavily involved with work, it seems," she said.

"It's important," I said. I knew immediately that this was the wrong thing to say, because Meg would interpret it as though I had implied that she and Diane were *not* important.

After a moment of silence, Meg continued. "I'm getting the real feeling that Diane is becoming much more communicative, John. I think we have an opportunity here. But even she . . . even Diane is concerned about all the time you're spending at work, and the way your behaving, and . . . "

"Diane is picking up on your feelings and expressions, Meg," I said irritably. "Surely you can see that."

"I don't think so, John," she said softly. "The three of us need to spend some time together. And not at the club, or on the boat. Just . . . together."

I sighed. "Sure, Meg," I muttered.

"This weekend?" she asked.

"This weekend. I promise."

"Thank you, John," she said. "I'll see you tonight."

"Tonight," I acknowledged, and hung up the receiver.

The moment that the yellow telephone light blinked off, my door opened, and Cheryl stepped inside.

"Dr. Summers . . . There's a police lieutenant here to see you," she said.

"Police . . . " My heart jumped. I wondered if perhaps Diane had gotten into some kind of trouble . . . if that was why Meg was so insistent . . . "Ask him to come in, Cheryl," I told her.

"All right." She started to leave.

"Oh, Cheryl . . . wait!" I said.

"Yes?"

"On my calendar," I told her. "Put a big note on Saturday and Sunday -- *Meg and Diane.*"

Cheryl smiled. "I sure will." She opened the door wider, and ushered in the lieutenant.

I stood behind my desk as he entered. He was a tall, bald-headed man, with a scowling expression. He watched as Cheryl closed the door. Then he walked across the room, displayed his badge, and gave my hand a quick shake.

"I'm Lieutenant Joe Chadwick, Doctor," he said.

"Hello, Lieutenant," I said. I pointed to the chair opposite me. "Won't you be seated."

"Sure." He sat heavily in the chair.

I sat down and moved some folders to the side of my desk. "What can I do for you?" I asked.

"Plenty, I hope," he said.

"Does this have anything to do with . . . ah . . . with my family?" I asked.

"What?" He squinted, and then shook his head. "No. No, it's about an investigation I'm involved in," he said.

I heaved a sigh of relief. "Then what do you want from me?"

"I need some information about one of your patients," he said.

"One of my patients?" I asked.

"Yes. He just left a few minutes ago," said Chadwick. "Peter Lumen."

I sat back in surprise. I couldn't imagine why the police would want to know about Peter. "I don't normally give out information about my patients . . . even to the police," I said.

"This isn't a normal situation," said Chadwick. "This is an investigation into a very serious matter."

"Serious . . . in what way?" I asked.

Chadwick's eyes narrowed, and his scowl turned into a faint smile. "I don't normally give out information about my cases . . . even to psychiatrists."

"Then I guess we're at an impasse," I said with a smile.

Chadwick shifted in his chair and rubbed his hand across his chin. "Peter Lumen is under investigation . . . as a suspect in the string of prostitute murders," He said slowly.

"What?" My hands instinctively slapped down on my desk, and moved my chair backward. "You can't be serious!"

"I'm always serious, Dr. Summers," said Chadwick.

"But how can you possibly think that . . . "

"We've had him under surveillance," he explained. "We know that he's gone to the raunchy part of town where the murders have all taken place."

Peter's ill-timed escape from reality last week . . . "Is that all?" I asked. "Surely you don't think that one visit to a seedy hotel is grounds for . . . "

"No . . . no . . . no . . . " Chadwick raised his hand and shook his head slowly. "We've observed Peter Lumen in that part of town three times in the last three weeks," he said. "And I'm sure you're aware that the most recent murder took placed during that time period."

"Three times . . . " This information shocked me. It wasn't that periodic clandestine visits and illicit encounters are unusual in cases of schizophrenia. But I thought I would have detected something during that time that would have alerted me to this repeated behavior in Peter.

"You didn't know about that, I take it?" asked Chadwick.

"Just . . . just one," I said.

"Well that observation, coupled with the fact that he is under psychiatric care, makes him a prime candidate for suspicion, don't you think?"

"No . . . " I mumbled. Then I shook my head, and pulled myself forward. "No, not at all, Lieutenant," I said emphatically. I mean . . . surely you know . . . Peter Lumen is a preacher!"

"Hmph!" Chadwick shifted in his chair again. "You think that makes a difference? You think preachers can't be criminals?"

"It's not that," I said. "It's just that . . . "

"And he's not even a real preacher," he continued derisively. "He's one of those television evangelists."

"What difference does that make?" I asked.

"Look, Doctor . . . surely you know about all the corruption that goes on in those ministries," he said.

"That's an over-generalization," I insisted.

"Well, I know plenty about this guy specifically," continued Chadwick. "My aunt is really into this stuff, you know. She's sent this guy thousands of bucks. And for what? So she can get this silly computerized form letter that promises his personal prayer, love and concern."

"It sounds as though you should perhaps disqualify yourself from participating in this investigation, Lieutenant," I suggested.

"Hey! My feelings about his so-called ministry have nothing to do with this case," he said gruffly. "I just used that as an illustration."

"All right." I observed him quietly for a moment. "Nevertheless . . . No. No, Peter couldn't be involved," I said.

Chadwick glowered at me briefly. Then he reached into his coat pocket and pulled out three photographs. Then he leaned forward and placed them in a line before me on my desk.

"These are from the last three murders," he said. "Look at them."

The photographs were gruesomely similar in one respect: in each one, on a bed, lay the lifeless, crumpled form of a woman.

"Look at the walls above the beds," directed Chadwick.

Scrawled in broad, painted letters . . . each picture carried a different ominous message: *SINNER! . . . CURSE OF SODOM! . . . REPENT OR DIE!*

"The spray paint can was left at the scene each time," said Chadwick. "But it was a common brand, so we can't get anything out of that. But the messages certainly do suggest some kind of religious fanatic, don't they?"

"It's possible," I said.

"At any rate, we have sufficient grounds to warrant getting whatever information we can from you about his psychological problem," he said.

"It's just that . . . there's nothing relevant," I told him.

"Doctor, it would be very easy for me to get a court order to force you to make all of your records immediately and totally available to me," threatened Chadwick. "But I'd much rather conduct this investigation on a . . . cooperative basis. Wouldn't you?"

I knew that Chadwick had the power to do precisely what he said. And I certainly didn't relish the idea of having all of my files pawed over by the police."

"Wouldn't you, Doctor?" Chadwick repeated.

"I'll . . . ah . . . I'll help you all I can," I mumbled.

"Good!" Chadwick pulled a pen and small pad out of his coat pocket. "Now . . . what were you treating him for?"

"Schizophrenia," I told him.

"Schizophrenia? And you don't think that's relevant?" he asked in disbelief.

"Not necessarily," I said.

"You mean you don't think one of his personalities could be violent?"

"You have a mistaken, or at least distorted understanding of schizophrenia," I told him. "The schizophrenic does not typically have multiple, unrelated lives. The split is manifested by different aspects of his personality becoming unusually magnified or de-emphasized in an attempt to deal with a disturbing and painful environment."

"And couldn't one way to deal with a painful environment be through murder?" he asked.

"It's just highly unlikely," I said. "Schizophrenics are actually less dangerous than the population as a whole. To others, that is. Their suicide rate, of course, is higher than . . . "

"No . . . " Chadwick waved his hand disapprovingly in front of me. "Don't get sidetracked on that one." He sat back and passed his hand slowly over his bald head. "You've spent quite a bit of time with him in therapy, haven't you?"

"Yes."

"What does he talk to you about?" he asked.

"His primary problem centers around disturbing dreams, and paranoiac delusions," I told him. "And his evangelistic personality is not a fanatical view of life, but rather a protective shield against some hidden fear."

"Which is . . . " he prompted.

"I haven't discovered it yet," I admitted.

"So . . . this hidden fear . . . " he mused. "It could be a hidden *secret*, too, couldn't it?"

"Yes."

"A secret that is so shocking . . . so hideous that even you can't detect a hint of it," he continued, gesturing grossly.

"If it were anything like murder, I would have found a clue," I insisted.

"But you didn't find a clue to his multiple visits to hooker village," he said.

"No."

"And did you even know that Peter Lumen isn't is real name?" he asked.

"I assumed that it was not," I said.

Chadwick smiled. "Then you didn't know that his real name is actually Peter Watkins."

"No. I didn't know that," I admitted. I sat forward eagerly. I thought perhaps that I could glean as much information from the lieutenant as he could from me.

"What *do* you know?" he asked. "What about his parents?"

"He's told me only that his mother is dead, and that his father is a mechanic," I responded.

"Well, he told you wrong, then," said Chadwick, smiling. "His mother is *not* dead . . . and his father *is*."

"Hmm . . . "

"Hmm," Chadwick mocked. "And his father wasn't a mechanic, either," he continued. "He was a tent revivalist in Arkansas."

Chadwick's last sentence drifted across my perception, and lay momentarily suspended, as my array of inferences about Peter shifted slowly into a new perspective. I raised my hand to force a pause in his statements. This was so significant! And this was surely the fact that Hatcher had been so reluctant to reveal. But why?

"I take it from your expression that this information is a complete surprise to you," said Chadwick.

"Yes," I said tentatively. "I mean . . . not that it doesn't fit in with his pattern. But . . . yes."

Chadwick raised his hands and shrugged slowly. "Then other surprises could be hidden out there, too, couldn't they?"

"Of course," I agreed. "But not murder, Lieutenant. That would *not* fit in with his pattern."

"I've been in police work long enough to know that patterns can be much more complex than initially perceived," said Chadwick. "Now, as I said before . . . I could get a court order and pull your files for one of our department shrinks to look over. But,

I'll be candid with you, Doctor. I think you'll be a lot happier . . . and that I'll make progress a lot more quickly if we can work together on this."

"What do you want me to do?" I asked.

"You know what we're looking for," he said. "You're the psychiatrist. You should be able to . . . I don't know . . . ease the conversation toward topics which might give you some clues to work with."

"I'm reluctant to manipulate my therapy for external motives," I said.

"Hey, doctor, if your patient is involved in murder, I can't see that this would be considered an external motive," said Chadwick with hostility.

I sighed and sat back in my chair. He was right of course. It was just that I was so positive that his suspicions were ill-founded. "Very well. I'll see what I can find out," I said finally.

"Good!"

"But my discovery process will go much more rapidly if you can share some information with me," I added.

"Like what?"

"Like . . . his parents' names," I said. "And his mother's address."

Chadwick broke into a wide grin. "Sure. Why not." He removed a slip of paper from his shirt pocket and read from it. "His father's name was Jason Watkins . . . and his mother is Pearl. The address is on here, too." He tossed the paper onto my desk.

"Thank you," I said, placing my hand over the slip of paper.

"I'm sure I don't have to tell you, Doctor, that this information that I've shared with you is strictly confidential," he said. "Under no circumstances are you to say anything about the investigation to Peter, or to his mother."

"I understand."

"Well, then . . . " Chadwick clapped his hands together and stood. "I think we're through here for today." He slid the chair aside, and headed toward the door. "Keep in touch with me, won't you?"

I stood and followed him. "Of course. Oh, Lieutenant . . . "

He turned back. "Yes?"

"Tell me . . . How were the women killed?" I asked.

"Beaten . . . and then strangled," he said slowly. He walked back toward my desk. "The murder weapon was actually left behind in the last case. Let me show you." He took me by the arm and pointed to the three photographs still laying on my desk. "Look at this one," he said, placing his large finger on the photo.

I looked at the crumpled woman lying on the bed. Something was wound around her neck. "It looks like a belt," I said.

"It is," said Chadwick. "It's a snake-skin belt . . . with the buckle torn off." He released my arm and turned toward the door again. "We got some feelers out on it. It may mean something."

"Yes . . . "

"Keep in touch," repeated Chadwick, and he stepped through the door and closed it behind him.

I circled my desk, sat again, and pulled the slip of paper and three photographs closer. I could see the markings clearly now -- the pattern of the snake skin on the belt. I was positive that Chadwick was mistaken about Peter. Nothing in my therapy had given me the least hint of this kind of violent behavior. But there had been so much that he hadn't revealed. Peter's multiple visits to downtown . . . his name . . . his parents. I felt a sudden surge of resentment that Chadwick was able to obtain so many facts that remained hidden from me, and I wondered, if I had done a better job of ancillary investigation myself, whether I could have discovered these myself . . . and other hidden things . . .

I hated this . . . the vague, yet overpowering feelings of doubt, creeping into my consciousness. It happened so seldom, but when it did, it made me realize how fragile people's perceptions are. I was a skilled, successful psychiatrist. That fact was branded indelibly on my consciousness. But one countermanding revelation, and the sense of assurance can trickle away like rivulets from the estuary of a stream and merge with the merciless, nondescript sea.

I glanced at the picture again, and I had to close my eyes in revulsion. The image of the dead woman hung momentarily before my eyelids, and then was replaced by my recollection of Peter's dream. The crumbling stairway, leading to the flaming mandala . . . and the snakes leaping out from the walls . . . their buckles torn off . . .

I forced my eyes open abruptly and sat upright. Then I gathered the photos and the slip of paper, and placed them in Peter's folder which still lay conspicuously on top of the others on the edge of my desk. I decided to take the folder home with me tonight and study it some more . . . after dinner.

15

The one-day break in therapy didn't seem to have any effect on Peter. He arrived for his session Friday afternoon, calmly told me that he'd had a restful night, and lay compliantly on the couch. I had so many questions spinning in my head that it was difficult for me determine how to sequence them in order to break him out of his false, self-protective state, and yet not send him tumbling into a catatonic reaction. I would find whatever information I could for Chadwick, but I wasn't going to let that consideration drive my therapy. I had planned to organize today's session around a video recording of Peter's presentation, so I took the remote control device for the VCR out of my bottom desk drawer and placed it in my pocket. Then I walked over to the chair near the couch, and sat at Peter's head.

"You look very relaxed, Peter," I said. "Are you ready to begin?"

"Of course," he replied.

"I believe that you're at a point where we can begin to make good progress," I continued. "You know that our task is to help you make contact with your true self, and bring it clearly into view."

"I believe you told me once that all of us have different selves," said Peter. "And that our task was to find a way to make them work in harmony."

"That's right," I agreed.

"Well, I believe we've accomplished that," he said. "I think our task now is more one of . . . oh . . . preventive maintenance." He laughed lightly.

"What shall we prevent, Peter?" I asked.

"Fear, doubt . . . " He circled his hand vaguely and then let it drop.

"We haven't spoken much yet about the time you spent downtown last week, Peter," I said. "How do you feel about that now?"

"That was a long time ago," he muttered.

"Still, you must have some recollection," I persisted. "Why did you go?"

"It's part of my regular ministerial duties," he said.

"Oh? In what way?" I asked.

"It's an outreach," he explained. "Most of those people don't go to church. And they seldom watch television. It's an outreach," he repeated.

"Do you go there often?" I asked.

He ran his fingers aimlessly through his hair. "I've made several evangelistic journeys."

"What do you think about Rebah?" I asked.

"Who?"

"The woman you visited last week," I said.

"You mean *Mary*?" he asked.

"Well, you referred to her as *Mary Magdalene*, I believe," I agreed. "But wasn't that just a symbolic Biblical relation, for ministerial purposes?" I asked, leading him.

He nodded slowly. "Of course," he agreed. "Rebah."

I nodded. "What do you think about Rebah?" I repeated.

"She was kind enough to let me stay with her during my meditation," he replied. "I'm afraid the details of my conversation with her are not too clear, though, because the messenger visited me again that night."

"The messenger of God?" I asked.

"Yes. The first time . . . when I was a boy . . . it was frightening," he explained. "But now I know what it is, and I just let it happen . . . let it flow. The tingling, from the center outward . . . Sometimes it's painful, of course. But I must allow it, because it's my divine duty."

"Do you often feel the pain?" I asked.

"Probably . . . whenever I'm visited," he replied.

"Does that ever make you angry?"

"You can't be angry with God," he said.

"Anger isn't controlled by judgments, Peter," I said. "It's a feeling. Do you ever have feelings of anger while you are on these evangelical journeys. Toward anyone?"

"I suppose . . . of course."

"Terrible anger? Violent anger?" I probed.

He passed his fingers through his hair again. "The forces of evil and disbelief are rampant. I rage against them. I rage . . . "

"How do you rage?" I asked.

"In my mind . . . in my spirit," he mumbled. "There are so many examples in society today. It's easy to be violent in your mind."

"Do you ever fear the results of your rage?" I asked. "Do you fear that you might become physically violent?"

"No. My selves are in harmony," he said. "That's what control is all about."

I didn't want to push this line of questioning too far. I was already leading him too much to obtain a reliable response. I had to break through his composure. Then perhaps he would exhibit an accurate reaction. I pulled the remote control from my pocket, pointed it toward the monitor on the wall and turned on the power.

"Can you see the television screen on the wall across from you?" I asked.

Peter looked toward the monitor and nodded as the flickering gray illumination appeared.

"When I visited your service last week, I bought a video tape of the presentation that I previously attended," I said. "I thought we might use it today to help us construct some personality images."

Peter shifted on the couch, and turned his head toward the center of the room. "That's outdated information."

"Still, I think it may be helpful," I said. "Don't you want to look at it?"

"Whatever you want," he said without turning his head.

I started the video of the service, but muted the sound. I had previously advanced the tape to thc point where Peter made his entrance. The picture appeared, and Peter's white-robed figure stepped out from the crack in the rock behind the falls and walked down the winding path to the front center portion of the stage. I activated the sound as the congregation chanted, "Peter . . . Peter . . . Peter . . . " and Peter turned his eyes to the screen abruptly in response.

The video continued as Peter raised one arm to the side and shouted, "Cry!", and the crowd responded, "Salvation!" Then Peter raised the other arm to the side, and shouted again, "Cry!" and the crowd answered, "Salvation!" Finally Peter raised his head toward the ceiling, and placed both arms high above his head and called emotionally, "Cry!" And the lingering sound of the congregation's final "Salvation!" echoed from the speakers.

I pushed the pause button, and the image of Peter remained on the screen, transfixed, his head raised, his arms above his head. Peter shifted on the couch again, and placed a closed fist against his mouth.

"You probably don't often get an opportunity to view the services, do you?" I asked.

"It's outdated information," he muttered.

I disengaged the pause, and Peter's voice continued: "Bless you all!" . . . "This is life. This is about life, isn't it? All of you out there, you're here because you're alive. Alive! And God wants us to live fruitfully and abundantly."

I paused the video again. This was a better view. Peter was reaching toward the congregation, and the expression on his face was one of fervent encouragement."

"You are really very effective in your messages," I told him. "Do you prepare a great deal beforehand?"

"It's the Spirit," he responded. "It comes to me."

"I know that some ministers that I've spoken with tell me that they spend hours preparing their sermons."

"Then they have not experienced Christ as the innermost possession of their souls," he said, with an almost mechanical intensity.

Peter's eyes remained fixed on the screen. I sensed that this would be the appropriate time to introduce the critical revelation. Since I had learned about Peter's father from Chadwick, I thought that Peter's temple presentations may consist of transforms of his father's words, and that forcing this realization might bring him to a recognition of the truth.

"Did your father use a similar format in his tent revival meetings?" I asked casually. But I knew that my voice was trembling slightly, since I had no idea what response this might elicit.

Peter merely shook his head, though, and spoke slowly and deliberately. "My father is a mechanic."

"Your father, Peter," I persisted. "Jason Watkins."

"My father is a mechanic," repeated Peter more loudly.

"He was a tent revivalist in Little Rock, Arkansas," I said emphatically. "Your father is Jason Watkins."

Peter began to stir, so I activated the video again, and his voice resounded from the speakers: "I want you to begin today by looking inwardly. . . . To the very core of your being. God is there. Can you see Him? He's waiting to serve you, as He's told us so many times. Do you have a hope? God hopes it, too. Do you have a wish? God wishes for you."

I paused the video again. "Did your father use those words, too, Peter?"

Peter sat up suddenly. Perspiration beaded heavily on his face. He glanced toward the monitor, and then toward me, and then back to the monitor again. Then he clenched his fist, and tapped his thumbnail nervously against his teeth. His eyes narrowed, and then he slowly pointed to the paused image of himself. "Oh . . . you mean *his* father," he said, with a crack in his voice. "Yes. *His* father is Jason Watkins. But *my* father is mechanic. He fixes things . . . he fixes things . . . "

A surge of excitement rose from the pit of my stomach. I realized that I was on the brink of tearing off his mask. I quietly stood up, went to my desk, and retrieved a hand-held mirror from the bottom drawer. Then I returned, slid my chair over in front of Peter and sat. His eyes were still directed toward the screen.

"Do you know him, Peter?" I asked. "Do you know the man on the television screen?"

His eyes narrowed. "Sometimes . . . "

I held the mirror up in front of his face. "Look, Peter. Look in the mirror."

He jerked his head toward the mirror, and then down.

"No, Peter. Look into the mirror," I insisted.

He slowly raised his head and complied.

"And now look at the television screen," I directed.

Peter looked at the screen, and then back at the mirror. He repeated the visual comparison three times, a look of fear growing on his face.

"They are the same, Peter," I told him. "You are Peter Watkins."

"No!" Peter suddenly grabbed the mirror from my hand and threw it violently across the room, where it slammed against the wall, and fell shattered to the floor. Peter pressed his lips together. Then they parted in a faint smile, and he raised an eyebrow. "Seven years bad luck!" He shook his head. "Tick, tack . . . step on a crack . . . "

I muted the sound, let the video advance to a point at which the congregation was showing on the screen, and then paused it again. "You have thousands of followers, don't you, Peter?" I asked, pointing toward the screen.

He glanced toward the image and nodded jerkily.

"You must reach many more people in one service than your father ever dreamed of," I said.

Peter looked at the monitor again, and his lips moved silently as he appeared to be counting with his finger. Then he shook his head and lowered his hand. "Too many," he said.

"That should make you feel good," I told him. "Your father would say that you are very successful."

"Success is meaningless," he muttered.

"What . . . the thousands of followers?"

"It doesn't matter," he said expressionlessly.

"Why do you say that?" I asked.

"They're sheep," he said. "They're just blind, dumb sheep."

"They are your followers, Peter," I said.

"They are followers of nothing!" shouted Peter, and his eyes were wide with an intense, unexpressed rage.

"What do you mean by that, Peter?" I asked.

He merely glanced toward the screen, and then back toward me. "They are followers of nothing," he said more softly.

I was so close to pulling the scales from his eyes . . . yanking the hidden terror from the deep recesses of his repressed unconscious. I had to maintain the intensity . . . not let him revert to his blocking technique. But at this moment, I felt a strange tingling fear . . . a vague desire that the truth should remain hidden.

"I don't understand how you can say that, Peter," I continued cautiously. "This is your mission. You were appointed."

"Appointed and anointed," he chanted.

"Then they cannot be followers of nothing," I insisted. "You are their link with God."

Peter lowered his eyes and began shaking his head slowly from side to side.

"You said it . . . you were appointed by God," I reminded him.

Peter did not respond, but moved his head with growing intensity.

"You were visited by God's messenger," I continued. "And you are doing God's work . . . and you are taking God's Word to your followers, and . . . "

Peter raised his head toward me abruptly, and his eyes were filled with fear. He grasped my arms. "There is no God!" he whispered harshly. Then he raised his face toward the ceiling and bellowed loudly, "There is no God! There is no God!"

He began shaking me violently, and my finger fell on the resume button, and the sound of his voice from the video merged with his continuing cry . . . "I want you to concentrate on your dream . . . Concentrate on your dream. God wants you to have it." And then the music streamed forth, and Julie's singing now blended with Peter's agony . . . "Only in my dreams did I imagine the Lord. Only in my dreams was He real. Silly as it . . . "

I pulled my arm free from Peter's grasp and turned off the power to the VCR. The screen became black, and the sound from the speakers ceased abruptly, but Peter's voice across from me continued the agonizing, pleading cry . . . "There is no God! There is no God! " . . . And his voice slowly diminished to a harsh whisper again, and then faded to silence as he slumped back into the couch, his lips still moving inaudibly.

I tried to speak, but the power of this awful recognition was so overwhelming that my words caught in my chest, and then trickled out in a heavy, involuntary sigh. I breathed deeply in an attempt to stifle my reaction. This was Peter's hidden secret . . . the hideous suppressed truth that had cast him into the unlikely, bizarre denial personality. This was the moment that I had wished for. This was the sublime instant of catharsis which stripped the evil of self-deception from the subject. As I looked at the huddled figure before me, though, I wished for a moment that I could turn back the discovery . . . restore his illusion. But the veil had been rent, and Peter had confronted the horror of his demon.

"All right, Peter," I said finally. "That's all right. Don't pull back. This is good. You've found your secret . . . brought it out. That's good, Peter," I repeated. "I can help you now."

"Help . . . "

"Of course," I assured him. "Because healing can only begin when the disease is discovered. You must talk with me now, though, Peter," I said. "You must try to answer my questions."

He sat without moving and blinked slowly.

"Our feelings about our parents can be a powerful, subtle controller in our lives, Peter," I said, hoping to find some avenue to lead him into communication. "And we are all victims of unwarranted guilt based on notions that our parents will not approve of something we do . . . or something we believe."

I paused for moment, hoping for some responsive sign. But there was none.

"Naturally you believe your father would be angry over what you have just told me," I continued. "Is that an accurate statement?"

Peter did not respond, but he raised his eyes toward me.

"The hardest and most valuable lesson we learn in life is that we must not be controlled by our parents' value systems, Peter." I said. "And you have allowed yourself to be controlled by your father's notion of God."

"There is no God . . . " Peter said dispassionately.

"But there is a . . . a spiritual sense," I said, grasping to verbalize some vague response to his sense of loss. "Surely you have discovered that . . . developed it in your work. I mean, your followers . . . "

"They are followers of nothing," he said slowly.

I struggled to put together a relevant, helpful image from Jung's treatment of the deep, historical spiritual drive of mankind. I had to find a way to help him convert his unbearable idea into some productive conception. "The products of spirituality are as varied as the individuals who possess them," I said. "This doesn't mean that the product does not exist. Your conceptualization of God is different from that of your father. But it's just as valid."

He shook his head.

"It's the internal notion that counts," I said. "For your father it was an omnipotent external being; for you, it may be the unconscious expression of the concealed divine motive. Either way, the *archetype* of God exists."

Peter sat forward suddenly, and placed his hands on my knees. "Do you really believe that God can be replaced by an archetype?" he asked intensely.

I tried to back away, but he held me firmly. He was attempting to shift control again. I had to turn it back. "What . . . what do *you* believe, Peter?" I asked.

"No. What do *you* believe, Doctor?" he persisted. "You're the doctor, Doctor. You have opened Pandora's box. Now either close it . . . or justify it!" He leaned closer. "What do *you* believe, Doctor?"

"What . . . what do you *want* me to believe, Peter?" I asked.

"I've already ripped out my guts for you!" he shouted.

"I know . . . I know . . . " I tried to remain in the position of the disinterested therapist, but he made it very difficult. His wrenching cry was such an indictment that it had been my leading . . . my insistence that had brought this feeling forth. If I were in his place I would be asking me the same question. I would want to know. But I wasn't in his place . . . couldn't allow myself to be put in his place. But his presence was so overpowering, that our unconscious thoughts seemed to direct themselves in a merged state toward some undefined primal need.

Peter's figure blurred before me, and my thoughts seemed to tumble automatically from some prerecorded psychiatric dialog. "You have confronted the truth, Peter," I told him. "That is the important thing."

A strange pleading look appeared in Peter's eyes, and he lowered his voice and moved closer. "But, of course . . . I could be mistaken, couldn't I? I could be mistaken. What do you believe, Doctor?" He leaned close to my face and whispered hoarsely. "Is there a God, Doctor? Is there a God?"

He was so close to me that his face was a complete blur. But the words . . . those words . . . They jolted my recollection of the past, and the shadowy features before me revealed a scene long forgotten. It was my tenth birthday. It was to have been such a happy day, but Lloyd left home that day, and my father was angry, and they argued. Lloyd was just searching . . . asking . . . He leaned close to my father, too, and held tight to his shirt. And they were his words . . . "Is there a God, Pop? Is there a God?" But my father pushed him aside, and told him that he would spoil my birthday party with his idiotic questions. But Lloyd persisted, and asked again . . . And then my father just told him he could believe anything he wanted . . . that it didn't matter. My mother was crying, and she tried to soothe Lloyd. She told him everything would be all right if he just didn't talk about such things. But

Lloyd left, anyway. I must have gotten a present for my birthday. I always got a present. But I couldn't remember what it was . . .

I felt myself being pulled closer to the blurred form, and then Peter's harsh whisper fell directly into my ear: "Is there a God, Doctor? Is there a God?"

"It doesn't matter . . . " I heard myself muttering. Then I placed my hands on Peter's arms and shoved him back. "It doesn't matter," I repeated. "I mean, you can believe anything you want. You're in control. It's all in what you define. The spirituality remains. The archetype exists."

Peter removed his hands from my knees and sat erect on the edge of the couch. He sighed deeply, and his eyes filled with tears. "Thank you, Doctor," he said haltingly. "I guess that means . . . there isn't . . . any . . . God . . . " He stood and walked slowly to the end of the couch.

He hadn't been listening. I had tried to formulate the spiritual awareness concept as clearly as possible. I raised my hand toward him, and tried to find another way to express it. But before I could speak, Peter turned toward me, and thrust his pointed finger toward my face.

"Judas!" he shouted. "Betrayer!"

"No . . . Peter . . . "

"Judas! Betrayer!" he shouted again, and he backed away from me with his finger still pointing.

His words rang in my ears, and forced my eyes into a blurred reaction, and I struggled to bring his features into focus. I grasped the arms of my chair for support. He wasn't listening . . . and now his image was fading. A shaft of light appeared behind his form. He had opened the door to the outside office. I wanted to stop him, but I couldn't release myself from the chair.

"Judas! Betrayer!" he shouted again. And then the shadowy figure slipped out, but the voice continued, growing softer as he left . . . "Judas! Betrayer! . . . Judas! Betrayer!"

Another form passed through the door, and came toward me. There was an aroma of perfume, and a soft hand fell on mine, and a higher voice called out . . . "Dr. Summers . . . Dr. Summers . . . "

I breathed deeply, and forced the strong smell of perfume into my lungs, and the pungent sensation lingered in my nostrils. I squeezed my eyes shut and shook my head forcibly from side to side, and stammered, "I renounce you . . . I renounce you . . . " When I opened my eyes, the features came into focus. It was Cheryl. She was squatting down before me, a terrified expression on her face.

"Dr. Summers . . . Are you all right?"

"Is he gone?" I muttered.

"Yes. He went running out of here like he'd done something terrible," she said. "That's why I wondered . . . I mean, should I call 9-1-1, or something?"

I began to chuckle at her question. And then the relief of Peter's departure and the exhilaration over my regained awareness forced their way out in a siege of unrestrained laughter. He had taken control of the session again . . . yes. But I had again pulled myself out of the mire. I had the strength. I had the ability.

"Isn't there something I can do, Dr. Summers?" asked Cheryl.

"No," I said. And then I thought. "Yes . . . yes. Sit down . . . there," I said, pointing to the couch.

Cheryl gave me a perplexed look, and then sat on the couch.

I needed more time. Just a few more moments. The recollections still circled my mind like hungry buzzards. Cheryl was reality. I looked at her . . . long and hard. Finally, all of the external relationships fell into place. I took a deep breath and nodded. I knew that Peter would return on Monday. I had opened a gaping wound, but his false self would quickly cover it and place him gently into the comforting zone of denial. But I had found his hidden secret. Now I had to build on it . . . lead him into every unwished-for area in his life that lay screaming for release. I would have to talk with his mother . . . find out everything about his rich, perplexing past.

"Do you want me to just sit here, Dr. Summers, or what?" asked Cheryl.

"No. I want you to get me a plane reservation, Cheryl," I said. "The earliest possible flight tonight to Little Rock, Arkansas."

"Little Rock . . . "

I nodded. I didn't know how much time I'd need, so I decided to allow the entire weekend. "Schedule the return flight Sunday evening," I said.

"Do you think . . . " she began.

"Don't question, Cheryl," I said irritably. "Just go make the reservations."

She stood up, and walked nervously out of the room.

I pushed myself to a standing position. The blood rushed to my head, but the moment of physical discomfort felt good. I quickly pulled my briefcase out of the closet, and placed Peter's folder inside. Then I hurried into the outer office. Cheryl was on the telephone, but not speaking.

"Did you get them?" I asked.

"I'm on hold," she said.

"All right . . . listen, I'm going on down to the airport," I said. "I'll call you from there to find out the ticket information."

"All right," she said.

I opened the outside door, but I was halted by Cheryl's voice.

"Oh, Dr. Summers," she called.

I turned back. She had a worried look on her face, and she held the point of her pencil lightly on my calendar.

"Your wife and your daughter," she said. "You had this weekend scheduled for them."

I was plagued by a sudden surge of guilt . . . or irritation. I couldn't tell which. It wasn't their fault, of course. But this had to be done. "Call Meg for me, will you Cheryl?" I said. "After you get the tickets. Call Meg, and tell her that I had to go out of town for something . . . unavoidable."

"Are you sure you don't want to talk with her yourself?" she asked.

"Call her, Cheryl," I insisted. "Tell her it was . . . unavoidable."

I opened the door and stepped outside. A blast of warm summer afternoon air hit my face, and my eyes accommodated quickly to the bright sunlight and focused on the welcome signs of reality. Peter hadn't been listening. It really didn't matter. You can believe anything you want. The archetype exists. As long as you're in control . . . it really didn't matter.

16

No one at the motel in Little Rock had any idea how to find the address that Chadwick had given me for Pearl Watkins' home. She lived in a town called Willow Meadow. A truck driver laughingly told me that this town was a suburb of a suburb of a suburb. He thought that it must be somewhere near one of the small rural settlements twenty-five miles north of town. The next morning, I purchased a map of the area, and pointed the rental car in the general direction that he had described. I wasn't in particular hurry, but I was eagerly looking forward to meeting Peter's mother. It's not that I expected some magical explanation to his condition to present itself, but this was the most important aspect of Peter's life that was still unknown to me. Schizophrenics often inherit or acquire a predisposition to respond in incomprehensible ways, and their split from reality frequently begins in their childhood as an escape from some unbearable situation.

None of the freeways leading out of Little Rock appeared to lead to my destination, so I stayed on the narrow rural highways, stopping every ten miles or so in hopes of finding more specific bearings. Finally, on the third stop, a service station attendant told me that Willow Meadow could be reached by taking the turnoff five miles further up the "main" highway, which was, itself, just a narrow country road.

The road to Willow Meadow was a narrow, bumpy gravel lane. Addresses were only occasionally listed in front of the widely scattered homes, but I gained enough information from them to assure myself that I was heading the right direction. I saw nothing that looked like a meadow. The area on both sides of the road was thickly covered with intertwined bushes and vines. The infrequently interspersed willow trees were dry and gnarled. They did have shoots of green mistletoe dangling from them, though, and I was reminded of the flourishing symbiotic foliage in Bernadette's greenhouse. The willows did not flourish here, however. The parasitic plants had completely drained them of their existence.

I saw a small, run-down shack at the end of a dirt driveway, and I calculated that it must be Pearl's address. I pulled into the drive, and came to a halt about twenty feet from the house. I stepped out of the car, and the hot, humid late-summer-morning air pressed in on my body. I started to walk toward the house, but two vicious-looking dogs rushed out from behind an adjacent shed. They stood between me and the dilapidated porch with their teeth bared, and growled threateningly. A screen door squeaked open, and a disheveled woman stepped out.

"Who ya for?" she yelled.

"I'm here to see Pearl," I said. "Pearl Watkins."

"That's me. Who are you?" she asked with a frown on her face.

"My name is John Summers," I said.

Pearl's frown was joined by a suspicious glare.

"I'm . . . I'm a friend of Peter's," I said.

"Peter? *My* Peter?" she asked.

"Yes."

She reached into the pocket of her shabby dress and pulled out a crust of bread. She tore off a piece of it and tossed it toward the shed. The dogs turned immediately, ran to the bread, and began fighting over it. Pearl motioned for me to come, and I hurried across the dusty yard and onto the porch.

"John, ya say?" she asked.

"John Summers," I nodded.

"Hmm . . . " She opened the screen door and beckoned for me to follow her into the house.

The door led directly into a tiny, cluttered living room. An old woman sat in a tattered overstuffed chair, watching a game show on a small, black-and-white television.

"Who is it, Pearl?" asked the woman without turning around.

"A friend of Peter's, mother," said Pearl, letting the screen door slam behind noisily us.

"Good morning," I said to the woman.

Pearl's mother turned away from the television and scowled at me for a moment. "Hmph!" She returned to her viewing.

"Here . . . " Pearl bent over a worn straight chair, and brushed some newspapers off of it onto the floor. "We don't get much company. Sit." She pointed to the chair, and then sunk into a torn divan beside it.

"Thank you," I said. I turned the chair so that I could face her, and sat. I brushed a fly away from my face, and wiped the perspiration from my forehead with the sleeve of my shirt.

"No so humid where you're from, I guess," said Pearl.

"No, it isn't," I agreed.

"Sweat is good for the system," said Pearl's mother. "Some people . . . they don't sweat . . . they die with all that inside 'em."

"I guess . . . " I mumbled passively.

"So . . . why ya here?" Pearl asked me.

"I was . . . I was in Little Rock," I said evasively. "I thought Peter would want me to stop in . . . say hello."

"Peter don't care about us," said Pearl's mother. Then she suddenly slapped her leg and laughed raucously as a bell began ringing on the game show.

"Can you turn it down a little, Mother?" asked Pearl.

"After this is over," mumbled her mother.

"I haven't seen him for ten years, ya know," Pearl told me.

"No, I . . . "

"He writes now and then, though," she added. "I know he's on the TV there. Is he doin' good?"

"Oh, yes. Very . . . very good," I told her. "He's extremely successful."

"Ya hear that, Mother?" asked Pearl over her shoulder. Then she turned back, and a wide smile crossed her face. "I knew it . . . when he was a boy. I prophesied that he'd be a rich, famous evangelist some day. Is he rich and famous?"

"Yes, he's . . . " I glanced at their shabby surroundings. "He's very successful."

"Well, if he's so rich and famous, we sure ain't seen none of it!" said Pearl's mother gruffly without looking away from the television.

"It's the Lord's money, Mother," said Pearl. "It's for doin' the Lord's work."

"We ain't seen none of it," repeated Pearl's mother.

"Are you still living in the same house as you were then?" I asked.

"Same," said Pearl. "Nowhere to move."

"I forgot . . . " I ventured cautiously. "Does Peter have any brothers or sisters?"

Pearl shook her head. "He's my only child," she said. "I used to tell him . . . I'm his only Pearl and he's my only jewel!"

"I guess he spent a lot of time with his friends, then," I ventured.

"No. Peter was a good boy," said Pearl. "He didn't have no time for that. He was with his father. And he helped me a lot."

"Hmm . . . " I glanced around the small room. One door led out into a small kitchen. The only other door was closed. "Peter's room was back there, I guess?" I asked curiously.

"There's only one bedroom," she said. "Me an' Mother share it now."

"Listen to the question!" shouted Pearl's mother toward the television. "If you'll just listen to the question you can answer it!"

"So we was real close," said Pearl, continuing the previous thought. "Me an' Peter . . . an' Jason."

"Peter's father?" I asked.

Pearl nodded.

"He was an evangelist, too, wasn't he?" I asked.

She nodded. Then her eyes brightened, and she sat forward. "Ya wanta see some pictures?" she asked.

"Yes. Yes, I would," I said.

"I don't get a chance to show 'em much any more." Pearl rose and walked across the room. She pulled a ragged photo album from a cluttered shelf, returned and sat again, placing the album on her lap. "Peter's father was a healer," she said. "A divine healer. He knew miracles."

"Miracles are in your head," carped Pearl's mother. "That's where healing comes from."

Pearl frowned at her mother and shook her head. "My mother, she reads a lot in that . . . *Mind Science*, ya' know," she said slowly. "She never did cater much to Jason's calling."

"There ain't no such thing as a *calling,"* continued her mother, without turning away from her game show. "It's in your head. The healing's in your head. I showed you the books. You just don't listen!"

Pearl sighed heavily. Then she turned back toward me and opened the album. "Most of this is earlier," she mumbled, flipping through a few pages. "You wouldn't be . . . " Then she stopped and tapped her finger lightly on a large photo which filled an entire page. "This is where it started," she said. "Look at that."

The quality of the photograph was not the best, but it clearly displayed a large tent with the sign bearing the phrase, *SALVATION TONIGHT!* hanging over its entrance. A large crowd of people spilled out of the overflowing tent.

"He sure used to bring 'em in!" said Pearl. "They always came."

"You said he was a healer?" I asked.

She smiled, turned the page, and pointed to a picture of Jason preaching. He was a tall, haggard looking man, but even in the grainy photo his eyes blazed with intensity. She pointed to a group of pictures on the facing page that showed Jason working with a number of individual people -- kneeling with one, embracing another. In one photo, a person was standing beside him with his hands raised high above his head, and Jason appeared to be tossing away a crutch.

"Now, here's where Peter starts," she said, turning the page. "He was just about ten when he started gettin' up there and puttin' the fear of God in people's hearts. See . . . " She patted a group of pictures lovingly.

I studied the photographs on the next two pages carefully. Several showed Peter from a distance, reaching out toward the hundreds in the tent. The close-ups were more revealing. Even though he was only ten, his facial expressions and gestures displayed many of the same characteristics that he still utilized in his Light on the Rock messages. That was a significant discovery. I thought that Peter's charismatic evangelistic personality could easily have been formed at this early age, and his rejection of it might well relate to some other aspect of his father's ministry.

"Did Peter enjoy doing this?" I asked her.

"Oh, yes!" she exclaimed. "He knew he was anointed . . . even then."

"But, I mean . . . did he like what he was doing?" I asked.

Pearl closed her eyes and laid her head back slightly. "I remember once I was sittin' in the front row," she said wistfully. "Peter was about fourteen then, I think. He was speakin' so smooth, an' strong! It was like I could see Jesus himself steppin' off that stage an' fillin' me with the Holy Spirit!"

"But I guess . . . what I mean is . . . " I mumbled.

Pearl lowered her head and opened her eyes. "Did he like it? Why would he not? He was anointed."

"I see."

Pearl continued flipping through the pages. Each set contained a few photos of Peter, and his size gradually increased as she proceeded, until he was nearly as tall as his father. Then she turned to a page which didn't contain any photographs. Instead, at the top was a crudely printed phrase: *Jason's Accident*, and underneath that, a date . . . fifteen years ago. Pearl sighed and passed her hand softly across the date. Then she slowly closed the album.

"Jason's accident?" I questioned.

"Car . . . " she explained. "Fifteen years ago. He was killed. It was a terrible loss."

Loud laughter issued from Pearl's mother again, as the bells rang loudly on the game show. "They got it!" she shouted. "Eleven thousand!"

"Where did it happen?" I asked.

"In Little Rock," she said. "So dangerous in the big city. He knew that. But he drove anyway. And it happened."

"*Really* dangerous!" rasped her mother.

"I'm sorry," I said. "And Peter was only . . . what . . . fifteen then?"

Pearl sighed and nodded.

"A boy needs his father," said Pearl's mother. "I showed him in the books. He wouldn't listen."

"But Peter was such a comfort to me after that," said Pearl without responding to her mother's barb. "That's when I knew the Lord had listened to me. Peter started carryin' on his father's business. I prophesied that he would. He was such a comfort to me after that. He took his father's place. He was my only jewel . . . " She let her voice trail off slightly, as she gazed toward an undefined point on the wall.

If Leonard were here, I knew that he would be jumping on this last bit of narrative. Pearl definitely was expressing a potentially carnal view in her description of Peter, and a Freudian analysis would certainly capitalize on the possibility of an incestuous relationship as the root of the psychosis. But I remembered Bernadette's caution: we mustn't jump to the obvious interpretation, because that will invariably be wrong. After all, this was why I was working on a case that Leonard had given up on.

Pearl turned toward me and spoke pointedly. "Are you in the business with him?" she asked.

"What?"

"Are you part of his ministry?" she asked.

"Oh. No," I replied. "No. I'm a doctor."

"Another healer!" scoffed Pearl's mother. "It's the same thing."

I was glad that I hadn't told them that I was a psychiatrist. I thought that would really have set the old woman off. But there was so much here! I pushed my mind to gather the information . . . organize it and categorize it so that I could remember it later. I wished that I had brought a small tape recorder.

"Why are they the same, Mother?" asked Pearl.

Pearl's mother pointed at me. "He's a medicine doctor . . . Jason was a witch doctor!"

"Jason was a divine healer!" Pearl said emphatically.

"Healing is in the mind!" said her mother, finally turning away from the television set. "I showed you in the book. There's ways to handle feelings and physical things without going to others."

"Jason worked for God," said Pearl.

"A boy needs his father," said Pearl's mother again. "That's why I had to help. You remember . . . when Peter had his nightly problem. I was the one who had to give him the ice-water bath."

I sat forward abruptly at the mention of the ice-water bath. This was the traumatic treatment that Peter had referred to in relation to Leonard's therapy. It had stemmed from some abusive remedy imposed by his grandmother.

"They were just dreams, mother," said Pearl. "Every boy has dreams."

"Not them dreams," said her mother. "His father should've dealt with it. But I fixed it. I fixed it." She shifted back in her chair, leaned her cheek against her fist, and squinted her eyes toward the television set.

Pearl rose slowly from the divan and took the photo album back to the shelf. As she replaced it, I noticed that on the shelf above was a row of video tapes. I wondered if Peter had sent her tapes of his services.

"What are those?" I asked, pointing.

"What?"

"On the top shelf," I said. "They look like video tapes."

"Oh . . . those," she said. "Jason had movies made of some of his revivals. Then, after he died, a friend of ours made them into television tapes . . . gave them to me." She shook her head. "I don't have a machine to play them on, though, so they don't do me any good."

"Do you suppose . . . " I stood and walked over beside her. "Do you suppose I could take one of those . . . or borrow it. I think Peter would like to see it."

"Hmm . . . " Pearl looked at me absently. Then she turned, and passed her hand slowly across the row of tapes. She pulled one from the set and read the notation on its edge. "I remember this day," she said. "Peter was twelve. Jason had the fire of God in his voice . . . and Peter was like . . . it was like looking in a mirror."

"I would really appreciate it if . . . I'd be happy to pay you something for it," I told her.

"I wouldn't know what price to put on it," said Pearl.

"They're worth something," said Pearl's mother. "Remember? Your friend told us . . . they're very expensive."

"I don't know," said Pearl.

"Here . . . " I took out my wallet and removed a fifty-dollar bill. "Here. Takes this." I gave Pearl the bill.

"All right." She took the bill, put it in the pocket in her dress and handed the video tape to me.

"Fancy doctor," mumbled Pearl's mother. "You prob'ly could've got a hundred."

"I think I should be going," I said. "Thank you for spending some time with me. I'll tell Peter that we met."

"He's my only jewel," muttered Pearl.

I waved absently at the back of Pearl's mother and stepped to the door.

"Here . . . take this." Pearl handed me a crust of bread. "Just toss it," she said. "They'll go after it and let you alone."

"All right." I stepped out onto the porch and gave the bread a toss toward the shed. The dogs were lying directly in front of me. They stood slowly, bared their teeth, and then turned and trotted over to retrieve their reward.

Once I had arrived back in Little Rock, I headed directly toward the public library. I knew that they would have past newspapers available on microfilm. I obtained films for the major newspapers for the time of the automobile accident and loaded the viewing machine. I didn't have to look beyond the first reference. Jason must have been fairly well known, because the article appeared on the first page. The headline was fairly innocuous:

LOCAL EVANGELIST AND COMPANION KILLED IN AUTO ACCIDENT

But the lead paragraph of the article summed up the devastating facts:

> The bodies of Jason Watkins, popular rural tent revivalist, and his female companion, Patricia Sims, were pulled from the wreckage of Watkins' auto, where it had plunged into a rain-swollen culvert. An autopsy revealed that both people had been drinking heavily. Ms. Sims was known by police to have been a prostitute. Family members were unavailable for comment.

17

It was eight-thirty the next night by the time I arrived home. The door was locked, and as I walked into the dark house, I realized that Meg and Diane weren't there. They rarely went anywhere on Sunday evenings, and I couldn't imagine where they could be. A fleeting thought passed through my mind that Meg had been so angry over my leaving town that she had taken Diane off somewhere for the weekend, and I momentarily savored the irritating taste of that contemplation. Then I realized that it was better this way; I needed some time alone anyway. I turned a low light on, and tossed my jacket and the video tape that I had gotten from Pearl on the couch. I went to the bar and fixed myself a drink. Then I picked up the remote control for the video recorder and turned on the power. The flickering white light appeared on the television screen, and cast a soft glow about the room. I walked over to the television, inserted the tape, and then returned deliberately and sat in the corner of the long couch. My eyes passed slowly over the plush upholstery, and I recalled the tattered furniture in Pearl's shabby house. I couldn't imagine why Peter hadn't done more for her. But then, of course, he had claimed that she was dead.

I hunched back further into the couch and took a long drink. It had been a busy weekend, and a tiring plane ride. It felt good to be home.

I pointed the remote control toward the television screen and pressed the start button. After a moment the flickering glow was replaced by the image of people's heads, and, in the distance, a dimly lighted stage. A small choir stood at the side, singing and clapping their hands. The video was clearly made from an amateur's film of the service. Portions of people's blurred figures periodically appeared, and the image was irregular and unsteady. A young boy stood on the other side of the stage, clapping his hands in rhythm. The picture wasn't clear, but I was certain that it was twelve-year-old Peter. At the conclusion of the song, Jason Watkins stepped out from behind the choir and moved to the center of the small stage. He was clearly recognizable from the pictures I had seen of him. His tall, lanky frame moved clumsily into place, and his fierce eyes slowly scanned the crowd.

"We're here for salvation tonight!" called Watkins, in a high, forceful voice.

The crowd responded with calls of "Amen! . . . Hallelujah!"

"We're here to praise this town and praise the people in it!" he continued. "Do you believe me?"

"We believe ya', brother . . . Praise the Lord!" responded a few in the crowd.

"The Lord told me to come here," said Watkins. "He told me there were hurtin' people here, and it was my duty as His messenger to come and fix things!"

The congregation continued to punctuate his sentences with periodic sighs, chants, and responses of praise.

"Now the first time I'm in a town, I always give my credentials," Watkins told them. "Because you gotta know who's bringin' the Spirit. Well, I'm here to tell you . . . it came to me some twenty years ago. I was standin' on my daddy's porch one night, lookin' up at the sky, when, all of a sudden, a flickerin' light shot down an' stood before me!"

The crowd responded in awe.

"I thought I was a goner, for sure," continued Watkins. "But I could see a sort of mouth open up, and then that light started talkin'! And it told me I shouldn't be afraid, because it was an angel sent from the presence of the Almighty God, and that it came to tell me that I had the gift of divine healing that I should take to the people in the world!"

Peter stepped out toward the edge of the stage and raised his arms. "Praise God! Heal the world!" he shouted, and the congregation echoed a supportive response.

"But before we can be healed, we gotta be *clean*!" shouted Watkins, pointing threateningly toward the crowd on the last word. "The Lord knoweth how to deliver the godly out of temptations, and to reserve the unjust unto the day of judgment to be punished!" he shouted. "He knows them that walk after the flesh in the lust of uncleanness. People who speak evil of the things that they understand not, they shall perish in their own corruption! All you with eyes full of adultery, who cannot cease from sin . . . you're cursed children. You have forsaken the right way. You have gone astray, following the way of Balaam!"

"Amen! . . . Save us from our sins!" cried the people.

"You are overcome with sin!" Watkins cried. "You must remove it from you . . . tear it out! As our Lord said . . . if thy hand offend thee, cut it off: it is better for thee to enter into life maimed, than having two hands to go into hell, into the fire that never shall be quenched!"

"Yes, Lord . . . " murmured a few people.

"And if thy foot offend thee, cut it off," continued Watkins. " And if thine eye offend thee, pluck it out!" he added. "You vipers!" he pleaded. "How can you escape the damnation of hell?"

The crowd moaned.

"How can you escape the damnation of hell?" he repeated. Then he turned toward Peter, and beckoned for him to approach. "A little child shall lead them, the Lord said," he said. "A little child shall lead them."

Peter stepped to the front of the stage. He glanced momentarily toward his father, and then he began to speak emotionally. "Some of my schoolmates came up to me earlier tonight, and asked me to go with them to the wicked city."

Several in the crowd responded with cries of, "No . . . The devil's in them . . . The curse of Sodom . . . "

"But I told them I had to come here tonight," said Peter. "I had to come here tonight . . . and be about my father's business!"

The congregation responded with resounding praise.

"'Cause my father was chosen by God," continued Peter. "An' he's here to save you an' heal you. An' you must listen to him . . . an' heed his words. 'Cause it's the voice of God . . . callin' you to repent!"

The image jerked violently for a moment, and then stabilized, as heads bobbed back and forth, and hands were raised in loud clapping. Then the holder of the camera apparently moved into an aisle, because the stage became more visible. Peter had stepped aside, and Watkins was pushing a box on rollers toward the center of the stage. He stopped, placed his hands on the table-height box, and closed his eyes. A hush fell over the crowd.

"Lord, help me find the true believers," said Watkins. "Let me find those worthy to be saved! For you told me, go into all the world, and preach the gospel to every creature. He that believeth and is baptized shall be saved; but he that believeth not shall be damned. And these signs shall follow them that believe: in my name shall they cast out devils; they shall speak with new tongues; They shall take up serpents; and if they drink any deadly thing, it shall not hurt them; they shall lay hands on the sick, and they shall recover!"

"Praise God!" shouted Peter.

Watkins eyes remained closed, and he raised his arms above his head, and opened his mouth. Then, slowly at first, but rapidly increasing in speed and volume, strange syllables issued forth: "Vasta loito. Rakiri memto, staltror, tantal, vasaito, laporto. Mostoro kantolo, beloro hordo lasisai. Do marta, lebntentantala!"

Low murmurs of awe erupted from the crowd.

Watkins opened his eyes and slowly lowered his arms. Then he removed a covering from the box and set it in the floor beside him. "They shall take up serpents . . . and it shall not hurt them!" he said to the crowd. Then, slowly, he lowered his arms into the box. He brought them forth again, and in his hands were two large rattlesnakes.

The crowd responded wildly with weeping and praise. Peter stepped back away from the box. He glanced at the crowd for an instant, but then his eyes darted back to the snakes, and he stepped back again.

"It shall not hurt them!" repeated Watkins. Then he frowned toward Peter, and held one of the snakes out to him.

Peter jerked his head toward the crowd again, and then back toward his father. But he did not get any closer.

"A little child shall lead them!" said Watkins. He walked slowly over toward Peter. Then he held out one of the snakes and wrapped it slowly around Peter's neck, and he placed the head of the snake against Peter's face, and its tongue darted in and out against his pale skin.

Peter stood motionless, his eyes unblinking.

"A little child shall lead them!" repeated Watkins. Then he slowly uncoiled the snake from Peter, and returned to the box. "Who of you shall be saved?" he exhorted the crowd, holding the snakes before him. "Come forth! Come forth and prove your worthiness!"

Peter glanced at his father again, and then stepped toward the front of the stage. He closed his eyes for a moment, and then opened them with a look of determination on his face. He was clearly blocking the horror of the experience from his conscious recognition. "Who of you shall be saved?" he called. "Come forth and speak in the Spirit to prove that you are true believers . . . and the serpents shall not harm you!"

The choir began singing, and a few people stepped into the aisle in front of the camera and headed for the stage. They walked slowly up and joined Watkins. Then, one by one, they closed their eyes, laid their heads back, and began to utter incoherent syllables. As they did this, Watkins handed them the wriggling reptiles, and they continued with their loud, unintelligible chants. Peter swayed back and forth and clapped his hands in rhythm, and the crowd joined him, and chanted and wept in response.

The screen suddenly reverted to a flickering glow. The video tape had come to an abrupt halt. I absently pressed the rewind button and listened while the sound of the twirling tape merged with the buzz emerging from the speakers. I had found the explanation for at least part of Peter's dream. Clearly the snakes jumping out from the walls and wagging their tongues at him referred to his father's fanatical practice. And Watkins' fire and brimstone messages could have implanted a powerful fear which might have been translated to the images of the fire and Satan.

But I didn't know how to relate the presence of the mandala. And the image of the tongues having been ripped out . . . I realized that every dream was, at its root, some manner of wish fulfillment, but I could not match this image with any direct or indirect motive that I had discovered so far in Peter's case. Jung had written some about the dismemberment motif, and its link with the archetype of the god hero, but a link in this regard would be somewhat far afield. There was, of course, a more direct reference in something that Watkins had said: "If thy hand offend thee cut it off . . . and if thine eye offend thee, pluck it out!" Pluck it out . . . pluck it out . . .

I heard the front door open, and Meg and Diane's voices in the foyer.

"Oh, hi, dad."

I looked behind me and saw Diane standing in the entry to the entry to the living room. Meg stepped up beside her and turned on a brighter light.

"Well, I see you're back," said Meg coldly. "What's that all about?" she asked, pointing to the television.

"Hmm?" I glanced toward the screen and saw the flickering glow. "Oh. I was watching a video." I turned off the VCR, and turned back toward them. "Where've you been?" I asked. "I thought maybe you and Diane might have run away for the weekend."

"No. *We* don't do that sort of thing without telling our family," she responded bitingly.

"Mom . . . " Diane whispered harshly.

Meg sighed heavily. "We were at church," she said.

"What?"

"Lloyd and Kate invited us," she explained. "So we went to Lloyd's church, and then out for ice cream."

"Oh . . . I see."

Meg walked around to the front of the couch and stood glaring at me, her hands on her hips. "Do you have a problem with that?"

"No, I don't have a . . . " I began.

"Because I have a *real* problem with the way you disappeared this weekend," she shouted, tears forming in her eyes.

"I didn't disappear, Meg," I said. "Didn't Cheryl call you?"

"Oh, yes . . . Cheryl called me," said Meg sarcastically.

"Well, then . . . "

"I wish you could have gone with us tonight, Dad," said Diane. I looked around, and saw her leaning against the back of the couch. Her eyes darted furtively between Meg and me. "We had a real good time."

"You really make it very clear what you think of this family, John, when you have your secretary do your dirty work," Meg continued angrily. Then she tossed her arms wildly to the side. "Your *incompetent* secretary, at that!"

"Mom . . . come on . . . " urged Diane.

"Come on?" Meg said to Diane. "Tell *him* to come on."

Diane threw her arms in the air. "I give up!" She turned and stalked out of the room.

Meg pressed her eyes shut. Then she clenched her fist and brought it up against her lips.

I sighed deeply, rose and walked to the television. "You were acting childishly, Meg," I said.

"Is that your psychiatric opinion, Doctor?" she asked caustically.

"Meg . . . " I turned and raised my hand to calm her, and I saw a dim reflection of our two figures in the smoked mirror on the wall. "I shouldn't have said that," I mumbled. "I'm sorry."

"We have to stop arguing in front of Diane," said Meg.

"We have to stop arguing . . . period," I added.

"We have to . . . " Meg shook her head in frustration. "What is it, John? We've always had trouble communicating, but for the last month . . . What's the matter with you?"

I raised my eyebrow and shook my finger at her.

"Oh, I know all your lectures about give and take . . . and a two-way road, and . . . " She sighed heavily. "All right, then. What's the matter with *us*? Here's an easier one . . . What's the matter with *me*, John? What's the matter with *me*?"

"There's nothing . . . " I began. How could I tell her what was wrong, when I didn't even know myself. I understood her anger at my having stolen our time together. What was the magic cycle . . . knowledge, understanding, acceptance, action . . . Where was I? Where did I want to be. "No, it's not you, Meg," I admitted to her. "I have made it harder on you for the last month. I know that. It's this case, Meg. It's . . . "

"Then drop it!" she said.

"No, I . . . "

"Or at least steal some moments from it," she pleaded. "That's all we ask, John. Can't you give us some moments?"

"Yes . . . Of course," I mumbled.

"Please . . . "

"Yes."

She looked at me with a pleading gaze for a moment. Then she turned away. "I'm going to bed." She turned back. "You coming?"

I nodded. "Right away."

Meg turned back again and walked out of the room.

I started to follow Meg, but then I stopped in front of Diane's door. I tapped lightly. "Diane . . . " She did not answer, so I pushed the door open slightly and knocked again. "Diane, can I see you for a minute?"

"I'm here," she said sullenly.

I pushed the door open and stepped into the room. Diane was lying on her bed fully clothed, her crossed arms pressed tightly against her stomach. I moved closer to her. "You planning to sleep that way, or do you have another engagement tonight?" I asked lightly, trying to break through her hostility.

"What difference does it make?" she asked.

"Look, Diane . . . your mother was feeling . . . "

"Don't try to explain how mother was feeling, Dad," she said angrily.

"But I . . . "

"You always have to turn these things into some kind of analysis!" she said bitterly. "Talk about yourself!"

"Myself . . . "

"How were *you* feeling?" she asked.

I felt the surge arise again -- the overwhelming temptation to tell her that her question was not appropriate . . . that *I* must ask the questions . . . She wouldn't understand, but it was true. I couldn't let my feelings interfere. I had to retain control of the situation. Otherwise, I couldn't fix things.

Diane looked at me impatiently for a moment. Then she shook her head and continued. "Sometimes I think I should have been a boy."

"Why?"

"Then I could have been a better friend," she explained. "You know . . . done more of the things you like. The boat racing, the hang-gliding, the dirt-bike . . . "

"No, Diane," I said. Although once, I recalled, I had taken my dirt bike thirty miles into the deep forest, and camped for the night. I remembered thinking at the time that it would have been nice to have someone with me . . . a son . . . a daughter, even. The cool air, the smell of the campfire. We could have spent time together, then. We could have talked about . . . about what?

"What do you think, Dad?" she asked. "Do you sometimes wish I was a boy?"

"No," I said simply.

"Well, anyway . . . we had a good time tonight," she said. "Maybe sometime you can . . . "

"Maybe," I interrupted. Then I smiled and waved at her. "You get a good sleep." I turned and walked out of her room.

"Good night, Dad," she said as I left.

I closed the door softly behind me, and leaned back against it. The image of Meg and Diane together with Lloyd and Kate floated vaguely before me. Had a good time, Diane told me . . . twice. I felt a sudden surge of resentment rise from my stomach, and a swallowed hard to suppress it. Why shouldn't they have a good time with my brother and his wife? They deserved it. I had been so busy lately . . . After I got Peter's case more under control, I could arrange for more family time. But I couldn't even think about it any more now. I was very tired, and tomorrow was the beginning of another busy week.

Meg was already asleep when I got into bed -- or was pretending to be. That was fine with me. I turned on my side, and within a few short minutes I had fallen into a deep sleep myself. I seldom dream. And when I do, the images are usually some fleeting relationships to activities of the preceding or following day. I often considered them my nighttime repeat calendar. But tonight was different. The strangest aspect of the dream was that I felt all the while that I had conscious control over its events. I had control, and yet . . . it was out of my control. It was like . . . the ocean. And the ocean was there, in my dream, rolling uncontrollably toward the horizon. But I had mastered it. The water was choppier than normal, but as the speed boat dashed across the crests of the waves, I made if fall slowly and softly into the cushions of foam, and then I thrust it ahead. Meg and Diane were beside me, and they were laughing. But then dark clouds appeared in the sky, and the ocean tilted . . . first one way, and then the other, sloshing itself wildly into a huge circle. And it spun round and round, carrying the boat with it. Then the center of the circle dropped, and the ocean became a gigantic funnel. I tried to tell Meg and Diane to be careful, but they were laughing so hard that they couldn't hear me. A shaft of light pierced the sky, and I looked up and saw a huge white cloud in the midst of the black ones. And then the white cloud parted into a mouth, and the lips reached out, revealing the nose, and eyes. It was my father, and he looked down at us, and he began to laugh, too. I could hear Meg laughing that Diane was going to get sick, and I looked, and saw her vomit into the funnel of water. And then the funnel opened up, and the shaft of light fell into it, and became a raging fire. I tried to turn the boat back to the shore, but it was held captive in the whirlpool. And then, from the direction of the setting sun, a white horse suddenly appeared. And Lloyd was riding the horse, and smiling. And he galloped up, and shouted, "If thy wife offend thee, pluck it out!" And he grasped Meg, and placed her on the horse behind him. And I shouted, "No!", but Lloyd just laughed, and called out again, "And if thy daughter offend thee, pluck it out!" And he reached out and took Diane, and placed her on the horse with Meg. And they were laughing . . . all three of them, now. And they rode off into the blinding light. And the cloud that was my father growled, and cursed at them. But he poured his light down on me, and it joined the flames. The boat began to be drawn into the vortex, and the heat from the flames rose and seared my skin. I squinted my eyes against the blinding rays, and through the slits between my eyelids, I could see the outline of a circle stairway in the whirlpool, and my boat followed the stairs as they fell irresistibly toward the warmth and the glow and the excitement of the fire.

A low, bellowing scream pierced my consciousness, and I reached out to grasp the gunwales of the boat, and they fell harmlessly on the cool, smooth linen of the sheets. I forced my eyes open, and realized that I was sitting up in bed, but the whirlpool still raged around me. I heard a vague sound near me, and I struggled to see, but the darkness was too blinding. There was a form . . . somewhere between the whirlpool and the setting sun. I shook my head, and then forced my eyes to focus. It was Meg's face, and behind her, the sun . . . no, the light . . . the light on the night stand. I trembled violently, and reached out for my pillow, and I heard the galloping hooves of a white horse in the distance . . . and above . . . my father's laughter . . .

"John! John! What is it?"

"What . . . what . . . " The sounds died down. I grasped my pillow, and wiped it across my sweaty face.

"John . . . It's Meg! Wake up!"

"Meg . . . " Yes. It was all right now, because my lips were moving, and I could hear them . . . I renounce you . . . I renounce you . . . And then, the whirlpool was gone.

"Are you all right?" she asked.

I reached out and grasped her hand and held it tightly in both of mine. I had the sudden urge to count her fingers . . . make sure she was real.

"Are you all right?" she asked again.

"Yes," I whispered. "Nightmare . . . I had a nightmare."

"I never remember your having one like that," she said.

"No . . . never," I muttered.

She leaned close to me, and placed her other hand gently on my shoulder. "Do you want to tell me about it?"

"Hmm?"

"Your nightmare," she said. "Do you want to tell me about your nightmare?"

I felt suddenly as though I were on my own therapy couch, asking myself questions. I couldn't allow this. I had to regain control.

"No. I'm fine," I said.

Meg frowned slightly. Then she squeezed my shoulder, and pulled her other hand from my grasp. She turned off the light, and lay down with her back to me.

I breathed deeply and eagerly drank in the obscurely visible details in the familiar room. The feeling had been so strong at the beginning of the dream. I had control . . . and yet things were not in my control. How could I be in control and, at the same time, out of control. The recollection of the images passed vividly before my conscious perception. I had the feeling that, at this instant, should I desire, I could initiate the nightmare again. And yet, I knew that, once it was initiated, I could not stop it from following its own momentum toward my threatened destruction.

I trembled suddenly as a dreadful sense of excitement rose from the pit of my stomach. It was just like the session with Peter, when his actions had forced me into the frightening images from my past . . . and the momentary departure from reality in the oppressive heat of Bernadette's greenhouse. I could control those situations. But could I control my nightmares? I felt as though I were balancing on the edge of the precipice again, but there was no carpet beneath to hold me captive. Other forces were struggling to bring me down, and they were warring with my skills. It was terrifying . . . it was exhilarating . . . That's what Bernadette had said about walking along a curb at the edge of a cliff. Bernadette . . . I thought perhaps I should see her again . . . seek her counsel . . . But then the hideous shadow of doubt crept before my eyes, and the excitement fell tediously like a trapeze artist into a cushioned safety net. No. This was my challenge . . . my murky adventure. And I would renounce my demons by myself.

18

Peter was very compliant at his sessions the next three days, as I had predicted that he would be. I had opened an extremely painful recognition, and his denial pattern had leaped in to cover the injury. But he was behaving now autistically, almost robotically. I realized that I could break through this crust again easily, with the knowledge that I had gained from my visit with his mother, but I had as yet not found the appropriate moment to cut into his psyche again. I tried to rationalize my reluctance by assuming that he was not psychologically ready yet for another cathartic experience, and even that I didn't want to do anything that would prejudice my inquiry into the possibility of Peter's involvement in the murders. But I knew that the problem really lay within myself. It soon became clear that the sessions were being almost totally driven by my own counter-transference. Elements from my nightmare became merged with my analytic questioning of Peter, and I became more and more inundated with feelings of my inadequacy to deal with Peter's psychosis. I knew that this was not an unusual state of consciousness for psychiatrists in situations like this, but I was unable to deal with it by myself. I decided to follow the instinctual notion that passed through my mind after having wakened from my nightmare. I would see Bernadette, after all.

It was about eight o'clock Wednesday night when I stepped through the vine-covered entryway to Bernadette's house. She must have heard me drive up, because, before I could knock, the dark wooden door swung open, and she beckoned for me to follow her into the house.

"John, I'm so glad to see you again!" she called warmly. "Come in."

"Hello, Bernadette," I said as I stepped into the dark foyer.

Bernadette swung the door shut. "'Come into my parlor,' said the spider to the fly," she chuckled.

Bernadette's living room was a clutter of papers and books. A variety of stone and metal figurines rested on mismatched tables throughout the room, and the flickering light of five or six large candles augmented the dim glow from a bulb inside an old amber lamp shade. It seemed oppressively hot in the room, and I suddenly realized why: flames danced across a newly placed log in the fireplace.

"It's the middle of summer, Bernadette," I said, pointing to the fire. "You surely aren't cold, are you?"

"No. I built the fire for our consultation," she said.

"What?"

"See . . . " She pointed above the fireplace. A large wrought-iron mandala hung on the wall. It was similar to the one Peter wore around his neck.

"I got that in Mexico several years ago," she said. "When you called to say you were coming tonight, I brought in logs for the fire, and hung the mandala. It's a symbol of the universal consciousness. And if we're going to make progress with our discussion of your patient, we need to merge our thoughts with the symbols that drive his dream fantasies."

"Hmm . . . "

"Come . . . sit!" Bernadette tossed a few newspapers off the high-backed maroon couch facing the fireplace, and pointed toward the end cushion.

"You really want to see me sweat, don't you?" I said as I sat.

"Here . . . this will help." She turned on a small table fan and pointed it toward the fire, and the flames moved back slightly, driven by the flow of air. She sat at the other end of the couch, and laid one leg up casually before her. "Now, when you called me, John, you said that you had learned something new about your patient's parents."

"That's right," I said. "I discovered that his father was a tent revivalist who handled snakes as part of his ceremony."

"Ah! The serpents in his dream!" she said enthusiastically.

I nodded. "And I also learned that his father was killed in an auto accident fifteen years ago . . . while in the company of a prostitute."

"Well, those facts, individually or in concert, might have led to his repression," she said. "How did he react when you told him what you knew about his parents?"

"I . . . I haven't raised the issue yet," I admitted.

"Oh?" She tilted her head and raised an eyebrow. "Why is that?"

I had come to Bernadette because of my feeling of inadequacy over this matter, but I wasn't ready to admit it to her. "I'm not sure he's ready yet," I hedged.

"Ready for what?" she asked.

"For another cathartic experience."

"*Another*, you say?" she said with a smile. "Then you have uncovered something. Excellent! Tell me about it."

I tried to bring Friday's session with Peter clearly into focus, and, for some reason, I was blocking the details surrounding our emotional discourse. Instead, I felt driven to gather more information from Bernadette of a general nature -- something that would help me in my commitment to Chadwick.

"You're not going to make me coax you, are you John?" she asked coyly.

"No. I just need to establish a perspective first," I said.

"That sounds like a typical university professor's response," she joked.

"You've treated many schizophrenics, haven't you?" I asked.

"In my career?" She nodded. "Several hundred, in some fashion or another."

"Have you known any of them to be capable of . . . violence?" I asked.

"What type of violence?" she asked.

"Extreme violence . . . murder," I said.

"My!" Bernadette shifted slightly, and placed her arm on the high back of the couch. "Well, many of the patients I worked with *thought* they were capable of violence. In fact, a young woman I have in therapy right now is a case in point. She has dreams of giving birth to many unwanted babies. And then she has wakeful delusions that she is a killer of babies."

"But they are just delusions?"

"Of course," she said. "I have interpreted the children to be her own rejected feelings of dependence, stemming from her relationship with me. I was able to lead her to a recognition of that, and her feelings of violence subsided."

"Have you found that generally to be the pattern?" I asked her.

"Generally," she said. "But, of course, there are always exceptions to the rule. I have treated several schizophrenics who were, in fact, murderers."

I sighed and sat forward slightly. "I told you, of course, that my patient is an evangelist," I said.

"Yes, you did."

"Would that . . . would that make a difference?" I asked.

Bernadette chuckled softly. "In which direction?" she asked.

"Well, I . . . "

She placed a finger to her lips. Then she pointed toward the mandala above the fireplace. "All things are in all people," she said. "Good and evil . . . demons and angels . . . Christ and Satan. The motivations for murder are many and varied. And the occasions for the act are sometimes as perplexing as the psyches of the perpetrators."

"But let's say, for the purpose of discussion . . . a successful, sincere preacher," I proposed.

"The crusaders were successful and sincere," she said, and she laughed softly. "But tell me," she continued after a slight pause, "is this the awful secret that you're reluctant to reveal? Is your patient a murderer?"

I shook my head, and motioned for her to give me more information. "Just give me your opinion," I said. "How likely is it?"

"Well, in some ways, less likely," she said. "But, on the other hand, another motive may be added?"

"What's that?" I asked.

"Well, for the religious zealot, for example, any act can be committed in the name of God," she explained. "Even murder."

"He doesn't believe in God," I blurted out.

Bernadette raised her eyebrow, and let her arm slip slowly down from the back of the couch "Really? So *that's* the hidden secret."

"Yes."

"That's very intriguing!" she said slowly. "The primal scream of disbelief!"

"Perhaps."

"Well . . . is he like Nietzsche, then. That is . . . " She leaned forward and spoke intensely. "Did he once believe . . . and then renounce his faith?" she asked.

"I don't . . . I don't know yet," I said.

"That may make a difference, you see," she said. "The foundation of his reality shaken to its base . . . no supports, nothing to cling to except the rage remaining from the desolation . . . "

"I don't know yet," I repeated.

"Tell me your discovery process," she said.

"I forced him to look at his role," I said. "His role in relation to his followers. That's when it happened. He said they were followers of nothing . . . because there was no God."

"I see . . . And how did you respond?" she asked.

"I tried to get him to recognize that, even without a belief in God, he did, in fact have a substitutionary spiritual awareness -- the archetype of God," I said.

"And . . . " she probed.

"And . . . " She was not going to let it rest at that. But this was the point of my blockage. The image of Peter sitting across from me was crystal clear, but his words were mixed with my own response to them. "He sat across from me," I said finally. "He asked me if I really believed that God could be replaced by an archetype."

"Ah . . . He turned the session!" she said.

"Yes."

"How did you regain control?" she asked eagerly.

"Regain . . . " But Peter's pleading voice still throbbed in my consciousness . . . You have opened Pandora's box. Now either close it . . . or justify it! . . . What do *you* believe, Doctor? . . . Is there a God, Doctor? Is there a God?

"He kept asking me," I said. "Is there a God . . . Is there a God . . . "

"Yes . . . yes . . . " She nodded excitedly. "And you were able to relate that question to some fact from his history?"

I shook my head slowly. "You see . . . Lloyd . . . my brother . . . When I was ten years old . . . He asked my father the same question. The pressure was intense. His need was so close . . . "

Bernadette leaned forward and placed her hand on my arm. "So you were held captive in a state of counter-transference," she said.

"Yes . . . for the moment."

"Something that powerful is never for the moment, John," she said softly. "So . . . your response was your father's response."

"Yes," I said. "I told him . . . It didn't matter, that he could believe anything he wanted."

"Yes. And then?" she coaxed.

"And then I told him that the spirituality remains. The archetype exists."

"But, of course, that answer did not satisfy him," she said.

I shook my head slowly. "He called me a Judas," I muttered.

Bernadette emitted an ecstatic squeal, clenched her fist, and stood abruptly. "This is outstanding!" she exclaimed. She walked over and leaned against the fireplace. "I haven't dealt with a Judas archetype for years!" She turned back toward me, and reached out aimlessly. "Tell me about your feelings after that, John. Did you *feel* like a Judas?"

Her question caught me by surprise. I had intended to discover facts about Peter, not spend time talking about *my* feelings. But I was suddenly filled with a surge of relief that someone was eliciting my emotions related to this episode. I sighed, and leaned back against the couch. "I thought at first that *he* had betrayed *me*," I said. "I mean . . . I had been seduced into letting him take control of the session. And it wasn't the first time. It was almost as though it was some hideous plot to abolish my defenses against this happening. Yes . . . I first felt that he had betrayed me."

"And what changed that?" she asked.

"I'm not the patient," I replied. "I'm responsible for what happens in the sessions. I knew that something had happened inside of me . . . something that I couldn't completely deal with. I had let my unconscious slip itself into my role. I could have avoided it." I shook my head, and then spoke deliberately. "I'm the responsible one. I'm the betrayer."

"Are you, then, responsible for his non-belief?" she asked.

"No, I couldn't . . . " I mumbled. But Peter's pleading figure still confronted my vision . . . His harsh whisper . . . But, of course . . . I could be mistaken, couldn't I? I could be mistaken. What do you believe, Doctor? Is there a God? "No, I couldn't be," I told her. "He can't lay that one on me. No one can take on that kind of responsibility." I shook my head to clear the echo of Peter's words. "He just . . . He just didn't want me to turn God into an archetype. Lloyd said the same thing about Christ."

"Your brother?" she asked.

"Yes. He told me that Christ is not an archetype." I leaned forward again. "Are we taking too much on ourselves with that, Bernadette?" I asked. "I mean . . . who's to say, for example, that my brother's religious view isn't just as good as my father's. Why must there always be an archetype?"

"That wasn't a case of this religious view, or that religious view," said Bernadette with a sudden intensity. "Your brother hurt your father. Charles had provided for him, and Lloyd rejected him. His fundamentalism was an affront." She stopped speaking abruptly and lowered her head.

I looked at Bernadette standing beside the fireplace, and the waves of heat from the flickering flames made her image seem to quiver in the radiant light. It took a moment for me to shift from my self-revealing mode to one of questioning. I couldn't imagine her being aware of all this personal information about my family.

"How did you know all that?" I asked.

"What?"

"About my father, and Lloyd," I said. "I mean . . . Lloyd's fundamentalism, and the notion that it was an affront . . . That's my father's opinion," I told her. "How did you know about it?"

"Well, I believe I told you, John, that your father handled my legal affairs for many years," she explained. "We became rather good friends during that time. And we often discussed mutual problems." She laughed lightly. "I'm sure your father thought he was getting free psychiatric advice."

"But why would you remember that obscure reference?" I asked.

She walked back to the couch and sat beside me. "You're avoiding my questions, John," she said with mock irritation. "We really need to get to the bottom of your counter-transference. You've clearly internalized aspects of your patient's psychosis. And even though you can rationally abrogate responsibility, you will unconsciously assume accountability for that aspect of your psyche that identifies with his."

"It has never happened before," I said.

"You have never had a case like this before," she said. "So, please . . . continue. Other than the feeling of being a betrayer, what other manifestations have occurred?"

"The dream . . . " I mumbled. "I've never had that before, either. Not like that . . . frightening . . . overpowering . . . "

"Oh, John!" Bernadette suddenly took both my hands in hers and squeezed tightly. "Do you realize what you're on the brink of?"

"What . . . what do you mean?"

"You have the opportunity of a lifetime!" she gushed. "You're on the brink of psychotic experience! And you have the knowledge and skill needed to relish it . . . learn from it . . . and escape from it!"

"I don't look at it that way," I said.

"You must!" she insisted. "So many times, the idiotic interpreters . . . even in the Jungian school . . . so many times, they look upon the reports of their patients as nothing more than a chaotic jumble. But, you see, they haven't been there. They have no idea of the richness that experience can bring. They have no concept of the truth that can be derived from the other side of reality. But you, John . . . you're on the precipice. And you have the ability to walk the line . . . and step back." She leaned closer. "Be honest. Haven't you been aware of the excitement of the experience?"

How could I deny it? That was the overpowering recollection of the sessions during which it had taken place . . . the sense of excitement at having actually slipped into a brief hysterical state, and pulled myself back by the power of my own conscious will. But that was before the nightmare.

"You must have been aware of it," she continued to push me.

"But why are you so . . . I mean, how about you, Bernadette?" I asked. "You're so intense about it. Have you had the experience?"

She smiled and sat back slightly. "Only artificially, I'm afraid."

"What?"

"I've placed myself in self-induced hysterical states occasionally through the use of hallucinogenic drugs, but . . . "

"Are you serious?"

"Don't look so shocked, John," she said. "Many psychiatrists have experimented with hallucinogenic drugs to give them insight into the mind of the psychotic."

"People on the fringe . . . " I began.

"Fringe . . . precipice . . . " she said. "No matter. If the end result is increased insight, then it has been worth it. But I always realized that the chemically induced experience couldn't hold a candle to the real thing."

I couldn't believe that Bernadette -- my learned mentor from the institute -- had resorted to mind-bending drugs to help her gain knowledge about the mind of the schizophrenic. Of course I was aware of the practice being carried on by a few controversial psychiatrists, but I never imagined that she would be one of them.

"But I haven't experimented with them for years, John," she continued. "My old body's too fragile to go through the excitement anymore." She laughed and moved back away from me. "But now . . . tell me about your dream!"

I just looked at her without speaking for a moment. I couldn't refocus my recollections after that sudden, unexpected shock to my image of her.

"Come on, John," she urged. "Tell me about your dream."

"We were in my boat," I began reluctantly. "Meg, Diane and I. And there was a giant whirlpool, pulling us down. And my father was in a cloud above us, laughing. But Lloyd came on a white horse, and rescued Meg and Diane."

"Interesting!" she said.

"And then . . . there were stairs leading to the bottom of the whirlpool," I continued. "And a fire was waiting for me . . . and it was warm . . . and exciting."

"Yes. Of course . . . of course!" Exclaimed Bernadette. "The stairway and fire in the whirlpool are transforms of your patient's dream, of course," she said. "That would be worthy of exploration."

"I know."

"But now . . . your father in the clouds, and the laughter . . . " Bernadette smiled and nodded. "That could be very significant. I suspect it reflects you feeling of overdependence on him."

"Overdependence for what?" I asked.

"Well . . . you told me that he had set you up in private practice, and supplied you with a majority of your patients to begin with," she explained.

"Yes, but I don't . . . "

"Well, and add to that the fact that he had guaranteed your acceptance at the institute, and had arranged with me to work with you, and assure your success . . . "

"Wait a minute!" I stood abruptly. "What are you talking about, Bernadette? I got a letter . . . inviting me to attend the institute."

"Well, yes, but . . . " She laughed self-consciously.

"And I didn't need anyone to *assure my success*," I added. "I was a good student."

"Well, of course, John," she said. "As it turns out . . . you were a fine student, and the administration finally realized that your acceptance had been all right, and . . . "

"All right? Are you telling me that if my father hadn't pulled strings with the administration, and arranged for you to *tutor* me . . . that I wouldn't have been accepted at the institute?"

"Well, I . . . I thought you knew that, John," she mumbled. "I'm sorry. I'm really sorry."

I turned angrily, walked to the fireplace and pounded my fist on the wall. I heard a rustling noise, and then I felt Bernadette's hand on my shoulder.

"Really, John," she said softly. "You turned out to be one of my favorite students. It doesn't really make any difference now, does it? It really doesn't matter."

I had a brief vision of my mother trying to soothe Lloyd that day, after my father told him that it didn't matter. But this was different . . . Bernadette was the soother and the teller . . . as I had been with Peter. I was the Judas . . . and so was Bernadette.

"Don't hold this against your father," said Bernadette softly. "Look at the result."

"It's the deception . . . " I mumbled.

"That's a harsh word," she said.

The heat from the fire rose in radiating waves, and undulated past my body. The flickering flames began to take on shapes . . . my father, my mother . . . and Lloyd, flickering away from the log like a disobedient child . . .

"He shouldn't have treated Lloyd that way," I heard myself muttering.

"Oh, now John . . . "

I thought it was Bernadette's voice that I heard, but I couldn't be sure, because my perception was still locked on the fleeting, darting images.

"Your father has a healthy detachment from spirituality, and you should try to emulate it . . . "

I shook my head, and pushed myself away from the fireplace. "I have to go, Bernadette," I said.

"So soon?"

I walked toward the door, and the sudden relinquishment of warmth momentarily chilled my body.

Bernadette walked up behind me and grasped my arm. "We need to work together, John," she said. "You're going to need guidance through this period. You're on the brink of a thrilling adventure . . . but you're going to need guidance."

"You mean I need a mentor again, Bernadette . . . to assure my success?" I asked bitterly.

"Don't harbor hostility, John," she murmured. "You're better than that."

I sighed deeply, squeezed her arm gently, and then opened the door and stepped out onto the vine-covered entryway. The warm night air seemed cool and refreshing in contrast to the raging fire in Bernadette's living room. I stepped forward into the night, but her words followed me like locusts in the wind.

"Call me the moment you have another experience, John," she said. "You know that I'm right. You know that I'm the only one who can lead you through this successfully. No one else has had the experience. The universities don't teach everything you need to know . . . not even the institute. Remember Paracelsus. He knew. He knew that a doctor must seek out old wives, gypsies, sorcerers, wandering tribes, and outlaws. A doctor must be a traveler, John. Paracelsus knew that. You know that, too. And you know that I am your best and only guide. You have a wish hiding in you somewhere . . . something unbearable to you. And I'm the only one who can carry your delusion into reality."

I held my hand up without turning around, and Bernadette stopped talking. I nodded, and stepped out into the coolness of the night. Bernadette was right about one thing -- I did need help. I knew that before I even came to her. There was no way that I could objectively evaluate the effect my counter-transference was having on my analysis of Peter . . . or on my own mental health. The time had come to have another analyst observe one of my sessions with Peter, and evaluate my effectiveness. I found myself cringing at the sudden clear recognition of this. But I knew after tonight's experience that Bernadette was not the one. I decided that I would call Leonard tomorrow . . . and ask him to observe Peter's session on Friday.

19

Leonard arrived on Friday shortly before the time for Peter's appointment. I had given him only a day's notice, but he was flattered that I had called on him to evaluate my session, and he willingly rescheduled some of his own appointments to allow time for the observation. I was glad that Peter had not arrived early, though. I didn't want him to see us together. I greeted Leonard warmly, and ushered him into my office.

"I really appreciate your coming on such short notice, Leonard," I said.

"I have you down in my book for a return favor," he replied, smiling.

"Here . . . let's just sit there." I pointed to the single chair at my desk, and pulled another one alongside it.

"I'm glad you aren't going to put me on the couch," he joked as he sat.

"Maybe afterwards," I said. I laughed and sat beside him.

"I'm really impressed with your commitment to this case, John," said Leonard. "I mean . . . flying all the way to Arkansas to obtain information about Peter's family."

"But it really paid off," I said.

"Oh, definitely!" he agreed. "And it's not just the background about his father, and the video tape. His mother and grandmother promise to be powerful developmental factors as well."

"Yes."

"And I'm sure you've considered this . . . and rejected it," he added, smiling. "But I really think you need to investigate the possibility of an incestuous relationship with his mother."

"I have considered it . . . and I have rejected it," I admitted. "Not necessarily as a potential additive aspect, but I don't see it as the major factor in his repression."

"But when the signs are so clear . . . "

I lowered my head and glowered at him.

Leonard sat back and placed both hands up in a gesture of surrender. "I promise to have an open mind."

I smiled and nodded. "Besides . . . " I said casually, "I haven't told you everything."

"Oh?"

"It seems that Peter is being investigated by the police," I said.

"Really? For what?"

"For the string of prostitute murders," I told him.

"Whoa!" Leonard sat up abruptly, and grasped the arms of the chair. "I expected something like parking tickets! Are the police serious?"

"Very," I told him. "You see, he has been observed in the red-light district several times."

"That escape syndrome is not uncommon," he said. "Especially for someone whose denial of the lustful tendencies is almost a requirement of his job."

"I know. And I told the detective that, and tried to soften his suspicion. But he seems intent on pursuing it."

"Hmm . . . " Leonard shook his head. "I agree with you. In the three months I spent with Peter, I didn't see anything that would result in that great a departure from the normal pattern. He had plenty of signs leading toward *self*-destructiveness . . . but not murder."

There was a light tap on the door. I looked up to see Cheryl step in and close the door quietly behind her.

"Excuse me, Doctor," she said softly. Then she looked at Leonard and giggled. "I mean . . . *Doctors.* Peter is here for his appointment."

"Thank you, Cheryl," I said. "Tell him I'll be ready in a minute."

"All right."

"And, of course, you're to say nothing about Dr. Butler," I reminded her.

She smiled, nodded, and placed her finger to her lips. Then she stepped quietly out and closed the door behind her.

Leonard watched her leave, and then he laughed lightly. "I'm sorry, John," he said. "I don't see what your problem is. I think she's absolutely charming!"

"Well . . ."

"But . . . to each his own, I suppose."

I nodded, and then stood and replaced the chair. "I'm going to ask you to observe undetected from the adjacent room."

Leonard stood and joined me. "Yes, you mentioned that," he said. "I'm not sure that I agree with that arrangement, but, of course, I'll be glad to do whatever you think is best."

"I really think it's necessary at this point," I assured him.

"Just take care that he doesn't find out about it, though," he warned me. "That could really damage the state of trust that you've established."

"I know."

"So . . . " He clapped his hands together. "I presume that is the observation room," he said, pointing toward the door with a full-length mirror on it. "That must be one-way glass."

"That's right," I said. I walked over to the door and opened it. "It's relatively sound-proof, too, but I wouldn't make any loud noises," I said.

"I understand." He looked inside the small room and nodded. "That'll be fine." He stepped inside, waved, and closed the door.

I waved toward the mirror, and nodded. Then I walked to my office door and opened it. Peter was sitting in the waiting room with a pensive look on his face.

"All right, Peter. I'm ready now," I said.

He looked up expressionlessly, rose, and stepped slowly into my office. The golden mandala still hung conspicuously around his neck, and he grasped it lightly as he moved. I closed the door and watched him as he walked directly to the chair in front of my desk and sat.

I walked over to the front of my desk and leaned on it. "How are you today, Peter?" I asked.

"Very calm . . . very calm," he mumbled.

"I see that," I said. "Did you have the dream again last night?"

"Of course," he said quietly through clenched teeth. "It fits me now . . . like an old shoe."

"Well, I think we may be able to resolve some aspects of it today, Peter," I said. "I've gathered some information that, I believe, will help you."

He looked up at me with a fleeting look of anxiety. Then he shook his head. "It fits me now . . . like an old shoe," he repeated.

"I think it's time to think about getting rid of your old shoes, now, Peter," I said. "What do you think?"

He sighed heavily and shrugged. "Go ahead," he mumbled.

"Over here, though," I said, pointing to the couch.

He glanced at the couch, and then toward me. "I don't want to lie down today," he said with a frown.

"It really will be much more effective for the initial phase of the session," I told him.

"I have this headache, you see," he said vaguely. "It's better if I sit."

The session was starting out on the wrong foot, but I didn't want to do anything that would block his willingness to talk. "Very well," I said.

Peter stood, walked to the couch and sat at the end. I pulled a chair around in front of him, and glanced toward the door to the adjacent room to be sure that Leonard still had an unrestricted view.

"We had a good discussion about reality yesterday, Peter," I began. "I think we should begin today right where we left off. All right?"

"Of course," he said noncommittally.

"All right. What is your name, Peter?" I asked. "Your *real* name."

"Peter Daryl Watkins," he said almost mechanically.

"Good," I said. "And your father . . . "

"Jason Watkins," he said irritably. "The same as yesterday."

"And his occupation is the same as yesterday, too, Peter," I said. "What was your father's occupation?"

"Mech . . . " he began. Then he frowned and slumped down slightly.

"Your father was a tent revival preacher," I prompted him. "An evangelist . . . just like you."

"No one is just like me," he muttered.

"Acknowledged?" I asked, ignoring his irrelevant remark.

He nodded. "An evangelist. But I also told you yesterday that this information is not important. It has nothing to do with my nervousness, or my dreams . . . or anything."

"Oh, but it does, Peter," I said. I pulled the remote control device from my pocket, pointed it toward the television screen and pressed the power button. The flickering white glow appeared on the screen. "We're going to look at another video today, Peter," I said.

"Another temple service?" he asked.

"No. This is different," I said. I activated the video, and paused it immediately at the spot that I had prearranged. The twelve-year-old Peter stood at the side of the stage, his hands poised to clap, and Jason Watkins stood in the center, his finger pointing threateningly toward the audience.

"What . . . " Peter sat up abruptly, and studied the frozen image. "Where did you get that?" he asked with a quavering voice.

"That doesn't matter right now," I told him. "What matters is that there are things here that will help you."

"I don't need . . . "

"But it will require you to take a journey, Peter," I told him. "I want you to be prepared for that."

He didn't respond. He just sat rigidly, with his eyes transfixed on the screen.

I pressed the resume button, and the video commenced. Peter sat without moving while his father gave the testimony about his heavenly visitation, and his exhortation of the crowd to forsake the way of Balaam. But then his father's voice became softer, and called . . . "A little child shall led them . . . " and the small boy stepped to closer to the camera. Then Peter sat back again, and turned his head away.

"You must continue to watch, Peter," I insisted. "You must continue to watch."

He turned his head slowly back, and watched as the small figure told about his friends, and the wicked city. But when his father pushed the large table-height box toward the center of the stage, Peter began shaking his head violently, and he rose from the couch.

"No, Peter!" I stood in front of him and prevented his movement. "This is going to be painful . . . but it's necessary," I said. I placed my hands on his shoulders and pushed him slowly back into a sitting position.

"They shall take up serpents . . . and it shall not hurt them!" issued Watkins' crackling voice from the speakers.

I took up the remote control device again, and paused the image on the figure of Watkins holding the snakes in his hands.

"From this point, Peter . . . you must see," I said.

Peter turned his head slowly toward the screen again, and I pushed the resume button. The noise of the crowd increased as Watkins moved about with the snakes, and then stepped toward the boy. Peter slumped down in the couch again, and thrust his fist against his teeth, but I placed my hand on his shoulder, and prevented him from turning away, as the tall man held out one of the snakes and wrapped it slowly around the boy's neck, and placed the head of the snake against his face. I pressed the pause button again, and held my hand on Peter's shoulder. He was trembling, but his eyes were wide, staring at the image on the screen.

"That is you, Peter," I said. "That boy is you . . . when you were twelve years old. You know that, don't you?"

Peter merely nodded, and took a quick, heaving breath.

"Do you think anyone would have reacted differently to that horrifying experience?" I asked. "What you did then . . . what you're doing right now . . . is natural, Peter. It's natural fright over a fearful situation."

"It shall not hurt them . . . " he mumbled.

"Not physically," I said. "But this did hurt you emotionally, Peter," I said. "The serpents in your dream, Peter! Surely you can see that. This explains that aspect of your dream!"

"The snakes will not hurt me," he continued to mumble, holding his eyes steadily on the image before him.

His response was not what I had anticipated. I pressed the resume button again, the video continued, with Watkins continuing to speak, and incite the crowd.

"Who of you shall be saved?" called Watkins. "Come forth and speak in the Spirit to prove that you are true believers." And as the choir began singing, the people stepped into the aisle, and onto the stage, and joined Watkins. And they closed their eyes, laid their heads back, and began to utter the strange, incoherent syllables.

"No . . . " Peter now turned away again, and his head began to jerk from side to side.

I quickly pressed the pause button. "What is it, Peter?"

He merely shook his head in response.

I glanced up at the television screen, and saw the somewhat blurred image of the half dozen or so people, their heads thrown back, their mouths opened in irrational speech. I resumed the video, and a few bizarre syllables became audible.

Peter reacted with more violent trembling. "The snakes will not hurt me," he repeated, more loudly this time.

The snakes were clearly a disturbing aspect in his unconscious, but they were not the overpowering one. I halted the video, and Peter sighed in relief. I suddenly realized what it was that was setting him off. Quickly, I pressed the rewind button, and a high-pitched squeal issued from the speakers as the images tumbled chaotically backward. I stopped it as the figure of Watkins, his hands held high above his head, appeared on the screen. And then I resumed the video, and listened to Watkins' pleading voice.

"Vasta loito. Rakiri memto, staltror, tantal, vasaito, laporto . . . "

"No!" Peter screamed, and thrust his body forward, but I restrained him.

" . . . Mostoro kantolo, beloro hordo lasisai. Do marta, lebntentantala!" continued Watkins.

I stopped the video again. Peter was perspiring profusely, and tears streamed from his eyes.

"Peter . . . " I placed my hand again on his trembling shoulder. "Peter . . . tell me about this."

Peter's eyes didn't move, but he began stammering in a forced voice. "Who of you shall be saved? Come forth and speak in the Spirit to prove that you are true believers. Who of you shall be saved . . . who of you shall be saved . . . "

"Is that it, Peter?" I asked. "Your father's speaking in tongues? Is that what bothers you?"

"Not for them that can . . . " he replied. "Not for them that will be saved."

"Who, then?" I asked.

"Satan!" he cried suddenly. "He is not in the spirit. And the serpents . . . Man shall have dominion over them. For they cannot speak in the Spirit. For their tongues shall be torn out and they shall grovel like slime upon the ground!"

"Peter . . . "

"And those of you who cannot speak in the Spirit will grovel with the serpents . . . and your tongues will be ripped from your mouths . . . and you will slip with them into the eternal fire . . . the everlasting fire . . . "

This was surely the source of the image in his dream, but I didn't understand the meaning of it. I placed both hands on his shoulders and shook him. "Peter . . . Peter! What does that have to do with you?"

He looked up at me, and his eyes were filled with fear. "I cannot . . . I cannot!" he cried. "I cannot speak in the Spirit!" He burst into tears and slumped into the couch.

A sudden rush of relief passed through my body. This was so obvious . . . and yet so obscure! And it would surely be easy to deal with. "Peter . . . Peter, listen to me . . . Your father . . . What do you think of your father?"

"He fixes things," he said. "People need healing and he fixes them so they can have the Spirit . . . but he can't heal everyone . . . "

"Peter . . . Your father was wrong," I said.

"No . . . " He began shaking his head again.

That was not going to work. I had to pull the issue away from his highly charged emotional attachment to his father. I remembered attending a seminar on speaking in tongues several years ago. *Glossolalia* was the scientific term for it. I struggled to recall some of the significant facts.

"Listen, Peter," I began. "This . . . this *speaking in the Spirit* as you call it . . . I learned something of that in my studies."

Peter did not respond, but his head became still.

"It's known as *glossolalia*," I said casually. I thought the use of this scientific term would help to defuse his emotional response.

Peter nodded slowly without looking at me.

"And here's another interesting fact," I continued. "A number of psychiatrists have studied people who engage in this practice. And several of them made an interesting discovery that, I believe, relates to you." I paused purposely, attempting to elicit an evocative response.

"What . . . " he said absently.

"They discovered that skill in glossolalia, and the ability to be hypnotized are closely linked," I said with deliberate emphasis.

Peter's eyes narrowed, and he sat forward slightly.

"They found," I continued "that people who could not be hypnotized . . . could also not speak in tongues."

He began shaking his head slowly.

"That's the absolute truth, Peter," I said. "I can show you the references. That's exactly your situation, isn't it? You said that Dr. Butler tried, several times, to hypnotize you. And he never succeeded. I think it's clear now that the reason for that is . . . you simply don't have the required psychological makeup to allow that type of . . . well . . . experience."

Peter closed his eyes hard and pressed a few remaining tears from them. Then he wiped the sleeve of his shirt across his face and sat straight up. He opened his eyes, and resumed his calm, detached posture.

"Do you understand what that means, Peter?" I asked him.

"Of course," he said quietly. "I always knew that, of course. I know that some members of my congregation continue to practice it. I allow it . . . as a courtesy to them. Belief in the gifts of the Spirit, like the belief in God, is an illusion, naturally. But I must allow my followers to nurture this false belief for the time being, because they haven't arrived yet at my elevated state of awareness."

His last statement made me think that Peter had internalized my suggestion that he had indeed developed a spiritual sense to compensate for his loss of belief in God, but I couldn't be sure. "This *elevated state of awareness*, Peter," I probed. "Is this the spiritual sense that we talked about before?"

"Spiritual . . . " He frowned slightly. "That's a broad term. It implies moral correctness, doesn't it? And, of course, people must be good and bad for there to be moral correctness, mustn't they? Good and bad . . . good and bad . . . That's why Christ must remain only a symbol. He has that flaw in his character, you see . . . the absence of evil." He jerked his head abruptly toward me. "But then I told you that before, didn't I?"

"That's all right, Peter," I said eagerly. "Tell me again."

"Well, his character is flawed by the absence of evil," he repeated. "I presume that is because he had no father."

"What do you mean?" I asked.

"He had no father . . . Christ had no father . . . " he mumbled. "Christ was the son of God . . . and God does not exist . . . my doctor told me . . . " He paused for a moment raised an eyebrow toward me. "So Christ has no father."

"Your doctor told . . . " I began to challenge this direction in his logic, but then I decided that I had a much better opportunity to lead from his introduction into the crux of his problem. "Do you think that people without fathers are flawed by the absence of evil?" I asked.

"Only Christ figures," he responded without hesitating.

"Why is that?" I asked.

"No model," he said. "They have no model."

"Did you not have a model, Peter?" I asked cautiously. "Your father . . . "

"My father is a mechanic," he said quickly.

"No, Peter," I followed immediately. "Your father was an evangelist. And your father is dead."

Peter closed his eyes momentarily and sighed deeply.

"Your father is dead, Peter," I repeated slowly.

He opened his eyes again and shrugged. "But of course, everyone dies, don't they? That's another flaw."

"What do you think about your father's death, Peter?" I asked.

Peter pursed his lips and emitted a low moan, and then he turned his head away from me.

"How did your father die, Peter?" I asked.

"Hmm?"

"How did your father die?" I repeated.

"My mother killed him," he said slowly.

I had to thrust my fist into the pit of my stomach to prevent my excitement from revealing itself. I felt that I was so close to the cause of his psychosis! I had to choose my questions very carefully.

"Your mother killed him . . ." I repeated casually.

"Yes."

"But you told me that your mother was dead," I said.

"Soul-dead," he said quickly. "My mother is soul-dead. She was dealt with."

"Dealt with . . . "

"My father was a mechanic. He fixed things," Peter said deliberately. "Don't you think the person who killed my father should be dealt with?"

I paused for a moment before proceeding, and then chose my words carefully. "Was your father flawed?" I asked.

"My father fixed things," he said.

"Then your father did not have the flaw that Christ had?"

"Hmm?"

"Your father had the capability of good and evil," I suggested.

Peter got a strange, strained expression on his face. "I didn't say that."

"But he wasn't flawed, Peter," I pressed quickly. "He could make mistakes. He *did* make mistakes. He was at fault."

"No . . . no! You don't understand," he said. He turned away from me.

"But I do!" I had to continue him in this direction . . . no matter what the cost. "I do, Peter," I said emphatically. "You think I don't have a father?"

"You're a doctor," he said.

"I have a father, Peter," I said. "And I always thought my father could fix things, too . . . " Fix things, too . . . fix things, too . . . I sat back for a moment, as the words reverberated past my conscious recollection, and drifted away into some long forgotten memory. "But I discovered that this wasn't always the case. He wasn't flawed, either."

Peter was staring at me with a look that combined disbelief and eager pleading for clarification.

"And I'm not flawed, either, Peter," I said, struggling to continue the metaphor. "I am frequently at fault . . . as a father, I mean. I have a daughter . . . and many times, I fail her . . . fail to respond to her needs . . . "

Peter sat forward abruptly and placed his hands on my knees, and I knew immediately that I had gone too far.

"How do you feel about your father, doctor?" he asked.

"No, Peter . . . That's not what . . . "

"And how does your daughter feel about her father . . . and about her father's father . . . " He leaned close, and his eyes locked fiercely onto mine. "Every good father must be flawed . . . else the father's fathers will be lost for the lack of their fathers . . . "

"Peter . . ."

"What does your daughter think about her father, doctor?" he asked passionately. "Does she love his flawlessness . . . Does she lust after it?"

Peter's words were loud and sharp, and the nearness of his eyes forced the image into a blur of color . . . and for a moment they looked like a giant whirlpool, swirling in the midst of on undefined ocean . . . And Lloyd rode up on his giant white horse, and plucked them from the offending flawlessness, and the rode off laughing . . . and their laughter joined the laughter of my father, and my father's father . . . and my father's father's father . . . .

"No!" I pushed myself back and shook my head violently. "I renounce you . . . I renounce you!"

I heard a silly giggle, and I looked up to see a clearing vision of Peter's smiling face.

"Doctor . . . doctor . . . doctor . . . " he mocked.

I ripped Peter's hands from my knees and pushed him back into the couch. "Your father, Peter . . . "

"My father is a mechanic," he said, still smiling.

"Your father was killed in an automobile accident in the company of a prostitute!" I shouted. "Acknowledge!"

"Words . . . words . . . words . . . "

"Acknowledge!" I repeated, and I shook him sternly to grasp his attention.

"Prostitute . . . " The smile disappeared from Peter's face, and he slumped back into the couch. "It doesn't matter . . . Someone must be dealt with."

He was silent. I took a deep breath, and glanced about the room to assure myself that my vision had completely cleared. Peter was compliant again. Nothing more would be served by our continuing today. We had accomplished a great deal.

"Peter . . . " I said softly.

"Yes?"

"That's all for today," I told him. "You may go now."

"Of course." He rose slowly from the couch, and headed toward the door.

"Try to give some thought to our session tonight, Peter," I said.

"There are so many thoughts," he mumbled. "Which thoughts would you like me to give some thought to?"

"About your parents," I told him.

"My father fixes things . . . and my mother is dead." He opened the door to leave, and then turned back. "Soul-dead . . . " His voice trailed off, and he left the room, closing the door behind him.

I leaned back and heaved a sigh of relief. Then I made a gross beckoning gesture toward the adjacent room, and crossed to the chair behind my desk and sat.

The door to the observation room opened, and Leonard appeared. His head was moving slowly back and forth, and his complexion was ashen. I pointed to the chair across from me, and he walked over slowly and sat.

"Do all your sessions go like this?" he asked with a sly grin.

"I never know . . . from day to day," I said with an air of fatigue.

"Well . . . Where shall I begin?" he asked.

"Whatever strikes your fancy," I told him.

Leonard sat back, glanced toward the ceiling for a moment, and then dropped his eyes slowly toward me. "I'm sure you know that a potentially damaging counter-transference has taken place," he said.

"I know . . . I know."

"And, of course, your reference to your own father . . . your own daughter . . . " He shook his head. "Well, that just leads to inappropriate personal involvement with your patient."

"I'm always aware of that, Leonard, even before it occurs," I admitted. "And yet it always seems to open up new avenues . . . new exposures."

"But are they his exposures . . . or yours?" he asked.

I merely shook my head.

"And, then . . . " He tossed his hands to the side. "You may think this is merely mechanical."

"Go ahead," I urged him.

"Letting him sit facing you during the therapy," he explained. "That just encourages his parallel participation . . . makes it much easier for him to grasp control . . . like he did for a moment today."

"Yes."

"And I'm sure you don't want that to happen again," he said.

"No. Of course not," I agreed. But that wasn't the truth. That was the problem with this abortive relationship. I *did* want it to happen again. Not rationally . . . almost not consciously. But that was the action that created the instant of excitement -- the brief departure into the realm of psychosis. And no matter how great was my intellectual rejection of the counsel that I had received from Bernadette . . . I knew that she was right about me in this respect.

"I think you should shift Peter to another therapist for a while," said Leonard. "You've made a great deal of headway, but it looks as though the closeness of it all has reached a point of counterproductivity."

"Perhaps . . . "

"I'd take him myself," he continued, "but I don't think he'd respond to my therapy now that he's had the rich Jungian style!" He laughed, and then he became somber as he continued. "Seriously, John . . . You're walking a tightrope here. I detected a definite potential for danger -- both to you and to Peter. You really should consider a shift . . . temporarily, at least."

"I'm sure you're right, Leonard," I said. "I'll give it some thought."

"I hope you don't think I'm being presumptuous," he said apologetically. "I'm sure that your aware of everything that I've told you."

I put my hand up and smiled. "Being aware of things that someone tells you does not mean that you shouldn't be told," I said.

"There you go with another brilliant observation!" He slapped his hand lightly on the desk and stood up. "Listen . . . I'd better get out of here and let you do some recapitulation work."

"Yeah . . . I guess I should," I agreed. "Thanks for your help."

"I enjoyed it, John. I really did." Leonard was at the door now, and he turned back with a sober expression on his face. "There's another suggestion that I'd make, John. We all need it from time to time. I think you should have some analysis yourself. I'd be glad to do that for you if . . . "

"We'll see," I said.

He smiled and nodded. Then he turned, and tapped his hand on the door knob. He turned back slowly, with a thoughtful look on his face. "You know . . . I told you that I didn't think Peter was a likely candidate for the prostitute murders."

"Yes."

"Well . . . " He glanced toward the now empty couch. "Now I'm not so sure . . . " He glanced back to me, shrugged, and left my office.

I agreed with everything that Leonard had said . . . even his ambivalence about Peter's capacity for extreme violence. If I were in his place, evaluating myself, I would have arrived at precisely the same conclusions. But I realized that my rational reactions were being driven by more powerful forces . . . and I wasn't sure that I could counteract them.

"Oh, John . . . "

I looked up to see Leonard's head in the slightly open door. "Hmm?"

"Cheryl asked me to tell you that your brother is on the phone," he said smiling. Then he leaned in farther and threw me a cupped whisper. "I tell you, John . . . She's charming!" He laughed and backed out, closing the door before him.

I reached over and picked up the receiver. "Lloyd?"

"Hi, John. Hope you're not busy."

"No. Just finished for the day," I said. "What can I do for you?"

"Well . . . " There was an unusually long pause. "I'm sure you know that Meg's talked to me and Kate."

"She and Diane went to church with you last week," I said.

"Yes. And . . . well . . . Meg is worried about you, John."

"Look, Lloyd . . . "

"I know, I shouldn't be butting my nose in," he said. "But you're my brother, John, and . . . well . . . I guess I claim prerogative."

I sighed. "Go ahead. This has been my day for it."

Lloyd paused again, and then continued. "I really would like to speak with you. And I thought, since we all had such a good time last week . . . maybe you'd like to come with us this Sunday night. As it turns out, I'm having guest speaker -- a Christian counselor. I thought you might find that interesting."

Sunday night. At this point the only thing I wanted to do on Sunday was go to the temple again . . . find out what effect today's session had on Peter's public behavior. And yet Lloyd's call was so opportune. I had to grasp whatever pole star I could find in the next weeks of my dealing with Peter. Lloyd could help me evaluate . . . help me learn about Peter's spirituality . . . or his rejection of it.

"What do you say, John?" he asked.

"Actually, Lloyd, I could use your help," I said.

"Anything," he said impetuously.

"Well, instead of my going to your church Sunday night . . . will you come with me to Peter Lumen's temple?" I asked. "I could really use your advise."

He was silent for a long moment again. "Well, I'll tell you, John, I hate to invite a guest speaker and then run out on him."

"I understand," I said.

"But, hey! What are brothers for? Sure. What time?"

"I'll pick you up about six-thirty," I said.

"All right. See you then," he said, and hung up.

"Bye . . . " I said aimlessly, after the connection had been broken. I placed the receiver back in its cradle.

The door swung open a crack, and Cheryl poked her head inside. "Dr. Summers . . ."

"Yes, what is it, Cheryl?"

"It's not quite five yet," she said. "But I have an appointment with a lady barber. I wondered if I could . . . "

"Of course, Cheryl," I said. "Go on . . . "

She beamed. "Thanks!" She backed out quickly and closed the door.

"Lady barber . . . " I mumbled. Then I began to giggle uncontrollably. Leonard was right. She was charming.

20

Lloyd and I arrived at the temple at a little before seven Sunday night, and it looked as though we should have gotten there an hour earlier. The auditorium was completely packed, and people were standing in the lobby, peering over others' shoulders through the broad doorways.

"Sorry," I told Lloyd. "It's been crowded before, but nothing like this."

"The power of television!" said Lloyd. "I knew that his healing services always drew thousands. I should have suggested we come earlier."

"Have you been to his services before?" I asked.

"No, I never have," he said. "I've seen him on the tube a couple of times. But this . . . " He gestured toward the expanse of the temple. "The broadcast doesn't do it justice. It's unbelievable!"

"Pastor Summers!"

Both Lloyd and I turned in the direction of the calling female voice. It was Julie, stepping around people, and heading toward us with a broad smile on her face.

"Pastor Summers!" she repeated, and walked directly to Lloyd. "Hi! What are you doing here tonight?" She grasped his hand warmly and squeezed it.

"Well . . . Julie!" said Lloyd with a shocked look on his face. "Julie Peters! This is a real surprise."

"Yeah . . . " she mumbled.

"John, Julie used to go to my church," said Lloyd. "Her parents still do."

"Really?" I said.

"Julie, this is my brother, John Summers," said Lloyd, introducing us.

"Julie took my hand and tilted her head slightly. "We've met, haven't we?" she asked.

"Well, I spoke with you at the sales counter four weeks ago," I said.

"Sure, but . . . "

"And I've been here a couple of times since," I added.

She snapped her fingers. "I know! I saw you with Brother Greg and Brother Kyle," she said.

"Probably," I said.

"Sure! You're . . . " She looked as though she had made a forbidden recognition. "Oh, sure. You're Dr. Summers." She swallowed visibly and raised and lowered her eyebrows. "I don't know why I didn't make the connection. You two look alike . . . kind of . . . "

"I have more hair," I joked.

"Give yourself a little time," returned Lloyd.

"Listen, do you two have a place to sit?" asked Julie.

"Right here," said Lloyd.

"No! Look, I have places saved for when I meet people," said Julie. "Why don't you come and sit with me."

"Sounds great!" said Lloyd.

"Good! Come on!" she responded.

Julie smilingly excused herself to the crowd of people standing at the doorway, and led us through. We followed her briskly to the side aisle, and all the way to the front of the auditorium.

"She seemed a little embarrassed to see you, John," said Lloyd.

"She probably doesn't want me to know that she's aware of Peter's therapy," I said. "*Brother* Greg and *Brother* Kyle haven't been too charitable about the situation," I added sarcastically.

"I see," he said knowingly.

Julie directed us to a spot in the front row near the center. She moved between us, and we sat just as the choir began singing the now familiar chorus to *Light on the Rock*.

The lead-up ceremony with Hatcher and Wingate was even more passionate than it had been in the morning services that I'd witnessed. The choir punctuated their rousing claims of successful salvations and healings, and the audience joyously joined them in song and praise. I was surprised to see that even Lloyd seemed taken up by the service, and he was participating willingly in their emotional response. Then the colored beams of light fell on the mountain, and Peter emerged and exhorted the congregation in the threefold responsive chant of Cry . . . Salvation!

"We're here for healing tonight!" called Peter, in a high, forceful voice.

The crowd responded with calls of "Amen! . . . Hallelujah!"

"We're here to praise this town and praise the people in it!" he continued. "Do you believe me?"

"We believe you . . . Praise the Lord!" responded a few in the crowd.

This exchange sounded strangely familiar to me. Then I remembered that it was almost identical to the lead-in that Jason Watkins had used on the video of the tent revival service.

"And I know you're here because you believe that I was called by the messenger of God to heal you," continued Peter. "And you're right! But you first must realize that you also are living stones. He said, you must be perfect as I am perfect."

I noticed that Lloyd had taken a small pad from his pocket, and was jotting down hurried notes as he watched Peter.

"But you can't be perfect if you are filled with imperfections," said Peter. "You also have been chosen as selected vessels. The Lord said, 'You are gods, and all of you are children of the most High.' So you must cleanse yourself of your imperfections. And you can do that by recognizing that you are perfect, even as your Father in Heaven is perfect. Do you believe that?"

"We believe!" cried a few in the congregation.

Peter placed his hand to his ear, and repeated, "Do you believe that?"

"We believe!" shouted a larger number.

Peter thrust forth both clenched fists. "Do you believe that?" he cried.

"We Believe!" responded the congregation in a tumultuous, reverberating voice.

The crowd then suddenly became deathly silent, and Peter began to deliver his message. This one followed his usual line. He exhorted the people to recognize the hidden power within them, and revel in it. But this time, he spoke even more glowingly about the divinity within each person, and the need to express that divinity. "You don't have a God living in you . . . you *are* one!" he claimed. Then he emotionally implored them to realize that God wanted them to be gods . . . that he wanted them to be exact duplicates of Him. The congregation responded silently, but emotionally to his words, and they swayed and nodded in agreement with his exhortations. But all was directed toward their need to cleanse themselves of the imperfections within them -- those aspects of their minds and bodies that are not godlike. Then, at the climax of his message, his words again sounded vaguely familiar.

"The Lord knows how to deliver the godly, and to reserve the unjust unto the day of judgment!" he shouted. "He knows those who walk after the flesh in imperfection. People who think evil of themselves, because they understand not, will perish in their own corruption! All you with eyes turned away from your own divinity cannot cease from the sin of self-denial. You are cursed children. You have forsaken the right way. You have gone astray, following the way of Balaam!"

"Amen! . . . Save us from the sin of self-denial!" cried the people.

I realized what it was now. His words were a paraphrase of Watkins' passionate plea. And the response of the crowd was also similar. But the elements of the message seemed so different.

"I can save you if you will save yourselves?" cried Peter. "Are you ready?"

"Yes!" responded the crowd.

"Are you ready?" he repeated fervently.

"Yes . . . yes! . . . yes!" replied the people.

Peter raised his arms, and the people became suddenly silent. Then soft music began to play, and Peter turned and walked toward the waterfall. He sat on a flat, chair-height rock near the water, and bowed his head. The lights in the auditorium dimmed, and extinguished, leaving the stage in a soft, shimmering glow.

"Excuse me," whispered Julie.

"Hmm?" asked Lloyd, leaning toward her.

"I have to go up for a few minutes," she said. "I'll be back."

"Oh. Okay," he whispered.

Julie stood quietly and walked toward the center stairs leading to the stage. She picked up a cordless microphone from a stand, and stepped noiselessly up the stairs. Then she walked back toward the waterfall, and stood across from Peter.

Peter looked up at her momentarily, and then he spoke softly but firmly without moving, over the softly rising strains of music. "Look into your hearts," he said. "Look into your memories. Find your hidden wounds. Seek . . . seek them out . . . seek them out . . . " He lowered his head again.

The music raised and paused in introduction, and Julie raised the microphone and began to sing in low, plaintive tones.

Whenever I'm afraid,
Whenever I'm alone,
I think about His saving grace,
And all the love He's shown.
Whenever I have doubts,
I fall upon my knees,
And pray that He will show the way
To heal my memories.

Heal me! Let me feel Your hand.
Gently lead me to the River Jordan,
Where the sacred waters flow
Across the land.

Heal me! Wash away my sin.
Let me witness all your cleansing power.
If I follow you,
My life will just begin.

But sometimes I am still afraid.
Life is hollow. It's so hard to follow.
Sometimes all that I can see
Is an empty life for me.

Heal me! Take away my fears.
Let me know that I can live completely,
In a life with no more pain,
And no more tears.

The music faded subtly as Julie walked quietly back to the front of the stage, stepped down the stairs, and replaced the microphone. The final melancholy notes were played as she sat between us again.

"That was beautiful, Julie!" whispered Lloyd.

Julie just smiled faintly, and lowered her head.

"Let me take away your pain!" cried Peter, who was still seated on the rock by the waterfall. "Let me take away your tears!" He raised his arm and beckoned slowly toward the congregation. "They offend you!" he continued. "Let me tear them out!"

A line of a dozen or so people had already formed at the center stairs, and as Peter concluded his invitation, the first person mounted the stage and walked quickly to him. It was woman who appeared to be in her seventies. She knelt and bowed her head before him.

"What is your illness?" asked Peter.

"I just need to recommit myself to the healing waters," she said with a raspy voice. "You healed my arthritis last year . . . but every now and again, I need to exercise more faith. I pray for more faith!"

Peter placed his hand slowly under the stream of falling water. Then he brought a handful of it out and cast it over the woman's head. "Your faith will sustain you!" he said.

"Yes . . . " The woman nodded. Then she stood and started walking toward the side stairs. "Yes," she continued. "I can feel it . . . I can feel it!"

Another woman had now reached Peter's side. She was younger -- perhaps forty. And as she knelt, she held her head up with a pleading look, and placed her hand on his knee.

"Your soul is in pain," said Peter. "I know it."

"Yes . . . It's this hatred," said the woman. "I have this terrible hatred for my parents. It's destroying me!"

"Your divinity must not be marred by bitterness," said Peter, reaching for another handful of water. "Renounce it!" he said, placing his hand and the water on the woman's head. "Cast your hatred into the deepest recesses of your hidden memories and renounce it!" He held her head in both his hands and smiled at her. "You are healed!"

The woman nodded and stood slowly. "Thank you! Thank you!" she murmured, and she walked away nodding and murmuring inaudibly.

A middle-aged man was now kneeling before him, his head bowed low. Peter placed both his hands on the man's head, raised his face, and closed his eyes.

"This man has a hidden wound!" he cried ardently.

"Yes . . . yes . . . " mumbled the man without looking up.

"Your soul can't tolerate it," said Peter. "Tear it out!"

"I am . . . " He raised his head toward Peter. "I am . . . an adulterer!"

A low gasp rose from the crowd. Peter merely smiled and nodded. Then he pressed his hands harder against the man's head, and shouted, "Praise God!"

"Praise God!" cried a few in the congregation in response, and then the call was echoed by many.

"Tell it! Tell it!" cried Peter. Then he looked into the congregation. "Is your wife here to accept you after your cleansing?"

"My wife is not a follower," said the man.

Many in the congregation uttered murmurs of disappointment.

"But you are, and you have come to cleanse your memory!" said Peter.

"Yes. But it happened so many times . . . and with so many wicked women!" wept the man.

Peter reached under the falls with both hands, filled them, and poured the water over the man's head. "There are many hidden faults," he said. "Yours is cleansed by your action. The fault is no longer yours." He pressed his hands against the man's head again, and addressed the congregation. "There are many hidden faults driving this man. Others are to blame for his fall." He thrust his pointed finger toward the crowd. "Who among you would cast the first stone?"

Murmurs of negation rose from the congregation.

"Others are to blame here," said Peter. "This man is forgiven . . . but those who drove him to sin will be dealt with!"

The man took Peter's hands in his and kissed them. Then he turned and stumbled toward the stairs.

I glanced over toward Lloyd. He was frowning, and his head was moving slowly from side to side. Julie was intent upon the service, and tears filled her eyes.

The line had grown to about twenty, and Peter dealt with each person who came forward in the same way -- questioning, cleansing, forgiving, and dismissing. Through it all, the congregation was silent, but tearful and supportive responses were commonly expressed.

Finally, the last person walked off the stage. Peter rose slowly from the rock and walked to the front center portion of the stage. As the lights in the auditorium began to come on, he raised one arm to the side and shouted, "Cry!"

"Salvation!" responded the crowd with a deafening roar.

The light in the auditorium was now about half-full as Peter raised the other arm to the side, and shouted again, "Cry!"

"Salvation!" answered the crowd, even more loudly.

Then the lights in the auditorium shone brilliantly, and Peter reached both arms forward, and gazed intensely into the front row and called emotionally, "Cry!"

"Salvation!" returned the congregation, with a tumultuous, lingering sound.

Peter did not lower his arms, and his eyes remained fixed -- directly on us. The music commenced, and the choir began singing the chorus of *Light on the Rock*, but Peter did not move. I had the feeling that his unblinking eyes were riveted to mine. I felt perspiration bead on my forehead, and I tried to blink, but I was unable to. The image was precisely the same as the one I had pressed the pause button on . . . Jason Watkins . . . his lanky frame leaning threateningly toward the camera, and his fierce eyes scanning the crowd. But the snakes were no longer in the box. There were dozens of them, and they crawled about his body, and cast themselves into bizarre tangled patterns about his head. And now the image became one of Medusa . . . and her eyes still pierced my consciousness as she petrified me with her deadly gaze . . . And the circling colored lights fell heavily on the rocky mountain and the water spewed forth on the unhealed multitudes . . .

"Light on the rock . . . light on the rock . . . " The words fell vaguely past the accompanying instruments.

"John . . John . . . " It was Lloyd's voice . . . or Peter's . . .

I forced my eyes shut, and then let them open again. Peter had turned away, and was just now slipping between the crack in the rock.

"Rock, rock, Give us . . . Light!" The music exploded from the speakers in the final chords as the choir concluded the song.

"Well, what do you think?" It was Julie. Her voice faded slowly into my conscious perception.

"Hmm?" I breathed deeply, and wiped the perspiration from my forehead.

"Did you like the service?" she asked.

"Oh . . . yes. Yes," I mumbled.

"It was really nice of you to let us sit with you," said Lloyd.

"Oh, sure!" she said.

Wingate reappeared on the stage, squinted in our direction, and then hurried down the stairs. "I thought I saw you out here, Lloyd!" He took Lloyd's hand and shook it warmly.

"Hello, Kyle," said Lloyd.

Wingate then took my hand and looked first at Lloyd and then at me. "So . . . I never put this together. But you must be brothers."

"I'm afraid so," laughed Lloyd.

"Well, Doctor," said Wingate with a raised eyebrow. "I see you've been doing a little evangelizing yourself!"

"Whoa!" Lloyd raised his arms in protest. "Just visiting, Kyle!"

They both laughed, and Julie joined them.

Wingate grasped Julie's arm warmly. "I never did apologize for our having stolen Julie away from you, did I?"

"Nope."

"I guess I never did explain, either, Pastor Summers," said Julie hesitantly. "I mean, I ever told you why I started coming here."

"Oh, that's all right, Julie," said Lloyd. "That's your decision. But, yes, I guess I would like to know why, now that you mention it." He laughed lightly.

"Well, I really liked you, and everything," she said. "It's just that the services here were . . . well . I don't know . . . more spiritual."

Lloyd shook his head. "Well, I will admit . . . they have a lot more pizzazz!"

Julie suddenly looked embarrassed. "I hope I didn't hurt your feelings."

"No, absolutely not," said Lloyd emphatically. "No, listen, there's a lot I can learn from the charismatics. We need to compete with so much nowadays . . . with television and all. You're right. I need to evaluate my services."

"Well . . . " Julie grimaced slightly and shrugged.

"But the really important thing is what you believe, Julie," said Lloyd. "I hope you never lose that."

"Oh, no!" she said enthusiastically. "God seems so much more important to me now. Peter says that happens when you finally realize that He's just a natural part of you, and that when you love yourself, you love God."

"Well . . . " Lloyd glanced toward Wingate.

"Listen . . . I have to get back to the sales counter," said Julie abruptly. "You should come back and buy a tape of the service, Pastor Summers. Maybe that would give you some ideas."

"Yes. I think I'll do that," said Lloyd softly.

"Well . . . " Julie smiled and waved. "See you later!" She bounced off.

"That's not part of our doctrine, you know," said Wingate slowly as Julie left.

"Hmm?" asked Lloyd, turning toward him.

"' . . . When you love yourself, you love God,'" said Wingate.

"I hope not," said Lloyd with a half smile.

"It's just Peter's exuberance, you know. He wants people to feel good about themselves in their faith."

"That's important," said Lloyd.

"And pertinent," said Wingate with a smile. "Well . . . listen . . . I have to meet with some new members." He patted Lloyd on the arm. "Come again!"

"I will," said Lloyd.

Wingate gave my hand a quick shake. "Dr. Summers . . . " he turned and hurried out of the auditorium.

We had driven for nearly a mile, and Lloyd still hadn't spoken, so I decided that I'd better try to elicit some kind of response from him.

"Well . . . what do you think?" I asked.

"Hmm?"

I snapped my fingers several times. "Are you awake?" I asked.

"Oh . . . " He shook his head, and shifted toward me. "Yeah . . . sorry, John. I was just thinking."

"I don't know what you thought of the service," I said. "But I noticed you were really getting into it there at times."

"You're right," he said. "The vibrance of the presentation is very appealing. Julie's comment really helped me tonight. I do need to work on my services."

"Then what is it that you object to?" I asked. "Do you think the people are all off base, or . . . "

"Oh, no!" he replied. "No, I suspect the majority of the people in the congregation are sincere, believing Christians."

"Then what's wrong with . . . "

"It's the messenger," said Lloyd. "And his message."

"Explain," I said.

"Well . . . " Lloyd chuckled. "I couldn't believe his reference to Balaam."

"'You have gone astray, following the way of Balaam!'" I quoted.

"Yeah."

"His father used the same quote," I said. "I heard it on a video."

"The tent evangelist?" he asked.

"Yes."

"Sure. But he quoted the scripture correctly, I'll bet," he said.

"And Peter didn't?" I asked.

Lloyd shook his head. "And that's what makes it so ironic. Peter is, himself, following the way of Balaam!"

"Explain," I said again, motioning with a circling hand.

"Well, Balaam was a diviner, a priest, who was hired by Balak, the king of Moab to place a curse on the Israelites. The thing is, he tried three times, and God kept turning the curse into a blessing instead. I guess I see a relationship here. A lot of people at Light on the Rock are receiving a blessing, despite . . . "

"Despite Peter's curse?" I asked.

"Well, you see, Balaam finally realized that all he'd have to do is seduce the Israelites into idolatry . . . and they would *bring themselves* under God's curse."

"And you think Peter is seducing the people into idolatry?" I asked.

"Definitely," said Lloyd. "The whole approach to self-divinity . . . the God within . . . the Christ consciousness . . . That's all idolatry. It's worshipping other gods." He nodded adamantly. "Definitely. The way of Balaam is seeking only to make a market of his gift. And that is exactly how I see Peter Lumen."

"But Wingate said that was just his exuberance," I said.

"Kyle has to defend Peter," said Lloyd. "But I'm sure if he really thought about it, he'd agree with me."

Lloyd was right. Wingate had clearly expressed this concern about Peter's presentation when I met with him and Hatcher.

"And he would surely agree that Peter was improperly quoting scripture," continued Lloyd. He reached into his pocket and pulled out the tape of the service that he had purchased. He slipped it into my car's casette player, and the low music was replaced by nearly inaudible sounds from the service. He pushed the fast-forward button several times, and the normal narrative was periodically interrupted by a high squealing noise.

"Ah . . . Here it is," he said. "Listen."

He turned up the volume, and Peter's voice from the service issued from the speakers. "The Lord know how to deliver the godly, and to reserve the unjust unto the day of judgment!" he shouted. "He knows those who walk after the flesh in imperfection. People who think evil of themselves because they understand not will perish in their own corruption! All you with eyes turned away from your own divinity cannot cease from the sin of self-denial. You are cursed children. You have forsaken the right way. You have gone astray, following the way of Balaam!"

Lloyd stopped the tape. "Imperfection? People who think evil of themselves? The sin of self-denial?" He laughed and shook his head. "Absolutely not! That's a perversion of scripture."

"Hmm . . . "

"Here, let's hear it again . . . " He rewound the tape slightly, and the squealing noise reappeared.

"No, that's all right," I said. "I get the idea."

He turned off the power, and the car became filled with a welcome silence.

A sudden perverse notion struck me, and I laughed.

"What's the matter?" asked Lloyd.

"Maybe Dad would like this church better than yours," I joked.

"No chance!" he said. "He's not a good Catholic, and he sure wouldn't be a good charismatic. No . . . Pop isn't spiritual enough for this kind of religion." He sat back in the corner of the seat, and crossed his arms in front of him. "But you didn't ask me to go to this service just to give me a new spiritual experience. You told me you needed my advice."

"Yes, your advice . . . " I had almost forgotten. After seeing Peter in this dynamic, collected role, it was difficult to reengage my analytic awareness of his problem. "Apart from his theology . . . tell me what you think of Peter Lumen's personality," I said.

"Well, it really comes to the same thing," he said. "The Peter Lumen at the Light on the Rock Ministry is a false front. I guess I'd have to say that, to me, he is the epitome of Balaam -- the prophet for hire. And to me that implies insincerity, and deception." He chuckled lightly. "I don't know who hired him, though."

"Maybe he hired himself," I mumbled.

"What?"

"Just . . . ah . . . nothing," I said.

Lloyd raised an eyebrow. "What a minute!" He sat forward. "Is Peter Lumen . . . both Balaam . . . *and* Balak?"

"Well . . . "

"He's schizophrenic, isn't he?" he asked with sudden intense interest.

I couldn't believe that Lloyd could have picked up on that from such an innocuous hint. I hated having my patient-client privilege placed in jeopardy again, but Lloyd's perception was uncanny. And as long as he had guessed it . . . I thought I may as well capitalize on it.

"I guess you'd rather not tell me," he said. "But it certainly makes sense."

"No . . . You're right, Lloyd," I said. "I must say, though, that I'm impressed by your diagnostic ability. I know some psychiatrists who would need thirty hours of therapy to arrive at the same conclusion."

"Well, I'm really not all that good," he said. "It's just that Peter's personality fits in so well with a theory that I did some work on while I was in seminary."

"What's that?" I asked.

"Well . . . the split between the true self and the false self . . . outer reality and inner seeking . . . It's all really so clear in the context of the spiritual search."

"How do you mean?" I asked.

Lloyd shifted in his seat. Then he clasped his hands tightly together. "All of us have many selves. Right?" he asked.

"Sure, but . . . "

"But God didn't intend for them to be floating out in some nebulous ethereal portion of space, searching for meaning," he said. "He meant for them all to be confined within his divine plan . . . working together . . . unified." He illustrated by raising his fingers from the closed fists and wiggling them.

"And . . . "

"And without God, there is no unifying purpose, and the selves drift out desperately in search of . . . nothing." He separated his fists and let his hands float outward, the fingers squirming aimlessly.

"Well, I don't know about that, Lloyd," I said. "That would mean that everyone who didn't believe in God would be schizophrenic.

"Only the seekers," said Lloyd pointedly. "Only the seekers."

Lloyd had made a very perceptive point. I knew that Jung definitely placed a significant link between schizophrenia and the spiritual search. I recalled my latest meeting with Bernadette, and her comment after I'd revealed Peter's loss of faith. The primal scream of disbelief, she had said . . . is he like Nietzsche, then . . . did he once believe . . . is he like Nietzsche . . .

"Nietzsche . . . " I mumbled inadvertently.

"Precisely!" said Lloyd.

"Hmm?"

"Nietzsche," he said. "He was a seeker. And once he'd rejected God, look what he was left with. Have you read his narrative of the madman?"

"Well . . . "

"The madman jumped into their midst and pierced them with his eyes," Lloyd began quoting from memory. "'Whither is God?' he cried; 'I will tell you. *We have killed him* -- you and I. All of us are his murderers. . . . God is dead. . . . How shall we comfort ourselves, the murderers of all murderers? . . . Who will wipe this blood off us? . . . Is not the greatness of this deed too great for us? Must we ourselves not become gods simply to appear worthy of it?'"

As Lloyd spoke, the piercing significance of Nietzsche's words turned in my stomach. I did recall this quotation. Bernadette had referred to it as an illustration of a prime existential response to absurdity. But in this context . . . in this place . . . at this moment . . .

"Only the seekers," repeated Lloyd. "There is no choice. If they reject God . . . they must themselves become God. And *that* is what Peter Lumen is trying to do . . . and what he is urging his followers toward." He sat back in the corner of the seat. "Anyway . . . that's my theory," he said. "I think it has merit, but, of course . . . " He laughed lightly. "Of course, I'm biased."

I squinted my eyes against the glare of oncoming headlights. The driver of the vehicle honked his horn as he passed, and the sound swooped downward as our two cars diverged.

"No, Lloyd," I muttered. "It does . . . " I wiped the perspiration from my forehead with my shirt-sleeve. "It does have merit. I never . . . I don't believe I ever thought of it quite that way."

"*Everyone* should be a seeker," he said intensely. "The answer becomes so clear then . . . so clear."

I didn't know quite what Lloyd meant by this last statement. The search for meaning was anything but clear. But I knew the tilt in his voice. I could tell that if I pursued the conversation at this point, it would turn into a discussion of the need for religious commitment. So I let it drop. He had made a brilliantly perceptive evaluation of Peter, though, and I knew that I could put that to good use in my analysis.

Lloyd shifted nervously in his seat. "You know . . . Diane is seeking," he said slowly. "And Meg is also."

The uncomfortable churning in my stomach commenced again. I would like to have gotten through this evening without reference to what a poor job I was doing with my family life, but this was going to be the lead-in to that.

"I don't know if Meg told you or not," continued Lloyd. "Kate and I are holding a little retreat in the mountains for the high school kids. We'll be leaving Monday night and coming back on Friday evening. Amy's going, of course, and so . . . we invited Diane to go with us."

"No," I said. "No, Meg didn't tell me."

"Well, we just arranged it this morning. And you were at the office," he said. "I guess she didn't get a chance."

"I guess not," I mumbled.

"Anyway . . . Diane seemed really enthusiastic about going," Lloyd continued. "It's going to be kind of like camping out, you know."

"Really?"

"Yes. And Amy's looking forward to spending some time with her."

"That's nice." But the churning merely increased. I was hit with the sudden reflective odor of a campfire, and the recollection of sitting by it with Lloyd when I was only eight, and his telling me how life was so . . . mysterious. And the sounds and smells lingered on my consciousness like an old shoe. But we were both boys. That's what made the difference. That's what Diane meant the other night when I talked to her . . . What do you think, Dad, she asked me . . . Do you sometimes wish I was a boy? . . . But she still wasn't a boy, and she was going, anyway. And Lloyd would be there . . .

"Anyway, I hope that's all right with you," said Lloyd.

"That'll be fine, Lloyd," was all that I could say. "That'll be fine."

21

It was about nine-thirty when I arrived home. I knew that Meg and Diane must be there, because the lights were on, but as I walked into the living room, I didn't see them. Then I heard talking and laughter coming from Diane's room. I went into the hallway and glanced through the open door. Two suitcases and some clothes were lying on Diane's bed, and she and Meg were standing before the open closet.

"Hello! Anybody Home?" I said, tapping on the door lightly.

Diane spun around and smiled. "Oh, hi, Dad!"

"Hello, John," said Meg, looking over her shoulder. "I'm glad you came right home tonight." She tossed another outfit onto the bed.

"Well . . . " I looked at the growing pile of clothes. "What are you two doing?" I asked.

"Getting Diane ready for her camping trip tomorrow," said Meg. Then she lowered a blouse that she was inspecting. "Did Lloyd tell you about it?" she asked.

"Yes."

"I would have told you, but you were at the office all day," she said.

"I know."

Meg nodded and returned to her task.

"I thought you and Diane went to the service with Kate tonight," I said.

"We did," said Meg. "We got back about an hour ago."

"Oh . . . "

"I wish you could have been there, Dad," said Diane excitedly. "This guy was really . . . what was his name, Mom?"

"Tad McIntyre," said Meg.

"Yeah. Anyway, he was really neat!" she exclaimed. "He's a counselor. Maybe you know him, Dad."

"No . . . "

"He's not a psychiatrist, Diane," said Meg. "He's a psychologist."

"What's the difference?" she asked.

"He's not a doctor," I explained.

"They called him *Dr. McIntyre*," she said.

"Well . . . I mean . . . he has a degree, but he's not a real doctor," I explained.

"Oh . . . " Meg frowned slightly, then she shrugged and shook her head. "I didn't think I'd enjoy it when Uncle Lloyd first told us about it. But he was good!"

"That's nice, Diane," I said vaguely.

"There were a lot of kids there, too," she continued. "And he really knew how to keep our attention. I mean . . . he was *funny*, you know. But he knew how to talk to us so we'd listen to what he was saying."

"Hmm . . . "

"And he had a lot of great ideas about how to help the family," she continued eagerly. "He's written a book, too. I thought maybe we could get it, and read it together."

"Well . . . maybe," I murmured. The churning in my stomach had ceased when I dropped Lloyd off, but now it was starting up again. I knew exactly what it was. This terrible feeling of inadequacy that arose whenever I heard of someone else succeeding in areas in which I had failed. I hated the feeling. And I hated even more the realization that I had a complete and accurate intellectual understanding of my emotions . . . and I still could do nothing about them.

"I think it's called *Today's Dynamic Family*," said Diane. "Have you heard about it?"

I shook my head. "I wrote a book once too, you know," I reminded her, somewhat pettishly.

"John . . . " Meg frowned at me and shook her head. Then she pulled another outfit from the closet and held it out toward Diane. "Maybe this one would be good to take, honey," she said. "I don't know how cold it's going to be."

"I don't know . . . " Diane sighed heavily. Then she turned to me. "What do you think, Dad?"

"Hmm?"

"You know about camping," she said. "What do you think I should take?"

"What do I think . . . " She asked me that last Sunday night, too. And her words still clung to my memory . . . What do you think, Dad? Do you sometimes wish I was a boy? And now she was going camping . . .

"What do you think, Dad?" Diane repeated.

"I don't know . . . " I was having difficulty collecting my thoughts. I wanted to respond . . . be . . . adequate . . . But I couldn't relate. "I don't know," I repeated. "Why don't you just call Lloyd, Meg. He knows about these things. Or, maybe . . . Dr. McIntyre!"

"John!" Meg scolded again.

"I don't know," I said again. I saw the disappointed expression on Diane's face, and I wanted to wipe it clean . . . replace it with . . . anything. But I couldn't. "I don't know," I mumbled again. I shrugged and walked out of the room.

The light from the bedroom cast my shadow onto the floor of the hall as I walked toward the living room. And then it gradually disappeared as the general lighting from the rest of the house met it, and absorbed it. I stopped, and walked backward a few steps, reestablishing the faint silhouette. And then I walked forward slowly, and watched as it disappeared again with each step . . . the head . . . shoulders . . . upper body . . . The image was so simple to create. And each semblance relied on the angle and intensity of the light source . . . and the position and will of the shaded body. But without the light, there was nothing. Or perhaps there was something . . . something that was invisible . . . a mysterious shadow cast forth by the light of the darkness . . . Jung's *lumen naturae*, the light of the darkness itself, which illuminates its own darkness -- a darkness which only his own internal darkness can comprehend. But the darkness was invisible. How can anything invisible have the power to comprehend? Peter Lumen . . . the light on the rock . . . But Lloyd thought his light was the darkness . . . a darkness with the power to deceive . . .

I felt a cold moisture pressing against the palm of my hand. I looked down and saw that I was holding a drink. My arms leaned on our bar, and the glass was there . . . but I hadn't gotten it! I hadn't mixed this drink. Or, at least, I didn't remember having mixed it. I reached out with my other hand and tested the arm that held the glass to assure myself that it was mine, and then I laughed giddily at the thought of what I was doing. Of course it was my arm! Of course I had mixed the drink. It was something I had done so often . . . why should I necessarily remember every detail . . . every . . . But I couldn't remember anything about the incident. Not the intention, the movement to the bar, getting the ingredients . . . nothing! The hand holding the drink tingled slightly, and I reached out the other hand again and pinched it, and a dull pulsation crept up my arm.

"John, what is the matter with you?"

"Hmm?" I looked up and saw Meg standing beside me.

"Couldn't you see that Diane was just trying to establish some kind of successful communication with you?" she asked. "Why did you turn her off?"

"I . . . I don't think I . . .

"And now *this*!" Meg pointed at the glass in my hand. "I would think that a chance to talk with your daughter would take precedence over having a drink. Especially on a Sunday night when you've just returned from a religious service!"

"This isn't a religious thing, Meg," I said. "This is . . . this is . . . " I struggled against the desire to tell her that I hadn't even been aware that I had made the drink . . . tell her that I couldn't be held responsible for everything . . . not for everything. But I realized that would be wrong. That would be a sign of weakness. This was a fluke. It wouldn't happen again. I had to be strong. I had to be responsible. "This is just a drink," I said finally, and I raised the glass to my lips, and took a sip of the pungent liquid.

Meg sighed deeply, and tears suddenly formed in her eyes. "Please, John! Tell me what's happening to you. What's happening to us? We just can't talk about anything anymore!"

"I've just . . . I've just been so busy," I mumbled.

"No. It's more than that, John," she said. "That's why I wanted you to talk with Lloyd. That's why I thought . . . tonight . . . " She wiped the back of her hand across her eyes. "What did you and Lloyd talk about tonight?" she asked. "Can you tell me?"

"Seekers . . . " I mumbled absently.

"What?"

"Oh . . . seekers," I repeated. "The spiritual search . . . You know."

"Well . . . " She smiled slightly and nodded. "That's good, John. What did you discuss about the spiritual search?"

This was the wrong configuration again. Meg was asking the questions . . . and I wasn't even in my office. This wasn't a family issue. It was . . . it was a professional interchange.

"What did you discuss?" she asked again.

"I just asked Lloyd to come with me to give me his professional opinion about this patient I'm treating," I said.

"Peter Lumen," she said.

"Yes . . . " I didn't remember telling Meg Peter's name. "Yes," I said. "Peter Lumen. That's what it was all about. I needed to compare Jung's notions with contemporary evangelistic thought to help me formulate a more valid diagnosis and plan of action. The is a very difficult case. I need all the help I can get."

The tears welled in Meg's eyes again, and she shook her head slowly. "This is a very difficult case, John!" she said, gesturing broadly between us and toward Diane's room. "And unless you can put aside your office cases long enough to give us some of your precious treatment time . . . your going to lose these patients!" She turned abruptly, and strode back toward Diane's room.

"You're not listening to me!" I called after her. "I was trying to tell you what we talked about." I sighed heavily. "You're not listening to me," I said to myself.

I left the bar and walked over and collapsed on the couch. I couldn't understand what Meg was so upset about. She and Diane had an enjoyable evening, and Diane was going to camp. I didn't know what girls needed at camp. I'd only gone with Lloyd. Girls were different. But then why did I tell them to ask Lloyd what to take? And that counselor . . . A creeping irritation fell on my skin as I recalled my inappropriate response to Diane's question about him. But I was right about one thing: I *had* written a book, too. It was called *Archetypal Considerations in Post-Freudian Analysis.* It was never published, of course, but several of my colleagues had read it, and told me that they'd found it helpful. I'm sure Diane never read it. Meg tried once, but she couldn't understand the technical points. Still . . . that was a peevish thing for me to have said.

I thought I felt the tingle of irritation on my skin again, but it was too pronounced. My arm jerked suddenly in reflexive action, and I felt a few drops of cold liquid drop onto my leg. I had forgotten that I was still holding my drink. I quickly raised the glass to my lips and drained it. I squeezed my eyes shut and jerked my head as the strong aroma of the alcohol forced its way past my nostrils and throbbed momentarily behind the bridge of my nose. I set the glass on the table, and searched the surface of my arm in the dim light to find the gnat, or spider that was creating the troublesome sensation. I couldn't see anything, but I was sure that there was something there, because the prickling had now spread across my entire arm. I slapped at it violently, and the pain thrust itself deep into the tissue. Then I grasped my wrist and squeezed it tightly. The prickling subsided, and I breathed in relief.

I heard the faint sound of laughter from Diane's bedroom. I couldn't understand why Meg was so upset. They were happy . . . and Diane was going to camp. Every now and then, amid the laughter, I could make out a word . . . *Mother . . . Lloyd . . . camp . . . Dad . . .* Or was it *Tad*? And then the laughter again . . . so easy. No matter. They were occupied, and I had to recapitulate my consultation with Lloyd. He'd made some good points about Peter. But his theory . . . schizophrenia as a reaction of the spiritually minded seeker who'd rejected God . . . that was too simple . . . The human mind is more complex than that. It reaches out into myriads of uncharted segments of reality. And it was my responsibility to plot those . . . understand them. Tad McIntyre could never do that. He wasn't a real doctor. Why couldn't Diane understand that? But how did Lloyd know so much about Peter from so little knowledge? Only the darkness should be able to comprehend its own light. And what did it matter if Peter did engage in a perversion of the scripture? He still healed, didn't he? But I didn't believe that . . . not for a minute. Otherwise he could heal himself. He could treat . . . himself . . .

The laughter rose again from Diane's room, and for a moment it was held captive in the faint whirling that now passed through my head from the alcohol. I closed my eyes, and the whirling increased, and I could feel a darkening at the center of it, and a warmth rose from the bottom of the tiny point which was its source. The laughter grew, and the shadowy figures of Meg and Diane before me on the boat pulsated in and out of view. But then a gleam of white shot across the bow, and I could see Leonard in a white coat . . . and he looked at me with a stern face . . . and his words were slow and somber: You're walking a tightrope, John, he said . . . I detected a definite potential for danger. . . . I think you should have some analysis yourself . . . I'd be glad to do that for you. No . . . not from a Freudian. But Bernadette wanted to, also . . . We need to work together, John, she said. You're going to need guidance through this period. You're on the brink of a thrilling adventure . . . but you're going to need guidance. And she began to laugh, and her laughter joined that of Leonard's. But Meg and Diane were plucked up by Lloyd, and they rode off together under the gray cloud of my father's laughing face. That was it . . . Diane didn't really want my opinion. She didn't mean, "what do you think, Dad?" . . . She meant, "what do you think, *Tad*?" . . . That's why she wanted his book and not mine. And Leonard . . . he admitted it . . . I think you should shift Peter to another therapist for a while . . . I'd take him myself . . . You have a spiritual need . . . No, that was Lloyd. What were they trying to do to me? The laughter from Diane's bedroom now grew to a deafening roar . . . and I knew that they were all in there . . . and their laughter thrust itself purposely and mercilessly toward me.

"No!" I shook my head violently and sat forward on the couch. "What am *I* doing to me?" I mumbled. I cupped my hands in the vague shape of an imaginary book and thrust them hard against my face. "This is so stupid!" I whispered harshly. "This is textbook! I'm having an idiotic paranoid reaction! Stop it! Stop it!" I pressed my hands closer and rubbed the nonexistent pages of the book deeply into the microscopic path of my vision, and the cleansing words tumbled forth, but became lost in a blur of nonrecognition. "I renounce you . . . I renounce you . . . " I mumbled. My hands were trembling, but I held them cupped, and drew them slowly away until the blurred words resolved themselves . . . and then disappeared.

I breathed deeply, placed my trembling hands down, and felt them fall against the hard surface . . . I opened my eyes and looked about in disorientation. I wasn't on the couch. I was at the bar again. And another full glass stood before me. A shaft of fear crossed my spine. Either I had returned from the couch without knowing it . . . or I had never left the bar. No. I had drunk the other glass. I could still taste its aroma behind the bridge of my nose. This was not a good night . . . this was not a good night . . .

The voices of Meg and Diane rose in laughter again . . . and then subsided, like the boat gliding past the crests of the waves on the way to the whirlpool. Bernadette . . . you knew . . . the others will never understand the richness that experience can bring . . . They have no concept of the truth that can be derived from the other side of reality. But you, John . . . you're on the precipice. The precipice, Bernadette . . . Yes, but how do I translate this awful fear into that rare and mystical excitement again?

The laughter rose again. I raised the glass and drank its contents, and the buzz of lost awareness permeated my perception, and the laughter fell into a nondescript buzzing . . . like the faint sound of many distant horses, galloping through the raging foam of some dark and forgotten sea.

22

A few minutes remained before Peter's arrival, so I pored eagerly over my notes from the last few sessions to find the best avenue for exploration which would ensure the avoidance of his grasping control of the session again, as he had done on Friday. Leonard was right in his concern about the potential for danger in this therapeutic relationship. I *was* walking a tightrope. And after my frightening delusional departure last night, I was about ready to turn Peter over to someone else . . . anyone else. It wasn't just because of what Leonard had said. The psychiatric literature was full of warnings against succumbing to the temptation to slip into the manic state of consciousness in an attempt to gain a better understanding of your patient. But this morning I had awakened refreshed and energized, and the transient state of fear was replaced by newly formed feeling of invigoration. The seizures of doubt and ambivalence that had plagued me last night had disappeared.

It seemed as though the rest of my sessions today had passed by with lightning speed. I was sure that this was partially due to the fact that Cheryl was not here. She had called in this morning to tell me that she had a bad sore throat, and didn't want to risk . . . as she put it . . . infesting anyone. I was just as glad. Cheryl was my link with reality; and that was a crutch that I didn't need today.

I thought I heard a rustling sound, and I looked up to see Peter standing in the partially open doorway.

"Oh, Peter," I said. "Come in . . . come in."

He glanced behind him. "Your girl isn't here."

"No. She's out today," I said.

"And the door . . . "

"So that people will know to come in," I explained. I closed his folder and set it on the corner of my desk, and beckoned for him to enter.

Peter pushed the door slightly, stepped slowly in, and returned the door to its original partially open position. Then he walked over and sat quietly in the chair opposite me.

"How are you today, Peter?" I asked.

He leaned back with a haughty expression, and placed his chin on his thumb. "I don't know," he said.

"Did you dream again?" I asked.

Peter shrugged without changing his position. "That wasn't it."

"Then what?"

His eyes narrowed, but did not blink. "I need to know the purpose of your visit last night."

"At your temple service?" I asked.

He nodded slowly. "There were two of you," he said deliberately. "And you detained my singer."

"No, Peter," I told him. "Julie just asked us to sit with her."

"And . . . who was the other person?" he asked.

"That was my brother," I said. "He's a minister."

Peter's eyes widened again, but did not blink. He dropped his hands to the arms of the chair. "Then he's a part of the conspiracy."

"What conspiracy, Peter?" I asked.

"There is only one conspiracy," he said slowly. "The conspiracy against the chosen one. They want to steal the first fruits . . . and replace me with someone else." His eyes narrowed again. "Another minister."

"No, Peter. My brother already has a church," I assured him. "He doesn't need another one."

"False comfort," he said. "He must stay away from my singer. She is still pure. She must not be misled."

"Why do you continue to suspect a conspiracy, Peter?"

"Asked he innocently," said Peter mockingly.

I ignored his sarcastic remark. I leaned back in my chair, and tapped my finger rhythmically on the desk. "Why?" I asked again.

"Why . . . why . . . why . . . " he mumbled. "Why the cross? Why Judas?" He raised his eyebrow and stared at me without speaking.

"Go on, Peter," I urged him.

"I must expect it," he said. "I'm a Christ figure, you know. I must expect a conspiracy." His hand reached up aimlessly and fondled the golden mandala which hung from his neck.

"Will that protect you from the conspiracy?" I asked.

He picked up the mandala and stared at it. "Perhaps . . . " He said slowly. Then he placed his finger in the small square in the center if the figure. "It's my nerves, you see. I'm here . . . " He tapped the square. "And my nerves radiate outward . . . and God . . . " He moved his finger to the outer circle, and traced around it three times. "God feels them . . . draws them in . . . He's attracted by them."

"And the mandala in your temple?" I asked him.

"The rock is its center," he said. "And the rock is Peter. But the rock radiates an invisible energy. And God feels that, too . . . He's a part of it."

"But you told me . . . " I began cautiously. "You told me that there is no God."

Peter shifted nervously in his chair, and turned his head away.

"Do you remember telling me that, Peter?" I asked him.

He turned his head abruptly back. "How could I not remember something like that?"

"Do you still believe that?" I asked.

"Perhaps . . . " He shifted in his chair again. "Perhaps God will be resurrected."

I had no idea where his thought pattern was leading him, but I felt an overpowering drive to lead him more deeply into areas of discomfort. It was the only way that I could make him dependent upon me again, and reinstate the dynamics of the therapy.

"Yes . . . perhaps he will be resurrected," Peter repeated almost inaudibly.

"Resurrected from where?" I asked.

Peter shifted in his chair and looked away again. Then he looked back with a faint smile on his face. He pointed is finger vaguely toward me. "From the thoughts of those who love him."

"Do you love him, Peter?" I asked.

He narrowed his eyes again, and ran his hand aimlessly across the mandala. Then he turned his head toward the television monitor, and fixed his eyes on the blank screen.

"Do you love God, Peter?" I asked deliberately.

"Don't you remember what you told me?" he asked. "How can I love something that doesn't exist?"

I suddenly regretted having allowed this session to commence with him sitting in the chair opposite me. There really hadn't been a good opportunity to make the transition to the couch, but here he was too free to turn away. I could not easily control the interchange, and Peter had developed many strategies for reinstating his composure.

"What about your followers, Peter?" I asked, pressing for some kind of instability. "Your followers clearly love God, don't they?"

"Because they don't know," he said softly.

"Know what?"

"The terrible trick that God has pulled," he mumbled.

"Trick . . . "

"We live . . . and we die . . . And in between, we are plagued by devils." He turned back from the television monitor slowly and slumped in the chair.

"How about your father?" I asked, attempting a different course. "Was your father plagued by devils?"

"Of course . . . "

"But he was a healer," I said.

"Yes."

"Did you love your father?" I asked.

"I and my father are one . . . " he mumbled. Then he jerked his head up. "Of course I loved my father!"

"Are you ready to talk about the accident . . . his death?" I asked.

"His death . . . "

"Before you can be restored to health, you'll have to be able to talk about that," I told him.

"I *am* restored to health!" he said resolutely. "I think I told you that already."

"Then tell me about your father," I urged him. "Tell me about his accident."

Peter closed his eyes momentarily. Then he opened them again, and sat up rigidly in the chair. He placed his hands together and placed them under his chin in a thoughtful pose. "It occurred fifteen years ago last April twenty-third," he mumbled. Then he began reciting, with dry, mechanical accuracy, words identical to those I had read in the newspaper article . "The bodies of Jason Watkins, popular rural tent revivalist, and his female companion, Patricia Sims, were pulled from the wreckage of Watkins' auto, where it had plunged into a rain-swollen culvert." He paused and closed his eyes.

"Who was Patricia Sims?" I asked.

"Ms. Sims was known by police to have been a prostitute," he said, quoting again.

"Why was he with a prostitute?" I asked.

"It was part of his outreach," said Peter. "He frequently spent time with the underprivileged. He was a healer. He healed their memories."

It was clear that Peter had placed the newspaper account of his father's death deep within his unconscious. He had already pulled forth the parts that he could justify. I had to coax him into revealing all of it. "What did the autopsy reveal, Peter?" I asked.

He slumped down slightly and began to fidget. "I . . . inconclusive . . . "

"No. It was not inconclusive," I said emphatically. "What did the autopsy reveal?" I repeated.

Peter sighed heavily. Then he sat forward and placed both hands on my desk "The autopsy revealed that . . . that both people had been drinking heavily," he recited stiffly.

"How do you explain that?" I asked.

"Outreach work can be very demanding," he said quickly. "There are reasons . . . There is nothing inherently evil in the evil brew . . . Some things are difficult to understand."

"Did your mother understand the reasons?" I asked.

"No . . . "

"And your grandmother?" I pushed.

"My grandmother was unavailable for comment," he said mechanically, paraphrasing the newspaper article.

Peter's cloaked responses were interfering with the possibility for a productive interchange. It seemed to me that, since I had forced his recognition of this incident at Friday's session, he had manufacturing another level of repression. I knew that the fact of his father's relationship with a prostitute must be weighing heavily on his unconscious. Leonard's suggestion that Peter might be more capable of violence than either of us initially thought crossed my mind, and I decided to push again in this direction. If there were some link between his father's illicit encounter and Peter's psychosis, it could have manifested itself in hidden desire for retribution.

"You must have been very saddened by your father's death, though," I began.

"Of course."

"And it would be only natural for you to have placed the blame on someone," I continued.

"Judgment is a fierce responsibility," he said.

"But we all judge when persons close to us are harmed," I told him. "It's a natural, reactive occurrence."

"A fierce responsibility . . . " he mumbled.

"Try to remember your feelings at that time, Peter," I said. "Do you recall . . . Let me see . . . what was the woman's name again? The woman who was with him?"

"His female companion . . . Patricia Sims," he recited.

"Yes. Do you blame Patricia Sims for your father's death?" I asked.

Peter straightened his posture, and placed both hands rigidly on the arms of the chair. Then he spoke coldly through pursed lips. "My father was doing service in the field. That was his outreach. It would be presumptuous of me to judge the implications of his ministry. If the harlot was guilty of anything . . . then she will be dealt with."

"By whom?" I asked.

"She will be dealt with . . . " he muttered. He closed his eyes.

"And similarly," I began slowly. ". . . if your father were guilty of anything . . . "

Peter's eyes popped open. "My father was a healer!"

I leaned forward and spoke intensely, in an attempt to yank Peter out of his mode of repression. "Your recovery hinges on your accurate reflection of this memory, Peter. You must reject your delusions!"

Peter clutched at the arms of the chair, and a faint smile appeared on his lips. "Of course." He placed the palms of his hands toward me, and then moved them outward. "My delusions are hereby rejected!" He paused for a moment with his arms outstretched, and then he returned his hands to the arms of the chair. "You see? My recovery has been accomplished."

"No, Peter," I said. "You're still denying." I reached into the bottom drawer of my desk and pulled out a hand mirror.

"I thought I destroyed that," said Peter.

"I bought another," I told him.

"Oh . . . "

"Are you going to destroy this one, too?" I asked.

"Of course not," he said. "My delusions are rejected."

I reached across the desk and handed the mirror to him. "Very well. Then look at yourself in this mirror."

Peter took the mirror, and turned the reflective surface slowly toward his face. Then he brushed a few stray hairs off his forehead.

"Who are you looking at?" I asked.

"Peter Lumen," he said softly.

"What is his real name?" I asked.

"A.K.A. Peter Daryl Watkins," he said deliberately. "But Peter Lumen is the real person now. Peter Lumen was called by the Messenger. Peter Lumen is the healer. Peter Lumen is . . . "

"The judge?" I interrupted.

Peter lowered the mirror and glanced at me with narrowed eyes. Then he placed the mirror on the desk and moved his head slowly around the room. He stopped as his eyes fell on the mirrored door to the adjacent observation room. "Do you really think my delusions haven't been rejected?" he asked. "Then you should have placed me before *that* mirror."

Peter stood abruptly and crossed over to the doorway to the observation room. He stood rigidly three feet before it, and brushed at his shirt. I could see his reflection from where I sat. The same faint smile was on his face.

"Who do you see?" I asked.

"Peter Lumen," he responded.

"But is that really you?"

Peter placed his palms out again and swept them apart before him. "All my delusions are hereby rejected!" In the process of this gesture, his hand brushed across the mirror. He stepped closer and observed a smudge that he had made. Then he leaned close to the mirror, reached out rapped on it with the tips of his fingers.

"What is it, Peter?" I asked.

He lifted his face so that his reflection was directed toward me. He raised his eyes in a questioning expression. Then he quickly dropped his hand to the knob, turned, and pulled the door open.

"No, Peter! That's not . . . "

But it was too late. He had already pulled the door completely open, and was now inspecting the small observation room. He turned his head to the side, and stepped back as he saw the back of the mirror. He moved closer, and placed one of his hands on the other side of the door, and gazed at the image of his hand through the one-way glass.

"That room is not part of our therapy session, Peter," I said, struggling to defuse his discovery.

"But it is being used in the conspiracy, isn't it?" he asked threateningly.

"Conspiracy? No, Peter. There is no conspiracy!" I insisted.

He smiled slyly and wagged his finger at me. Then he stepped inside the small room, and pulled the door shut in front of him.

"Peter . . . " I walked toward the door, and saw my own reflection walking toward me.

"I can see you!" called Peter from the room mockingly. "I can see everything in your office . . . everything! And I can even hear you!"

I heard a light knocking behind me, and I turned around to see Diane standing in the doorway.

"Dad . . . excuse me," she said.

"Diane! What are you doing here?" I asked.

"Your secretary wasn't there," she said apologetically. "And the door was open, so I just . . . "

"No. I mean, why are you here . . . at my office?"

"Uncle Lloyd and Aunt Kate are outside in the car," she said. "We're on our way to the camp. I just . . . " She pushed the door open and walked slowly toward me. "I just wanted to say good-bye."

"Oh . . . of course . . . "

The door to the adjacent room opened suddenly, and Peter walked aggressively into the room. "Well . . . who have we here?" he asked.

"Oh . . . I'm sorry," said Diane. "I didn't think anyone was here."

"That's perfectly all right," said Peter. "I'm a colleague." He thrust his hand toward Diane. "My name is Dr. Lumen."

"Oh . . . Hi!" Diane took Peter's hand. "I'm Diane . . . I'm his daughter."

"Well!" Peter placed his other hand on Diane's and pressed it firmly. "Of course. He's told me so much about you!"

"Diane, I think that . . . "

"Did I hear you say that you were going to camp?" Peter asked Diane, ignoring my attempt to abort the conversation.

"Yes . . . with my aunt and uncle," said Diane.

"Oh!" Peter glanced furtively toward me. "That would be the minister."

"Yes," said Diane.

"Which camp are you going to?" asked Peter.

"Moon Lake," said Diane. "It's in the mountains."

"Oh, yes. I'm very familiar with Moon Lake in the mountains," said Peter. "It's beautiful up there. Beautiful!"

"Diane, I really appreciate your coming by," I said, placing my hand on her shoulder. "But you'd better not keep Lloyd and Kate waiting."

"No . . . " Diane gave Peter's hand a final shake and pulled hers free from his grasp. Then she turned to me. "'Bye, Dad . . . " She stepped forward and gave me a quick hug. "I'll see you Friday night."

"Sure," I said, returning her embrace. "Have a good time."

Diane nodded. Then she waved at Peter. "It's nice to have met you, Dr. Lumen."

"And you, Diane," responded Peter through a faint smile.

"Bye . . . " Diane waved at me, and left the office, closing the door behind her.

"You have a lovely daughter, John," said Peter softly.

"What?"

"I said . . . you have a lovely daughter, John," he repeated.

An irritating tingling feeling swept across my arms. "I think it's important that you continue addressing me by my last name, Peter," I said.

"You may call me *Dr. Lumen* if you wish," he said.

"No. You must continue to call me *Dr. Summers*," I said.

Peter merely smiled, and stepped closer to me. "Tell me, John . . . Is that the daughter who is giving you all the trouble?"

"No . . . there is no trouble, Peter . . . " I said. "There is no trouble."

Peter shook his head slowly. Then he stepped over to the desk and picked up the hand mirror. He walked back and thrust it toward me. "You must reject your delusions!"

I took the mirror from Peter and let it drop to my side. "There is no trouble, Peter. And we are here to deal with you . . . not me."

"Physician . . . heal thyself!" he said loudly.

"There is nothing to heal," I said.

Peter cocked his head, and pointed directly toward the mirror. "Remember . . . I'm a healer of memories." He reached out with both hands and forced the mirror up before my face.

"There is nothing to heal, Peter," I repeated. But the reflection of my face in the mirror revealed a disturbing visage of doubt. I tried to lower the mirror, but Peter held it firmly before me as he continued speaking.

"That's why they're called delusions," he said. "But I could tell. I held her hand, you see. I could feel it . . . the rebellious urge . . . the sinful spirit! And you've sent her out in the company of your brother . . . the conspirator? I'm surprised at you, John."

I forced the mirror down. "Peter, you must drop this line of conversation immediately!" I tossed the mirror onto the couch.

"Be careful!" he said with mock concern. "Seven years bad luck! Tick, tack . . . step on a crack!"

"No bad luck . . . no problem," I said firmly.

"John . . . John . . . John . . . " He sighed deeply and shrugged. "But then, it's your conspiracy, and you'll have to deal with it.

"No, Peter, I don't . . . "

"I have my own conspiracy to deal with," he said abruptly, and turned and headed toward the door.

"What do you mean by that, Peter?" I asked.

Peter glanced toward the adjacent room. "Hmph!" He opened the office door and started out. Then he turned back and smiled at me. "If you have trouble rejecting your delusions, John . . . call on me. I've had experience with these things, you know. I'm a healer. I can fix things."

"Peter wait . . . our session . . . " I walked quickly toward him. I couldn't let him leave at this level of interchange. "Our session tomorrow. Don't forget."

"Of course." He paused, and looked at me condescendingly. "Of course, John. You can trust me. You *must* trust me. I'll be here . . . to help you." He stepped suddenly outside and slammed the door shut behind him.

"Peter . . . " I stepped up to the closed door and slammed the palms of my hands against it. The dark wood spread out before me like a black sky, and I clutched my fingers at the flat surface to prevent me from falling. I thought I could hear Peter's voice from the outer office . . . I'll be here . . . to help you . . . Or it may have been a fleeting recollection. I shook my head and slapped my hands hard against the door, and the palms of them tingled from the smack. I couldn't believe that I had botched this session so badly. If Diane just hadn't come . . . perhaps I might have defused Peter's discovery of the room. I should have locked that door . . . should have . . . should have . . .

It must have been Peter from the other room that I heard, because now his voice came again . . . loud and clear. "It's your conspiracy, John. You'll have to deal with it!"

I threw open the door just in time to see the outside door slam shut. I thought I heard the sound of laughter . . . but I couldn't be sure. I stepped backward and breathed deeply to counteract the dizzying sensation that was now clouding my perception. A sudden surge of hostility rose from my chest. The memory of Peter's voice, telling me that I'd have to deal with my conspiracy, and that I shouldn't have sent Diane off with Lloyd . . .

I shook my head forcefully in rejection of my feelings and walked to my desk. I couldn't let myself be thrown into a state of anxiety by Peter's problems. And it was his problem. He was the one who suspected the conspiracy. And he was the one who was planning to deal with it. The recollection of his statement repeated itself in my memory. What was it? A threat . . . or just an idle response to his delusion? I walked behind my desk and sat. Peter's reaction to the possibility of his blaming the prostitute for his father's death was inconclusive. But he had called her a harlot. That reference would surely fit in with the biblical warnings painted on the walls.

I reached out and let my hand fall on the telephone receiver. I knew that I should call Chadwick. It had been nearly two weeks since his visit. But I had nothing to tell him . . . only that I had once again let Peter step into the controlling role in our analytic interaction.

I pulled my hand away from the telephone. Then I called through the open door. "Cheryl, would you . . . " I stopped abruptly as I recalled that Cheryl was not here today. And then I suddenly realized my error. I had been relieved that she wasn't here today since it would allow me to abandon what I considered an unnecessary link with reality. But when I was dealing with Peter, reality was my ally. I had to be the one to maintain the channel to the real world . . . force him to address it on my terms.

I opened my top desk drawer and pulled out a small adhesive note pad. I removed my pen and, in large letter, printed the phrase, TAKE CONTROL! I tore the top sheet off the pad and stuck it on Peter's folder. Then I put the pad back in my desk drawer, replaced my pen, and sat back leisurely in my chair. The trip to Moon Lake would take nearly four hours. I closed my eyes and entertained some fleeting thoughts of Diane in the car with Lloyd and Kate . . . talking . . . laughing . . . They would have a good time together. That was all right Peter said it was beautiful at Moon Lake . . . Peter said it was beautiful.

23

Cheryl was still sick the next day, but I asked her if she could come for the last hour just to clear up some paper work. That really wasn't the reason, of course. After yesterday's experience, I realized more than ever the need for me to retain my detached, objective role with Peter. And for all her shortcomings, Cheryl always provided that bit of untainted authenticity that allowed me to maintain at least a window out of the ever-present potential of delusional turmoil. I had asked her to come in at three forty-five, and at precisely that time, the outside door opened, and Cheryl stepped inside. She looked over to where I stood in the doorway to my office and waved.

"Hello, Cheryl," I said. "I appreciate your coming in for a while today. I hope you're not feeling too sick."

"No. I'll be all right," she said in a harsh, gravely voice. She coughed and stepped over to her desk.

"There isn't a lot to do," I said. "It's just that . . . "

"That's all right Dr. Summers," she said. "I felt bad about not being able to be here yesterday afternoon. It's important to have someone else in the office . . . especially with Peter." She coughed again.

"Yes . . . yes, that's right," I agreed.

Cheryl set her purse down on the floor, and moved a stack of folders from the center to the side of her desk. Then she glanced at the telephone. "Oh, Dr. Summers . . . You didn't pick up a message."

"What?"

"There's a telephone message," she said. "It must have come in last night, or before you got here this morning."

"I don't know. I didn't check it today," I said.

Cheryl pressed the rewind button, and the recording device emitted a high-pitched hum for a few seconds. Then there was a click, followed by a moment of silence that seemed to be punctuated by a deep slow breath. Then a deliberate voice issued from the tiny speaker. "Hello, John. This is Peter."

"What?" Cheryl looked up and grimaced.

"Shh!" I placed my finger to my lips and stepped closer to her desk.

"It's seven a.m. Tuesday morning," the voice continued. "I'm afraid I won't be able to be in for our session today. I need some time to relax. I plan to go to the mountains . . . get some fresh air. I thought perhaps I'd go to Moon Lake. It's beautiful up there. I might even stop off and see Diane while I'm there . . . look after things. You have a nice day, won't you . . . " His voice stopped, and the device clicked to a halt.

"What does he mean by . . . " began Cheryl.

I raised my hand to silence her as the shallow electronic tones of Peter's voice reverberated in my head. I glanced toward my office door, and the image from yesterday flashed across my consciousness . . . Diane, here to say good-bye . . . and Peter standing before her, pressing his hands hard against hers. And I could still hear his low threatening words -- "I held her hand, you see. I could feel it . . . the rebellious urge . . . the sinful spirit! And you've sent her out in the company of your brother . . . the conspirator? I'm surprised at you . . . John . . . John . . . John . . . it's your conspiracy, and you'll have to deal with it."

"Dr. Summers, would you like me to . . . " Cheryl began.

But the recollection of Peter's words, and the image of Diane suddenly merged in a hideous sense of fear, and I exploded with rage. "No! I have to stop him!"

"Dr. Summers . . . "

I did not acknowledge Cheryl's voice. I had already crossed the room, thrown open the door, and dashed out into the hot blast of summer air.

The late afternoon traffic made it difficult to get out of town, so I tried to make up as much time as possible once I reached the open road. Still, it was eight o'clock when I finally turned onto the gravel road leading to the campground at Moon Lake. Darkness had fallen, but a full moon hovered over the crest of a distant peak, and its soft rays cast a shimmering glow across the softly lapping water in the lake. I pulled my car to a halt next to Lloyd's in the spacious parking area, and got out. Several cabins lay in the trees fifty yards away, but there were no lights on. I thought I heard the faint sound of laughter, and I noticed a flickering glow in the distance. I looked around to verify that there were no other signs of activity, and then I ran toward the light.

As I approached, the laughter ceased, and voices began to sing. I hurried around a turn in the trail, and I saw a roaring fire. In the radiant light behind the flames I saw twenty-five or thirty young people, sitting on stepped benches which appeared to have been carved out of the adjacent rocky hill. They all held their hands in the air, with a single finger projecting, and they smiled and swayed back and forth as they sang . . . "This little light of mine . . . I'm gonna let it shine!"

I stopped beside a tree and squinted as I searched the rows for Diane. I finally saw her. She was in the front row, and she was participating enthusiastically, her eyes fixed on the song leader . . .

My gaze suddenly shifted to where she was looking. The song leader . . . His back was turned to me, but the image hit me with stark immediacy -- the muscular figure beneath the tight-fitting turtle-neck shirt, and the flowing, sandy-colored hair . . . He swayed in rhythm with the young people, and urged them on.

The feeling of rage exploded within me again, and I pushed myself away from the tree and burst into the fire pit area. "No!" I shouted.

I heard screams from the rows of young people, and my vision was suddenly darkened by the searing heat from the fire, but I could still see the outline of his body before me. I grasped him by the arm and spun him around. "No, Peter! You can't . . . "

But the face before me was that of a frightened high school boy. I dropped my hand from his arm, and he backed away with a look of terror in his eyes.

"Daddy!"

I looked across the shimmering waves of heat and saw several dark figures running toward me. I stepped away from the fire, and I could barely discern the features of Diane, Lloyd and Kate.

"Daddy! What are you doing?" Diane reached me first. The tears on her face glistened in the flickering light.

"Here, John . . . let's step out of the heat."

"Hmm?" I felt Lloyd's hand on my arm, and I stumbled along with him with Diane and Kate beside me.

"Come on, John," Lloyd urged me.

I stopped abruptly and turned back toward the rows of figures. They were all watching . . . silent. The frightened leader had returned to his place by the fire, and he was running his hand through his flowing, sandy-colored hair. "Where is he?" I asked.

"What?" asked Lloyd.

I turned toward him and repeated, "Where is he?" I took Lloyd by the arm and shook him. "Where is he?"

"Where is who, John?" asked Lloyd.

"What are you talking about, Daddy?" cried Diane.

"Peter . . . " I turned back and searched the campfire again. "Peter . . . " I repeated.

"Peter Lumen?" asked Lloyd.

I nodded. "Where is he?"

"He's not here, John," said Lloyd. "What made you think that Peter Lumen was here?"

"What made me . . . " I repeated mindlessly.

And over the sound of my own confusion, Peter's voice still echoed in my ears: "I might even stop off and see Diane while I'm there . . . look after things . . . "

"He's not here, John," repeated Lloyd softly.

Of course . . . Peter had tricked me. He'd found another way to gain control of me . . . a hideous, frightening way.

"Go on, Mike!" called Lloyd to the boy. "Take them through another chorus."

The boy started singing, and the others joined him. But some of them were laughing. I could hear them.

"Daddy . . . I don't understand," mumbled Diane. Her expression . . . I'd never seen it before. Confusion . . . no . . . fear . . .

"Diane, I . . . " I reached out and placed my hands on her shoulders. "He tricked me . . . " I pulled her close to me, and I felt my tears falling against her hair. I wanted to tell her that everything was all right . . . comfort her. But I couldn't now. He had tricked me. It was hideous . . . frightening. And the laughter was there . . . and all I could do was mumble . . . "I'm sorry . . . He tricked me . . . "

"It's all right, John," said Lloyd. He placed his hand on Diane's shoulder. "Kate, why don't you and Diane go on back to the group. John and I need to talk."

"Sure, Lloyd," said Kate. She smiled broadly and took Diane by the hand. "Come on, Diane."

Diane stepped back away from me and nodded. Then she turned and walked away with Kate.

"I'm . . . I'm sorry, Lloyd," I said.

"Hey, no problem!" He smiled, and slapped me on the arm. "Come on. Let's go down by the lake."

"Yeah . . . yeah, that sounds good." I followed him along an unseen path. The overhanging trees obscured the moon, and my eyes still hadn't accommodated from the penetrating light of the campfire. But Lloyd was in front of me, and I followed the sound of his footsteps.

"You haven't been to this campground before, have you?" he asked.

"No."

"I really love it here!" he said. "When you're in the city, with all the noise and dirt . . . It's easy to forget."

"Yeah . . . " We were quite a distance from the campfire now, but the smell of the burning wood still lingered in my nostrils. That was the most striking memory, it seemed, of the time I had camped with Lloyd when I was eight . . . the smell of the campfire.

"Here we are," said Lloyd.

We stepped out from the overhanging trees, and the bright moon shone over the hill. I could hear the water lapping lightly against the rough shoreline.

Lloyd brushed a few rocks from a section of ground. "Let's sit." He sat down, and motioned for me to join him.

"All right." I sat beside him, and breathed deeply to allow the moist lake-side air to fill my lungs. I glanced back toward the campfire as I heard the faintly recognizable words of the song in the distance.

"Don't let Satan blow it out," said Lloyd.

"Huh?"

"That's the verse they're singing," he explained. "But they substitute the action for the word. You know . . . 'Don't let Satan . . . '" he puckered his lips and blew. "' . . . . it out. I'm gonna let it shine!' Just a good old camp song," he said.

"I don't know it," I said.

"No . . . I guess not." He turned back and leaned forward on his knees. "Tell me about Peter Lumen," he said after a moment. "Why did you think he was here?"

"He left a message on my phone this morning," I explained. "He said he was coming up here."

"What brought that on?" he asked.

"I'm afraid I've really botched my responsibility with his case," I said. "I've allowed him to learn details about my personal life."

"Like . . . Diane, and the fact that she was going to be here this week?" he asked.

"Well, that was accidental," I said. "But . . . yes."

"Hmm . . . And the schizophrenic personality can be very threatening," he said. "You never know what bizarre actions they are going to take."

"That's right." I hadn't told him about Peter's being a suspect in a murder case. There was no need for that.

"I don't know as much about that kind of psychosis as you, of course," said Lloyd. "But I did study the topic pretty extensively while I was in seminary. I think I told you about my theory."

"Yes."

"I guess the characteristics are pretty common, though," he continued. "People who are withdrawn, and yet tend to exhibit high-risk behavior. And I guess the sudden shifts from depression to feelings of omnipotence are prevalent, too. And I guess many times there are symptoms of paranoia."

"Yes . . . those are some common danger signs." I shifted uncomfortably, and turned toward Lloyd.

"And the delusions . . . and dreams . . . " He shook his head. "That would be terrifying!"

"Yes, it . . . it would be."

"I think it would scare me to death . . . to deal with them, I mean." Lloyd picked up a pebble from the ground, and looked at it aimlessly as he rolled it slowly between his thumb and finger. Then he dropped the pebble, and looked at me intently. "I think I'd be concerned that I'd be . . . I don't know . . . drawn into all of it somehow."

I tried to look away from him, but I found myself glued to his intense, questioning eyes. Lloyd was always able to do this . . . even when we were younger. He had the uncanny ability to read my emotions . . . understand my fears. I always attributed it to the fact that I looked up to him as the protective older brother. But we weren't children anymore. And this was none of his business.

I picked up a stone, and flung it far into the lake. I waited for a moment, and then listened for the silent splash. "But there are many historical aspects to take into consideration, too," I said clinically. "In Peter's case, he has a really strong feeling of rejec-tion by his father. He has a deep unconscious fear that he isn't living up to his father's religious expectations. And so . . . he's rejected them. But it's difficult to discover how deeply the rejection lies."

"I can sure relate to that," said Lloyd.

"You mean . . . with you and Dad?" I asked.

"Yeah."

"But you keep telling me that Dad isn't religious," I said.

Lloyd smiled. "And that was *his* expectation for me."

"Hmm . . . " I tossed another stone into the lake. "So how did you get over your feeling of rejection?" I asked.

"I haven't," he said softly.

"Then . . . how do you deal with it?" I asked.

"There just came a point in my life when I discovered that I had to make my life right with God . . . with or without Pop's acceptance."

"Well, I just wish Dad could understand you, and accept you the way you are," I said.

Lloyd shook his head. "Pop will never accept anyone he can't control."

"I don't know," I said. "I think he accepts *me*."

Lloyd smiled and shrugged.

"What do you mean by that?" I asked. I'm sure Lloyd knew that was a rhetorical question. I knew exactly what he meant, and the knowledge of it was like a dagger. My father had "arranged" for my education and private tutoring, had paid the bill, had set me up in practice, and supplied me with the majority of my patients. "Never mind," I said caustically.

"Anyway, that's where it stands," said Lloyd. "And I'm at fault, too, because I reject the controls."

"But, of course, Dad wouldn't accept that statement," I said. "He says you've become part of a very controlling, dogmatic, fundamental religion."

"That's because he doesn't understand what it means to have a personal relationship with God through Christ," said Lloyd. "Man is completely and absolutely free. Pop doesn't understand that, because he doesn't understand the concept of a non-controlling love."

Lloyd's lead-in to the familiar religious topic made me feel uncomfortable. I picked up another stone, and passed it back and forth between my hands. "Why don't we just talk about Peter?" I asked. I flung the stone into the lake.

"Sure." Lloyd picked up a stone larger than mine, and tossed it several yards farther.

"Hey! Unfair advantage!" I joked.

"What can I say?" laughed Lloyd. Then he became serious again. "Peter's father was very controlling also, I suspect."

"From what I could learn . . . " I had a fleeting recollection of the video of Watkins in the Tent revival . . . approaching Peter with the snake . . . wrapping it about him . . . forcing him to address the congregation . . . and then the rejection of the truth of Peter's faith for his inability to speak in tongues. "Yes. He was very controlling," I said.

"Well . . . it's easy for people to get their earthly father and their Heavenly Father mixed up," said Lloyd.

"Sure," I agreed. "The father/god archetype is . . . "

"Forget the archetype!" said Lloyd abruptly.

"Terminology!" I responded testily. "Don't get so upset by my terminology! Just think of it as a symbol. I mean . . . Peter has a dream that I have to interpret, too. That's the same thing."

"Maybe," he muttered.

"Maybe? What do you mean by that?"

"Well, there may be a great deal more in his dream than just a symbol, too," said Lloyd. Job certainly realized that: 'In a dream, in a vision of the night, when deep sleep falls upon men, while slumbering on their beds, Then He opens the ears of men, and seals their instruction.'"

"Ahh . . . " I cast my hand disgustedly toward him. "You explain it with Biblical symbols . . . I'll explain it with father/god archetypes. To each his own!"

Lloyd shook his head. "Your earthly father . . . Peter's earthly father is a *person*! And at some point in his life, Peter had to make a decision to reject his father's controls. But if he still had his earthly father all mixed up with his Heavenly Father . . . that rejection could have led to his schizophrenic split."

"Come on, Lloyd . . . " I said with mock displeasure. "I don't tell you how to interpret the Bible!"

Lloyd frowned at me for a moment. Then he searched the ground, and picked up a small forked branch that had fallen. "Look . . . " He held the branch up so that I could see it. "This is life," he said.

"Looks just like a branch to me," I joked.

He smiled, and pointed his finger at me. Then he placed the finger at the base of the branch. "Whether we're searching, or just wandering, we're part of God's plan . . . and he wants us to follow Him." He illustrated by climbing up the base of the branch with two fingers. "But now . . . " He came to the fork in the branch and stopped. "Talk about freedom . . . This is the greatest freedom! At some point in our lives, we all come to the fork. Some people get here when they're very young . . . some when they're very old. I got here when I was twenty-two."

"What's *here*?" I asked. "What's the fork?"

"It's when you discover that life isn't just about crawling along the dry stick until it ends," he said. "It's when you make the conscious, willful determination."

"Determination . . . "

"Either God exists . . . or He does not exist," explained Lloyd.

I swatted at my arm and brushed away an ant. Then I crossed my legs in front of me and turned away from the lake and sat facing Lloyd. This type of discussion really made me uncomfortable, particularly when talking with someone as dogmatic as Lloyd. But I still had the strange feeling that there was something very significant here for Peter's case. "It's not as simple as that, Lloyd," I said. "There are customs, and rituals . . . symbols and . . . "

" . . . and archetypes," he interrupted.

"Well . . . yes."

"Bottom line, John . . . " He placed his finger at the fork again. "Either God exists . . . or He does not exist. Until you've tussled with that basic question, you have not reached the fork."

An uneasy feeling began to creep up the base of my spine. I didn't really want to talk about basic questions. I would leave that to the theologians. I was more interested in the related spiritual symbols and rituals that might be impacting Peter's personality. But I could see that Lloyd wasn't going to give up on this issue, so I decided to let him pursue it. "All right," I said finally. "Make your point."

"Where is Peter?" he asked."

"Hmm?"

Lloyd pointed below the fork, on the fork, and up each branch of the fork. "Where is Peter?" he repeated.

"Where is . . . I don't . . . " I focused my eyes intently on the single dry stick branching into two, and I recalled suddenly the traumatic moment of catharsis . . . Peter's pleading cry . . . *There is no God! There is no God!* . . . And his voice slowly fading to silence as he slumped back into the couch, his lips moving inaudibly.

"There is no God . . . " I mumbled. "That's what he said."

Lloyd's head dropped slowly. Then he raised it, and placed his finger on the right fork of the branch. "All right," he said slowly. "So . . . somewhere here . . . "

"But it's not as simple as all that!" I said loudly. "And I told Peter that, too," I said.

"What did you tell him?" asked Lloyd.

"I told him . . . there is a . . . a spiritual sense," I said, recalling that wrenching moment. "I told him that it was the unconscious expression of the concealed divine motive that was important. Either way, the *archetype* of God exists."

"Did he accept that?" asked Lloyd.

"Did he . . . I don't . . . "

"What did he say when you told him that?" he asked.

"He said . . . " I mumbled, struggling to recall. "He asked me if I really believed that God can be replaced by an archetype."

"And what did you tell him?" asked Lloyd slowly.

"I didn't . . . I didn't answer him."

Lloyd sighed heavily. "And did it end there?" he asked.

"I . . . I don't have my notes with me."

"You don't need your notes for this, John," said Lloyd. "Surely that must have been the single most significant session in your therapy."

"It was just . . . "

I didn't have my notes. If I'd had my notes, I could have responded accurately . . . competently. But instead, the terrible memories of that moment flooded into my consciousness, and overwhelmed my rational considerations. I could still feel Peter's strong hands clutching at my knees . . . and his pleading harsh whisper . . . "Is there a God, Doctor? Is there a God?"

"It was . . . " I repeated softly. "It was very significant."

"How?" he asked.

I sighed and looked out across the lake. "Do you . . . do you remember the day you left home?" I asked.

"Oh, yes," said Lloyd.

"Do you remember what you asked Dad that day?" I asked.

Lloyd nodded. "Apparently you do, too, John. Why don't you tell me."

"You asked him . . . 'Is there a God, Pop? Is there a God?'"

"And what did Pop say?" Lloyd asked deliberately.

"He said . . . he said it didn't matter."

"Yes," said Lloyd. "I remember . . . very well."

"Lloyd . . . "

"Yes?"

"Peter asked me the same thing," I said.

"And what did you tell him?"

"I told him . . . it didn't matter," I mumbled.

Lloyd crossed both legs in front of him, and turned toward me. He leaned forward and spoke intensely. "And what did Peter say to that?" he asked.

"He thanked me," I said. "And he said that he guessed that meant . . . there isn't . . . any . . . God . . . "

"Yeah . . . " Lloyd swallowed hard. "That's what I thought, too . . . when Pop told me that."

I trembled lightly as a shudder crossed my spine. I suddenly felt ashamed for having revealed so much to Lloyd. I picked up a large stone, stood up, and cast it far out into the lake. After a few moments a dull splash resounded. "This is all very confidential, you know," I said.

"Of course," said Lloyd, without moving.

"I mean . . . of course it was a significant session," I said. "It was the single most important repressed element in his life. And once that was out, it allowed me to plan for dealing with it . . . finding substitutes . . . "

"Oh, John . . . ." Lloyd stood beside me and held out the forked branch. "All the substitutes are on this branch." He pointed to the right fork. "And our true selves . . . the persons that God wants us to be . . . are on *this* branch." He placed his finger on the left fork. "And the more we follow substitutes, the farther we will get from God . . . and the more split we will be from our true personalities."

I looked at the craggy piece of wood before my eyes. Lloyd was so dogmatic. It wasn't as simple as all that. I impulsively reached forward and grabbed the branch from Lloyd. Then I tore off the right branch and let it fall to the ground.

"It isn't as simple as all that, Lloyd!" I said loudly. I held the remaining part of the branch far behind me, and thrust it hard. It spun noiselessly through the air, hovered for a moment, and then fell with a silent splash into the darkness of the lake.

"John . . . " Lloyd held me by my arms, and turned me toward him. "All of us have many roles that we perform . . . professional, husband, father, friend, brother, self-fulfilling . . . And if these are all performed in God's will, and with God's plan, they will be healthy and productive. But if they are performed apart from God . . . and especially in the search for some substitute for God . . . they will fall into chaos . . . and ultimate destruction."

I let my eyes return Lloyd's intense stare, and I waited patiently as he finished his statement. Then I shook my head. "It isn't as simple as all that," I repeated. "And besides, your premise is wrong. It's *my* will that determines what roles I perform. I'm in control of my life . . . my destiny. And that has to be the basic direction. That's where strength comes from. That's the meaning of character."

Lloyd shook his head. "That's the legacy we got from Pop."

"Well . . . what's wrong with that?" I asked. "Why should we have to rely on external power? That's weakness."

"I used to believe that, too," said Lloyd. "But then I realized that I was never so strong . . . as when I acknowledged how completely and utterly weak I was . . . without God!"

I pulled my arms away from Lloyd's grasp and headed back up the dark path toward the campfire. Lloyd stepped quickly up beside me, but we walked in silence. They were all still there, and as we approached, I could hear the growing swells of another song . . . "Nearer, my God, to Thee . . . Nearer to Thee . . . " I stopped behind a tree and searched for Diane. She was in the top row now, sitting next to Kate. Her eyes were closed, and she was singing.

"We have an extra cot in our cabin, John," said Lloyd. "You will stay, won't you, so you can spend some time with Diane tomorrow?"

"What?"

"Stay . . . cot . . . Diane . . . tomorrow . . . " Lloyd's lips weren't moving, but the words still moved about in my mind like some cascading fall. I turned away from him and struggled to focus on the raging campfire. The boy with the flowing sandy-colored hair was still there, and he was coaxing, and urging them to sing, and they followed . . . "Nearer, my God, to Thee . . . Nearer to Thee . . . " And then he turned toward me, and his face twisted and he became Peter, and he laughed, and the others joined him.

"No . . . " I heard myself whispering.

"Stay . . . cot . . . Diane . . . tomorrow . . . " Lloyd's words flowed in irregular pitch and volume, and as I turned to him, his face became disfigured in the shadow of the flames.

"No!" I pushed Lloyd aside. Then I turned and ran toward the parking lot. The moon had risen higher now, and its welcome rays pushed their way through the overhanging branches of the trees. Then I stopped abruptly as I came to a fork in the path. I couldn't remember which way to go . . . And Lloyd's harping words were chasing me . . . tussle with that basic question . . . right . . . or left? The shrubbery was low in the center, and I pushed my way through it, avoiding both paths. Finally, to the left, I saw the parking lot, and I struggled through the thickening shrubs, across a bridge of stone, and ran to my car. The door wasn't locked. I thrust it open, fell inside, and closed it behind me. Then I pulled the key from my pocket, inserted it in the slot, and turned. The warm throbbing engine roared, and I laughed suddenly in recognition of how wrong Lloyd had been. I was in control! And in four hours I would lead myself down the mountain . . . and into the comfort and security of my own home.

I pressed the electric window control, and the window to my left lowered slightly. I could still see the flickering campfire in the distance . . . and hear the faintly discernible words . . . "Nearer, my . . . " I quickly pressed the up button, and the window shut, and renounced the unwelcome sound. Diane would be all right. Lloyd and Kate would see to that . . . But what would Meg say when I returned home? There would be questions . . . and explanations . . . She probably expected this, though . . . probably some conspiracy with Lloyd and Kate to get me up here . . . make me stay . . .

I slapped my hand angrily against the dash board in rejection of my irrational thoughts. I had to be careful of my actions . . . bizarre . . . Even Lloyd understood . . . common characteristics . . . withdrawn, high-risk behavior, depression, omnipotence, paranoia, delusions, dreams . . . dreams . . . dreams . . .

Why was I punishing myself? Lloyd wasn't a real doctor. He was just a minister. I couldn't let myself be diverted from my goal. Of course I couldn't stay tonight. I didn't have time for that. I had misinterpreted Peter's motives tonight. I had to be ready. I would go to the office . . . sleep there . . .

I put the car in reverse and backed quickly out of the parking slot. I could see the moon clearly in an opening in the branches of the trees. There was a slight mist around it, and it seemed to be whirling . . . and then the white moon became a burning, reddish glow, and it spun deeper, and deeper . . . "Nearer, my

God . . . " No. Lloyd said it was Job . . . "A deep sleep falls upon men, while slumbering on their beds. Then He opens the ears of men, and seals their instruction."

I shook my head and the moon regained its clarity. I would sleep in my office tonight . . . be ready for tomorrow.

24

I returned to the office late after lunch the next day. It had been an exhausting morning. Naturally my experience last night hadn't helped . . . or the long drive back. I hadn't returned until after 1:00 A.M. And I had lain on my therapy couch for only half an hour when I had realized that spending the night in my office probably hadn't been the best decision. But it had been my decision, nonetheless, and I had seen it through. Besides, it wasn't just the lack of physical rest. My patients' lives are so complex. And I have to understand them . . . deal with them. At the conclusion of each session this morning, I had recalled the absurdity of Lloyd's simplistic theory about the origin of the schizophrenic split from reality. I was angry with myself for having become embroiled in a discussion of his fundamental beliefs.

I pushed the door open, and walked quickly into the outer office. Cheryl looked up and smiled brightly at me.

"Hi, Dr. Summers," she said with difficulty over the lingering hoarseness. "You're back late today."

"Yes, I had some . . . yes . . . " I mumbled.

"Your wife called," said Cheryl. "She said . . . well . . . " She shrugged self-consciously.

"What?"

"Well . . . she seemed kind of upset," explained Cheryl. "She said she really wanted you to be home on time tonight. Something about the two of you . . . and your daughter."

"Yes. Yes, of course I will," I said with some irritation.

"Dr. Summers . . . "

"Yes?"

"Your wife is really a nice lady," she said. "And I've met your daughter a couple of times, too. She's neat."

"Thank you," I said curtly.

"I know my dad always used to be busy all the time," she said slowly. "And I really missed . . . you know . . . spending time with him."

"How old are you, Cheryl?" I asked.

"Twenty-seven," she responded.

"My daughter is sixteen," I said firmly, and I turned and headed toward my office.

"Yes, sir," said Cheryl quietly. "Oh . . . Dr. Summers!"

I turned back at the door. "What?"

"Mrs. Masters was scheduled for two," she said. "And she called in to cancel for today."

"Hmm . . . " I glanced at my watch. It was nearly two now. "What time is Peter scheduled?" I asked.

"At three," she said.

"All right," I said. "I'm going to work in my office until then. Don't disturb me until three."

"All right, Dr. Summers," said Cheryl.

I passed through the door and closed it behind me. I felt myself sigh with relief. I wasn't looking forward to dealing with Mrs. Masters' neurotic complaints, anyway. She was suffering from delusional hypochondria, and I had frequently been tempted to prescribe a placebo just to quiet her idiotic ravings. I started toward my desk, but then a renewed wave of exhaustion swept over my body. I sat down on the therapy couch and yawned. Then I kicked my feet up, and laid my head back on the stiff cushioned arm. A slight dizziness passed across my forehead, and the faint aroma of wine still lingered in my nostrils. I chuckled at the fact that it had been Lloyd's irritating presence at lunch five weeks ago that had made me break my rule about drinking during working hours. Each day since then, I had deliberately had a glass of wine in rebellion against his sanctimonious attitude. It was silly, of course, but all of us need a little diversion now and then. And Lloyd was so inflexible. Our discussion last night made that very clear. I could still see him holding that gnarled branch in front of me. Either God exists . . . or He does not exist . . . "To be, or not to be . . . " I mumbled, and then I laughed lightly. How could Lloyd relegate the richness of the schizophrenic personality to so naive a distinction? Naturally there was a spiritual tie with schizophrenia. Jung was well aware of this -- particularly in the area of religious symbolism. But the archetypes were interwoven with multiple layers of intricate, interrelated facets. The spiritual essence was a conglomerate of these unconscious images. There was no rational basis for Lloyd's fatuous allusion. Things were so much more complex than that. So much more . . . complex . . .

I felt a dull throbbing sensation on the bridge of my nose, and a wakeful surge swept through my head. I opened my eyes slowly, and focused on the clock across the room. It was two forty-five. I stretched my arms out and sighed deeply.

"Hello, John. Did you have a good rest?"

"What?" I bolted abruptly to a sitting position. Peter was sitting directly across from me . . . in my analyst's chair.

"Wakening from an afternoon's nap can be disconcerting, can't it?" he asked.

"Cheryl!" I called.

"She stepped out for a few minutes," said Peter. "To the ladies' room, I believe. So I took the liberty of beginning early."

"Early . . . " I was still not fully awake, and our interchange took on a bizarre flavor.

"And I was eager to see how you enjoyed your trip to the mountains yesterday," he added derisively.

"Mountains . . . " That did it. I squeezed my eyes together for a moment, and breathed deeply to dispel the last vestiges of drowsiness. "How did you know what I did yesterday afternoon, Peter?" I asked.

Peter sat back in the chair, and tapped his fingers lightly together. "I was watching from across the street," he said. He glanced across the room, and then back again. "It was almost as good as a mirrored door."

I frowned at him, and shook my head slowly. "Why, Peter?" I asked him. "Why did you do it?"

"I initially did consider going to the mountains," he said. "And Moon Lake is so beautiful!"

"No, Peter," I said. "It was a purposeful action directed at me. I need to know why you did it."

Peter sighed. "Curiosity," he said deliberately. "And, since I'm not a cat . . . " He chuckled slowly.

"Curiosity about what?" I asked.

He leaned forward and whispered harshly and haltingly. "I wanted to see . . . if you could experience . . . fear!"

That word certainly summed up my feeling as I ran from the office. But I couldn't let him have the satisfaction of knowing that he had succeeded. "What makes you think that I was experiencing fear, Peter?" I asked him.

Peter sat back again and smiled. "People in a state of stark terror are very easy to read," he said softly.

I had never observed Peter in so threatening a mode, but, at the same time, he was evincing a strangely sane posture. That reaction wasn't unusual, of course. Schizophrenic's will often "play at being sane," particularly in instances in which they are feeling at odds with their therapists. But he was carrying forward today, a deliberate action that he had initiated yesterday to throw me off balance, and I had to discover the reason.

"What you did yesterday, Peter . . . " I began slowly. " . . . was not productive."

"Oh, I think it was very productive," he responded.

"Why do you say that?" I asked.

"Any action leading to the revelation of truth is productive," he said.

"What truth was revealed by that action?"

Peter smiled and shifted in his chair. "In due time, John. In due time."

"You're still calling me by my first name, I see," I said.

"Of course."

"That's not an advisable practice, Peter," I said. "Unless, of course, you believe that you are now cured."

"How could I be cured?" he asked loudly. "You've only been treating me for seven weeks!"

"Then . . . you're acting," I suggested cautiously.

"No. I feel good today, John," he said. "I feel good!"

"Why?" I asked. "Because you sent me on an eight-hour trip?"

He leaned forward again and shook his head. "Because . . . what I suspected . . . was substantiated."

"What's that?"

"We . . . you and I . . . we have a kinship," he said.

"I am your therapist, Peter," I said.

Peter raised his palm and shook his head. "No. We have a kinship. We are very much alike, the two of us. We are both healers . . . and we both play with peoples' minds."

"I'm a psychiatrist," I reminded him.

"What does that mean?" he asked. "That you've gone to this or that college, and learned . . . " He shifted in his chair.

"Well . . . "

"You have that on me, I'll admit," said Peter. "I'm sure you're aware of my lack of schooling."

"No, I'm not." And I wasn't. That was one aspect of his historical background that I hadn't learned.

"From high school to healer in one easy jump!" he said. "But for ten years . . . I've read, John. I've read extensively." He smiled and passed his hand across an imaginary title. "*Sermons that inspire* . . . and, of course, philosophy, and history, and poetry . . . I love poetry . . . " He sat forward and spoke intensely. "And don't you think I've read everything that has been written about the schizophrenic?"

"I suppose."

Peter sighed and sat back. "I apologize for placing you in that position, John, he said slowly. "It wasn't kind, I know. But I had to be certain, you see. I've seen it so often in your eyes . . . in fleeting moments."

"What?"

"We're so alike, John," he said. "We have a kinship."

"No, Peter. I'm the psychiatrist, and . . . " But his eyes were burning, and I turned my head away. I tried to evaluate my reactions with Peter . . . see what I was doing which was revealing those feelings. Bernadette knew . . . she knew the truth that can be derived from the other side of reality. She knew that I was on the precipice. And Leonard had warned me . . . potentially damaging counter-transference . . . inappropriate involvement . . . But they didn't bother me. They were my colleagues. It was a sort of shared concern. But Lloyd knew also. That was the most disturbing . . . until now.

I breathed deeply and turned my head back. "Sometimes these things occur, Peter," I said with forced calmness. "It's called counter-transference."

"I know," he said.

"And the therapist . . . assimilates some of the fears and behavior patterns of the patient . . . in the process toward recovery . . . "

Peter smiled and shook his head slowly. "Only if there are similar experiences . . . shared fears . . . " He leaned forward and whispered harshly again. "You have demons, too, John! You have demons, too!"

I tried to turn my head away again, but it was as though his words were circling on a steel band through my head, holding it in place. Perspiration formed on my forehead, and I wiped it away clumsily with my fingers.

"But that's good, John," continued Peter. "Because that made it possible for you to help me renounce *my* demon."

"You mean . . . your father," I said.

"No! My father is not my demon!" he said sternly. "It was my father's fear. My father's absurd faith! I was able to reject that finally. And there was a kind of . . . peace in the rejection. And you gave me that peace, John."

"But we didn't finish, Peter," I said. "After rejection there must be re-fulfillment. Death, and rebirth. I told you . . . there is a spiritual sense. That is the classic Jungian explanation."

"Perhaps Jung was wrong," he said.

"No," I insisted. "Surely you should know. You experience it. You used it. Your message to your followers exudes the creation of the divine self."

"We are so alike, John," he said slowly. "We are both healers . . . and we both play with peoples' minds."

"No, Peter . . . Nature abhors a vacuum," I said. "Expel the non-useful, yes . . . but recovery lies in the successful spiritual replacement."

"What is successful, John?"

"I . . . I must ask the questions, Peter," I said weakly.

"But before you can ask the questions, you must know the answers," he said. "We are so alike, John. What do you love?

What is successful for you? Do you love speed? Do you love danger?"

"I love . . . "

"But afterward . . . what is there?" He adjusted his chair slightly to afford a direct view of me. "Why didn't you study poetry at the institute, John?" he asked. "That's the true psychology. Why didn't you study Swinburne?"

"Swinburne . . . "

Peter thrust both his hands out suddenly. "Listen!" He closed his eyes, and began to recite, slowly and passionately:

From too much love of living,
From hope and fear set free,
We thank with brief thanksgiving
Whatever gods may be
That no life lives for ever;
That dead men rise up never;
That even the weariest river
Winds somewhere safe to sea.

"Why didn't you study Swinburne, John?" he asked again. "That's the true psychology."

"I . . . there wasn't time," I mumbled irrationally. "And, besides . . . there are reasons. There are explanations. Your father, Peter. Your reactions to your father's beliefs and actions were . . . "

"Is that the sum total of *your* life, John?" he asked. "Do your reactions to *your* father's beliefs and actions explain *you*?"

"I must ask the questions . . . "

"You must have the answers!" Peter whispered loudly.

"But there are reasons . . . there are explanations . . . " I said.

"What's the bottom line, John?"

"What . . . " I was in a clear, rational interchange. This was undeniably Peter's question. But the image that flashed through my mind was from last night, at the lake, and Lloyd's insistent distinction. But Peter couldn't be referring to that simplistic distinction . . . he couldn't . . . "What do you mean by that, Peter?" I asked.

"Beyond all the reasons and explanations . . . What's the purpose?" he asked.

"Life is . . . it's so complex, Peter," I said, struggling to find an answer that would lead him from this state of frustration to a new level of awareness. "And there are so many complex experiences . . . It's beautiful!"

"And beauty is its own reward?" he asked slowly.

"Only in terms of . . . the journey . . . "

"Toward . . . " he coaxed me.

I closed my eyes momentarily to formulate a productive answer. Peter was leading toward a healthy realization of the complexity of life, and I had to find the best way to ease him over the hump . . . But I was startled out of my contemplation by Peter's roughly grasping my knees again. I opened my eyes and saw him leaning close to me, his eyes burning with intensity.

"Bottom line, John," he whispered. "Just tell me! We are so alike, you and I. Just tell me your bottom line . . . and that will help me. Is there a God, John? Is there a God? Surely you have an opinion!"

The session had reverted to where it was nearly two weeks ago. Peter was addressing me with precisely the same question. Nothing had changed . . . not in Peter. My reaction was muddied more, of course. That was Lloyd's fault. I closed my eyes, and I saw his idiotic stick before me again, branching off into the darkness. His theological premise had no place in my psychiatric therapy session, but the terminology was so similar, that I had to battle with myself to avoid using that experience as some kind of constructive referent. But there was nothing constructive about it. Peter must learn to recognize the complexity . . . just as I had. Otherwise, he would never be whole.

I wiped the perspiration from my forehead again. I was beginning to feel like I did in the session the Leonard had observed. I hated the feeling of failure that inevitably arose from these control-shifting occurrences. Something . . . beyond my control. It was clear that my continued presence at this point was nonproductive. I put my hands on Peter's shoulders and pushed him back. "Peter . . . I understand your confusion. I even understand your action yesterday," I said deliberately. "It's this pesky counter-transference. I tried to deny it's effects at first, but I'm afraid it's gotten the best of us."

"What are you saying, John?" asked Peter softly.

"I was warned about this," I said, "but I thought I could rise above it. But I can see now that I'm not serving you well."

"But you have," he said.

I shook my head. "Only to a point. There's a barrier, now, Peter."

"What is the barrier, John?" he asked.

"It doesn't matter," I said.

"Beauty is its own reward," said Peter vaguely.

"The important thing is to find the best therapeutic experience for you at this time," I continued. "I believe spending some time with another psychiatrist for a while would be very helpful."

"I see." Peter sat back quietly. His eyes were expressionless, but the feeling of deep disappointment radiated from him.

"Just for a while, Peter," I reassured him. "Just until I can deal with my own reaction to this barrier."

"Who do you recommend, John?" he asked.

"Well, ordinarily, I wouldn't . . . " I began, and then stopped momentarily. "You've already spent some time with Dr. Butler, though. He's a brilliant therapist. I think you should give him another chance."

"Dr. Sigmund, eh?" He smiled faintly, and then shifted in his chair. "He knows nothing of the father/god archetype, of course."

"What . . . " I was startled by his use of this term. But, of course, he said he had done extensive reading. "No . . . well, but we can carry on with that . . . later, you know," I said haltingly.

Peter slouched down in his chair. Then he narrowed his eyes, and looked at me without speaking.

"What do you say, Peter?" I asked.

"What are you afraid of, John?" he asked slowly. "What are you afraid of?"

I heard a light knocking, and the door to my office swung open.

"Dr. Summers . . . " Cheryl stood in the doorway with an apologetic look on her face. "Oh, I see you're in session. I'm sorry. I stepped out for a minute, and I guess I just didn't . . . "

"That's all right, Cheryl," I said.

"Yes, that's quite all right, Cheryl," said Peter. He rose abruptly from his chair and walked toward her. "I was just leaving, anyway."

"Oh?" Cheryl looked questioningly toward me.

"Yes. We're through for today," I said.

"We're colleagues, you, know, Cheryl," said Peter. "John and I . . . We're both healers . . . and we both play with peoples' minds."

"Oh . . . " Cheryl chuckled softly. "That's cute!"

"That'll be all, Cheryl," I said.

Cheryl nodded and stepped back into the outer office.

Peter placed his hand on the knob and started to follow her. Then he turned back and smiled. "Have you seen that bumper sticker, John?"

"What?"

"The one that says, *THE ONE WHO DIES WITH THE MOST TOYS WINS*?"

"Yes . . . Yes, I believe so," I said.

"How many patients have you had in your career, John?" he asked.

"How many? I . . . I don't know."

"Say . . . a thousand?" he asked.

"I suppose," I said.

Peter smiled broadly. "I've had millions! I win!" He left the office, and pulled the door closed firmly behind him.

I breathed deeply . . . and then exhaled, and I listened to the rapid expulsion of air as it passed through my lips. I felt a sudden calmness . . . a sense of peace. But then a tightness formed around my chest, and I breathed in again to replace the rejected air whose life-giving oxygen had been spent. I had counseled so many people seeking to escape from destructive relationships. The pattern was always the same. At the point of dissociation there is always a feeling of sadness . . . a sense of loss, no matter how cancerous the union was. Inertia . . . that was the term out of physical science. Things just keep revolving . . . But Peter had been right about me. I could patronize Bernadette, fool Leonard, avoid Lloyd . . . and lie to myself. But Peter . . . that mirrored reflection of the subconscious aspects of my personality. All this time I had tried to pass it off as a counter-transference which I could recognize, confront, and deal with. And I would deal with it . . . except . . .

I glanced toward the blankness of the closed door. A momentary terrifying thought crossed my mind. Suppose I needed Peter . . . suppose, despite all the pernicious mutual feeding of anxiety . . . there was something there . . . some bizarre symbiotic relationship. But which of us was the willow . . . and which was the mistletoe?

There was a knock at the door, and Cheryl stepped in, more quickly this time, and walked over to where I was sitting.

"Dr. Summers, I know you didn't want to talk while he was here," she said. "But I hope I didn't cut things short by coming in like that."

"Don't apologize, Cheryl," I mumbled.

"He was acting kinda strange," she said. "I mean . . . natural, but, for Peter . . . strange." She sat down and leaned toward me. "Are you all right, Dr. Summers?"

"What?"

"Are you all right?" she repeated. "Can I help you?"

"Help me . . . " That's what Peter had said . . . Just tell me your bottom line . . . and that will help me . . . But he missed the point. It wasn't that at all. It was his father. "It was your father . . . " I mumbled.

"What?"

Then I realized the problem. I was still sitting on the couch . . . and she was sitting in my chair! "You don't belong there!" I shouted.

"What?"

"You belong here!" I stood up and pointed to the couch.

"Oh . . . well, I didn't . . . " Cheryl winced through a smile and shifted gracefully to the couch.

"Now . . . " I sat in my chair, and leaned toward her. "It was your father. Tell me about your father."

"Oh . . . " She swallowed, and then smiled and continued. "Well, I told you that my dad always used to be busy all the time, and I really missed spending time with him."

"What . . . " I looked at Cheryl, and suddenly began to laugh. "No. I didn't mean *your* father. I meant *my* father."

"What?"

"I'm sorry, Cheryl," I said after I had stopped laughing. "My father. Yes. That's the key . . . if there is one."

"I guess . . . " she said with a puzzled look on her face.

I stood and headed toward the door. "There are no more sessions today, are there, Cheryl?" I asked.

"No. Peter was the last one."

"I'm leaving now, Cheryl," I said. "I'm going up to my parents' place."

"All right," she said. "Oh . . . Dr. Summers . . . "

I turned back. "What?"

"Don't forget . . . your wife called, and . . . "

I raised my palm to silence her, and hurried out the door. Peter had overstated the case. Our kinship was strictly coincidental, and tenuous at best. To begin with, our fathers were nothing alike. And the best way to cement that knowledge in my unconscious was to take these vibrant reflections . . . now . . . and bathe them in the reality of the true relationship I had with my father. I knew that he always took Wednesday afternoons off, so it was likely that I would find him at home. I opened the outside door, and headed quickly toward my car.

"Dr. Summers!"

"What?"

"Dr. Summers . . . May I speak with you for a minute?" Lieutenant Chadwick stepped out from behind a large van and walked toward me.

"Oh . . . Lieutenant. How are you?"

"Well . . . " He shrugged. "That depends. It's been a couple of weeks, and I haven't heard from you. So I thought I'd better pay you a visit."

"Yes," I said. "Well, these things take time."

"You just had a session with our friend, apparently," he said. "I saw him leave just a few minutes ago."

"Yes."

"Well . . . what's your opinion?"

Which opinion was he referring to? Two weeks ago? Today? Last night? I could identify at least five different points in time during which my opinion regarding Peter's potential for violence shifted radically from one extreme to another. What was I to tell him?

"My original opinion was that he was non-violent," I told him.

"Tell me something I don't know," he said sarcastically.

"This is a very complex case, Lieutenant," I said. "I haven't found anything that would lead substantially to a firm conclusion . . . "

"Give me your gut-level feeling, Doctor," he said. C'mon . . . Bottom line."

"What?" That phrase again . . . and then Lloyd and Peter merged momentarily in the demanding plea with Chadwick.

"I mean . . . either Peter Lumen is a murderer . . . or he is not," said Chadwick. He leaned closer to me, his coat parted, and in the nearness, took on the appearance of a gnarled, forked branch.

"It . . . it isn't as simple as all that," I mumbled.

"Well, at some point, you're going to have to stake a claim . . . make a decision," said Chadwick.

"It just seems . . . Surely there are some other suspects out there," I said.

"Sure, there are," said Chadwick. "I could even make a case against you."

"What?"

"Well . . . you have been observed in that area several times in the last three weeks," he said smiling.

I had a momentary recollection of the sights, and sounds, and smells of downtown. I hadn't even given my trips any thought. But since I had gone there to pick up Peter, I had driven through the district several times. It was perverse, I know, but the memories from my high school days still retained a sense of excitement, and merely passing through the dark, dirty streets rekindled that feeling. I had no idea that I would be under surveillance.

"I was just doing research," I told Chadwick.

"Research about Lumen?" he asked.

"Yes."

"Well, then that must mean you have some suspicions," he said.

"No. Just research," I said. "Is there anything else?" I asked him.

He shrugged. "Just keep in touch, Doctor. Keep in touch." He waved and walked away.

I stepped quickly to my car, unlocked the door, opened it, and slipped inside. The interior was oppressively hot, but I pulled the door shut. The silence gave me A sudden sense of relief. And I knew that, at the touch of a button, I could regain control of the environment, and make it conform to my bidding. But then a cold shiver passed across the bubbles of hot perspiration on my forehead. I recalled Peter's question . . . What are you afraid of, John? What are you afraid of? But what's to fear . . . if dead men rise up never . . . and even the weariest river winds somewhere safe to sea . . . No, Peter . . . it isn't as simple as all that.

25

I pulled my car to a halt on the broad circular drive in front of my parents' huge house, got out, and walked up the steps leading to the massive double entry doors. I pressed the doorbell, and I could hear the faint four-fold chime from inside the house. After a few moments, one of the large doors swung open, and the frail-looking gray-haired maid answered the door.

"Yes . . . Oh, hello, Dr. Summers."

"Hello, Hillary," I said. "Are my parents here?"

"Your mother's in the kitchen," she said, swinging the door completely open.

"Thanks." I brushed past her and headed through the wide hallway toward the kitchen.

"Dr. Summers . . . "

I stopped and turned around to see Hillary a few steps behind me. "Yes? What is it, Hillary?" I asked her.

"Ah . . . " She pointed vaguely toward the kitchen and frowned. Then she shook her head slowly. "Never mind." She left the hallway and walked quickly into the living room.

The kitchen was bright and spotless. A large bay window extended out into the back yard. My mother stood there, with her back to me. I walked up to her quietly, and placed my hands on her shoulders. "Hi, Mom!"

"Oh!" She jumped suddenly, and turned her head back. "Oh, John! You startled me so!" She turned around completely and gave me a brief one-armed hug. She was holding a drink in the other hand.

"Sorry. I thought you heard me come in," I said.

"No. I was preoccupied, I guess," she said.

I thought I knew what Hillary had started to tell me. My mother looked terrible. She was wearing a dirty house coat, her hair was uncombed, and her eyes had dark circles under them.

"Are you all right, Mom?" I asked her.

"Of course, John . . . of course." She took a sip from her drink, and turned back toward the window.

This wasn't a completely uncharacteristic condition for my mother. I had seen her this way on several occasions during the last ten years. My father had become increasingly involved in his law practice after I left home, and this sometimes led to disagreements between my mother and him. This usually resulted in her paying less attention to her personal care and drinking more for a short period of time. My father wasn't the easiest person in the world to get along with, and I sympathized with my mother to a degree over the way he treated her. On the other hand, she tended to rely on him too greatly for a degree of affection that he seemed unable to give. I recalled the many times that I had actually held her in contempt for what seemed to be unrealistic demands on his time and attention. I often thought she should have gotten a job. But, of course, my father would never have allowed that.

I remembered that I was not here today for the purpose of a social call. I had lived in this house since I was a baby. The greater part of the history of the early development of my personality lay within this home, and if I were to find the slice of my psyche that was creating the overpowering, unwanted bond that I'd developed with Peter, it would surely be here. But the discovery process required an absolutely objective approach, otherwise I would be participating in some mindless return to childhood. That shouldn't be difficult. My mother was exhibiting classic neurotic behavior today. Recognition of that would help me to hold firmly to my role as therapist.

"Is Dad here?" I asked.

"Yes. He's out at the pasture," she said dryly. "He's hired a new boy to train the horses. He's out there now . . . working with him."

"Good. Let's go out and see him," I said.

"Me?"

"Sure. C'mon," I said. It was important that they both be there. It was primarily my father's influence that I needed to explore, but the interaction between the two of them had certainly also been a factor.

"I don't know . . . " My mother glanced down at her garment and frowned.

"You're fine, Mom," I said. "C'mon!"

My mother sighed. Then she followed me slowly out the kitchen door onto the spacious patio. The pasture was about fifty yards directly ahead of us. The late afternoon sun was setting to our left, and as we walked across the lush grass toward the gleaming white fence, the rays trickled through the leaves of the trees and cast speckled shadows on the ground.

My father had constructed a large raised lanai against the pasture fence. This made it easier for him to observe the working of the horses, and converse with the riders. It was covered with a bright candy-striped roof, and was completely outfitted with patio furniture and a wet bar. My mother and I ascended the four wooden steps leading to the lanai. My father stood leaning on the pasture fence with his back to us, a battery-operated megaphone hanging from his hand.

"Charles . . . John is here," said my mother.

"Hmm?" He turned around and frowned momentarily at her. Then he looked at me, and his face brightened into a toothy grin. "John! What a nice surprise!"

"Hello, Dad," I said.

"You're just in time," he said enthusiastically. "We're working with a new gelding." He beckoned for me to join him. "Come watch."

I walked over and joined him at the waist-high fence. It was shorter than I remembered, because, as a boy, I had placed my chin on the top rail. The trees in the pasture were definitely larger, though. But somehow the vibrant green leaves had given way to a dull olive hew. Several trees near the fence displayed bare branches with dry curling bark. Long, robust mistletoe hung from many of them, in stark contrast to the dying hosts.

I heard a loud electronic click, and I saw my father raise the megaphone to his mouth and call out into the pasture.

"Change leads! Change leads!" he shouted. "Don't let him get away with that!" He dropped the megaphone slightly, but he kept his eyes intently in place.

In the center of the two-acre pasture, a slight boy rode on a large black thoroughbred. He turned his head momentarily as my father called to him, and then he leaned forward slightly and directed his attention again to his riding.

"Incompetent . . . " muttered my father. Then he raised the device to his lips again and called angrily. "The animal feels your lack of will! Come over here! Come over here!"

The boy pulled the horse to a walk, turned, and headed toward the platform. My father's voice through the megaphone sounded very familiar. I had learned to ride in this pasture. And my father had used the same technique in training me.

The fence trembled slightly as the flank of the horse brushed against it. The boy appeared to be about sixteen. He glanced at me with wide eyes and nodded briefly, as he brought the animal to a halt in front of us.

My father set the megaphone down. Then he grasped the reins of the horse and pulled it closer to the fence. "Here. This is the problem." He reached up and turned the boy's shoulder roughly around. "Take off the hat!"

The boy reached up and removed a small cap that he was wearing. A sudden memory flooded my mind. A leather strap encircled the boy's head. Three straps dropped from the sides and back of this to a halter which was fitted tightly about his chest. Yes . . . I had worn the same device. I had completely forgotten.

"If you're not erect, the horse will not be erect," said my father. He reached for a buckle in the small of the boy's back. He muttered angrily as he released it from its present setting. Then he pulled the strap down two more notches. The boy's head jerked back suddenly. "Now try to look down!" said my father.

The boy pulled his head forward, but the strap restrained him.

"Good!" My father secured the strap in this position. "I shouldn't have to do this for you. You know what's up and what's down."

The boy mumbled in assent, and replaced his cap.

"Now take him around again in figure-eights . . . ten minutes," said my father. He gave the horse a slap on the flank, and the powerful animal trotted off with his rider.

"Have a seat. I'll fix you a drink," my father told me. He slapped me on the back, and headed toward the wet bar.

"Yeah . . . okay." I turned first and watched as the boy led the horse toward the center of the pasture, his head held rigidly in an upright position. I was about his age when I had worn the halter. I couldn't imagine why I had forgotten. As I watched now, I could feel distinctly the press of the circular strap around my head, and the restraining yank against the halter as I frantically tried to look down in an attempt to establish my balance and perspective. I remembered my father trying to use that with Lloyd, too, when he was learning to ride. But he had refused.

"Double scotch and soda . . . right?" asked my father.

"Yes. That's right." I walked over and joined my mother at the table. She had already refilled her drink, and was sitting quietly, sipping it.

"Here we are!" My father brought our drinks over, and sat beside me.

"Thanks." I took a large swallow from my glass, and the familiar bitter aroma passed through the roof of my mouth into my nostrils, and lingered at the bridge of my nose.

"Louise, didn't you get dressed at all today?" he asked exasperatedly.

"I wasn't feeling well, Charles," she responded absently.

"The better you look, the better you'll feel," said my father. "That's always been my motto."

"Yes," she answered vaguely, and took a large swallow from her glass.

"Well, John, it's been a while since you've watched the horses work," said my father. "Does it bring back memories?"

"Yes, it really does," I told him.

"You were a natural," he continued enthusiastically. "I never had to remind you to change leads."

"Sure you did, Dad," I corrected him. "Lots of times." I could still hear his angry voice shouting right, or left . . . and my trying to force my head past the restraining strap so that I could see what he was talking about. "Lots of times," I said again, and took another large swallow from my drink.

"Well . . . maybe so," he conceded. "But you learned eventually. And didn't you just love it?"

My father was always so strong. That's what I had always admired about him . . . still did. His strength, courage . . . and character. But I was here to explore the truth about myself today. I had to force it out of my memory and deal with it.

"Didn't you just love it, John?" my father asked again.

"Well . . . no," I mumbled. "I really didn't, Dad."

He set his drink down and glowered at me. "What? What are you talking about?"

"It was always so . . . hard, and restrictive," I said, gathering courage.

"Ahh . . . " he said derisively.

"And you always seemed so angry," I added. "I think that was the worst part."

"A little anger is always part of the training process," he responded. "This is an angry world. And you've got to learn to deal with it. I'm sure you'll admit that my training paid off when you got out on your own."

On my own . . . That phrase suddenly dug at me. I remembered Lloyd's snide glance last night that reminded me that I wouldn't have anything except that my father had arranged for it or paid for it. And of course . . . even my mentor.

"Don't you agree, John?" asked my father.

"I'm not sure that . . . " I began, and then stopped.

"What?" he prodded.

I finished the remainder of my drink. "I'm not sure that I really ever got out *on my own*," I said.

"What are you talking about, John?"

"It's all from you, Dad," I told him. "You paid for my education, you set me up in practice. You even gave me most of my clients."

"No more than any father would have done for a bright son," he said.

"Maybe not so bright."

"Hmm?"

"I spoke with Bernadette Keating last week," I said.

"And . . . "

"I found out that you did more than just handle her legal affairs," I said.

My mother suddenly sat forward, and spilled some of her drink on the table. "I told you it would come out!" she shouted.

"Shut up, Louise!" uttered my father threateningly.

"You always told me that there'd be no harm . . . that it was over with," she continued, and tears began to form in her eyes.

"I told you to shut up!" he shouted. Then he leaned forward. "Why don't you tell us what you're talking about, John."

I didn't know what was going on. I couldn't imagine my mother being so upset over such a . . .

"What did Bernadette tell you, John?" asked my father.

I pulled my eyes slowly away from the frightened face of my mother, and was met by my father's demanding expression. "We were discussing my education," I said. "And she told me that you pulled strings with the administration at the Institute to get me in," I said. "And arranged for Bernadette to tutor me . . . that otherwise . . . I wouldn't even have been accepted."

My father raised his eyebrow toward my mother, slapped his hand heavily on the table, and sat back. "Well, Louise . . . "

"I'm . . . I'm sorry . . . " mumbled my mother. "I'm sorry, John."

"What for, Mother?" I asked her. "What were you talking about?"

"Never mind," my father said gruffly.

"No! I think I have a right to know," I said. "It's important that I know!"

My father reached out and took our glasses. "You need a refill, John. I'm not sure about your mother." He stood clumsily and went to the wet bar.

"It happened such a long time ago, John," said my mother softly. "I'm sorry. It was stupid of me to mention it."

"Mention what?" I asked in exasperation.

"Your father's . . . your father's affair . . . with Bernadette," she mumbled.

"What . . . " I tried to continue my questioning, get clarification of . . . But I was completely stunned.

"It happened such a long time ago," she said again. "It ended . . . well . . . before you entered college. It's over with. It should be forgotten."

"Did . . . did Lloyd know about it?" I asked her.

She sighed deeply and nodded. "That was one of the things that . . . well . . . set them off."

"He never told me . . . he never told me . . . " I mumbled.

"No. Lloyd wouldn't," she said.

"Here!" My father's large hand appeared suddenly before me, placing a refilled glass on the table. Then he reached over and placed a drink in front of my mother. "The other drink *opened* your mouth. Maybe this will *close* it!" He sat down and drank quickly from his refilled glass.

"This is . . . this is . . . I'm not sure I know how to deal with this," I told him.

"There are reasons for things like that happening, John," he said impatiently. "You're a psychiatrist! Surely you know that!"

Of course I did. With other people. And that's what I was supposed to be doing today . . . viewing my father and mother with the staunch objectivity of a clinical expert. But this was such a departure from what I had expected. My father had always been the epitome of morality. That had always been his final, victorious statement to Lloyd when they had gotten into a discussion of the need for a good religious foundation. My father had always insisted that he didn't need religious rules to show him what was right and wrong, because he knew, and he always did the right thing. And I thought that he did. But Lloyd knew better . . . and he never told me. He knew before he left home . . . before he asked him . . . "Is there a God, Pop? . . . Is there a God?" I thought that didn't really matter. That's what our father had said. And I believed that. But I suddenly felt an overpowering need to know . . . what he *believed* . . . to know his *opinion*.

I leaned forward slightly, and I heard myself speaking uncontrollably . . . "Is there a God, Dad? Is there a God?"

"What?" My father's form was close again, and his eyes were deep and piercing.

"I just . . . It's important to know what people think," I mumbled. "It's important for me to know what you think. You don't have to actually *know* . . . It's just . . . Do you have an opinion?"

"Oh, for . . . " My father pushed himself abruptly away from the table.

"Charles, can't you . . . " began my mother, the tears now streaming down her cheeks.

"I don't believe it!" interrupted my father. "I don't know what's gotten into you, John! You sound just like Lloyd!"

"I just thought . . . It's important for me to know . . . "

"I'm very disappointed in you, John," he said angrily. "I thought you had more intelligence than that!" He turned his head suddenly toward the pasture. "And look at *that*!" He rose abruptly from his chair, strode to the railing, and picked up the battery-operated megaphone. He placed it close to his lips and pressed the trigger, and a loud electronic click issued forth. Then his voice followed . . . loud, harsh, and scornful. "No, you idiot! You change leads in the middle of the figure . . . not at the beginning of it! Do it again! Do it again!"

I felt my mother's hand on mine, and I turned to see her tear-stained face, pleading.

"Mother, why can't he . . . "

"It will be all right, John," she said. "Just don't talk about such things."

"What things, Mother?" I asked. "God . . . or Bernadette?"

"Just . . . just don't talk about such things," she said.

"That's what you told Lloyd."

"And that's part of it, you see," she said. "He and his father have such a different opinion. But your father is a good man, John."

"I always thought so," I said. "But this has been a very . . . a very difficult thing for me to learn about. I needed him, Mother. I needed . . . his strength . . . his character . . . "

"Your father is a good man, John," she repeated.

I glanced at my father, leaning threateningly over the white railing. Then I looked back at my mother and shook my head slowly. "What's the measure, Mother?" I asked. "What's the measure?"

My mother smiled faintly. Then she sat back, raised the loose sleeve of her house coat to her face and wiped the tears away. She sat forward again, and patted me on the hand. "You know what? You should go talk to Father Sheen," she said.

"What?"

"You remember . . . Father Sheen," she said. "He's been at the church since you were a baby. He baptized you, in fact. He's still there, John. You should go talk to him."

"Why?"

"He'll tell you," she said. "Your father is a good man. Yes. Your father is very . . . religious-minded. Lloyd never could see that. But you ask Father Sheen. He'll tell you." She patted my hand again. Then she rose slowly, walked down the four steps to the lush lawn, and headed back toward the house.

"You don't need to *see* to feel the lead of the animal!" shouted my father through the megaphone. "You are the master . . . be in control! Don't disappoint me, young man! Be the master! Be in control!"

I thought my father had just filled my glass, but it was half gone. I raised it quickly to my lips and drank the remaining portion, and a few drops spilled out and cool liquid penetrated my shirt and their moisture touched my skin. I held the empty glass before me, and I chuckled as I considered it a cylindrical crystal ball. I squeezed my eyes shut and shook my head in reaction to the residual pungency of the drink. No . . . pure clinical objectivity. I set the glass on the table and moved it slowly . . . ever so slowly . . . away from me, until the rays of the sun trickling through the trees fell at the precise angle . . . yes. They were together again. From the left, the figure of my mother, moving slowly toward the house; and from the right, my father, leaning against the rail, shouting into the megaphone. And I was there, in the center. But my face was distorted by the imperfection of the glass. And it could as easily have been . . . anyone. But my mother looked rather like Pearl. She was so trusting also . . . And in the blurring image, my father's leaning figure became lank, and the cord dangling from the megaphone looked like one of Jason Watkin's hissing serpents as he shouted to the crowd. I could understand Peter's father . . . his son had fallen away . . . couldn't show the spirit. But why was my father disappointed in me? He wasn't even religious. But Lloyd told me . . . That's an expectation, he said . . . That's an expectation.

"Now you're doing it!" My father's harsh amplified voice echoed in my ears. "Left . . . right! Left . . . right! You're doing it, boy! You're going to make me proud of you yet!"

Of course you will, boy, I thought. All you have to do is take control. You'll learn the trick . . . just like I did. No one can ever really control a horse. Even Freud knew that. It's like the poor ego, struggling with the id. No one can ever really control the horse. You just carry its wishes into action. But my father never knew. It amounted to the same thing. Just don't question . . . He was proud of me, too, until I questioned. But the idol had cracked. I had to question that, didn't I? The hero had fallen. I had to question that. So long ago, my mother had said . . . it happened so long ago . . . But what is time . . . to the loss of perfection? I wished that I could find a stone . . . throw it in the lake, like last night. I had the answer then, when Lloyd asked . . . What do we do when a repressed element explodes? Deal with it . . . find substitutes . . . It was as simple as that. It was as simple as Lloyd's forked branch. But it wasn't simple today. The idol had cracked. And now the cracked idol was disappointed in me. I had lost control. And now I couldn't even be as good as fallen hero.

I turned the glass on its side and spun it, and the reflections of the images merged suddenly into an indiscriminate montage of color . . . like a gigantic whirlpool, leading toward some unseen darkness at the bottom of the trickling rays of the sun.

26

It was about six-thirty when I pulled into our driveway and parked beside Meg's car. The drive home had given me time to put my experience with my parents into perspective. I had definitely not acted from an objective, clinical viewpoint, as I had intended. Instead, I had exhibited a typical textbook reaction to the encounter. The fact that I was so aware of that angered me all the more. And yet I still couldn't dampen the residual echo of my father's words . . . "I'm very disappointed in you, John . . . I thought you had more intelligence than that." But why? That was an idiotic reactive consideration. It was my father's character that had been chipped, not mine. But still, the hideous shadow of self-doubt hovered like a hot mist, and I couldn't shake it. I decided that I would take Meg out to dinner tonight. I would spend some time with her. She would like that, and it would allow me to get my mind on something less depressing.

I stepped quickly through the front door and nearly tripped. Two suitcases sat precariously in the center of the entryway. I leaned down and pressed in on them, and realized that they were fully packed. I was hit by a sudden sinking feeling.

"Meg . . . " I called softly.

There was no answer, but I heard the sound of dishes tinkling in the kitchen. I stepped around the bags and hurried through the hallway. As I passed through the doorway to the kitchen, I saw Meg there, putting some dishes away in the cupboard.

"Meg, what . . . "

"Oh!" She turned around with a startled expression on her face. "I didn't hear you come in, John." She returned to her work.

"I saw the bags in the hall, Meg," I said. "What's that all about?"

"I waited until six, and then I had a bite without you," she said, still stacking dishes. "I'm just cleaning up."

I glanced at my watch to verify the time. "What was the hurry?" I asked.

She closed the cupboard door slowly. Then she turned around, leaned against the sink, and folded her arms in front of her. "How was I supposed to know, John?"

"Know . . . what?"

She looked at the ceiling for a moment, and then lowered her head slowly. She had a strained expression. "You didn't come home at all last night, and . . . "

"I know. That was . . . "

"At least, before, you had Cheryl call . . . tell me . . . "

"I know," I mumbled.

"You just don't seem to realize, John," she said. "I'm so worried about you! And then, when Lloyd called this morning . . . "

"Lloyd called you?"

"Yes. He told me you were at the camp last night," she said. "That's why I called the office . . . to find out if you were all right. Didn't Cheryl tell you?"

"Yes, she told me," I said. "I knew I wasn't going to be that late. I stopped by my parents' place."

"I know that, too, now," she said crossly. "Cheryl told me when I called later."

I became suddenly very irritated. "You called again? She's going to think you're checking up on me!"

"It wasn't that, John. It's just . . . "

"And it irks me that Lloyd would call and get you all worked up," I interrupted. "I just . . . I just drove up to camp to see Diane. What's so bad about that?"

"Lloyd was just worried about you, John," she said. "And so was Diane. They said you were . . . depressed . . . upset."

"Ah . . . " I shook my head angrily, pulled out a chair, and sat at the round kitchen table. "There's nothing to worry about."

Meg walked over to the table, pulled out another chair, and sat beside me. "You have to know that's not true, John," she said. "The way you acted Sunday night . . . and then impulsively driving four hours up, and four hours back . . . for what?"

I forced a smile and shrugged. "I'm just an impulsive guy."

"John . . . I'm your wife! Talk to me!" Meg pleaded.

"I told you before, Meg," I said halfway apologetically. "It's this case . . . "

"That's what Lloyd said," she interrupted. "Can it really be that important?"

"Lloyd again?"

"How can a case be more important than your family?" she persisted.

"No . . . it's not." I forced my head toward her. There was no reason for her to act like this . . . especially now. But she didn't know yet. "That's why I told Peter," I continued. "Yesterday would be our last session for a while."

"Yesterday?" she asked with a puzzled expression. "But Cheryl said that Peter was in today."

"What . . . " I glanced out the window. The sun had not yet set, and its rays flooded the kitchen with early evening light. "What day is this?" I asked vaguely.

"Wednesday," responded Meg.

"No . . . I know that. I mean . . . " That was stupid! I glanced at my watch. "I mean . . . what time is it? Nearly seven?" Out of the corner of my eye I could see the puzzled expression on Meg's face. But I had made a natural mistake. It was the fatigue . . . after the long drive. And so much had happened! The days just seemed to merge imperceptibly into an uninterrupted continuum of time. "Yesterday . . . today . . . " I muttered. "Yes. It was today, of course." I turned back toward her and smiled. "Anyway, I told Peter that things were becoming unproductive, and suggested that he change therapists for a while."

"Oh, John, I'm so glad!" Meg leaned forward suddenly and grasped my hand. "I thought it was too much for you . . . "

"Too much for me?"

"I mean . . . taking too much time . . . "

I pulled my hand away and sat back. It was bad enough that my father told me that he was disappointed in me. Now even Meg was questioning my competence.

"John, I . . . " Meg sighed, and nervously bet at her finger nail. Then she flung her arms aimlessly. "I'm sorry. I'm trying so hard not to say the wrong thing."

"Wrong thing? Has someone been coaching you?" I asked sarcastically.

"Of course not!"

"Maybe Lloyd . . . or perhaps Leonard?" I asked.

"Of course not!"

"And now even Cheryl talks with you about my cases," I continued. "Who else knows about my problems?"

"John, please . . . "

"Well, what else am I supposed to think?" I asked. "I come home and find packed suitcases in the hall, and . . . "

"Those are for *us*, John!" she shouted. "Those are for us!"

"What . . . "

"Lloyd asked . . . I thought it was such a good idea," she said tearfully. "Lloyd asked if we could come back up to the camp tonight . . . both of us . . . spend the last two days with them and Diane. I thought it was such a good idea."

"I . . . I don't know."

"And when I talked with Cheryl . . . she said she could reschedule your appointments if you decided to go," she continued. "She said you could just call her at home tonight."

Meg had never meddled with my practice before. This really upset me, but I forced down a hostile response.

"I spoke with Diane this morning, too, John," she continued. "She was concerned about you, too, of course. But she was so excited about the experience she was having at camp."

"Of course! She's with Uncle Lloyd!" I said sarcastically.

"Don't be defensive, John," she said. "She was excited because she wants to share the experience with you . . . wants us to share it together."

All I needed was a little time . . . things would get better . . . especially now. But Lloyd was interfering again . . . not giving me a chance to fix things myself.

"It's something we've always needed as a family . . . " Meg's voice continued in a strange, distant tone. "Time together . . . Sharing things . . . the three of us . . . "

"The three of us and Lloyd," I mumbled.

"He's just trying to help, John," she said.

"Just like with Julie," I said suddenly.

"What?"

I couldn't explain it. The phrase just slipped out. Then I remembered. At the Temple . . . Peter had seen us sitting together. He said Lloyd would lead Julie astray. I told him he was mistaken. But now . . .

"Who's Julie?" asked Meg.

"Someone Lloyd misled," I muttered aimlessly.

"What?"

"I mean . . . might have . . . or . . . " I shook my head and shifted in my chair. "It's his religion," I said. "It's so . . . fundamental."

"That's what your father says," said Meg.

"Does that make it wrong?" And I heard the word echo repeatedly . . . wrong . . . wrong . . . wrong . . .

"You should give it a chance," she continued, ignoring my question. "You should listen to Diane. I've never heard her express such an interest in God."

"I've always given her the opportunity for spiritual expression," I insisted.

"No, John. This isn't an item for . . . philosophical discussion," she said, searching for words. "It's an experience. She said she had an experience. It was after you left last night. They were all around the campfire, praying. And she said . . . she asked Christ into her heart. And she had been so worried . . . frightened . . . about you. But then . . . she just had this feeling of . . . peace."

"Uncle Lloyd's quick fix!" I said angrily.

"John . . . "

"She's only sixteen, Meg!" I shouted. "Some people search all their lives before finding spiritual peace. And some never do! There are no quick fixes!"

"I want to go, John," she said slowly. "I want to give it a chance . . . I want to give *us* a chance. Is that asking too much?"

"It's so much more complicated than that," I muttered. "Why can't you all understand that?"

Meg pushed her chair back and stood slowly. "Diane is expecting me, John," she said softly. "And she would very much like to have you be there, too."

"It isn't that simple," I said, shaking my head slowly.

Meg sighed deeply, and tears welled up in her eyes. "So I guess you're not going, then," she said.

I shook my head.

Meg sighed again, and nodded slowly. "There's a praise service after Lunch on Friday," she said. "We'll be heading back after that. We'll probably stop somewhere for dinner. We should be home by . . . nine . . . or so."

"All right," I said.

Meg looked at me without speaking for a moment. Then she turned and walked out of the room. I heard the front door open . . . and close. The house was completely quiet, so I could hear the car door, also . . . and the engine starting . . . and the slip of the tires against the pavement.

I pushed my chair back, rose slowly, and walked into the hallway. In the entryway I saw the single suitcase. I walked past it into the living room and stopped at the bar. I got a glass from the shelf, and then pulled out the bottle of scotch and opened it. The strong aroma rose and invaded my nostrils, and I recalled the traumatic scene the last time I stood here . . . when? Sunday night? Had it only been three days? Meg was disappointed with me then . . . she would be tonight. But then, so was my father. I poured the glass full, then I recapped the bottle and replaced it. I took the glass, walked over to the couch and sat.

The silence in the house was becoming oppressive. I picked up a remote control device from the low table in front of the couch and pressed the power button. A small white dot appeared in the center of the television screen, and then grew to a gray flickering glow. I noticed that the controls were set for the video recorder. I activated the device, and the image of people's heads and a dimly lighted stage appeared. This was Watkins' video. I had brought it back from the office . . . when? Monday? Yes. I wanted to study it before Tuesday's session with Peter -- the session that never took place. It had been in here since then. Suppose Diane had seen it . . . No, of course not. She went to camp Tuesday. Or Meg? Surely she would have watched television since then? Was she watching the video? Why? She was meddling again . . . I sat back and took a large swallow from my drink as I again watched the events on the video.

"We're here for salvation tonight!" called Watkins.

"Amen! . . . Hallelujah!" responded the crowd.

"We're here to praise this town and praise the people in it!" "Do you believe me?"

"We believe ya', brother . . . Praise the Lord!"

I took another drink, and the strong liquor permeated the tissue of my mouth and momentarily deadened my sense of hearing. The image on the screen seemed to waver slightly, and I breathed deeply and hunched back further in the couch.

"I thought I was a goner, for sure," continued the voice of Watkins. "But I could see a sort of mouth open up, and then that light started talkin'! And it told me I shouldn't be afraid, because it was an angel sent from the presence of the Almighty God, and that it came to tell me that I had the gift of divine healing that I should take to the people in the world!"

"Divine healing," I mumbled. "Why not?" I took another drink, and then let my arm fall limply forward until the glass touched the table, and slipped away from my hand. Then I shifted my body around and lifted my legs onto the couch.

"You have forsaken the right way. You have gone astray, following the way of Balaam!" issued the voice of Watkins in slightly distorted tones.

"Lead Julie astray . . . lead Diane astray . . . lead Meg astray. No . . . no . . . no! I won't let it happen!" I mumbled.

"If thy hand offend thee, cut it off . . . "

I raised my arm and struggled to focus on my hand dangling before me. Then I chuckled softly, and let it drop to my stomach. I turned my head toward the television, and watched the bobbing heads of the crowd, and listened to the damning . . . soothing voice . . . a little child shall lead them . . . a little child . . .

The crowd was choppier than normal . . . no . . . the water. But then it wasn't. It was smooth, and swirling. Been here before . . . been here before . . . But quicker . . . so much quicker . . . Because Lloyd was already there, on his charging white horse . . . and Meg and Diane were with him. And my father was in the clouds, and he was shouting down at Lloyd . . . "No, you idiot! Change leads . . . Change leads!" And he reached down from the clouds and pulled at the strap, and Lloyd's head jerked backward. But then Lloyd yanked the halter from his chest, and threw it into the sea . . . and my father frowned and shouted . . . "I'm very disappointed in you, Lloyd. . . " But then my father smiled, because Bernadette was there in the cloud with him, and she smiled down at me, and said . . . "Tell me about your dream, John . . . tell me about your dream . . . "

Dream . . . yes, of course . . . relax. I'll wake up, soon. But for now, it's so real . . . so . . . terrifying. Because the vortex was there, and the spiraling steps of the swirling water carried me down . . . down . . . down . . . toward the flaming mandala. Chunks of ice fell from my father's face and tumbled in upon me, but they were gathered up in the soothing warmth of the fire and became the water. I could hear a calling from above, and so I looked. And I was there . . . the other me . . . And Lloyd was galloping around the edge of the whirlpool on his charging white horse with Meg and Diane behind him. And I beckoned to the other me . . . But I said . . . no . . . And the me below asked why. And Lloyd, on his charging white horse, called out in a loud and terrible voice . . . "If something offends thee, pluck it out!"

"Nothing offends!" I shouted. This is a dream . . . and the warmth of the fire is soothing."

But the other me called down, "What offends me? What offends me?" And the other me smiled and raised a finger to our head . . .

So I reached up with both hands . . . and yanked my head from the socket of my neck . . . and I screamed. I knew it was only a dream, but the head cried out for a moment, and then smiled at its freedom. And then it shouted up at the other me . . . "I'm an archetype . . . I'm so complex! I'm the pure essence of spirituality!"

But Lloyd looked down from his horse and cried, "No! Either God exists, or . . . "

But my head didn't let him finish. "He does not exist!" I shouted.

But Diane was crying, and she called out . . . "Yes, Daddy . . . Yes . . . I've brought him into my heart . . . It's so simple!" And she reached out to Lloyd and grasped the gnarled, branch, and stepped her fingers gently up the left fork.

But my head cried out and mocked her . . . "You're only sixteen! You're only sixteen! You're not a real doctor! It's too complex!" And I grasped my head and placed it back onto the socket of my neck, and I cried out in pain. But the fire was there . . . and it was warm, and soothing.

And so I turned to it . . . the fire and the mandala. And in the center was the face of my father, laughing, chastising me for being just like Lloyd. And I cried out . . . "No, Daddy . . . No! I've brought you into my heart! It's so simple!" And I reached out and grasped his sweaty hand and followed him deeper . . .

deeper . . . deeper into the fire. And behind me, my voice still rang . . . "No, Daddy . . . No!" But it wasn't me . . . It was Diane. And she tried to climb off the charging white horse and follow us . . . but Lloyd wouldn't let her come. He was leading her astray.

So I called for my father to help, but he said, "It's too late . . . " And I followed him until the sea above me turned into darkness, and the circle below became a searing white circle of light. And it reached out and grasped my gasping lungs, and I cried out . . . I cried out to the searing white circle of light . . .

I cried out . . . And the sound of my voice echoed through my ears, and the white circle of light flickered and glowed . . . and there was darkness on either side. I sat up. Then I reached out and grasped my head, and my ears still ached from the scream that fell from my mouth. My hands fell suddenly and grasped the hard upholstery of the couch . . . and I began to laugh. I was awake! Yes. But the circle of light . . . I knew it was the television monitor, but it was still there . . . searing and white. And the buzz from the speakers roared like the ocean. And I was awake . . . but they were still there. In the near darkness of the room . . . my mind told me . . . that is a lamp . . . that is a table . . . that is a chair. But in my residual perception the images remained, and Lloyd still rode around the room on his charging white horse, and he and Meg and Diane were laughing at me . . .

I sat forward and forced my head hard against the delusion of the flickering light. "I renounce you!" I shouted. "I renounce you! I renounce you!"

Then the flickering white light resolved itself . . . and became the face of Peter . . . in his trench coat and dark-colored sunglasses . . . "These pesky dreams . . . " he laughed. "I'm so busy . . . I need my sleep . . . If you could just prescribe something . . . " And his face grew, and his eyes darted out from the sunglasses, and they were filled with fear . . . And his mouth gaped, and shouted . . . "Pesky dreams! Prescribe! Prescribe!"

"Yes!" It was my voice . . . and the noise of it chased Peter back into the flickering light. "Yes!" I repeated.

I stood up, and stumbled out of the living room . . . through the dark hallway . . . and into the bathroom. The switch was there, and I turned it on. But the blinding light thrust its way into my eye sockets and clogged them with blindness. I reached forward . . . into the cupboard. I could fix it! I'm a healer! The packages were there . . . like the ones I gave Peter. I quickly grasped one of the packages, ripped it open, and tossed the pills into my mouth. Then I turned on the water . . . hard . . . and thrust my head under the cooling stream . . . and drank . . . and drank . . . and drank . . .

The walls of the bathroom merged with the darkness as I pressed the switch again, and I hurried back to the flickering light. But the suitcase was still there, in the hallway. I had forgotten . . . and I stumbled over it. And from somewhere in the living room . . . my father's voice . . . "You idiot! Change leads!" So I did, and I found my way again, toward the flickering, searing light.

The light . . . I knew I had to extinguish the light. My mind knew that . . . but I had removed my head, and my mind didn't know my heart's desire . . . But I could renounce my mind . . . overrule it! My eyes were still blinded from the bathroom light, and I couldn't see the remote control. I ran my hands wildly over the table . . . but which table? No time . . . I ran to the light . . . directly to the light. And its flickering glow seared my mind, and I ran my hands wildly over the screen, but there were no buttons . . . there were no buttons. Renounce! Behind the light . . . I knew . . . The cord. I could see it there . . . barely . . . in the flickering shadows. And I reached out and grasped it. But then the cord became a writhing serpent. And its head reached out and hissed at me, and I jumped back. But I knew . . . my mind knew . . . I could fix it. I held fast to the serpent's body, and its head jumped out at me, and it opened its mouth and wagged the stub of a torn out tongue.

"You offend me! You offend me!" My voice was clear and warm. And I yanked hard . . . and the flickering, searing white light hissed once more . . . and then died.

"Yes . . . " I could calm my voice now . . . control it. And the darkness enveloped me like a warm, soothing fire, and the excitement of it surged through my body. But the images were still there. I couldn't see them, but their voices still rang out in whispers of laughter. I would fix them . . . I *could* fix them.

I pointed invisibly into the darkness and got my bearings. My feet shuffled slowly across the foamy carpet until my shins bumped gently against the front of the couch. I sat and breathed deeply. My hands fell on the table. My glass was still there. I picked it up . . . and I calculated from the weight of it that there were still . . . Renounce the delusion! Calculate! Calculate! I calculated that there were approximately one and a third ounces of liquid. So I raised the glass to my lips . . . and the one and a third became zero.

The deafening roar of the scotch fell quietly upon my ear drums, and I chuckled at the warmth of it. The voices were still there . . . but I could fix that. I had fixed it for Peter, and I could fix it for me. Fast acting sedative. I saw to that. I'm a doctor.

No more pesky dream. Ten, nine, eight, seven . . . voices fading . . . six, five, four . . . no more flicker in the hollow of my mind . . . three . . . two . . .

27

I heard a distant ringing, and turned my head to escape the irritation of the sound. A rough texture thrust itself against my nose, and I recoiled. The ringing continued. I forced my eyes open, and the forms in the room began slowly to resolve. I was still on the couch. I pushed myself away from the soft back, dropped my feet to the floor, and sat up. My head began to throb, and the pulses of pain were punctuated by the continuing, periodic ringing. I turned my head in the direction of the sound. The telephone . . . on the bar. I shoved my body away from the couch and stood on wobbly legs. The bar was just a few steps away, and I stumbled toward it, and took the cellular phone from its base, extended the shiny steel rod, and turned the switch.

"Yes . . . " My mouth felt as if it were stuffed with cotton. I swallowed hard. "Yes . . . hello . . . "

"Dr. Summers?"

"Yes . . . "

"This is Cheryl."

Cheryl . . . What . . . I breathed deeply. The throbbing in my head had ceased, and now a dizzy swell passed over me, and then faded away. I moved my head slowly from side to side, and the features of the room finally began to clear in the dim light.

"Dr. Summers . . . " her soft voice continued.

"Yes, Cheryl. What is it?"

"I called a few times earlier, and no one answered," she said. "I was just wondering what you decided to do."

"To do . . . "

"Your wife said you might be going somewhere, and that you'd call me," she said. "But when you didn't come in this morning, I thought . . . well, I thought I misunderstood."

"This morning . . . "

"But I rescheduled your morning appointments, anyway."

"Cheryl . . . wait . . . What time is it?" I asked.

"It's eleven o'clock, and . . . "

"Eleven?" I rushed over to the large living room window. The heavy drapes were closed, and it was impossible to tell . . . anything. I reached high on the cord, and pulled. The drapes parted quickly, and a gush of bright sunlight suddenly filled the room. "You . . . you called earlier, you said?"

"Yes. At eight-thirty . . . and again at nine. And then a couple more times," she said. "I hope I didn't misunderstand."

"No . . . no, Cheryl." The events of the preceding night began to trickle into my memory. The dream . . . the terrible dream. But I thought that I had awakened . . . done . . . something. Yes. The television set was off, and the cord lay on the floor where I had thrown it. So I had been awake. I pulled the plug. And that means that I did go to the bathroom . . . get the sedatives . . . I shuddered suddenly at the thought of it. On top of all that alcohol! That was stupid! I could have killed myself.

"Are you all right, Dr. Summers?" asked Cheryl.

"Yes," I responded vaguely. I wasn't last night, though. I was terrible. That was the worst I had ever experienced . . . the absolute worst. But look . . . it was morning. And I had survived . . . by the sheer power of my will!

I reached up and pulled the cord down again, and the drapes opened completely. I walked over to the center of the window and looked out into the brightness of the day. It was a rebirth! And as the rays of the sun engulfed my body, a surge of power ascended from the base of my feet, and my hands and head tingled from the sensation.

"So will you not be coming in, then?" asked Cheryl.

Meg shouldn't have made that suggestion to Cheryl. It really wasn't appropriate . . . meddling in my business. But as it turned out . . .

I took a deep breath, and reveled in the feeling of well-being that swept over me. I couldn't believe that, after the horror of last night, I was actually standing here . . . breathing, and alive. But that was my doing! Why did I continue to doubt myself? I could accomplish anything. Meg shouldn't have meddled, but I could forgive her for that. She needed me, and so did Diane. I could fix things. I realized that now more than I ever had.

"Dr. Summers . . . "

"No, Cheryl," I said finally. "I'm sorry I didn't call you. I overslept. But, yes . . . I will be gone for . . . " My mind was celebrating its newly recognized power, but it struggled to resolve the mundane things. "This is Thursday?" I asked.

"Yes."

The days were still jumbled. But that would clear up. "Yes, Cheryl. I will be gone today and tomorrow. I'm going to spend some time with my family in the mountains."

"Oh, that's wonderful, Dr. Summers!" Cheryl said enthusiastically. "I'll call everyone, then."

"Thanks."

"You have a wonderful time!" she said.

"Thank you, Cheryl. I will."

"'Bye!"

"Good-bye, Cheryl." I slowly clicked off the switch, and shoved the aerial back into the receiver. Then I walked over and set the device back onto its base.

I walked into the hallway and saw the packed suitcase still there where I had stumbled over it last night. I felt like picking it up and leaving immediately, but I ran my hand slowly across my face, and I realized that I needed to shave first. I walked down the hall and into the bathroom. The torn sample sedative package was still on the sink. That was a good reality check. I picked it up and tossed it into the waste basket.

I removed my shaver from its case and turned it on, and the familiar high-pitched buzzing sound commenced. I held the shaver for a moment, and let the almost imperceptible vibration work its way through the palm of my hand.

But then . . . I looked into the mirror . . . and jumped back in horror! I saw my face. But it was on a head detached from my body! And it was laughing with dirty protruding teeth . . . and serpents dangled in the place of hair!

I threw the shaver hard against the face of the mirror, and it shattered, and pieces of it dropped and burst upon the sink. My shaver fell to the bottom of the basin, where it continued moaning in its familiar high-pitched buzz.

My back was pressed against the wall. This was absurd! After the drapes were pulled, and the sun streamed in . . . I had conquered the demon! My mind . . . my mind must regain control. This was just a residual hallucination. It was textbook! Nothing unusual. And I was a healer. I could renounce it . . . with the force of my will . . . the power of my mind . . .

I pushed my body away from the wall and stepped toward the shattered mirror . . . one . . . two . . . It was nearly all gone -- in useless pile on the sink. But in the corner . . . a triangular wedge. I placed my hands on the sink and pressed them down upon the slivers of glass. Then I leaned my head down slowly . . . toward the corner. First my nose . . . then the chin. I moved my face in all directions and viewed the reflection. Yes. I had renounced the demon. The serpents were gone, and my head was attached firmly to my neck. I viewed it with clinical, psychiatric objectivity. I pushed myself to a standing position, and pulled my hands up from the sink. Pieces of glass imbedded themselves into the thickness of my skin, and I brushed my palms together, and they fell into the basin, carrying with them tiny drops of blood. My blood! Good reality check.

But I suddenly realized that I had made another bad decision. No! That wasn't right. It was just an inappropriate conclusion, based on insufficient data. The dream, the residual hallucinations, the megalomania, and the hasty leap to terror . . . It was all textbook! But the difference was . . . I was the healer. I understood . . . everything. I was on the verge of deciphering that sliver of the collective unconscious that was impinging on my psyche. I had to push forward now . . . into all aspects of my personality . . . investigate, explore . . . understand. This was not the time for sharing. This was not the time for helping others. I had succumbed to an inappropriate rush of sentimentality. I couldn't possibly go to the mountains. Not now! There would be time for Meg and Diane . . . later.

I breathed deeply. Never before had I seen myself with such clarity. I had to seize the moment. My mind was racing. All the better! There were so many facts . . . so many experiences. The sum total of my existence was equal to the infinitely calculated exponential product of my past experiences. My research had just begun. The experience with Lloyd . . . so revealing! And my parents . . . My mother's life was contemptible, but it was part of me, and I had to accept it, and go on. But my father . . . that would be harder. But even now, as I stood before the shattered mirror, I felt confident that I could shatter the mirror of my past. But first I must view it -- the whole hideous reflection. For only then could I reconstruct myself in the resurrected state of perfection that I knew now that I was capable of.

I reached out and began aimlessly pulling together the slivers of glass. There were so many pieces. And without a single one, the state of perfection would be marred, the reflection would be incomplete. So many thousands . . so small . . . where to begin? My mother . . . she was pitiable, and yet . . . what had she said to me . . . when . . . yesterday, or was it a century ago? The moments . . . days . . . years . . . But all were important. What had she said? What had she said, as she raised the loose sleeve of her house coat to her face and wiped the tears away. A rush of excitement surged through my body at the clarity of my recollection. I could see her as she sat forward again, and patted me on the hand. Father Sheen . . . that was it. Yes. She told me I should go talk to Father Sheen. He understood my father, she had told me. Good place to start . . . yes.

I brushed a few splinters of glass into the basin, and they slid to a stop against the black body of my buzzing shaver. Then I stood tall, and breathed deeply. But there was an imperfection . . . somewhere. My nostrils flinched. Meg should have done a better job. I threw open the cabinet door, and the remaining corner wedge of mirror clattered to the sink. I reached out, grasped a can of spray deodorant and flicked off the cap. I couldn't tell the direction of the imperfection, so I pointed . . . up . . . *Pffft*! Too strong, but . . . hidden . . . better.

I held tightly to the can and hurriedly left the bathroom. I glanced at my watch. Noon. High noon! Time to see if Father Sheen can shoot the bad guys. The overpowering hiding aroma had died down, so I breathed in again. The imperfection remained, so faintly, and yet . . . it seemed to follow me down the hall. Of course! I had been so busy, made so many discoveries. Naturally there would be a glandular reaction. That was textbook! I pointed . . . left arm . . . *Pffft*! Right arm . . . *Pffft*! Temporary, of course, but it would pass. I tossed the spray can on the floor, and ran out the door.

We were members of the largest Catholic church in town. My father wouldn't have it any other way. And he was probably right. It was majestic -- the spires, rising high above the surrounding structures. And all the marble! As I entered the large foyer, I could *smell* the marble, and I recalled, as a boy, running my hand across the surface of one of the massive table tops and imagining what it would be like to build a house of these blocks.

The soles of my shoes slapped against the floor tiles, and the sound echoed throughout the entryway. The young girl in the office had told me that Father Sheen was performing a baptism, but that he should be finished shortly. As I entered the huge sanctuary, I could see him in front, on the raised portico, standing before a marble baptismal font. He was holding a tiny baby in his arms, and beside him stood a man and woman, their hands folded piously before them. I raised and lowered my feet carefully, and I walked silently down the aisle toward them.

Father Sheen reached out and gathered a few sprinkles of water from the font, and placed them on the baby's head. The infant squirmed, and cried for a moment, cloaking the first portion of the sacramental phrase. But then the child became still, and Father Sheen's voice droned out the remainder: " . . . in nomini Patri . . . et Filio . . . et Spiritui Sancto . . . Amen!" He raised the child, and kissed him on the forehead. Then he handed him to his eager, smiling parents.

The woman took the child, and the man took out his wallet, removed a bill, and handed it to Father Sheen. Then they mumbled something inaudible, turned, and walked down the carpeted steps. I passed them in the aisle as they were heading out. The baby looked very peaceful now, lying in his mother's arms. I imagined that I must have looked very much like that, when my father arranged for my baptism with Father Sheen. I couldn't remember, of course. I was just an infant.

Father Sheen replaced the cover on the baptismal font and turned around. He leaned forward and squinted slightly as he saw me at the base of the stairs. "Yes? May I help you?"

When I was a boy I always remembered him having a much heavier Irish brogue. Now it seemed to be just a touch. But differences are often magnified by the very young. He looked much the same. Older, of course, but he always had a heavily jowled face, and the frame of his stocky body hadn't changed.

"Are you here for confession?" he asked, stepping down the carpeted stairs.

"No. I just wanted to speak with you, Father." I extended my hand. "I'm sure you don't remember me," I said. "I'm John Summers."

He took my hand limply and squinted again. "John Summers . . . "

"Charles and Louise are my parents," I added. "You baptized me . . . many years ago."

His face brightened. "Oh, of course! We have a very large congregation, of course, and I can't possibly know everyone. But I remember your father. He's a very faithful contributor! He's the lawyer, I believe."

"Yes."

"Of course. I remember now," he said. "Both he and your mother. Marvelous people!"

"Thank you."

"And what is your business, John?" he asked.

"I'm a psychiatrist," I responded.

"Oh?" His heavy jowls fell into a frown, and he raised an eyebrow. "Not one of those Freudian people, I hope."

"No. I follow the Jungian school," I told him.

"Ah!" Both eyes raised, and his mouth held the syllable for a prolonged moment. "Yes. I'm familiar with Jung's writings. Excellent! Excellent! He was a good Catholic, you know."

"Well . . . " I didn't know whether my father had gotten this false idea here, or whether he and Sheen merely coincidentally shared this piece of misinformation. All I knew was that I would not correct him.

"So, John . . . May I call you John?"

"Of course."

"What can I do for you?" he asked.

Sheen didn't seem to know as much about my parents as my mother thought he would. But his interest in Jung provided me with a better approach, anyway. "I'm doing research for a case I'm working on," I told him. "And my success depends on . . . well . . . comparison of spiritual views held by people."

"Excellent! Excellent!" he whispered.

"For example . . . " I glanced up at the baptismal font. "The ceremony you just performed. The water . . . " Suddenly an image of Peter's temple flashed across my mind, and the flowing stream of water across the rocks . . . "It has a different significance for some, I believe," I continued. "Some of the modern movements use it for healing ceremonies, for example."

"I know. I know," said Sheen, shaking his head. "And that's a misuse . . . a mockery. But, of course, that's just *water."* He turned and pointed toward this font. *"This* . . . This is *holy water.* It has been sanctified. And it's for salvation, not for healing."

"I know."

"Surely you were baptized as an infant," he said.

"Yes. My father arranged for it," I said.

"Excellent! A faithful parent."

"But my father himself is . . . irregular, at best," I said.

"Many are," he said shaking his head.

"And my brother has followed another faith," I added.

Sheen nodded slowly. Then his eyes widened again, and he raised his arms. "Wait a minute! I remember that! He's a Protestant pastor now, isn't he?"

"Yes."

"I can't imagine why I didn't remember before. I'm getting old, I guess." He chuckled lightly. "But yes! That was the only time I actually spoke with your father in person, I believe. It must have been over twenty years ago." He shook his head. "My . . . time . . . " He sighed, and then continued. "Anyway, your father was very upset about your brother's decision, naturally. He asked if there wasn't something that I could do about it. You know . . . prevent him from going that direction."

"What did he expect you to do?" I asked.

"Well, I was never quite sure," he said slowly. "But I did tell him that I'd pray for his son . . . your brother. And so I did, of course. I prayed for his return."

"The case I'm researching . . . " I said. "I'm hoping some of my experiences will help me with it. I need to understand some of the motives . . . the spiritual needs. There are some similarities . . . between the case and my family, I mean."

"Well, if you follow the Jungian school, you have a good grounding in the spiritual consciousness of persons," he said. "Jung recognized the value of the Catholic religion, because of its sound, historical doctrine and symbols."

"I know."

"And anyone who attempts to construct a spiritual aspect of his personality apart from that . . . well . . . he's treading on dangerous ground."

Sheen knew enough about Jung, and enough about my father and Lloyd to be able to provide me with some valuable information. I was beginning to become excited at the prospect. But I had to be careful. I didn't want to elicit a defensively guarded response, so I decided to proceed in general terms.

"Many of the new charismatic movements, of course, seem to encourage that type of spiritual development," I said.

"Oh! The charismatic movement!" Sheen seemed suddenly more interested. "Well, I didn't want to make you think that all experimental exploration in the spiritual realm is incorrect, of course. The Catholic Church has a charismatic movement within it, as I'm sure you know. And there are many good Jungian principles at play in the practices that they are espousing. You mentioned healing before. We're doing a lot with the healing of memories, using solid Jungian doctrine."

"But wouldn't other charismatic movements be as acceptable?" I asked.

"Protestant, you mean?" he asked.

"Yes."

Sheen scowled and shook his head. "Outside the control of the Mother Church? Remember Jung's warning about the danger of individual exploration."

His words fell on my ears like slivers of shattered glass. All the pieces were here. My father, Lloyd, Peter . . . and Jung. The common factor, of course, was the universal, collective unconscious -- the overarching firmament of experience. But how to pull together the relevant pieces . . . make them mine?

"Much of the difference has to do with a person's view of the need," I said. "And the manifestations of that view."

"Of course . . . of course," he muttered.

"For example . . . for the purpose of illustration," I said cautiously. "My father seems not to have an outward need to express his faith. He tends to . . . to leave that up to the priests, I believe."

"That's why were here," he said.

"But he seems to hold the view that considerations about faith are . . . well . . . too complex," I added.

"They can be," said Sheen. "They definitely can be."

"Some of the charismatic leaders, on the other hand, seem to insist on dealing with it," I continued. "They encourage their congregations to recognize . . . to nurture their own inner power . . . their personal divinity."

"Well, there's a lot to that, of course," said Sheen. "The charismatic movement in the Catholic Church goes a long way toward building people's sense of the divine."

"My brother, on the other hand, tends to oversimplify things," I said.

"How is that?" asked Sheen.

"Well . . . " This seemed to be one of the critical issues for me. I had avoided the specific mention because of my fear of making Father Sheen become defensive. But I realized now it was my own bubbling turmoil over Lloyd's views that was causing me to pull back. But the scene was set now. I had to proceed. "Well, for example . . . " I shifted to the other foot, and chuckled lightly. "My brother likes to compare a person's spiritual walk with a forked branch," I said. "And he says that, at some point in our lives, we must all come to the point of this critical decision: Either God exists . . . or He does not." I chuckled again, and perspiration began to form on my forehead.

Sheen joined my in laughter. "That is a simplistic distinction, isn't it? Of course, we realize, that things are a lot more complex than that."

"Yes . . . yes . . . " I breathed deeply, and the smell of incense filled my nostrils. Surely he could provide a better view. A sense of stability.

"That's why it's so important to be under the loving arm of the Church," continued Sheen.

"But . . . for the purpose of illustration again . . . How should I respond to my brother . . . when he makes this simplistic claim?" I asked.

Sheen folded his hands in front of him, and swayed back and forth as he spoke. "Well, God is God, of course. But his image is so much greater than that. I am reminded of the French monk who developed the art of *visualizing* the Lord. He realized that it is the responsibility of the church to give reality to this awesome experience. And, of course, identification with God enhances the meaning of power in the individual. That goes without saying. And I'm sure you're aware of Jung's belief that it should be our task to reinterpret the Christian tradition in the light of the entry of the Mother of God into the heavenly bridal chamber. And that reinterpretation can be so complex, and varied. That's why it's so important to maintain the guidance of the Holy Church. Even in the visualization of Mary, as some Jesuit priests are doing in the pursuit of inner healing, the essence of God becomes an important aspect, you see. It's giving reality to the unseen Lord!"

His words were flowing confidently and dramatically, but I couldn't place them into any type of rational construct. I was sure he was addressing my question about Lloyd's simplistic approach, but I couldn't put the pieces together. And now I was becoming slightly dizzy from having stood so long, and Sheen's face was beginning to blur. I breathed deeply again, and the incense filled my mind, and cleared my vision momentarily. I would have to pursue even a more direct, perhaps more personal reference.

"I guess the issue arose for my brother when he was younger," I said. "He told me once that he had . . . " I was about to reveal the incident that my father had also repeated with me. But I had to keep it light . . . keep it general. "It was during some philosophical discussion, I believe," I continued. "He told me that he had asked our father if there was a God. And I believe . . . I believe our father made some statement to the effect . . . that . . . it didn't matter."

"Hmm . . . " Sheen scowled again, and stopped swaying. Then he smiled. "Well, your father is a good Catholic, of course," he said. "And that was probably just his way of rejecting the Protestant simplicity of the question."

"But, you see, my brother really wanted to know what he thought," I said.

"Well, I'm sure he suggested that your brother come and speak with a priest," he said.

That's what my mother had told me . . . go talk with Father Sheen. And Father Sheen was here now. The priest was here. "You're a priest . . . " I mumbled, almost without thinking. "For the purpose of illustration . . . my research . . . pretend I'm my brother . . . and you're a priest."

"Well, I . . . "

I breathed in the smoking fragrance again, and stepped closer to the stocky figure. "Is there a God, Father Sheen? Is there a God?"

His jowls twitched slightly, and then he chuckled, and began swaying again. "The reason for that recommendation, of course, as you know from your study of Jung, is for protection from the immediate religious experience . . . "

"My brother would say . . . it's a simple question," I persisted. "Is there a God, Father Sheen?"

"The saints . . . " He gestured broadly toward the large ornate statues lining the walls of the church. "The saints would testify . . . And all who have taken their babies to the Holy font . . . " He pointed lovingly toward the heavy marble bowl with its protective cover. "The Holy water, you see . . . If it were not for the wonderful history and ritual of the Holy Church, and all its sacraments . . . well, many would falter over that question . . . "

My eyes followed his hand to the baptismal font, and then my mind jumped forth and captured the image of the water inside . . . and the bowl was circular, and as he raised the protective lid for the child, the water began to churn, and whirl. A child shall lead them . . . that's what Watkins had said, and Peter came forth. But this baby was so much younger . . . and Watkins had a box, not a bowl. Perhaps that was the difference. That's what Sheen said . . . the Holy water . . .

My lips moved without my will again. "But my brother would say . . . Is there a God, Father Sheen? Is there a God? Don't you have an opinion?"

"Theological opinions are the realm of the church also," he droned.

"But my brother would say . . . " I realized suddenly that I had thrust my hands out and grasped him by the shoulders.

"Oh . . . " He placed his hand on my head and patted it gently. "I think I understand. I'm something of a psychologist, too, you know." He lowered his hand slowly and joined it with his other hand in a prayerful pose. "I think you need to go to confession, my child."

"Child . . . " No. Because a child shall lead them. And what is there to confess . . . and to whom . . . if there is no God.

"Come to confession," he urged. "And then pray to the saints!" He passed his arm slowly around the walls of the church again.

My eyes followed his arm as it passed by the stiff, inanimate objects lining the walls. And then they fell again upon him, standing there before me, swaying from his heels to his toes, smiling with that benign, confident expression. He was just another statue. I could see that. I backed away, and my eyes narrowed as I looked at him, and he became an object . . . rocking back and forth inanimately, his smile frozen in time, because of his failure to communicate . . . his failure to know . . . I continued backing . . . all the way up the aisle. And his statue lips cracked open periodically, and muttered . . . come to confession . . . come to confession. But he was only a statue. My eyes and my mind moved past him, and fell upon the water. The water was alive! I could still see it behind him, swirling in the huge circular bowl. The water. That was the divine, overarching firmament which would explain the complexity of me. I had to return to the water!

When I reached the foyer, I turned and ran quickly out of the church. I was oblivious to anything except my destination. My legs moved like the legs of a statue, unaware of their lifelessness, propelling me mindlessly toward my car. And I entered it like a child into the womb. But once there, I was in control again, and I directed it. I was in control again. But the silence in the car was oppressive, and I reached my hand out, and turned on the radio . . .

" . . . the day of judgment! He knows those who walk after the flesh in imperfection. People who think evil of themselves because they understand not will perish in their own corruption!"

I looked down, and I realized that the tape from Peter's healing service was still in the car. His words merged with the silence, and the car became alive and confused again.

"All you with eyes turned away from your own divinity cannot cease from the sin of self-denial. You are cursed children."

But I didn't want to hear this! This had nothing to do with the water!

"I can save you if you will save yourselves? Are you ready? . . . Yes! . . . Yes! . . . Yes!"

And my lips responded like the lips of a statue . . . No! . . . No! . . . No! And I reached down and pressed the reject button, and I renounced it. And the tape popped out, and I yanked it out, because it offended me, and I slipped it into the pocket of my shirt.

The water . . . The soothing, overpowering, controlling firmament of the water. My dream had the answer. That's what Lloyd said, wasn't it? Job . . . in a vision of the night, He opens the ears of men, and seals their instruction. People couldn't help me. They were like statues. But my dream could teach me . . . teach me . . . Yes. I would go to the water, and join with the blinding, bubbling turmoil of its darkness . . . the darkness behind the mirror. The pieces must merge . . . the pieces must fit.

28

The sea was like glass. It was perfect! Even at full throttle, my boat cut cleanly into the smooth surface, and carried me toward my destination. I was glad now that I had at least met with Father Sheen. He was a part of my past experience that I had to bring forth, in order to construct the complete picture. But he didn't have any more insight than Lloyd, or Bernadette . . . or even Peter. His spiritual awareness was so tied up with the saints and ritual that he couldn't possibly relate to my request for some meaningful response. I shouldn't have expected it. The result made that clear. My anticipation had become a sort of false reliance, which didn't allow me to exercise my own powers of control sufficiently to prevent my inaccurate perception of his words and his actions. No matter. I had quickly resolved the error. I had forcibly taken command of my own thought processes. It was becoming easier. All those emotional attachments . . . I had to renounce them. And yet, Peter had done that, too, and he wasn't healed yet.

I had given up too quickly with Peter. I knew that I could succeed with him. It was just this pesky counter-transference. Why did Bernadette see that as exciting? But she did warn me . . . she warned me about the precipice. But I hadn't seen Peter since . . . when? What day was this? Yes. Thursday. I hadn't seen Peter since . . . yesterday . . . just before my parents . . . just before Meg . . . All the other factors were crowding in on me as well. Was it really a counter-transference? Or was it, rather, a parallel psychotic response? Why was I still asking myself this question? Even Lloyd knew that answer . . . and he wasn't even a doctor. Peter and I . . . struggling together. And now I realized that even our fathers were so similar! That's why it was so important that I deal with it myself. I desperately needed the freedom of isolation and dissociation. My dream was the source of my healing . . . and my dream was the sea.

The bottom portion of the sun's disk touched the horizon. I was heading directly toward it. When I had first pointed the bow of my boat out of the inlet it was so much higher. It was as though it was following me . . . preparing for the rendezvous. I had calculated that, too. The sun was part of my plan. That's why it was so important that I be alone, without any interference.

I knew that Danny wouldn't be concerned. When he topped off my tank today, I told him that I might be gone for two days. That was a beautiful moment. There is such a feeling of security, and power . . . when pulling away from the dock with a full tank of fuel! That reminded me. I glanced down at my gauges. The needle pointed just above the half-full mark. There was still time.

I remembered the last time I had attempted this experiment. It was in my senior year in high school. It was just after Harold Palmer had been killed by the muggers. I didn't want to go downtown again for a while. My friends accused me of being chicken. I had to show them. I taken my father's boat out alone . . . toward the setting sun. I told them I could speed due west until the fuel was half spent, and then return. They agreed that was a sign of courage. But I had misjudged the distance and the tides. On the return trip, I got to within five miles of shore . . . and ran out of gas. I had to call the club on the CB . . . have them tow me in.

I lowered my hand to the controls to the two-way radio. I turned it on, and listened for the familiar electronic crackle. The screaming whine of the high-powered engine was too loud. It obliterated all other sounds. But all I'd have to do is stop . . . pull out the microphone . . . and call. A sense of shame suddenly swept over me. My failure to complete this trip successfully when I was in high school had been humiliating. My friends had accused me of not being able to go the distance . . . and they were right. I should have swam the rest of the way. I had the ability. I gave up too quickly. Perhaps I had given up with Peter too quickly, too. I had the ability. I could heal him. Why hadn't I gone the distance?

I reached down, grasped the microphone, and yanked it . . . hard. It offended me. The plastic device pulled free from the black cable, which fell back and dangled uselessly from the base unit. I pulled my hand back, and threw the microphone far out into the sea. It skipped once . . . like the rock in the lake . . . and then disappeared. I would not be humiliated again.

It had been just moments, it seemed. But now the sun had nearly disappeared beneath the horizon. I placed my hand on the throttle and tried to push it forward more, but it was already at his highest setting. I knew that, if I could just go fast enough, I could control the sun . . . make it remain as that harmless, glowing sliver. But that would be like chasing a phantom. I had often accused Lloyd of doing that . . . chasing after a God who wasn't there. I chuckled momentarily as I contemplated the appropriateness of the metaphor. The sun would be gone, and all the running in the world . . . No. That wasn't true at all. The sun wasn't moving . . . just the earth, spinning mindlessly away from the day. Throughout the night . . . the sun was still there, even though we couldn't see it. And in the morning, it would return. The metaphor wasn't any good at all. I must remember never to use it with Lloyd.

I looked at the fuel gauge again, and stepped slightly to the right so that I was in a direct line of sight. A sliver of the black mark showed beneath the red needle. I fixed my eyes intently on the needle. It was like the sun. It could pass across the sky all day without the slightest appearance of motion, but once it fell in close proximity to its destination, near the reality of the point of reference, it tumbled headlong. The black mark diminished to a thirty-second of an inch . . . a sixty-fourth . . . a one-hundred-twenty-eighth . . . If I'd had a microscopic device, I could calculate it more accurately. But then, the last sliver of the sun had also passed beneath the absorbing horizontal band of water. The parallel response was precise!

I abruptly pulled back on the throttle. The high whine of the engine suddenly changed to a low rumble, and the boat decelerated almost instantly, and then rocked from side to side. I reached forward and turned off the ignition, and the rumbling was replaced by the silent sound of water, lapping against the sides of the boat.

I leaned back against the cool plastic covering on the seat and placed my hands behind my head. The boat rocked gently in the undulation of the sea. I turned my head from side to side. All I could see was the flat, rolling surface of the water. I was completely alone, but I felt absolutely secure as I bobbed up and down in my tiny ark. And that's just what it was . . . the classic symbol. Just like Noah, during the flood. Everything else was dead. But from this diminutive box, life would again spring forth . . . as from the womb. I reached my arm over the edge, and dangled the tips of my fingers on the cool water. How far down from here? Ten thousand . . . twenty thousand feet? There were so many unseen things there . . . just like the unconscious. And the collective unconscious of forever merged these . . . made them sensible . . . to anyone who could merely decipher the myriad of eternal meaning. The mind . . . If I could only control the mind . . . discover all its hidden secrets. But it lay there like an iceberg, sloughing off bits of moisture in the heat of the sun, but protecting the gigantic unseen mass beneath the water. What a waste! But if all the icebergs of the world were to melt . . . the earth would be inundated.

" . . . on schedule, but . . . weather looks like . . . so what's your pleasure . . . come back . . . " The low hum from the CB was replaced by these sporadic, crackling words. Somebody out there . . . talking to somebody else out there. I couldn't respond, of course. I was glad. Otherwise I might be tempted.

I leaned forward to turn off the unit, and then I realized that the tape from Peter's service was still in my shirt pocket. I reached up and tapped the plastic case to verify this. I slipped the tape out of my pocket, and started to throw it over the side. It offended me. That's what I had said earlier. But why? We were parallel, he and I. What I learned of him, I learned of me. He carried terrifying shadows deep in the iceberg of his soul. And I . . .

A shudder suddenly came over me as I considered the possibility that there were other ghastly secrets lying beneath the surface of my conscious recognition. My mind rejected that thought. And yet, like the moisture sloughing off the surface of the ice . . . moments of insight had arisen . . . even now. It shouldn't happen that way. I was a healer. But so was Peter. There should be no concealments. I had even experienced therapy during the course of my training. Peter couldn't be hypnotized. But then, I suddenly remembered . . . neither could I! I always said that didn't matter, because a more accurate interpretation could be gained from the more readily censored medium of the dream. But now . . . I wondered. Perhaps there was a deeper probe.

I slipped the tape into the cassette slot. Then I pushed the rewind button, turned up the volume, and waited.

"We're here for healing tonight!" The amplifier in the boat was not very powerful, but Peter's voice resounded clearly, and forcefully.

"Amen! . . . Hallelujah!" responded the crowd.

"We're here to praise this town and praise the people in it! Do you believe me?"

"We believe you . . . Praise the Lord!"

"And I know you're here because you believe that I was called by the messenger of God to heal you . . . "

I suddenly gained a sense of clarity. Listening to Peter's voice allowed me to place myself in the clinical position again. But now there was no threat that he would take the controlling position. I sat forward in a responsive mode. This was the point, after all. The idea that Peter could perform so successfully as a healing evangelist, and yet believe that God does not exist was still the greatest puzzle to me. I knew that his calling was a sham, of course, but no more than the professions of many people. Lloyd, in his simplistic way, had attributed it to his using the spiritual search outside the realm of God's plan. But Lloyd didn't realize . . . or accept . . . that the spiritual sense remains. I just hadn't discovered Peter's spiritual sense. It must be there. I knew that from my study of Jung. Certainly Jung was aware of the implications inherent in the rejection of God. It was a sense. He called it the tremendum. And he knew that if the tremendum were rejected . . . it would merely reappear under another name. What was Peter's other name?

"But you first must realize that you also are living stones," continued Peter's voice. "You must be perfect as I am perfect."

But there was a qualifier. I had almost forgotten it, because I had concentrated so heavily on Jung's writings on therapeutic techniques. But he had developed a qualifier . . . in his writings on religion. What if . . . what if the tremendum does not reappear under the disguise of another name? In those cases, Jung believed that it would certainly return in the mentality of the one from whom the rejection had issued. And he stated that, since this is a matter of such tremendous energy, the result will be an equally important psychological disturbance in the form of a dissociation of personality.

"The Lord said, 'You are gods, and all of you are children of the most High.' So you must cleanse yourself of your imperfections. And you can do that by recognizing that you are perfect, even as your Father in Heaven is perfect. Do you believe that?"

"We believe! . . . We believe!"

Lloyd understood this aspect of Peter's character. I had to give him that. He realized that, having rejected God, Peter must try to become God. But what of that? Jung was aware of this syndrome. I'd studied it, after all. Jung knew about the rejection of God and the replacement in the personality. He used Nietzsche as an illustration of the intense personal inflation that can occur. Of course . . . Nietzsche died a madman . . .

"Do you believe?"

I thought that I had drifted mentally for several moments, but Peter's voice continued at the very next sentence.

"We believe . . . " The voices of the crowd in response were slow, and drawn out, and I turned my head slowly to see if there could be a problem with the tape player . . .

"Do you believe . . . "

And now Peter's voice droned slowly. I tried to reach forward, but my arm was tingling from having hung over the side of the boat, and I couldn't move it.

"Do you believe, John . . . "

"What? No! It can't . . . " I shouted. I wanted to turn it off . . . crush it. But my other arm was tangled in the steering wheel.

"What do you think, John?" continued his eerie voice from the speaker. "Is there a God? How did you replace the tremendum, John? How did you replace the tremendum?"

I finally pulled my one arm from the spoke of the steering wheel, and yanked my other arm off the side of the boat. And then I leaned forward and started to eject the tape . . . but Peter's voice was no longer there. Instead, there was music . . . low and soothing . . .

> Heal me! Let me feel Your hand.
> Gently lead me to the River Jordan,
> Where the sacred waters flow
> Across the land.

All right. Peter was gone. I had renounced him. I let my hands fall to the seat, and I leaned back again, and let the melodious tones comfort me. It was too bright now, anyway. I glanced from side to side, and I could still see clearly . . . the water . . . the water . . . the water . . . Too much light for hidden things. I would have to wait for the darkness.

I heard a dull clicking sound, and I slowly opened my eyes. My body moved gently from side to side, and a mild breeze passed across my face. I opened my eyes more, and I could barely make out the steering wheel before me in the darkness.

"We're here for healing tonight!"

I sat forward abruptly and focused my eyes on the light green light above the cassette. It had run through and restarted . . .

We're here to praise this town and praise the people in it!"

But how many times . . . I held my watch up and squinted toward the faint luminescence. It was midnight!

"We believe you . . . Praise the Lord!"

I reached forward and ejected the tape. Hours . . . How many hours had I slept? Or had I just . . . tuned out?

This was *too* dark. I hadn't anticipated . . . I liked it the way it was before . . . at the camp. Lloyd was there, and we sat by the lake . . . I searched the sky for the moon. It was full when I was at the lake. But that was a long time ago . . . or was it? No. This is . . . Thursday. That was Tuesday. Two days . . . only two days. The moon had to be there . . . somewhere. Then I saw it. There were no clouds earlier today . . . as I sped toward the setting sun. But now, the moon lay in hiding behind a dark cloud. There was just a sliver . . . peeking over the fluff of black. It was as though the impatient horizon had risen to meet it.

" . . . beautiful evening here . . . bet we're having a great . . . what's your ETA? . . . come back . . . " The channel was still intermittent, but the noise relieved my momentary surge of anxiety. I turned to another channel.

"Hi, Billy, this is Clear Star. Do you read me?... Read you, Billy. ... Heading for the southeast beds. Rendezvous there.... Four a.m.... "

Still nothing rational. I pressed the scan button, and let the device move its way through the channels, finding the occasional strong signals. I felt suddenly betrayed. It had been perfect until... I mean, my timing had been perfect. I was in control. I had reached my planned status at precisely the point of sunset. But the moon had fled behind a cloud. I had so much to think about. I needed that light. Not the sun ... not the direct ... but the moon. The reflected light. I could look at that ... learn the complexities.

"... advisory regarding the time of high tide is ...

"... This is the midnight half day run. We'll be in ...

"... and sunrise will be at six-sixteen ... "

Sunrise where? Here? A thousand miles north? Japan? I turned off the unit and listened again to the lap of water against the boat. Six hours. No. Not completely. Before it rises, the sky will glow, in eager anticipation. But until then ... the night.

I looked over the side of the boat and strained to see beneath the surface of the water. The night was supposed to reveal its hidden secrets. And I knew that it would ... if only I would invite them. But I was terrified. I didn't want to dream again. I didn't want to fall into the whirlpool. The elements had betrayed me... and I had betrayed myself. The sea was the source, but the sea was so ... infinite! I didn't know where to begin. I would have to wait for the other light, now. The moon had betrayed me. I would have to rely on the sun. But first ... I would have to survive the night.

I reached into a shallow pocket under the seat and pulled out a paper bag. For emergencies ... yes ... still here. I opened the bag, and pulled out a pint of scotch. It hadn't been opened yet. Just for tonight. Just to help me sleep ...

I slouched down in the seat, removed the cap from the bottle, took a large swallow, and replaced the cap. My senses dulled from the immediate surge of relief, but I could feel the light breeze caressing my face ... and I could hear the gentle sound of the water, whispering its secrets to the sky.

I closed my eyes and sunk lower into the seat. "I renounce you ... I renounce you ... " I mumbled. "See me through the night. I renounce you."

I shivered slightly, and I turned my face away from the glaring light. My back responded with pain as I turned on the hard surface. I realized that I was lying flat on the prow of the boat. I had no idea how I had gotten there. I sat up and stretched my arms to the side. The sun . . . it was completely up. I looked at my watch. It was nearly nine. I couldn't believe that I had slept so soundly, unless . . . I glanced into the cockpit of the boat. The bottle of scotch was there, precisely as it had been after I finished the single swallow.

I had done it! I had renounced the dream, and brought myself safely through the night! I stood excitedly, and turned directly toward the sun. I spread my arms, and let the rays bathe me in their warmth. I had transcended the demon. Of my own free will, I had manipulated the elements and the continuum of time. It was stupid for me to have been afraid! I could do anything!

I began to laugh uncontrollably, and pitch my body from side to side. Then I stopped, but the movement continued. I stumbled forward and grasped the edge of the windshield to support myself. The boat was pitching violently from side to side. I jumped over the windshield and toppled into the seat. All around me, the sea was calm. But in this spot, the water was churning, and heaving. And then the boat began to spin, and the water around it formed itself into a whirling vortex.

My mind knew better! This was not reality. My nightmare had betrayed me! It had waited until morning, and now it was here, forcing itself upon my state of partial consciousness. My mind knew better!

"I renounce you! I renounce you!" I shouted into the whirlpool. It had worked last night. Surely it would work today. "I renounce you!"

But the whirlpool grew larger, and spun faster and faster. And then the funnel opened up, and a shaft of light fell into it from the sky, and became a raging fire, and its flames roared past me into the silence of the day. My boat teetered, and the toppled from the edge, and became caught up in the downward spiral. I turned on the ignition and started the engine, and the roar of the machinery met the sound of the fire. I thrust the throttle full ahead, and pointed the boat up . . . away from the terrible suction of the whirlpool. But even against the force of the engine, I felt myself being pulled backward, slowly, down the stairway . . . toward the mandala . . . and the laughing, dismembered head.

"Daddy!"

I didn't have to look. This was a dream! My mind knew it. But my mind was terrified . . . and it couldn't control my thoughts . . . and I turned my head up, toward the edge of the funnel, and cried . . . "Diane! Help me! Help me!"

They weren't on the horse this time. They were kneeling at the edge of the funnel . . . Diane, and Meg, and Lloyd. And they leaned forward, and they called . . . "It's simple . . . it's simple . . . you can do it!"

So I stood up, and I reached for them, but part of me thrust itself downward, not upward, and I reached out frantically and grasped onto the wheel, and it spun, and spun, and I found myself turning about like a top, and then being cast again onto the cold hard plastic.

"Change leads, you idiot! Change leads!" It was my father. He was on the charging white horse now, and he rode madly around the rim of the funnel, kicking water over the heads of Diane and Meg and Lloyd. "You sound just like Lloyd! Leave that to the priest!" His voice rose and fell as he rode from one side to the other. But his head was straight and firm. The harness was firmly attached to his chest, and the straps were tightly secured to his forehead.

"Help me, daddy!" The words tumbled forth from my lips without my permission. I didn't want his help. I didn't need his help! I didn't need anyone's help. I tried to push the throttle ahead more, but it was at his highest setting. I held the wheel desperately against the churning of the water.

"You'll never realize how strong you are, John . . . " Lloyd had cast aside the spray of water, and he was calling down to me. "Not until you acknowledge how completely and utterly weak you are without God!"

"It's more complex than that!" I shouted through the fury.

"It's simple, Daddy!" called Diane. "It's simple!"

"Either God exists . . . " called Lloyd.

" . . . or He does not!" I shouted in return. I knew that game. He'd played it so often. "Suppose He does not exist!" I called to the funnel. But it was not the me in the boat. It was the hideous, dismembered head below. It rested gently in the flaming circle of the mandala, and it smiled at me, and coaxed me to follow.

"Suppose He does not exist," it repeated. "Nothing changes."

"The beginning!" called Lloyd in a voice that was weakening from the distance.

"The beginning!" I repeated from the boat.

And my dismembered head laughed, and shouted back at me, "Almost nothing changes! Forget the beginning!"

"And the ultimate power!" whispered Lloyd from afar.

"And the ultimate power," I repeated.

"You can find a substitute," shouted my dismembered head. "It will be almost as good . . . for a while . . . " And the head tipped back and laughed uncontrollably, and the serpents that dangled from it reached out and beckoned me with the stubs of their torn out tongues.

"No! It's a betrayal!" I shouted. "Judas! Judas!" And I turned from the laughter and reached my voice to the heavens, and shouted . . . "Help me! Help me!"

And my father scoffed and rode off on the charging white horse, but Diane, and Meg, and Lloyd reached out and grasped the boat, and began to pull. And I was afraid they were going to be yanked in with me.

"Let me go!" I shouted. "Save yourselves!"

"No one can save himself, John," said Lloyd. "He has already done it for us."

And their soft arms were joined by a shaft of light that reached down from the sky, and I felt the boat being pulled up . . . up . . . up . . .

I stood up and forced my body hard against the wheel, and held it tightly into the spinning edge of the funnel . . . and the vortex diminished . . . and disappeared.

"Diane . . . Meg . . . Lloyd!" I called. But they were gone, and my boat was spinning at full throttle in a tight circle. At the center of its turn pattern was a harmless, shallow, depression of foam. And I threw my head back, and cried to the heavens . . . "There is a God! There is a God! There is a God!"

The bow of my boat bumped gently against the front of my slip, and I killed the engine. I glanced at the fuel gauge. It registered empty. It had for the last thirty minutes. I sighed heavily. There was no way that I could have gotten back with the fuel that I had left myself . . . not without help. All the way back, Meg's statement about what Diane had said came back to me . . . over and over . . she had been so frightened. But then . . . she just had this feeling of . . . peace. I had never felt such a feeling of dependence . . . and yet such a feeling of power. But it wasn't *my* control. I wasn't even interested in control anymore. I didn't pretend to be able to understand it. I just accepted it . . . and thanked God for it.

"Good to see you back, Dr. Summers."

"Hmm?" I looked up to see Danny tying off my boat. "Oh . . . Hi, Danny!" I pulled myself slowly out of the boat and stood on the dock. My legs were weak, and they wobbled uncontrollably against the firmness of the wooden deck.

"Need to trade your sea legs in for land legs, huh?" said Danny laughing.

"Yeah. I sure do!" I said.

"Did you have a good time?" he asked.

Good time . . . I smiled at the recollection of the hideous . . . yet wonderful experience. "Yes, I did, Danny," I said softly. "Yes, I did."

"Well, if you don't mind my saying so," he said. " . . . you look terrible!"

"Hmm?" I glanced at my reflection in metal case on the dock. Then I rubbed my hand across my face to verify. "You're right," I said. I never did shave. And I hadn't had anything to eat since . . . when . . . yesterday noon.

"Well, you go ahead, Dr. Summers," said Danny. "I'll clean up here." He hopped down into the cockpit of the boat.

"Thanks, Danny," I said.

"Oh . . . here," said Danny. "Do you want this?" He held the bottle of scotch toward me.

I shook my head. There wasn't even a question in my mind. "No, Danny. Throw it away. I won't need it any more."

"Okay, Dr. Summers." He tossed the bottle into a trash bag that he had tied around his waist.

I started to go, but then I felt compelled to turn back. "Hey, Danny!"

"Yeah?"

"Do you know . . . There is a God!" I shouted.

Danny laughed. "Sure, Dr. Summers!" he called back. "Everyone should know that!"

"Yeah," I mumbled. "Everyone should."

But everyone didn't. Peter didn't. I had to tell him. He could experience the same . . . wonderful . . . powerful healing. How could he not have discovered it? I had to tell him. I rubbed my hand over my rough face again. First I would go home . . . shave . . . clean up . . .

I stretched my body several directions to remove the remaining kinks, and then I ran toward the parking lot.

29

When I had driven up the broad winding road toward the temple before, it was during the time of the services, and the street had been teeming with cars, and smiling young people in logo-imprinted shirts had provided needed direction. The lack of vehicles today provided a stark contrast. But this was definitely a time for contrast. I chuckled in amazement at the clarity of my recollections now . . . of everything. The most striking was my memory of this morning's hallucinatory episode. Always before, in retrospect, I had viewed these departures as sort of vague, indiscriminate dreams, which added somehow to the richness of my character, but which had little to do with the stability of my personality. But then, I had never actually admitted that they were hallucinations. This one was different. After my recognition of the blinding truth of God's existence, my departures from reality became suddenly completely understandable to me. This had been clearly brought to my attention when I arrived home. My suitcase still lay in the middle of the hallway; the shattered glass from the mirror was scattered all about the bathroom; and my spent shaver rested lifelessly in the bottom of the basin. And each element matched with my recollection of the related events. This had been a complete and accurate reality check . . . and a substantiating testimony to my unbelievably belated comprehension of the truth. I smiled as I recalled standing before the nonexistent mirror and admitting that I was a sick person . . . and that I couldn't stand alone. But even now, the surge of confidence continued to grow in strength. It was a paradox. Strength based on dependence. I couldn't explain it. I just knew that I possessed it.

There were several cars in the parking lot, so I thought it was likely that Peter was here today. I parked near the entrance, jumped out of my car, and ran toward the doorway. There was one fact that was clearly not delusional. My personality was indeed closely matched with Peter's, and our similar experiences and beliefs had served both as a stumbling block . . . and as a vehicle for cathartic revelation. But this was the ultimate catharsis -- the primal recognition from ages past. But it wasn't just some convenient myth, cast haphazardly into the corporate soup of the collective unconscious, as Jung had thought. It was the truth! I couldn't wait to tell Peter the good news! I laughed suddenly as I realized the appropriateness of this phrase. I had always scoffed at Lloyd when he used it. It had always reminded me of a street-corner panhandler.

A door at the end of the foyer was open, so I hurried through it into the vast auditorium. It looked so different with all the seats empty. It was not quiet, though. There were fifteen or twenty people, scurrying about in bustling activity. The area on the stage behind the choir risers was being outfitted with a rich purple tapestry. And six or eight young men were running cable to additional cameras in the aisles.

Greg Hatcher and Kyle Wingate stood at the foot of the stairs leading to the stage. They were speaking with the choir director. They stood with their backs to me, but as I approached them, I could clearly hear their heated conversation.

"Yes, they've known about it for two weeks. And, yes, we have practiced all the songs," said the choir director in a high, raspy voice. "But these aren't employees, Greg. They're volunteering their time. And a lot of them already had made previous plans for tonight."

"Then call some of the people who used to sing in the choir and quit, Wesley," said Hatcher.

"They don't know the songs," said Wesley.

"Just call them in, and put a robe on them," Hatcher said through his teeth. "I don't care if they sing. Just have them stand there and pretend!"

"Excuse me," I interrupted. "Mr. Hatcher . . . "

Hatcher spun about and glared at me. He raised an eyebrow and spoke sarcastically. "Well, Dr. Summers! How appropriate!"

"I need to see Peter," I said. "Can you tell me where he is?"

"We need to see him, too," he said mockingly. "Can *you* tell *us* where he is?"

"He's disappeared again, Doctor," said Wingate. "We haven't seen him since Wednesday morning."

"Oh, no . . . "

"He was supposed to have a session with you Wednesday afternoon," said Hatcher. "Did he show up?"

Wednesday. How could I forget? It was the time of my failure . . . I had rejected Peter . . . told him he should seek help from another psychiatrist.

"Did he show up, Doctor?" repeated Hatcher.

"Yes. He was there," I said.

"Well, did anything unusual happen?" he asked.

"Perhaps," I mumbled. "We had decided on . . . No. *I* had decided on discontinuing therapy for a while."

"What brought that on?" asked Hatcher.

"Things were becoming unproductive," I said. "It seemed like the right thing to do."

"His whole affiliation with you has been unproductive," said Hatcher. "Things were going very smoothly until he started seeing you."

"Cool down, Greg," said Wingate. "You can't blame Dr. Summers for this."

"Psychiatric therapy is never an easy process," I said. But I definitely felt a surge of guilt. Not for treating Peter, but for discontinuing the treatment. And, especially, for not having been there for him during the last two days.

Hatcher just raised an eyebrow and shook his head.

"But what's happening?" I asked, pointing to all the activity. "What's happening tonight?"

"It's a special candlelight service," explained Wingate. "Peter knew about it. We've been planning it for weeks. It's supposed to begin at nine p.m. -- five hours from now!"

"Well, perhaps he'll be here," I said.

"Perhaps doesn't cut it for this one!" said Hatcher. "This service is being broadcast as a tryout for our incorporation into a national religious network. It could mean millions! But now . . . with Peter's stupid behavior . . . it could all be destroyed!"

"It's going to be all right, Greg," said Wingate. "I told you that I could handle the service. Actually . . . the way that Peter has been, it might even be better."

"Better?" Hatcher placed his hands on his hips and glared at Wingate. "You don't seriously believe that, do you? This is a national broadcast!"

"No better time," said Wingate. "You know how far afield Peter has been getting lately. If he comes across that way tonight, our whole ministry could go down in flames."

A young man ran up and stood beside Hatcher with an expectant look.

"Yes? What is it Brad?" asked Hatcher sharply.

"We're ready to set up the close-up camera, Mr. Hatcher," he said. "I need to know where to place it."

Hatcher sighed deeply. He glanced down the center aisle, and then he fixed his eyes on the tree on the stage. "You're going to have to remain flexible, Brad," he said, turning back slowly. "If Peter shows up, we're going to want plenty of full-face shots. But if he doesn't . . . " He shook his head and glared at Wingate. "We haven't decided yet. You're just going to have to remain flexible."

"Okay." Brad started to leave.

"Oh, Brad . . . " called Hatcher.

"Yes?"

Hatcher narrowed his eyes toward Wesley, and looked up toward the choir risers. Then he turned back, and pointed toward Brad. "Bring out the choir's studio recordings of the songs we're doing tonight," he said. "And get ready to crank that baby up to full volume. We'll have the choir lip-sync tonight."

"What?" Wesley stepped toward him.

"You told me you wouldn't be up to full size," said Hatcher. "This will be a lot more dramatic."

"But they'll be able to . . . " began Wesley.

"Do it, Brad!" said Hatcher gruffly, pointing again toward the young man.

"You bet!" Brad turned and ran off toward the back of the auditorium.

"You shouldn't be making decision like this, Greg," said Wesley. "I'm in charge of the choir, and . . . "

"But who's in charge of the one in charge of the choir, Wesley?" asked Hatcher threateningly.

Wesley started to respond, and then he just dropped his head and bit his lip.

"Call your people in early, Wesley," continued Hatcher. "And have them practice moving their lips in time with the music!"

Wesley frowned toward Hatcher. Then he thrust his hands into his pockets, and walked up the stairs toward the choir risers.

"And you, Doctor," Hatcher said to me. "You find Peter . . . and have him get his body back here!"

"Did he say anything unusual to you when you saw him last?" I asked.

"No! And I'm not being paid to analyze his flaky comments!" He started to turn back to Wingate, but then his head snapped back as he looked behind us.

I turned back also, and I saw Julie running down the aisle toward us. When she saw me she stopped momentarily. Then she smiled and continued.

"I'm glad you're here, Julie," said Hatcher. "We have to work on some alternatives. Peter's not here."

"I know," she mumbled.

"I'm going to throw you in during the first offering," said Hatcher. "Just after the entrance . . . of whoever. I want you to find something that'll knock their socks off!" He turned back to Wingate.

"Brother Greg . . . I need to speak with you," said Julie.

"Not now, Julie," said Hatcher. "Kyle and I are in the middle of something. You just find that song, and then clear it with me before you get set up with Brad."

"But I . . . "

Hatcher frowned and shook his head. Then he took Wingate by the arm. "Come on! We have some scripts to write!"

"Right with you, Greg," said Wingate, and they left the auditorium.

"Dr. Summers . . . "

I smiled and nodded at her. "Hi, Julie."

"This is awful!" she said.

"Well, let's wait until . . . "

"He called me this morning," she said. "I tried to tell them."

"What?"

"Peter. He called me this morning," she repeated.

"Where was he?" I asked.

"He wouldn't tell me," she said. "I mean . . . he said he was everywhere . . . and nowhere."

There was too much noise, and the technicians kept running back and forth. I motioned for Julie to follow me, and we walked over toward the side entrance.

"What else?" I asked. "What else did he say."

"He sounded very strange, Dr. Summers," she said. "He seemed so calm . . . but he frightened me."

"How?"

"Well . . . he told me there was too much evil in the world. And I told him that . . . I knew. And that was why he was here . . . to heal people . . . to help them find redemption. But he said . . . " She shook her head slowly. "He said there *was* no redemption. What did he mean by that, Dr. Summers?"

My recollection of that episode was overpowering also. And it had been repeated so often . . . as though for my particular benefit. I could still see his pleading expression . . . and hear his voice . . . imploring . . . Is there a God, Doctor? Is there a God. And my absurd response! How could I have been so blind?

"What did he mean by that?" repeated Julie.

I sighed. "Peter is in the midst of a spiritual crisis, Julie," I said slowly. "And I'm afraid I haven't helped him much with it."

"Spiritual crisis?" she mumbled.

"What else did he say?" I asked her.

"Well . . . that there was no redemption . . . "

"Yes? And then?" I prodded her.

"And then he said something funny," she continued. "He said he'd just have to renounce it himself . . . that he'd have to deal with the evil himself."

That statement concerned me . . . significantly. I pressed my thumb and finger against the bridge of my nose and squeezed my eyes tightly shut as I tried to reconstruct a pattern of motivation.

"I told him he should go see you, Dr. Summers," she continued. "But he said he called, and you weren't there."

"I know . . . " I mumbled.

"I don't know if you were gone, or . . . "

"Yes. Yes . . . I was gone."

"But then he said . . . " She frowned and shook her head. "He said it didn't matter anyway, because you had already cured him of his delusion."

"Yes," I said, nodding slowly. "That's what he thought."

"What did he mean?" she asked. "What delusion."

"It wasn't a delusion, Julie," I said. "It *isn't* . . . it isn't a delusion."

"I don't understand," she said.

I raised my hand. "I'm going to try to find him, Julie," I said. "Are you going to be here?"

"Yes," she said. "Dr. Summers . . . what should I tell Brother Greg and Brother Kyle?"

"Just tell them . . . " I sighed and shook my head. "I don't know, Julie. I'll try to find him . . . try to have him back here for the service."

She nodded.

I waved to her. Then I ran out the side entrance and headed toward my car. Where I thought Peter was . . . I wished he would not be. There were too many links already. And now, having been rejected by me . . . it was difficult to predict what his reaction might be. I should have said something to Chadwick . . . but I really didn't know . . . there was really nothing definitive. Just his desperate loss . . . and the potential for hatred . . .

"Renounce it, Peter," I mumbled as I ran. "Just don't deal with it . . . Just don't deal with it!"

30

Downtown looked different. The lingering rays of the early evening sun crept cautiously through the outline of buildings and hovered over the bleak and filthy streets, which were nearly devoid of traffic. No heavily made-up women stood in front of the dilapidated hotel building now. They would wait for the security of the darkness. A single dirty, unshaven derelict sat on the stairway, but he merely looked up and cackled as I passed through the doorway.

The frail man with the smelly cigar was there again. He stood at the counter behind the heavy metal grating, and looked up casually as I approached him.

"Whatcha need?" he asked.

"I'm looking for my friend," I said.

"Everybody might be your friend around here . . . or nobody." he laughed noisily, and then coughed through the tightly clenched cigar.

"No. I mean, someone who . . . he was here about three weeks ago. With Rebah."

"Rebah?" The man leaned his head close to the grating and squinted his eyes. "Oh, it's you! The friend of the crazy man!"

"Peter . . . " I shook my head. "Mr. Smith."

"Names don't mean nothin' here," he said. "I s'pose you're here to pick him up again."

"Is he here?" I asked.

"If he ain't, what are you doin' here?" he asked.

I pushed away from the counter and started toward the stairway.

"No you don't!" he shouted. "That'll be twenty bucks!"

I glanced at the stairway. The huge man was not there, and no one else was in the lobby. "I'll be right back," I said.

"I know what you're thinkin'," he said. "Archie ain't here, and no one's to stop you. But who's to say he won't be when you come down. An' if you ain't paid . . . " He reached his hand through the bar, turned up his palm, and motioned greedily with his fingers.

I walked slowly back to him, reluctantly removed a twenty-dollar bill from my wallet and handed it to him.

"Much obliged!" he sneered

"Is Rebah still in the same room?" I asked.

"What's to move for?" He cackled again, and his laughter fell into a phlegm-filled cough.

I ran up the narrow stairs to the second floor, hurried down to the third door on the right and knocked. I tried to turn the knob, but the door was locked, so I knocked again.

"Rebah! It's Dr. Summers!" I called. "Open the door!"

I heard a click. Then the door swung open slightly, revealing a portion of her pudgy face. She acknowledged me by silently raising her eyebrows. Then she opened the door completely, and nodded for me to enter.

"Is he here?" I asked, walking past her into the room.

"Hmm?"

"Is he here? I repeated. "Peter . . . Mr. Smith."

She shook her head slowly. Then she walked over, sat on the edge of the bed, and deliberately removed a cigarette from a crumpled pack on the side table.

"*Was* he here, then?" I asked.

"Yeah . . . "

"All day again," she muttered. "I mean . . . since last night." She placed the cigarette limply between her lips. Then she slowly raised a small lighter, ignited it, and lit the cigarette. She laid the lighter down as she inhaled deeply. After a moment, she exhaled, and a trail of white smoke issued from her mouth and nose.

I could see that Rebah was very depressed, and almost non-communicative. I grabbed a chair, set it on the floor facing her, and sat. "I need to find him, Rebah."

She shrugged and turned her head away.

"Rebah . . . " I gently turned her head back and studied her hard face. "Are you all right? He didn't . . . he didn't hurt you, did he?" I asked.

"Hmm?" She scowled. "No . . . no."

"Or threaten you in any way?" I persisted.

"What do you mean?" she asked.

"I mean . . . You seem so depressed . . . I thought, maybe . . . "

"I'm just tired," she mumbled. She inhaled deeply of the cigarette again, and let the smoke out slowly. "He was here all night. Talking . . . and talking . . . "

"About what?" I asked.

"He was crazy . . . I mean . . . different," she said. "The other time he was here, he was just . . . I don't know . . . kinda pleading. He just needed somebody to talk to. And then he slipped off to sleep, or whatever."

"And this time?" I asked.

"he never stopped," she said. "i told him he should get some sleep, but he said he couldn't, because some kind of demons would come and chase him. And then . . . he kept . . . " She shook her head.

"Kept what, Rebah?" I asked.

"He kept calling me 'Patricia Sims.' I told him that wasn't my name, but . . . "

The name hovered momentarily on the brink of my recognition, and then it penetrated. Patricia Sims was the prostitute that his father had been in the accident with. I suddenly got a sick feeling in the pit of my stomach.

" . . . but he wouldn't listen," Rebah continued. "He kept saying that I should be cleansed because I came out from the water."

"What water?" I asked. "Did he say?"

"Yeah . . . " She chuckled lightly. "Something about a 'raging culvert.'"

The accident . . . He was placing Rebah at the scene of the accident. This was not a good sign. He was identifying Rebah with the woman that he held responsible for his father's death.

I pulled the chair closer. "What did he say to you, Rebah?" I asked.

"He just talked and talked," she muttered. "I can't remember."

"It's important, Rebah!" I pleaded with her. "It's really important."

She sighed. "Mainly he kept telling me I should move out of Little Rock and change my life before the big rock fell on me." She inhaled again, and shook her head in the cloud of released smoke. "But then, just before he left . . . I don't know. He changed. He started using a lot of big words. And he said it didn't matter anyway, because there wasn't any big rock . . . and so he'd just have to deal with it himself."

"Deal with what, Rebah?" I asked. "Did he tell you?"

She shrugged. "Evil . . . corruption, he said. And he kept talking about some big conspiracy. He said there had to be some kind of sacrifice, and the big rock wasn't there to help." She shook her head and looked away again. "I don't know. He didn't make any sense."

"That's all right, Rebah." I glanced around the room for a sign of anything that he might have left. My eyes halted on the wall above Rebah's bed. A single rose dangled upside down from a long stem which was stapled to the wall. "What's that?" I asked, pointing to the rose.

She looked at the rose. "Oh . . . He brought that to me and put it up there." She laughed. "He told me it was the symbol of a beloved woman. But he said he had to hang it upside down like that, because now I was spoiled. But he told me that, if I changed, he'd come back and hang it right."

"Did he say . . . did he say what he would do if you *didn't* change?" I asked.

She shook her head. "I guess I didn't give him a chance. I was so . . . " She shrugged. "He hired me for twelve hours. He came in at midnight. And it was noon . . . and I told him his time was up."

"And he left?" I asked.

"Well . . . yeah . . . after I told him . . . "

"What?"

"He's a nice guy," she muttered. "I shouldn't have talked to him that way."

"What way?"

"I thought he was being so high and mighty all of a sudden," she said. "I told him I was doing fine, and he should take his help to some people who really needed it." She sighed heavily. "So . . . I told him about *the hole.*"

"The hole?"

"I shouldn't have sent him there," she continued without responding. "He was a nice guy. It was stupid of me!"

"Rebah . . . what's the hole?" I demanded.

She frowned at me. Then she slowly raised her hand and pointed her finger toward the floor. "It's . . . down . . . under the ground. Some people call it the sewer, but it's not that. I think they were planning a subway once, and then stopped, or something. I don't know. I've never been there. A lot of people like it. It can be kind of a shelter, you know . . . for the homeless and all. But the drug dealers use it, too . . . they use it a lot . . . "

"Did he go there?"

"I guess. I showed him how," she said.

"Show *me*," I said impulsively. "Show *me*, Rebah. I have to find him."

She shook her head. "I can't. I shouldn't have showed him. If anybody finds out about it . . . "

"You have to help me, Rebah," I pleaded. "I can't tell you how important it is! I have to find him!"

She looked at me for a long moment with no expression. Then she sighed, snuffed her cigarette out in a dirty ashtray, and stood slowly. "Come on." She walked toward the door.

I stood up and followed her. "Where are we going?"

She turned back and placed a finger against her lips. Then she opened the door, stepped out into the hall, and looked both directions. Then she nodded, and beckoned for me to follow.

I stepped out into the hallway and pulled the door shut behind me. Rebah was heading away from the stairway. She stopped in the shadows and motioned for me to hurry. We walked past several rooms, and stopped at a narrow door just beyond an old pay telephone covered with scrawled messages.

"Here . . . " she said.

"Hmm?"

Rebah pulled the door open. It appeared to be just a messy linen closet. She reached up and pulled a chain, and a bare bulb filled the tiny area with a dim light. She slid aside a small cardboard cabinet, revealing what appeared to be a narrow door behind it.

"What is this?" I asked.

"It's a way to get down . . . to the hole," she said. "A lot of the old hotels around here have these. You can get to the hole from the street, too, but people don't like to. The cops know about those places, and they're always waiting for an easy possession pickup."

"But . . . I mean . . what is . . . "

Rebah reached inside the closet and pulled open the narrow door. The smell of stale air drifted into my nostrils. The light from the dim bulb revealed a few bricks, and a dirty stair landing, but beyond that was only darkness.

"It's about four stories down, I think," she said. "When you go, you gotta turn off this light, and close this door behind you.

I stepped into the tiny room, and then turned back to Rebah. I wondered if she were being completely truthful with me. I had no idea where she was sending me. But then . . . I had insisted. I studied her face in the faint light. It was so hard and expressionless. It was difficult for me to read her. I'd never had anyone like her as a client. And yet . . . the other time . . . Peter had all that money, and she hadn't touched it.

Rebah abruptly pulled her head back and turned her ear intently toward the other end of the hallway. Then she quickly grabbed the telephone receiver off its base. "Just a minute!" She whispered harshly.

"What . . . "

"Shh!" She closed the door on me.

I stepped back against the cardboard cabinet, and it teetered back and forth precariously. Then I heard the faint sound of footsteps, and a loud banging.

"I'm down here, Archie!" Rebah's voice called out.

I heard heavy footsteps approaching, and then the sound of the huge man's voice. "Rebah?"

"I'm making a phone call," said Rebah. "Go on in my room. I'll be there in a minute."

"Huh? Oh. Okay." The footsteps retreated. Then I heard a door open and slam.

The door before me swung open, and Rebah popped her head back inside. "That was Archie," she said. "He's here to collect. I gotta get down there."

"Are you going to be all right?" I asked.

"Yeah. Just get going!"

"Rebah . . . If Peter . . . my friend . . . if he should come again . . . " I didn't want to frighten her, but there were so many unresolved questions. "If he should come again, maybe you shouldn't see him."

A barely perceptible smile appeared on her lips. "That's what I thought when I sent him out," she said. "Because he was telling me things I didn't want to hear . . . didn't think I wanted to hear. I mean . . . I'm not Patricia Sims of course, and I've never been to Little Rock. But he was right about me, you know. I *am* spoiled now, and it feels rotten. Most of my friends tell me not to think about it, 'cause it's too late. But sometimes, I wish . . . I wish . . . "

"Just be careful, Rebah," I cautioned her. "There are terrible things happening around here. You never know."

"I guess we never know anything until it happens, do we?" She glanced toward her room, and hung the receiver back on its base. "I gotta go. But when you see your friend, would you tell him something for me?" she asked.

"What?"

She sighed and closed her eyes. "I think I'd like him to . . . I think I'd like him to come back . . . and turn that rose around." She smiled faintly again, and closed the door.

I stood silently for a moment, as I listened to the sound of her footsteps, and her door opening and closing. Then I turned my body around in the small linen closet. The narrow door at its back had swung shut. I pulled it open and shook my head at the reappearance of the dank aroma. I tentatively placed one foot on the first step, and I felt it slip on a heavy layer of dust. Then I looked up, and the sphere of light from the stark bare bulb blinded me. I reached and pulled the chain. The closet became completely dark, but the residual image of the glaring bulb hung before my eyes. I looked behind me. A slit of light was visible at the bottom of the door leading to the hallway. Darkness is so relative, I thought, when there's any light at all.

I stepped through the tiny door and placed both feet carefully on the dust-covered stair, and the door swung shut and slammed behind me. The residual sphere of light before my eyes had vanished. I placed my arms up to either side, and my hands fell on what appeared to be rough, unfinished bricks. The staircase was no more than three feet wide. That would help. I leaned forward slightly and squinted into the darkness. My eyes had definitely had enough time to accommodate. There simply was no light at all. Four stories, she had said. Well . . .

I began calculating how I would deal with any emergency that might arise during my descent. That had been my normal pattern -- plan my own way . . . prepare for all contingencies. But then, for some reason, the image of this morning's descent into my hallucinatory whirlpool sprang into my recollection. All the planning and contingency preparation in the world could not have retrieved me from that hideous episode. It had been something entirely different.

I breathed deeply, and realized that I was now apparently becoming accustomed to the aroma. I pulled my arm back and strained to see the barely luminous face of my watch. It was nearly seven. The sun would soon be gone, anyway. Or, rather, the earth will have pulled itself laboriously away from its light. In reality, the sun was still there, of course . . . brilliant . . . eternal . . .

A strange sense of what seemed an unearned confidence suddenly swept over my body, and I raised my head and gazed intently into the deep well of unseen light above me. "Help me . . . " I mumbled. "Help me."

31

The old stairway seemed to have been constructed with two flights for each floor. When I reached the first shallow landing, I continued forward, and ran headlong into the wall. From then on, I counted -- twelve steps, switchback . . . twelve steps, switchback. As I descended, the steps felt weaker, and periodically one would seem to crumble under the weight of my foot. My hands slid along the walls, and they were met by indistinguishable lumps, and occasional crawling insects. I began to receive the distinct impression that I was following the stairway in Peter's dream. I was searching intently, and yet falling aimlessly into the darkness. It was almost like exploring the hidden reaches of a disturbed mind. I realized that Jung must have struggled with a similar perception as he tried to formulate a rationale for the unknown, for he admitted that he initially did not know where that direction would lead. I wondered now . . . if he didn't know what lay hidden in the depths of the psyche, why he had insisted on a humanly perceivable concept, and manufactured the notion of the collective unconscious, populated with its myriad archetypes and symbols. I chuckled as I mused that, if this were a dream, he would interpret my journey as a descent to the subterranean mother of death. I realized now how far afield Jung had gone in his attempt to rationalize the obvious. Yesterday I would have participated in the apparent delusional qualities of this experience; but now I held them firmly in the grasp of my newly discovered reality.

If Rebah had been correct in her statement that my destination was four stories beneath her floor, I thought I should be getting close, for I was about to turn onto the eighth flight of stairs. As I slowly rounded the corner I saw a flickering light. The walls became faintly illuminated, and I could now see the filth that my hands had been rubbing against. I pulled them down and brushed the palms vigorously against my trousers. As I neared the bottom of the final flight of stairs, the light grew brighter, and I could hear hushed talking, and faint shuffling noises. I had become accustomed to the smell on the way down, but now the sickening stench of garbage and human waste overpowered my resistance, and I coughed uncontrollably.

A few feet from the base of the stairs, a small group of shabbily dressed people huddled around a small fire. As I walked past them, my feet splashed in murky puddles of liquid. I stopped and tried to determine which direction I should go. The area was dimly lighted by periodically placed fires and candles, each one apparently designating someone's stake to their portion of "the hole." It did appear to have been an unfinished subway tunnel, and it disappeared into the darkness in both directions from where I was standing.

A single man sat with his back toward me on a box a few feet from me, and I approached him. I thought that if he'd been here for a long time, he may have seen Peter.

"Excuse me . . . " I circled the box, and spoke again from the front of him. "Excuse me . . . "

"Hmm . . . " The man stood up slowly. He was a short, thin man. He had long, greasy black hair, and a pock-marked face. A black leather jacket hung open from his shoulders, and a single earring hung from his left ear -- a cross entwined with a serpent. I stepped back in disbelief. This was the man that Peter had gotten into the confrontation with in the hotel lobby! My initial reaction was to avoid him, but then I changed my mind.

"Yes . . . You should be able to help me, if anyone can," I said cautiously.

"What?" he asked in a raspy voice.

"My friend," I said. "I think he came down here. have you seen him?"

"Friend?" He wiped the back of his dirty hand across his face and squinted at me. Then he appeared suddenly to recognize who I was. He jerked his head to the right, and then to the left. Then he swore, turned, and bolted back to the entrance, and up the dark stairway.

"Wait!" I called after him. "I need your help!"

But he was gone. Low laughter rose from the group of people huddled around the fire.

I walked up to the laughing group. There were four men and two women. "Excuse me . . . " I said hesitantly. "Can you help me? I'm looking for my friend."

They did not respond. Finally one of the men looked up and glared at me. "You buyin'?" he asked.

"No. I'm just looking for . . . "

"He's just a seeker!" called an unseen man from the shadows. "Seek . . . seek, seek, seek, seek . . . " he crowed in an imitation of a bird.

"Then get outa here!" snarled the man on the floor.

The others looked up with a vacant expression on their faces and giggled. They were clearly in a drugged stupor. I would get nothing from them.

I decided to begin to the left. I didn't know why. I walked carefully across the damp floor, past the randomly placed groups of foul-smelling people. A tall, long-haired man stood in the shadows. I stepped closer to him, and strained to see if it might be Peter. I quickly realized that he wasn't.

"What are you lookin' at?" he asked. He held a plastic food container in his hands, and he was chewing the meat off a chicken bone.

"Nothing," I said. "I thought you were someone else."

The man frowned. Then he tossed the container on the floor and walked off in the opposite direction.

I heard the barking of several dogs, and people yelling. When I turned around, I saw the dogs. There were three of them. They had pounced upon the container that the man had thrown down. But the people were surrounding them, cursing, and beating at them with sticks.

"Go find a rat, you mangy cur!" yelled an old man.

"Hold him off!" cried a woman. She pushed her way past two other women, and grabbed the box.

"Yah! Yah!" The old man stomped his feet, and beat the stick on the ground. The dogs growled, and then turned, and slinked away.

The woman took the box and joined the old man. The others grumbled, and sat down again.

I quickened my pace and continued through the tunnel. He could be near, or miles away. I had no way of knowing. But I thought that he would respond if he heard my voice. If he would just step out of the shadows . . .

"Peter!" I called. "Peter! Are you here?"

"Shut up!" cried someone from the darkness. "We're tryin' to sleep!"

Then others joined him in shouting at me and cursing. A small group of seated men started to get up as I approached them, but I continued past them, and they settled back, laughing.

"Peter!" I called again. "It's . . . It's John!"

"Peter's gone to the john!" shouted a hag of a woman with a gravely voice, and she and the others around her screamed with laughter.

"Peter!" I shouted again, ignoring them as I passed. "It's important, Peter! I was wrong. You need to know . . . There is a God, Peter! There is a God!"

"There is a God, Peter!" Yelled a grimy man in a high falsetto. "He's coming to get you! He's coming to get you!"

"Pete . . . Pete, Pete, Pete, Pete . . . " screamed another. It sounded like the same bird imitator.

"I was wrong, Peter!" I cried as I continued my rapid pace. "There is more than a spiritual sense! There is a God, Peter! There is a God!"

A young girl in a filthy dress stepped out from the shadows and stood directly in front of me. "Are you looking for a spiritual sense?"

"What?" I stopped suddenly.

"Come into my temple!" she said in a low, sultry voice. "I can show you things in the spirit."

"No . . . "

"Come on, preacher . . . " She pressed her body against mine and leaned her face close, and her breath smelled of stale marijuana. "Come to my temple, and I'll show you my religious mysteries."

"I'm not a preacher," I said. I pushed her away.

She shrugged and scowled. "Don't matter . . . "

"But I am looking for one," I told her. "Have you seen him?"

"Come on . . . " She grabbed my hand and pulled me toward a large furniture crate. "I'll show you a preacher, preacher . . . "

"Have you seen him?" I asked.

"I've seen the glory!" she cooed, and coaxed me closer to the box.

"Tamra!" An older man stepped out from behind the crate and took hold of her arm. His large mouth hung open, revealing several missing teeth. He glared at me, and then he yanked the girl away. "He's an outsider! Can't you see that? He won't do us no good. He's jist lookin' for a fix . . . like the other one."

The girl scowled, shook her arm free, and leaned against the crate.

"'Other one,' you said." I stepped in front of the man. "What did you mean by that?" I asked.

"The other one," he repeated. "The other outsider."

"When? Today?"

He narrowed his eyes, and turned slowly away.

"No . . . Tell me!" I took his arm and turned him back. "When did you see him? Where is he?"

The girl pushed herself away from the crate and stepped up to the man. "He wants something," she said slyly. Then she leaned up against me and spoke through her stale breath again. "What do you want, preacher?"

"My friend . . . the other outsider," I said. "Where is he?"

The man smiled, and his remaining teeth glistened in contrast to the cavities. "What's it worth?" he asked.

I wasn't thinking when I came down here. I had several hundred dollars in my wallet. I couldn't show them that. I'd be ripped off for sure. I reached into my pocket, and found that there were several small bills there. I pulled those out, and then pulled out my other pocket to show that it was empty.

"Here . . . " I thrust the bills toward him. "Take it all!"

The man glanced at the girl. Then he reached for the money.

"Where?" I asked, pulling the money away from him.

The man chuckled, and rubbed his fingers together nervously. "Keeper . . . "

"What?"

"He went to see the keeper," he said slowly. "Keeper has what he wanted."

"Where do I find the keeper?" I asked, waving the bills in front of his face.

"He's at his lodge," said the man. Then he looked down the tunnel and nodded. "Twenty fires down," he said. "You'll hear the music . . . see the lights . . . "

"He got the beat!" said the girl, and she started swaying and clapping to an unheard rhythm.

"Twenty fires down," he repeated. "You'll see!" He snatched the bills from my hand, and he and the girl ran inside the crate.

I hoped that the man wasn't misleading me. But I had nothing else to go on. I ran through the tunnel, past the flaming pockets. One . . . two . . . three . . . Sometimes it was hard to tell. The miserable individuals hovered so low over the fires. Seven . . . eight . . . nine . . . There were candles, too. Did he mean those? Thirteen . . . fourteen . . . fifteen . . . Then I heard it in the distance . . . the loud, rhythmic beat. It reverberated from the walls, and grew louder as I approached. There was a light there, too, but it wasn't from a fire. The dingy ceiling of the tunnel shifted from blue . . . to green . . . to red . . . Then I saw the source. On top of a table-sized box was a large flashlight, with a color wheel attached . . . spinning.

The music was almost deafening. It came from a huge boom-box sitting on the floor near the light. Several muscular men sat on the floor of the tunnel and, adjacent to them, inside an isolated area lined with gaudy fabric, a skinny man wearing a bright silk coat sat on a purple beanbag.

I slowed my pace, and walked casually up to the men.

"Whatcha want, man?" asked one of them.

"I'm looking for my friend," I told him.

"No friends allowed here," said another man, laughing.

"Yeah, I know . . . " I mumbled. Then I glanced further up the tunnel, and I saw Peter! He was sitting in a small recessed area, his knees pulled up close to his chest. The outside of the flashlight beam just caught his face, and covered it with blue . . .

green . . . red . . . I turned away from the men and walked slowly toward Peter.

"Hey, don't go away!" shouted one of the men after me. "We'll find you a friend!"

Peter was leaning against the rough wall, and staring across the tunnel with a blank expression. His hands hung limply between his legs. Directly in front of him, sitting cross-legged on the floor, was a midget of a man with wisps of hair hanging from his face. He was swaying forward and backward and chuckling lightly.

"Peter!" I called to him.

"Don't disturb him," said the midget. "He's concentrating!"

I stepped between Peter and the tiny man and squatted down. "Peter! Look at me!"

Peter shifted his head slowly from the vague point across the tunnel. He raised his eyebrows slightly as he saw me. "Well . . . John," he mumbled. "How nice of you to join me!"

"I'm so glad I found you!" I said.

"And not a moment too soon," muttered Peter.

The tiny man cackled, and shifted his body across the floor until he could see Peter again.

Peter lowered his legs slowly, revealing his hands. One of them held a piece of rubber tubing, and the other . . . a hypodermic needle!

"Peter, what . . . what is this?" I asked, pointing at the needle. "What are you doing?"

"Let me see . . . " Peter said with a faint smile. "If I am not mistaken . . . when last we met, we concluded our relationship."

"No, Peter," I said. "Just a temporary break, and . . . "

"And I believe that we had also determined that I was the winner, because I had the most toys," he said. "I can't have you catching up with me, now, can I?"

"No, listen, Peter . . . We still have so much to do," I told him. "It was my fault. I got sidetracked in my shallow attempt to discover your spiritual sense."

"Yes. My spiritual sense," said Peter. "That's why I'm here, you see."

The midget cackled and shifted closer.

"What do you mean?"

"It's so much simpler than you ever imagined," said Peter. "See that man down there?" He pointed toward the skinny man on the purple beanbag. "He's the savior, you see. And he promised me that this would take me to heaven. He is my hero . . . And this is my heroin!" He chuckled. "It's so simple, you see."

"No, Peter . . . " I shuddered as I looked at the amount of liquid in the hypodermic. If he injected the entire amount, it would kill him. Then I realized that this is what he intended.

"It's so simple," Peter repeated.

I stood up, and looked toward the skinny man, and I realized that he had risen from the bean bag, and was walking slowly toward us. The muscular men on the floor stood and followed him.

"Behold the risen savior!" shouted Peter, holding the hypodermic needle toward him.

The tiny man laughed loudly. "Behold!" he echoed. "He'll take you to heaven, all right! All the way in one play!" He laughed again.

"What are you doin', crazy man?" asked the skinny man. "You rakin' me over?"

One of the muscular men stepped up beside him and pointed at me. "*He's* the raker," he said. "You want me to take care of him, Keeper?"

The skinny man shook his head slowly and backed away, his eyes fixed constantly on my face. "No! Ain't you got eyes?" He raised his arm toward me. "He's the man, stupid! He's the man!" He turned around and ran suddenly down the tunnel.

I stepped toward the running figure, and three muscular men suddenly toppled to the ground in front of me, and I tripped over them, and fell headlong into a puddle of smelly liquid.

"Oh, we're sorry, officer!" said one of the men. "We seem to have fallen right in front of you!" He and another man stood, and helped me to my feet. Then they laughed, backed away, and sat again in front of the spinning light. The skinny man had disappeared.

I sighed in relief. Their mistaking me for the law had probably saved my life. I turned back to Peter, and then I froze. He had the rubber tubing tied tightly around the upper part of one of his arms, and he was about to inject the needle!

"No, Peter! Stop!" I cried, running toward him.

"Ahh!" Peter placed the tip of the needle on a protruding vein and shook his head.

"All right!" I stopped, and squatted before him again. "All right, Peter. Just wait. Okay? Just let me finish telling you."

Peter looked at me and smiled faintly. "Of course, John. What's on your mind? Are you tired of your toys, too?"

"Why are you doing this, Peter?" I asked.

He shook his head slowly. "John . . . John . . . John . . . I'm surprised at you. You had the answers. You can't have lost them already."

"What answers?"

"Existence is merely a collection of archetypes," he said. "I'm so grateful to you for bringing that to my attention. I was still muddling through life with the vague hope that, perhaps, there might be some meaning. But that was absurd! You made me realize that!"

"But I didn't mean . . . "

"And, yes, I appreciate your attempt to define my reluctant spiritual sense," he continued without listening to me. "And that may be enough for some people . . . for a while. But surely you can see the difference in my case. I *was* the spiritual sense! I was *called.* Don't you remember?" Peter's eyes widened, and his voice rose in intensity. "And I yanked my insides out for my followers, and I showed them how they could be divine as well. But it wasn't enough, because my divinity betrayed me . . . and intruded on my dreams . . . "

"But this isn't the answer, Peter," I said. "How could this be the answer?"

Peter closed his eyes momentarily, breathed deeply, and then spoke with extreme composure. "It's all the corruption in the world, of course . . . and the conspiracy. It's so hard being responsible for the sins of the world, you see. There comes a point of diminishing returns."

"You are not responsible, Peter," I told him. "There is no way that you can be responsible."

Peter smiled and shook his head. "John . . . John . . . John . . . I'm surprised at you! Don't you remember your Jung? Christ couldn't do it by urging and punishing and pleading, either, could he? But sacrifice! That great motive hidden in the myths and religions of all time! Don't you remember your Jung, John. Sacrifice of others . . . sacrifice of many . . . sacrifice of the one . . . " He raised the hypodermic needle up, and gazed at it lovingly. "And through this cup as the receptacle . . . The maternal womb wherein the serpent dwells . . . and arises . . . justified . . . " He lowered his arm slowly and looked at me. "It's lonely, you see, John. It's lonely without God."

"But there *is* a God, Peter!"

He narrowed his eyes. "Hmm?"

"I was wrong," I said. "So terribly wrong! I know now. There is a God!"

"That's quite all right, John," he said. "I appreciate your effort. But you see, a very learned man, my psychiatrist, assured me that the existence of God is merely a myth . . . and archetype . . . some sort of individual divine sense . . . "

"Your psychiatrist was wrong, Peter," I pleaded. "I was wrong. I led you astray."

"Leading people astray falls into the realm of the false prophet, I believe," he said aimlessly. "And, of course, I know quite a bit about that topic. But I don't quite see how a non-prophet can be a false prophet. I mean . . . one who leads from somethingness into *nothingness* . . . rather than into a *pseudo-somethingness* . . . "

"Listen to me, Peter!" I pleaded. "I've discovered the truth!"

" . . . and then, upon the pretext of that discovery . . . " he continued without apparently acknowledging me, " . . . attempts to lead from nothingness back to somethingness . . . " He shook his head. "That's a dream, John. And so very much like my other dreams . . . prior to *the* dream, that is. But I had my voices, too. And the voices carried me from the heights of heaven, to the depths of hell, and then back again. Why should I listen to you? My voices tell me much the same . . . and they are part of me." He raised his head as if listening to some far-off sound. "And my voices tell me now that my mission is complete. And the God who is no longer . . . if He is a God . . . resides as a piercing light within my mind. And my only hope is to die . . . and be reborn into that light . . . fully transformed. The child of the child of the child . . . "

"That's a false light, Peter," I said.

"No. *I* am the false light, John," he said, pointing to himself. "My *light* cannot be false, because a light is a light is a light . . . "

"Tell them, Peter," I pleaded. "Tell your followers. Tonight."

"Tonight?"

"The candlelight service," I said. "They're waiting for you."

"Candlelight . . . " He narrowed his eyes and tilted his head. "A light is a light is a candle?" He sighed and shook his head.

"Julie asked about you, Peter," I said, struggling to find anything that would jolt him back to reality. "She's worried about you. She wants you to return."

"Julie?"

"Yes. I spoke with her this afternoon," I told him. "She wants you to come back. They need you."

A cold look of hate suddenly fell over his face, and he shoved himself stiffly against the wall. "Oh! Now I see! You're quite right, John. You *are* a false leader, aren't you? You've led Julie astray! My one pure hope . . . And now you're all part of the conspiracy!"

"No, Peter. That's not what I meant."

Peter dropped his head slightly and sighed. "For the sake of one righteous person, I could have departed . . . and left the rest to chance. But now . . . " He raised his head toward the ceiling and cried out. "I'm so tired of the responsibility! Why must I deal with yet another?"

"It's all right, Peter," I assured him.

He gave me another hateful look. Then he pushed himself slowly to a standing position. "Why must I deal with yet another?" he repeated, more softly this time. He tore the rubber tubing from his arm and dropped it to the ground. Then he flung the hypodermic needle across the tunnel, and started walking away.

I heard a chuckle and a shuffling noise behind me. It was the midget. He had retrieved the rubber tubing, stood up, and was running toward a crowd of clambering people who had fallen like jackals upon the needle that Peter had thrown.

"I'll show you the way!" cried the tiny man as he ran. "You'll have to watch out! That's from the prophet! Nectar of the Gods! I'll have to show you the way. Ten dollars a pop!"

Peter was walking rapidly, away from the entrance to the stairway. I ran after him. "Peter . . . wait!" I called. "You don't have to deal with things. Not any more."

He glanced back over his shoulder and continued walking.

I caught up with him, and placed my hand on his shoulder. "You don't have to deal with things any more," I repeated.

"With all the corruption in the world?" he muttered.

"There has always been corruption," I told him. "And there will always be. Surely your father knew that," I said, holding fast to his shoulder.

He stopped abruptly and turned toward me. "My father participated in it!" he muttered through his teeth.

"And what of Patricia Sims?" I asked.

Peter's shoulders dropped, and he looked away.

"What of Patricia Sims?" I asked again. "Was she also a participant?"

"Of course . . . a weak participant," he mumbled.

"And all the Patricias?" I pushed.

"Weak . . . weak . . . "

"What does that mean, Peter?" I asked.

He raised an eyebrow and leaned close to me. "The weak shall die. First law of evolution!"

I turned my head so that I could look directly into his eyes. His words were so condemning. But I was afraid that I had led him.

"It has to do with judgment, I believe," said Peter after a pause.

"But it's not your place to impose judgment," I said.

"Whose then?" he asked.

"God's . . . " I said deliberately.

"Somethingness . . . to nothingness . . . and back to somethingness?" He smiled. "I prefer not to be judged by nothingness."

"You must renounce the hatred, Peter," I said. "You must bring a halt to . . . to dealing with others."

Peter suddenly raised his finger in the air. Then he smiled and pointed at me. "Frost . . . That's it!"

"What?"

"Robert Frost," he said. "*The Road Not Taken.*" He clasped his hands in front of him and began reciting: "'Two roads diverged in a yellow wood, And sorry I could not travel both and be one traveler . . .'"

The image of Lloyd's forked branch suddenly thrust itself upon my consciousness. If only I could bring Peter to a perception of that example. "Yes! Two roads, Peter!" I said. "And you can't travel both. You must choose!"

But Peter wasn't listening to me. He was drawing aimlessly in the air and moving his lips inaudibly. "I can't seem to remember the rest," he said. "Perhaps it was not that one, after all. Perhaps it was *Stopping by Woods on a Snowy Evening.* Oh, yes, of course: 'The woods are lovely, dark and deep. But I have promises to keep, And miles to go before I sleep, And miles to go before I sleep.'"

"Two roads, Peter . . . " I began in vain, trying to urge him toward the other metaphor.

Peter sighed heavily. "Miles to go . . . before I sleep . . . " He mumbled. Then he looked at me with a forlorn expression and shook his head. "I'm so sorry that you're part of the conspiracy, John," he said softly. "But I understand you, because you're a false messenger, too. And all false messengers must be dealt with."

Peter turned suddenly, and ran at full speed down the tunnel.

"Peter! Wait!" I ran after him, but he had already gotten too far ahead. It was difficult to maintain focus on his figure in the shadows. But further ahead . . . perhaps fifty yards . . . was a glimmer of steady white light . . . not a fire. Perhaps this was the exterior outlet that Rebah had spoken of. I pushed myself to run faster.

"What's your hurry, seeker?"

Three large men had emerged from the shadows, and they stood between the light and me.

"I have to find . . . " I began.

"Pete . . . Pete, Pete, Pete, Pete . . . " mocked one of the men. It was the bird imitator again.

"Yes . . . " I said weakly.

"Ugh-ugh," he muttered, shaking his head.

The three men began edging toward me. I thought that I could run around them . . . reach the exit. But then, behind them . . . ten . . . fifteen others . . . waiting.

"What do you want?" I asked.

"Oh, John . . . John . . . John . . . I'm so disappointed in you!" mocked the man in a high voice, and the others laughed raucously.

"We don't want much," said another. "Just everything!" The men laughed again.

I began backing away from them, and my soles slipped on the wet floor as I retreated. I caught my balance, and then put my hand out toward them. "Look . . . if you'll just let me through . . . " I thought for a moment that, if I just gave them some money, they'd let me go. But I realized immediately that this was a vain plan. There were so many of them! They would have no compunctions about taking everything . . . and leaving me dead on the floor of the tunnel.

I reached slowly into my back pocket and pulled out my wallet. "Okay . . . Look . . . " I pulled all the bills from my wallet, and then opened it to show them that it was empty. Then I replaced the wallet, and held the bills out. "Look . . . Look . . . " I suddenly pulled my arm back, and flung the bills into their midst.

"Hey! What's he doin?" asked one of them. But he was immediately surrounded by the crowd of others, and they pounced on the money like jackals.

I turned around, and pushed my body into a full run . . . back toward the other end of the tunnel. The rhythmic sound of the boom box swelled, and then diminished amidst the circling blue, green, and red lights. My lungs were aching, and I began counting backwards to myself as I passed the fires. Eighteen . . . seventeen . . . sixteen . . . The sounds were so deceiving. I couldn't tell if the men were following me or not. Eleven . . . ten . . . nine . . . The water from the murky puddles splashed up and inundated the bottom of my pants legs, but I continued running. Four . . . three . . . two . . .

"Hey, preacher! Did you find your savior?"

I glanced to the left, and saw the girl by the crate, smiling, and wagging her finger at me. I had forgotten how far it was from here. I strained my eyes through the darkness. There was the other fire, I thought. They all looked alike, but this one must have been the first. There were four men and two women . . . lying in a stupor about the flickering flames. And just beyond them . . . against the dark wall of the tunnel . . . a darker cavity. It was the entrance to the stairway.

I ran into the sheltered area, and inhaled deeply in an attempt to regain my breath. I glanced up the tunnel. The men were nowhere in sight. They were apparently satisfied with their bounty. I suddenly laughed uncontrollably at the realization that I had been so grateful to relinquish several hundred dollars. "For the needy . . . " I mumbled. Then I chuckled at the thought that I could probably declare it as a tax deduction.

I took another deep breath, and my lungs responded with a welcome absence of pain. I turned and headed up the dark, narrow stairway. I placed my hands out to the sides and let them slide over the dirty lumps and spiders on the walls. I realized how much more appropriate this was, after all. I had descended into the depths of Hades through this portal. What better place for the resurrection?

32

Darkness does strange things to the senses. I retraced my route up the narrow stairway by counting the number of flights and switchbacks, but I couldn't remember whether my destination was *on* the eighth landing, or *after* the eighth landing. I fumbled about until my hand landed on a knob. I turned it and pushed, and the door gave way partially, and then slammed against something and rebounded. I shoved the door forward, and squeezed through the small opening. If this were the right place, I knew where the light would be. I reached up and passed my hand through the air until it fell upon the flimsy chain. I pulled it, and the light from the dim bulb filled the interior of the linen closet. The cardboard cabinet stood in the center. That is what the door had hit. I hadn't left it that way. The man with the earring must have come out this way, too, and moved it.

I pushed the cabinet aside, and glanced about quickly to verify that this was the place from which I had begun my journey. I couldn't resist the temptation to pull open the narrow door again, and peer down into the murky cavern. It would previously have been so easy to let my surrealistic experience slip into a vague, delusional recollection. But the reality of the events were vividly impressed on my mind. Peter had nearly killed himself. And now he was apparently off on some unconsciously-driven, revengeful action. The prostitute murders? I still had difficulty reconciling that action with Peter's personality. But his behavior just minutes ago was also unlike any I had witnessed. I had to find him as quickly as possible.

I opened the closet door and stepped out into the hallway. I heard the sound of talking, and I looked down the hall, and saw a group of uniformed policemen with their backs to me. They were standing outside the open doorway to Rebah's room. I hurried quietly down the hall, and pushed my way through them into the room.

"Hey! Where do you think you're going?" yelled one of them. He ran into the room after me and grabbed my by the arm and yanked me back toward him.

"I'm a friend," I said. "I need to know what's going on."

"Not now you don't," said the policeman.

"It's all right, sergeant. He's a doctor. Let him come in."

I shook my arm loose and looked inside the room to see Lieutenant Chadwick beckoning for me to enter.

"This is quite a coincidence, isn't it, Dr. Summers," said Chadwick with a knowing smile.

I walked into the room. "What happened here?" I asked.

But he didn't need to answer. Rebah sat hunched on the edge of the bed, where she was being attended to by a paramedic. She had swollen lips and a massive abrasion on the side of her cheek, and her gown was torn in several places.

"Rebah!" I ran toward her. "What happened?"

"Careful, Doc! Don't touch anything," yelled Chadwick. "We haven't dusted for prints yet."

Rebah made an unintelligible grunt and shook her head. Then she winced in pain and pulled her face away from the medic's hand.

I glanced at the table beside Rebah's bed. There was a can of spray paint . . . and a snake-skin belt. "What are you . . . "

I turned around and looked at Chadwick. Another man stood beside him, and as I saw him, I was startled by an immediate recollection of my trip down the dark stairway. It was the short, thin man with the greasy black hair, and the single serpent-entwined cross hanging from his left ear.

"It looks like your friend Peter Lumen is off the hook in the prostitute murder investigation," said Chadwick.

"What?"

"It seems we've caught the guilty party in the act," he said with a wry smile.

"You mean . . . " My eyes fell on the thin man.

A narrow smile crossed the man's pock-marked face, and he grasped the open edges of his black leather jacket and shifted his weight to one foot.

I glanced back at Rebah's bloody face, and an uncontrollable feeling of rage suddenly swept over my body. "You fiend!" I shouted, and I thrust my hands on his chest and pushed him back against the wall.

"Summers . . . Wait!"

I couldn't respond to anything except my anger. "Because of you, an innocent man has been suspected," I shouted. "Maybe even driven to . . ."

"Summers!"

I felt two pairs of hands pulling me back. I turned to see Chadwick and a uniformed policeman grasping tightly to my arms. The thin man scowled at me, stepped away from the wall, and straightened his jacket.

"Not him, Summers!" shouted Chadwick, pointing to the thin man. "He's a good guy! That's Inspector Zuckerman."

"Wh . . . what?" I muttered.

"From homicide . . . undercover," explained Chadwick. "He's been working on this case for three months." He nodded to the uniformed policeman, and they released my arms.

"I . . . I didn't . . . " I stammered, in a state of disorientation. I stepped forward and extended my hand to Zuckerman. "I'm sorry . . . "

"You're as creepy as your patient!" said Zuckerman without taking my hand. Then he leaned back against the wall.

I turned to Chadwick. "I really am sorry," I said. "But when you said that you'd caught the guilty party . . . "

"We have!" Chadwick pointed toward the other corner of the room.

Sitting on the floor, almost lost in the shadows despite his huge frame, was Archie! His knees were pulled against his chest and were held in place by his handcuffed wrists.

"Are you . . . are you sure?" I asked.

"As sure as we can ever hope to be," said Chadwick. "It's a lucky thing that Zuckerman did think you were a creep?"

"What?"

"When he saw you in the tunnel earlier . . . "

"Yes . . . "

Chadwick shook his head and chuckled. "Zuckerman knew that Lumen was secure for the time being in the hole," he said. "But when you suddenly appeared from the stairwell, he had this sudden premonition that you might have been up to something. That's why he took off like a jack rabbit." He smiled wryly at Zuckerman. "He definitely wanted me to tell you that he wasn't running because he was afraid of you." He laughed.

"Knock it off, Lieutenant!" muttered Zuckerman.

"But anyway," continued Chadwick, "when he came back up here, he heard noises . . . and he broke in just in time to see the beating . . . in progress!"

"That's . . . that's great, Lieutenant! That's . . . " I stepped toward Archie, and eyed him with disgust.

My rage was already spent, but Chadwick stepped between us, just in case.

"But . . . why?" I asked him.

Chadwick shrugged. "We'll know more later," he said. "My theory is . . . he was selling his protection services to the hookers for a neat profit. But that would only work if they thought they needed to be protected, wouldn't it? So . . . he created the incentive."

"That's terrible!" I said.

"And . . . if anyone tried to pull out . . . or, especially, if anyone gave him the idea they were leaving the streets . . . Well, they became good candidates for the next victim," he said. Then he turned toward the huge man and continued. "That accomplished two things, didn't it, Archie? Got rid of the defectors . . . and increased the demand for your services. Huh?"

Archie cursed and shifted clumsily on the floor.

"That's right, Lieutenant," said Rebah with a soft, slurred voice. "That's right."

I looked at Rebah. She was holding a compress against her cheek, and speaking through her swollen lips. "You shouldn't try to talk, Rebah," I said. Then I turned to the paramedic. "Is she . . . "

"She'll be okay until we get her to the hospital," he responded to my unspoken question. Then he turned to Rebah. "Are you going to need a stretcher?" he asked.

"Are you kidding?" Rebah chuckled. "I've taken worse than this from some of the vice guys!" She stood slowly, and then flinched slightly, as she placed one hand on her ribs.

"I think they're just bruised," said the paramedic.

"Yeah . . . " She stepped toward me, and forced her swollen mouth into a faint smile. "Anyway . . . the lieutenant was right . . . about Archie's reason," she said. "And you can tell your friend . . . it's all his fault!"

"Why is that?" I asked her.

"Because . . . it all began to make sense, you know," she said. "After I left you, I decided . . . This was the time. I'm gettin' out of this . . . for good!"

"That's great, Rebah!" I told her.

"Yeah . . . " She said sarcastically. "Well . . . Archie sure didn't think so! And when he started beating me with that belt, he almost had me convinced to change my mind. But then he pulled that can of paint out of his pocket . . . " She turned around and looked at the wall above her bed. "He was gonna spray right over my rose!"

The rose was still there, stapled upside down above her headboard.

"That's all right, Rebah," said Chadwick. "We'll take the rest of your testimony at the hospital." He motioned for the paramedic to lead her out.

"Just a minute!" I said. I walked past them, knelt on the edge of the bed, and reached for the rose. I carefully pulled the securing staples out with my fingernails. Then I walked back and held the rose out to Rebah. "Here, Rebah," I said. "Peter would want you to have this."

Her eyes narrowed, and she laughed lightly. "Right side up?"

I nodded, and urged her to take the rose.

Rebah looked at Archie and shook her head slowly. Then she looked back at me. "Thanks, Doc." She took the rose gently, placed the petals against her nose, and inhaled deeply. "Can life really be that sweet?"

"It can," I said.

She shrugged, and walked slowly out of the room on the arm of the paramedic.

"Well, I hate to say it, Doc," said Chadwick, "but I guess you were right about your patient."

"Hmm?"

"He's not a murderer, after all," he said with a shrug.

"I always believed that . . . " I mumbled. But simultaneously, I recalled with a strangely persistent anxiety the deep, vengeful look on Peter's face, and his determination to deal with . . . if not the Patricias, then what? The conspirators? Miles to go before I sleep . . . he had said as he ran toward the diminishing light . . . And his anguish at having to deal with yet another, before . . . before destroying himself . . .

"So I guess there's a first time for everything," said Chadwick.

"First . . . "

"In twenty-three years . . . I don't think I've ever been wrong when I was that sure," he said.

"Why were you so sure?" I asked him.

Chadwick smiled. "Police work *is* a science. But some-times . . . I just get this overpowering . . . feeling, you know . . . "

"Yeah . . . "

"But then . . . I've never dealt with a schizo like him before, either," he said with a smile. "I guess that made the difference."

His qualifying statement made me feel a little better, but the strength of his belief disturbed me. Chadwick was certainly no beginner in these matters, and my own anxiety over Peter's motives blended with his suspicions to form a new, bubbling source of torment. The fact that Archie was, in all likelihood, the prostitute murderer became almost irrelevant in my mind, as I mulled over Peter's deeply troubling statements.

"I wouldn't write him off too quick, Lieutenant," said Zuck-erman, stepping up to us. "He's still a creep."

"The world's full of creeps, Zuckerman," said Chadwick.

"Not like him," said Zuckerman. "A preacher . . . getting his kicks from visiting hookers, and buyin' *H* in the hole . . . "

Zuckerman's level of knowledge of Peter's activities in the tunnel shocked me. "How did you know all that?" I asked him.

"I'm not the only undercover cop around here, you know," he said.

"But if he'd injected that heroin . . . he'd be dead!"

Zuckerman shrugged. "To each his own."

"All right, Zuckerman. That's enough!" said Chadwick. Then he turned to me. "Don't let him rile you, Doc," he said. "He's a little callous. It goes with the territory."

"But how about you, Lieutenant?" I asked Chadwick. "Do you know what goes on in that tunnel?"

"Sure," he said casually. "The hole's been there since my father was on the force . . . and probably years before that."

"Why don't you do something about it?" I asked.

Chadwick suddenly became hostile. "Let's hear it again!" he shouted.

"I just don't see . . . "

"Hey! Our job is to catch the bad guys . . . and put them away, so they can't bother the good guys!" yelled Chadwick caustically. "We do the best we can at that. We can't change the world, Dr. Summers!" Then he sneered. "You want to know whose job that is?" He leaned close to my face. "Preachers . . . and psychiatrists!"

Our eyes met in a moment of shared hostility. Then the entire situation seemed suddenly absurd, and I began to laugh . . . and Chadwick joined me.

"Touche, Lieutenant!" I said.

"We'll do our job, Doc," he said. Then he patted me on the arm. "You go on home. You should be able to rest easier now."

"Sure . . . " I held my hand out. "Lieutenant . . . thanks."

He shook my hand warmly and smiled.

I turned and headed toward the door. I would not be going home, though. Not yet. I glanced at my watch. It was almost eight-thirty, and the candlelight service was supposed to begin at nine. I was sure that Peter would go to the temple now . . . after all his ramblings about a conspiracy. But Chadwick didn't know how right he was. I should go home. There were so many things I needed to make right with Meg and Diane . . .

I halted in the doorway for a moment, trying to sort out my thoughts. Then, almost without thinking, I turned around and called back to Chadwick. "Lieutenant . . . "

"Yeah?"

"Would you . . . " But I caught myself. What an absurd request I was about to make! I had stopped myself just before asking Chadwick to call Meg for me, and tell her that I'd be home as soon as I could. I had almost put into play the routine that I had fallen back on for all these years . . . get someone else to communicate for me . . . when I was too insecure to do it myself. That was going to stop!

"What is it, Doc?" asked Chadwick.

"Nothing . . . nothing." I turned back, and left the room.

I walked quickly down to the end of the hall, and lifted the grimy receiver from its graffiti-filled base. I fumbled in my pocket, removed a quarter and placed it into the slot. Then I reached up, and realized how old this device was, as I entered my number on the slowly circling dial.

At the first ring, I realized that Meg and Diane were probably not back from the mountains yet. And yet that seemed impossible, since so much had happened since Meg had left.

The ringing was interrupted by a soft click, and Meg's taped voice met my ears: "This is the Summers' residence. We aren't able to come to the phone right now. Please leave your name and number at the beep, and we'll get back to you."

I started to hang up the receiver . . . but then I felt suddenly impelled to say something . . . anything.

I listened for the beep, and then began hesitantly. "Meg . . . " I chuckled inadvertently. "Talk about one-way communication! But I guess I'm good at that. This has been . . . a very . . . extraordinary . . . day, Meg, and I can't possibly begin to explain it here. I just need to say . . . I want you to . . . to forgive me for the way I've behaved. And . . . " I leaned closer to the telephone base. "And the only thing good about this next message is that I'm delivering it. Because I'm calling to say that I won't be home . . . just yet. I really do have to talk with Peter again tonight, Meg. I have to go to his temple, and . . . and try to resolve some things. I can't tell you how important it is . . . but I want to . . . and I will when I see you." I started to replace the receiver, and then pulled it back again. "Meg . . . tell Diane and Lloyd . . . tell them how grateful I am to them . . . for helping you rescue me from the whirlpool! I . . . ah . . . I love you . . . " I slowly replaced the receiver in its cradle. Then I breathed deeply, and hurried down the hall.

33

I arrived at the temple by nine, but the parking lot was packed, and I had to park on the street, a half mile away. By the time I walked back, I could hear the muffled sound of singing inside the temple. Security guards were everywhere, and several of them were restraining an overflow crowd. I avoided this group, and hurried around to the side entrance. I told a guard there that I was Peter's doctor. He gave me a perplexed look, but he let me in.

As soon as I opened the inside door, the sound of the music was deafening. The auditorium was packed. People were standing, swaying back and forth, and singing loudly, and they were being led by the choir director, who stood in front of the choir that must have numbered well over a hundred. Security guards were inside, also, standing conspicuously in the side aisles. I saw Julie, in her long white dress, standing in her usual place in the front row. Several spaces were vacant near her, so I walked quickly up to her. She turned toward me, and greeted me with a wide smile.

"Dr. Summers! I'm so glad you're here!" she said.

"Is Peter here?" I asked her.

She nodded. "He got here less than an hour ago."

"Where is he?"

"Brother Greg and Brother Kyle took him," she said. "He looked terrible. They had to get him cleaned up and dressed."

"Yeah . . . How was he acting, Julie?" I asked.

"I didn't really get a chance to talk to him," she said. "They took him way so quickly. But he seemed very quiet. And he looked so . . . I don't know. Were you with him?"

I nodded.

"Where was he?" she asked.

I started to answer her, but then I shook my head. "It's a long story," I said.

Hatcher came into the side entrance and walked toward us. He carried a large two-way radio in his hand, and he was joined by two men and a woman. One of the men carried a mobile television pack. As he saw me, he frowned. Then he smiled broadly, took one of the men by the arm, and presented him to Julie.

"This is Julie Peters, the talented young lady I've been telling you about, Mark," he said. "This is Mark Langley, Julie. He's the representative from the National Christian Network."

"Glad to meet you, Mr. Langley," said Julie.

"My pleasure," said Langley, leaning close to be heard over the sound of the singing.

"And I'm sure you've seen Susan Masters on the evening news," said Hatcher, bringing the woman forward. "She's here with her camera crew to cover the service."

"That's wonderful!" said Julie.

"Looking forward to it," said Masters.

"You people can sit here with Julie," said Hatcher. "We left room for you."

The three people walked to the space to the left of Julie.

Hatcher walked deliberately around me, and stood at my right side. "Doctor Summers . . . " he whispered harshly.

"Yes?"

"I don't know what Peter got himself into . . . and I don't even want to hear about it now," he said. "But I'm going to tell you this . . . We finally got him calmed down and ready to perform. If you cause any problem tonight . . . I mean *anything* . . . I'll have you ejected so fast it'll make your head spin!"

"Why do you think I'll cause a problem?" I asked.

Hatcher merely smiled, and placed his finger on my chest. "You've been warned!" He turned away from me, raised the two-way radio to his mouth, and spoke in a low, deliberate tone. "Brad, I think we're about ready. After this number is over, bring up the soft intro for Kyle's entrance."

As if on cue, the choir director coaxed the congregation toward the final emotional strains of the song, motioned for them to sit, then he merged with the members of the choir.

A hushed noise arose as the thousands of people sat down. The television cameraman pointed meaningfully toward another man, who stood in the side aisle holding an identical set of equipment, and nodded. The other man pointed his camera toward the stage.

The low murmur in the auditorium was masked by the sound of soft music, and then the lights began to dim, until the only illumination visible was a soft light on the stage. Kyle Wingate stepped out from the wings, and walked briskly to the center of it.

"Good evening!" he called to the crowd.

"Good evening!" responded a few hundred.

"This is going to be a wonderful night! I can feel it in my soul! Amen?" he coaxed.

"Amen!" shouted a few respondents.

"I imagine some of you are wondering why we turned out all the lights," he continued. "Well . . . It's really very simple. That's how we all started, isn't it? We all started our spiritual walk in the darkness of ignorance! And that darkness must be cast aside, before any true healing can be accomplished. And how do we get rid of the darkness? With the light of God's Word!"

"Amen! . . . I hear you, brother!" responded a few members of the congregation.

I felt Hatcher shift beside me, and I vaguely heard his harsh whisper: "What are you doing, Kyle? Stick to the script!"

"Well, we're going to show how that happens tonight," continued Wingate. "When you came in tonight . . . all of you should have received a candle."

A shuffling noise arose, as people reached for the candles. I felt a tapping on my arm, and looked to see Hatcher handing one to me. I took it and placed it in my pocket.

"Now these don't do any good like this, do they?" cried Wingate. "They're just like our poor, dark souls . . . sitting there, waiting to be sparked into existence! Well, Jesus can do that for you! All you have to do is ask! And when you receive your light, you're not to hide it under a bushel, are you? No! You're to pass it on! Show His light to the world!"

Wingate took a step forward and nodded. There was repeated clicking noise, and then lights began to flicker in the aisles.

"We have our helpers out there," said Wingate. "They're standing there, waiting to pass on the light! But it's hard to receive, isn't it?"

Wingate's question was accentuated by a rise in the volume of the music. And then the choir began to hum in accompaniment.

"It's hard, because the darkness is so overpowering!" continued Wingate. "It's so hard to penetrate, because we don't know about the light. But it's there . . . the truth of God's Word. We just have to recognize it!"

Hatcher muttered again, and then he activated his two-way radio. "What's going on back there?" he whispered harshly. "Did Kyle lose his script? It's supposed to be *our* light . . . not *the* light!" He pressed his finger against his ear piece and listened for a response. "Well, is the mandala light ready? . . . What? What do you mean he decided not to use it? . . . " He shook his head disgustedly. "No, not now. We'll bring it up when Peter comes on." He let the radio drop to his lap, and passed a quick breath through clenched teeth.

"Are you ready to cast aside the darkness?" cried Wingate.

"Yes . . . yes . . . " responded a few.

"Then you have to be fully aware!" he shouted. "You have to feel it . . . see it . . . hate it!"

The music swelled in introduction to another number, and lights from the side fell on the choir, casting weird shadows about their eyes and mouths.

"Jesus is waiting to give you the light!" cried Wingate. "But close your eyes, first . . . and feel the emptiness of a life without Him!"

The music diminished slightly and the choir began to sing, softly at first, and then swelling in volume and emotion.

> There was darkness on my spirit.
> There was blindness in my eye.
> I didn't know I was so near it.
> All I could do was cry.

"Are you ready to cry?" asked Wingate emotionally. "Are you ready?"

> Cry Salvation!
> Though the darkness covered me.

"We're living in darkness! We're wallowing in sin!"

"Self-denial!" whispered Hatcher coarsely. "We're wallowing in self-denial!"

> Cry Salvation!
> And He heard my raging plea.

"Light your candles!" cried Wingate. "Spread the Word!"

At every aisle, workers leaned in toward the waiting congregation, and passed the flickering flames. And then each person passed it to the one next to him. And in moments the entire auditorium was aglow with thousands of tiny flames.

"Can you feel it now?" called Wingate. "Can you feel the power of the truth? Christ is the light! He died for our sins!

The lights rose on the choir, and they swayed as they sang to the loudly swelling music. Hatcher said they would lip-sync, and their lack of precise synchronization was evident, but no one in the congregation paid any attention to them. They were too involved in the emotion of the moment.

> Now I have Jesus in my spirit.
> I have His vision in my eye.

"Feel the light! Live the truth!" exhorted Wingate.

There is singing. I can hear it.
I want to raise my head and cry.

"Cry out for the joy of His love!"
Cry Salvation!
I was blind. Now I can see.
Cry Salvation!
I am free! I am free!

"You're free! You're free!"

I heard a sobbing to my left, and I turned to see Julie, leaning forward . . . straining to listen to Wingate's message. Tears streaked down her cheeks, and glistened in the candlelight.

"Is this . . . this the usual ceremony?" I whispered.

She shook her head slowly. "No. This is . . . wonderful! This is wonderful!"

A chill rose up my spine and cast a dizzying sensation across my forehead. Wingate was clearly not following Peter's typical pattern. This was not self-divinity. This was not the way of Balaam. This was . . . this was light . . . this was truth . . . But why was Hatcher so upset? He pounded his hand against his leg, and stared threateningly toward Wingate. The choir continued as though nothing had happened. They pressed their silent lips unwittingly against the unyielding cadence of the prerecorded music.

Cry Salvation! Cry Salvation!
There is no more night.
Cry Salvation! Cry Salvation!
See . . . There is light!

"It's the light of Christ in your lives!" cried Wingate. "Don't let anyone take it from you!"

Cry Salvation! Cry Salvation!
Let Him hear your voice.
Cry Salvation! Cry Salvation!
Lift your hands, lift your eyes.
He is there! Rejoice!

"Rejoice in your salvation! Rejoice in your salvation!" Wingate turned, and walked quickly off the stage.

Cry Salvation!
Cry Salvation!
Cry Salvation!

The music stopped abruptly at a feverish pitch. Then, almost simultaneously, the congregation began chanting: "Peter . . . Peter . . . Peter . . . Peter . . . " And they swayed back and forth, and the flames from their candles flickered in the motion.

I felt a movement to my right, and I turned to see Hatcher talking into the two-way radio. "The mandala . . . bring it up . . . quickly!"

Suddenly the multi-colored glass surrounding the mandala shone brilliantly, and, behind it, simulated flames flickered about its configuration. The choir moaned a responsive tone, and they swayed in rhythm to the plaintive melody.

"All right," continued Hatcher into the radio. "Ready . . . Now!"

At that moment, the stage became ablaze with light, and Peter stepped out from the crack in the rock behind the falls. He was wearing his flowing white robe, and his face appeared to be heavily caked with makeup. The chanting became louder as he walked down the winding path, and headed toward the center of the stage. Then Peter raised his head toward the ceiling, and stretched both arms out to the side, and the chanting stopped.

Peter remained in the position for several seconds, and a few in the congregation prematurely uttered, "Salvation," in response to Peter's anticipated demanding call. Then several began to shift about and whisper.

Finally, Peter lowered his head, and brought his arms slowly to the front. "How many have come for healing tonight?" in a loud, deliberate voice.

"Yes! . . . Praise God! . . . Heal me, Peter!" And the many respondents swayed, and the flames flickered above their hands.

Peter dropped his gaze to the front row, and narrowed his eyes against the brightness of the light. He slowly scanned the row of people, and stopped abruptly as his eyes met mine. "Yes, there are many here tonight who need healing," he said without taking his eyes off me. "Miles to go before I sleep . . . "

Hatcher twitched suddenly, and he leaned forward with the two-way radio held directly before him.

Peter looked out to the congregation again. "So many lights out there tonight . . . glowing on the outside. Do they flicker on the inside as well?"

People in the congregation began to shift nervously, but a few attempted to follow his pattern. "Yes, Peter . . . Yes . . . "

"But they're so fragile!" cried Peter. "They can be snuffed out . . . in the blink of an eye!"

"Amen! . . . Praise God! . . . "

"And . . . see . . . " Peter raised his head and stretched his arms out again. "I don't even have a candle! Just the cold truth of the searing lights . . . casting the horrible revelation on all of us here tonight! The hideous trick!"

Hatcher suddenly raised the two-way radio to his mouth, and spoke through his teeth. "Brad! Get someone backstage! Get hold of Kyle, and ask him what's going on. Peter isn't following the script either!"

"But sometimes the truth is hideous, isn't it?" continued Peter. "But then . . . " His eyes turned on me again. "A learned doctor once told me that the truth must be known . . . if there is to be healing!"

"Yes . . . Yes, Peter," I mumbled inaudibly. "But you haven't seen it yet."

"So we need the light!" cried Peter. "We need the light for the truth . . . and we need the light to expose the false messengers!" He spread his arms again. "And the light is on me!" he cried fervently. "*I* am the false messenger! I have deceived you! I can heal no one! And the light inside us can be snuffed out in the blink of an eye. There is no light! It is meaningless! We are all . . . meaningless!"

The crowd gasped, and began to whisper.

Hatcher grasped my arm roughly and pulled me toward him. "What's he doing, Summers? Do you know what he's doing?"

"I don't know," I told him. "You'll just have to . . . "

A bright light glared to my left, as the television cameraman turned his camera on Peter. Susan Masters had her hand on his shoulder, and was directing his angle. Hatcher pushed me back, cursed under his breath, and brought the two-way radio to his mouth again. "Brad! Be ready to bring the music up again!"

Hatcher stood and smiled nervously at Mark Langley. Then he walked past Julie and knelt in front of Susan Masters. "I don't know what's going on here, Susan, he whispered loudly. "You'll have to kill the broadcast!"

"Forget you, Greg!" said Masters with an excited smile. "This is news!"

Hatcher glared at her. Then he leaned over and whispered something to Mark Langley, who sat silently with a puzzled look on his face.

"But you see . . . I was searching for a *greater* light," continued Peter emotionally. I wanted it . . . needed it! But it was so faint . . . so . . . complex. It was like a vague archetype of some lost spiritual sense!"

Hatcher stood from his whispered conversation, glared at Peter, and then raised the radio to his mouth again. "Music, Brad! Loud!"

"Is there a greater light?" pleaded Peter. He turned around and walked slowly toward the waterfall, and then fell to his knees in front of the rocky wall facing the pool of water. "I need to know . . . for sure! Is there a greater light?"

The introductory chords to the song suddenly exploded in sound. Hatcher ran to the edge of the stage and motioned frantically toward the choir director. The man stepped quickly out from the robed figures, turned, and began directing the choir . . . barely in time for their erratically moving lips to fall into rhythm with the taped rendition.

"Faker! . . . Cheat! . . . You're a sham! . . . " echoed many in the crowd. And others began to talk angrily among themselves.

"I came to be healed, Peter!" cried a man on crutches, who was hobbling down the center aisle. "I came to be healed, you faker!"

"Yes! Faker . . . cheat . . . sham!" yelled others, and they began to step out from the rows into the middle aisle, and join the man on crutches.

Hatcher turned back and motioned for the security guards. A line of them quickly ran over from the side of the auditorium and formed a barrier in front of the steps to the stage.

Susan Masters jumped up excitedly and motioned for her other cameraman to join her. He ran over from the side of the auditorium, filming the guards as he came. Then he stationed himself a few feet away from her. She straightened her jacket, smiled, and pointed toward him.

The blinding light from the television camera shone directly toward us, and I turned away from it. But I could hear bits of the monologue from Susan Masters . . . "Surprising turn of events . . . Charges of fakery . . . What happened to Peter Lumen? . . . "

But the noise of the crowd soon overpowered her soft voice. There were several hundred at the front now, shoving against the line of guards . . . taunting, cursing. Suddenly, someone tossed a candle onto the stage. Then the practice quickly escalated, and hundreds of flickering flames flew through the air, and landed all about Peter. Then a tapestry near the choir suddenly caught fire. The singing people abruptly stopped, and began to run off the stage, but the song to which they had been moving their silent lips continued to resound above the turmoil.

Other areas of the stage caught fire -- furniture . . . carpet . . . even parts of the artificial tree. The crowd finally realized what was happening, and they began to scream and run for the exits. The security guards quickly formed a protective circle around the people in the front row. I reached out and grabbed Julie by the hand as we were shoved toward the side exit. There was already a crowd there, but the guards pushed, and thrust their fists into their backs, and we wedged our way through the screaming people . . . and out into the darkness of the night.

The mass of people kept moving, like a giant amoeba, toward the front of the temple. Others were still streaming out of the other exits. But within moments, a space was cleared between the noisy crowd and the building, and the line of security guards now held hands and inched us back further.

Susan Masters and her two cameramen still stood on the other side of the guards. Their lights were glaring, and she stood in front of one of the cameras, speaking excitedly and pointing. In the distance . . . the blare of sirens sounded in the night.

It had happened so quickly. I reached out to assure myself that Julie was still beside me. I pulled her into a small pocket of space. "Are you all right?" I asked.

"I . . . I think so . . . " But tears were streaming down her face. Then she looked around frantically. "No . . . " She broke loose and grabbed Hatcher, who was standing with Langley. "No . . . " she said again. Then she turned back to me, and grasped me arms. "Peter . . . Peter is still in there!" she cried.

"What . . ."

"I know it!" She looked around desperately again. "He's still in there! I know it! I know it!"

There were so many thousands there. How could she know? But I had the sinking feeling that she was right.

"Someone . . . " Julie pounded on several people in a frenzy. "Peter is still in there! Peter is still in there!"

But they just shook their heads . . . and looked toward the distant sound of sirens.

"All right . . . " I mumbled. "All right . . . " I waited until the security guards in front of me were not looking. Then I squatted down and crawled under their linked arms into the open area between the crowd and the temple.

"Hey! Where do you think you're going?" shouted one of the guards.

But I was already half way to the building by now. And as I glanced back, I saw that he wasn't following me.

"Daddy!"

"What . . . " I stopped abruptly and turned back toward the crowd.

"Daddy!"

My eyes scanned the front row of people in the direction of the voice . . . and then I saw them! It was Diane calling to me. And beside her were Meg and Lloyd. And suddenly my perception turned inward, and my vision became distorted. The crowd blurred . . . and then merged into a foamy whirlpool . . . and Meg and Diane and Lloyd were kneeling there at the edge of the funnel . . . reaching out for me. A sudden draft of hot air blew past the back of my neck, and I turned toward the temple. But it, too, had blurred, and transformed itself into the flaming vortex of my hallucinatory journey. But this was not a dream . . . it was not a hallucination. My mind was clear, and my will was my own. No, this wasn't a dream! It was a momentary, blinding recollection . . . a direction . . . a message! A chill of excitement suddenly crossed my spine, as I realized that all of the confused, misdirected incidents in my life . . . Peter's life . . . and the lives of any others who might be affected by this moment in time . . . had miraculously converged upon this one compulsive action of mine. And it wasn't even my action now! It was . . . obligatory!

I smiled faintly, and waved my hand vaguely in their direction. Then I turned, and ran into the burning building.

The fire was still mainly limited to the stage, and the sides of the auditorium toward the front, and the high ceiling gathered most of the smoke. But the flames were quickly working their way backward, and many seats were beginning to burn. The sound system was surprisingly not yet affected, and the blaring music blended grotesquely with the crackling sound of the fire. The choir loft was completely enveloped in flames, but, unbelievably, the area surrounding the waterfall was not. Julie was right. Peter was still there . . . kneeling in front of the pool.

I ran down the aisle and bolted up the stairs. The heat from the fire forced itself into my lungs, and I took shallow breaths to avoid the pain. Peter couldn't have heard me coming, but when I placed my hand on his shoulder and pulled him around, he looked up at me calmly and smiled.

"Peter! Come on! Get out of here!" I shouted.

He reached up, grasped my belt, and pulled me down suddenly beside him. "Well, John," he said with a distant look. "How nice of you to join me!"

"I'm not joining you!" I cried. "I'm rescuing you!"

Peter shook his head. "John . . . John . . . Weren't you listening earlier?"

"What?"

"I told you . . . I had to deal with yet another." He looked slowly about at the raging flames and shook his head. "I couldn't have planned it better myself! The conspiracy has been defeated. And now the false messenger may sleep."

"No, Peter! It's not necessary!" I cried.

"Sacrifice, John!" said Peter. "In the absence of God, the sacrifice of man is the ultimate spiritual message . . . "

"But God is not absent!" I shouted. "And your sacrifice is not necessary, because . . . " I struggled for words. Something that Lloyd had told me . . . "Because Christ made the ultimate sacrifice . . . for all of us."

Peter tilted his head slightly, and glared at me through narrowed eyes. "Well, Doctor . . . you mean . . . the *Christ archetype*, of course."

"Christ is not an archetype!" I shouted.

Peter raised his eyes and breathed deeply. Then he shrugged. "Well . . . in the absence of God . . . " He turned his face toward the water and shook his head. ""It's so complex!"

"Peter . . . " I flinched suddenly as a burning ember bounced off my back. I glanced up and saw that the curtains and hanging settings above the stage were a blazing inferno. "It's not complex, Peter," I said. "It's simple! Either God exists . . . or He does not."

"Yes . . . well . . . suppose He does not exist," he mumbled. "Nothing changes."

Those words echoed also from my recollection. They were part of my hallucination! I struggled to reconstruct it. "The beginning, Peter," I said. "What of the beginning?"

"Forget the beginning," he mumbled.

"And the ultimate power, Peter?"

"You can find a substitute," he said. "And it will be almost as good . . . for a while . . . "

"No, Peter!" I shouted. "That's a betrayal! The curse of Balaam!"

Peter turned around and gazed absently past me. "A doctor betrayed me once . . . " he mumbled.

"Yes, I did, Peter!" I cried. "You were right! I was a Judas!" I grasped him by the shoulders and shook him violently. "Ask me again, Peter! Ask me again!"

A strange puzzled look filled his eyes. "Surely we couldn't *both* have been mistaken . . . "

"Ask me again, Peter!" I repeated fervently.

I had reconstructed it -- that terrible, traumatic moment in our session two weeks ago! And his reaction was as I had hoped. A strange pleading look appeared in Peter's eyes, and he lowered his voice and moved closer. "What do you believe, Doctor?" He leaned close to my face and whispered hoarsely. "Is there a God, Doctor? Is there a God?"

"Yes, Peter . . . yes!" I shouted. "There is a God! There is a God!"

There was a sudden sound of exploding glass, and Peter and I both turned abruptly in the direction of the gigantic mandala, which had shattered from the heat, and spewed bits of colored crystal across the stage.

Tears welled up suddenly in Peter's eyes, and he began catching his breath in short, irregular gulps. Then he sat back with a strangely relaxed smile. But suddenly, he jerked his head upward, and then down again. He stood up, grasped me by the arm and pulled me up beside him. "Let's get out of here!" he shouted.

"Yes!" I laughed. "Yes."

At that moment, the deafening music suddenly stopped, and all I could hear was the roaring fire. We ran down the steps and up the aisle. The fire had reached the back of the building now, and as we moved under the overhang of the balcony, the captive smoke met us in billows, and the hot soot surged into my lungs. My eyes burned, but I felt Peter's hand still on my arm . . . and I sensed that we had passed through the inner door. The lobby was now burning, and we had to run across a flaming section of carpet. But the doors were there. I could barely see them, but I could feel the coolness of the night as we passed through. And then . . . my face and body became inundated by a stream of cold water, and I placed my hand on Peter's shoulder and shoved our way through it . . . toward the flashing red lights . . . in the midst of the swirling, raging foam of the whirlpool . . .

"Daddy!"

Yes . . . they were still there . . .

"Daddy!"

I reached out, and their hands were upon me. I pressed my eyes together tightly and shook my head to rid myself of the smoke and water. And when I opened them, I saw Meg . . . and she was crying. And Diane was clutching at my hand. But Lloyd knew better . . . He was smiling!

"Meg . . . I . . . " I suddenly began laughing. "I didn't really have this in mind when I called!"

"John . . . " The tears streamed from her eyes, and she shook her head. Then she began suddenly pounding her fists on my chest. "I hate you when you do these things! I hate you! I hate you!"

"I know," I said, pulling her into my arms. "But things will change now. I promise!"

"Are you all right, John?" asked Lloyd.

"Yeah . . . I'm really all right," I said.

He smiled. "I thought so."

I heard a cough, and I suddenly remembered Peter. He was standing silently, watching the flames escape tauntingly from the powerless streams of water.

Several figures ran across the clearing toward us. The first were Susan Masters and the cameramen. Behind them were Hatcher, Wingate, and Julie.

"Peter . . . " The glaring light came on suddenly, and Susan Masters straightened her jacket and walked up and stood beside Peter, facing the camera. "I'm standing here with Peter Lumen, now, who was just miraculously rescued from the burning temple." She turned to him. "Peter, this has been an extraordinary event! Tell me . . . all the things you said before . . . about your being a false messenger, and there being no light . . . What did you mean by that?"

Peter turned his head toward her slowly and smiled. Then he leaned over and whispered something in her ear.

"Huh?" she said questioningly.

"There is a God," he said quietly. Then he stepped closer to the camera, looked directly toward the light, and repeated more loudly, "There is a God." And then he threw his head back, and cried into the darkness of the night . . . "There is a God! There is a God! There is a God! There is a God!"

"Well, of course, but . . . " Masters laughed nervously.

"Excuse me . . . " It was Hatcher. He stepped between Peter and Masters and then turned toward the camera with a broad smile. "We're extremely grateful, of course . . . and we definitely do thank God for Peter's safe return!" He became suddenly very somber. "This has been a terrible tragedy, of course! But I promise you . . . all of you faithful followers of the Light on the Rock Ministry . . . We will rebuild the temple! We will be here for you! The healings will continue!"

I pulled Meg closer to me, and clutched at Diane's hand. I looked around for Lloyd. And then I saw him. A few yards away, he stood with Peter . . . talking. Julie and Wingate were with them. And above the agitated shouts of the crowd and the wild, indiscriminate roar of the fire, I could distinctly hear the faint sound of their joyful laughter.

EPILOGUE

This will be the last entry I make in Peter's case record. It has been two months now since the fire. I found it initially impossible to believe, but follow-up sessions have left no doubt: Peter's schizophrenia has been completely cured as a result of his traumatic recognition of the existence of God, and his newly developed commitment to Christ. I should not have found this so difficult to accept, since my own problem was resolved in an equally immediate manner. But then, I had never completely accepted the fact of my own psychotic behavior. This was partially due, of course, to my following Bernadette's warped logic, and assuming that it had been either a deliberate exercise of my will, or some spontaneous symbiotic manifestation of the counter-transference syndrome. Whatever the cause, it had become God's tool for breaking through my blindness. My healing has been graphically illustrated by the complete absence of delusions. I must admit, however, that, while my previously overpowering pattern of escapism has diminished, I still have to struggle against the urge to soothe my psyche with the habitual shot of whiskey. I'm no longer making excuses for this weakness, though. And my struggle has been aided by Lloyd's assurance that Christians aren't perfect -- they're just saved!

The apparent simplicity by which both Peter and I were cured of our schizophrenic conditions initially gave me cause to consider, somewhat selfishly, that if everyone suddenly became believers, I might lose all my business! I realized, of course, that this was a very unlikely occurrence. Besides, Lloyd assured me that there were plenty of neurotic Christians!

But the schizophrenic syndrome was qualitatively different from other psychological disorders. Lloyd was right, of course. Schizophrenia is a reasonable, logical manifestation, when a person searches for spiritual meaning outside the acceptance of the existence of God. And I saw so clearly now that Jung himself had skirted this issue without realizing the significance of it. He vaunted the tremendous importance of the "rebirth archetype," but he never recognized the healing power of truly being "born again." I used to mock this expression, but I realize now that there is no other phrase which better describes a person's resurrection into a new and meaningful life, from the state of spiritual darkness.

Peter broke his ties with the Light on the Rock Ministry, of course, as a result of his final message. He left immediately after the fire, and is now enrolled in a Bible College. He told me that, since he now recognizes the truth, he needs to learn all there is to know about it.

Peter's departure left a vacancy which was quickly filled by Kyle Wingate. Hatcher remained on, of course, as Business Manager, but with Wingate clearly in control. Wingate's last message in the temple seemed to spur him on to greater and higher confidence and inspiration. They are temporarily holding very successful meetings in a tent while the temple is being rebuilt, and they are anticipating a dynamic reopening. There is no reason to doubt that they will succeed. The essential ingredient wasn't the person of Peter Lumen; it is man's overpowering desire to find spiritual meaning. Wingate can definitely provide for that need.

The Light on the Rock services will proceed without Julie, however. She returned to Lloyd's church. She has become very active there, and is using her experience to help Lloyd make his services more dynamic and appealing. Lloyd's openness to these changes has frankly impressed me. He is by no means the narrow-minded fundamentalist that our father had denounced. Despite the method of delivery, however, Lloyd has remained staunchly insistent on the presentation of accurate Biblical truth. And that has also impressed me. And our regular attendance at his church has provided a powerful avenue for my own spiritual growth.

I think that, even more remarkable than the changes which have occurred in my life and the lives of those about me, is the paradoxical transformation of things which have not changed. Reality takes on a new perspective when viewed through the eyes of a believer. It contains the same frustrations . . . the same fears . . the same hideous aspects of life. But it is suddenly no longer something to be renounced, or escaped from. It becomes instead an opportunity for enjoyment, nurturing, and improvement in the context of a new and rewarding life. My recognition of this was quite ironic, because this is, of course, the ultimate goal of successful psychiatry. But like so many other goals, it had previously been illusory, and meaningless.

Meg and Diane arrived at this realization more quickly than I did, of course. And I had to admit that they had been more open and eager in their search. Diane has improved upon her reality by selecting new school relationships, and developing others at the church. My personal problem had forced Meg into a position of weakness; but now she is growing stronger and more outgoing in her own right.

That has provided another paradox which I should have understood in the context of those illusory psychiatric goals. Meg and Diane have both become significantly more independent in the last two months. And yet our mutual need . . . our family bond . . . has grown immeasurably in the process! It has to do with freedom. Lloyd had previously tried to describe to me the significance of Christian liberty, but it is like so many elements of knowledge which mysteriously combine to form that entity we call human intelligence: until we have it . . . we can't understand it. I wish my father could understand that kind of freedom.

Perhaps . . . one day . . .

Lloyd is planning a four-day Thanksgiving retreat at Moon Lake next month. I'm going to take Meg and Diane. I'm really looking forward to viewing that piece of unchanged inspirational reality through new eyes.

I must remember to have Cheryl schedule my appointments around those days. I can't imagine why I ever had any question about Cheryl's abilities. She is quickly turning into the most competent secretary I have ever had.